I0572873

A Pond of Blood and Lavender

CAROLINE CREWS

Startree BOOKS

Text Copyright 2025 © Caroline Crews

ALL RIGHTS RESERVED. This book contains material protected under the international and Federal Copyright Laws and Treaties. Any unauthorized reprint or use of this material is prohibited. No part of this book may be reproduced or transmitted in any form or by any means, electronic or mechanical, including photocopying, recording, or by any information storage and retrieval system without express written permission from the author/publisher, except for the use of brief quotations in a book review. This is a work of fiction. Names, characters, places, and incidents either are products of the author's imagination or are used fictitiously. Any resemblance to actual events, locales, or persons, living or dead, is entirely coincidental.

Cover & interior art by SG Designs

ISBN: 979-8-9987006-0-6

For my mom, who's always believed in my ability to tell a story and who gave me an assignment when I was grounded in 2009 that turned into my debut novel sixteen years later.

Contents

One

Rushing emerald water bubbled over the sharp-edged stones and lulled me into a blissful state until a branch snapped in the distant canopy. The hairs on the back of my neck rose. No one ever dared to come out this far. The River of La Mont was deadly, and the birds were venomous. It was the reason Mother and I had chosen to have our one-on-ones here.

Another snap, and I narrowed my gaze, hand tightening around the dagger at my hip. Beside me, Mother tensed. Her orchid-spiked nails painfully dug into the sleeve of my satin tunic.

Before worrying her further, I tuned in to the noises within the forest. Amid the songbirds' melodies and the rustling of leaves, heavy breathing marred the tune. I leaned over and whispered into Mother's ear, "Don't panic. But someone is watching us."

Mother's eyebrows knitted together, and purple mist began to overshadow her navy irises. Only here, in this secluded place, could she permit her true nature to show without worrying about losing her beloved citizens' loyalty.

"Are you sure? Nobody comes out here. Plus, they all know not to disturb us."

That last part couldn't be more true, at least since I became Mother's primary bodyguard two years ago at the age of sixteen. I took my role so seriously that everyone feared bothering us in any way or even upsetting me. Just them mentioning me being the queen's bastard son could put their lives at risk.

"Still, Aris's guards are daft." I wouldn't put anything past the king's loyal men.

"Ever since I announced Aris would be facing execution, you've been on edge." Mother patted my arm as if I were an innocent teenager, not her personal weapon. "If it's anything, you'll protect me. But I'm sure it's nothing. Just relax. Don't let your nerves ruin the best part of our day."

Inwardly, I groaned. Mother trusted the citizens of Astal and me too much. On the off-chance someone didn't love her, I'd handle them, no matter what—feelings be damned. That was why she had me. I did the dirty work. But even though she had ordered me to kill anyone who suspected our heritage or posed a problem to her, she forgot I had my limits.

I couldn't kill anyone important—like Aris's guards—or do anything that might raise suspicions and risk exposing us. If I ever did, she'd ship me back to Hellspace, the place of my nightmares. She'd never threatened it outright, but she didn't need to. We both knew it.

Despite my certainty that someone was out there watching, waiting, I bit my tongue, holding back my wariness. But before faking relaxation, I scanned our surroundings. Behind us, *nucha* trees with poisonous sap filled the forest. The mile-wide glowing river, separating the two kingdoms of this realm, flowed sluggishly, with metal benches and overgrown neon bushes lining either side. Several yards away, a gravel path zigzagged from the river, leading to the poorest village. Nothing looked off.

Perhaps she was right. My nerves were getting the better of me. Shaking off the discomfort, I leaned back against the bench again.

After several minutes, I lost myself in the intricate way the water trickled over the rocks and almost missed the flash of purple zip between two bushes. My magic stirred deep inside, and I straightened, nerves on high alert, as someone jumped in front of us. Mother's face paled, her fangs biting into her lip.

Shit. I knew someone had been lurking in the distance. I should've trusted my gut. I bounded up, my body concealing Mother within my shadow, and I nudged her foot, a warning to retract her fangs and hide the mist. This wasn't one of our guards. They waited back at the palace. It wasn't one of Aris's guards either. The intruder was a peasant.

My stomach turned rock hard. Had he seen her face? Her secrets?

"Why are you bothering your queen? It better be important."

The peasant bent down to fix his tights, grabbed a glob of mud from the trail, and flung it at Mother. "You're going to destroy us all, you wretched—"

Mother gasped as I darted behind him and fisted a chunk of his copper hair. "You insolent fool! How dare you insult your queen!" I yanked my blade out, and with a single fluid swipe, slit his throat. Warm blood coated my hand as he fell to the damp ground with a thump.

I stared at his lifeless form, feeling nothing. It was just another death. Another life taken to save Mother and our mission.

Resheathing my dagger, I glanced back at Mother. A lone tear trickled down her cheek, and mud covered her dark purple gown. Her empathy shone through. Mother cared, even when they wronged her. I didn't, not one bit.

I missed that.

"Mother." I stepped forward and brushed her lilac hair from her face. "Don't listen to him. You're the kindest woman in all the realms, dedicating your time to reuniting the kingdoms, the realms, and our people. You're saving us." After taking a deep breath, I added, "I know now is not the time, but as your bodyguard and confidant, I must know why a peasant attacked you. Aren't they loyal to you?" It made no sense that anyone would side with Aris and his lies. He had betrayed them.

"Not everyone knows why Aris is being executed. They won't know until the trial. Plus, it's nothing to worry about." Her jaw clenched as she stared at the peasant.

"From the death grip you have on the bench, I'd say it's something to worry about." I tilted her chin up to peer into her eyes. Anger, sadness, and pain flickered through them, and I cringed internally. This was my fault. I was her bodyguard. Preventing this was my job. "Mother, I'm here to protect you, but to do that, I need to know everything we're facing inside and outside the palace."

"Tartarus, it's just a stupid rumor."

I placed my hands on her shoulders. "Elaborate. Please."

Mother shrugged. "Aris is spreading lies to the guards, telling them they shouldn't trust me, that I'm determined to bring everyone under a reign of terror. I guess the rumors are reaching the villagers now."

My nostrils flared, and I dropped my hands, clenching them into fists as I paced. Mother was the savior, fixing the problems Aris never dared to. The list of reasons why Aris deserved to die a thousand deaths kept growing. It had started accumulating the moment I learned what his ancestors, those born from the Fire God, Aggeeshvar, did centuries ago. They had massacred almost everyone with demon blood. My and Mother's lineage. "Let me deal with him. He won't talk again once I'm finished."

"Son." She placed her cold hand on my burning cheek. "No matter how much I'd like for you to punish him, you can't."

With my booted foot, I swiped the wet grass near the bench. "Why not?"

"Because you can't be near him, especially not alone." Her mist hovered around me, my warning to watch myself. When we were angry, we both had a problem controlling our tempers.

"That rule shouldn't matter anymore." I raked my hand through my slicked-back hair. "He's behind bars, getting executed in a week. Who cares if he learns demon blood runs in my veins—or yours, for that matter?"

"It's obvious from what just happened that he still has influence over this kingdom. You're not about to leak our true heritage and give him more ammunition." She cocked her head to the side. "Not unless you want to risk our mission."

"You're right. I'm sorry, Mother." I dug the toe of my boot farther into the wet mush. It would've been nice, but I couldn't put everything we'd been working on in jeopardy.

Uniting the fractured realms would make Mother and I heroes to millions, and once we saved everyone, they'd realize not all demons, especially half-demons, were bad. We wouldn't have to hide anymore. This was also my chance to rectify the past and hopefully feel some glimpse of happiness in the future.

"It's okay, son. Soon, he'll get what's coming to him. The wait will be worth it." She wrapped her arms around me. We squeezed each other tight, our deepening breaths settling into a rhythm. All the while, images of Aris's future beheading flooded my mind.

She pulled away. "I need to change and clear my head. Please take care of this mess. Once finished, you can have the rest of the day off." After giving me a forced smile, she snapped her fingers and vanished.

I approached the dead peasant. He had dark skin, a tattered gray tunic, and a baby face. He couldn't have been older than twenty. I searched through the grungy metal *ghadee* wrapped on his wrist to see if he had a family. I'd have to write a fake condolence letter if so.

Static hummed around the fuzzy three-inch projections popping off the screen. I clicked the icon of his face, which pulled up his photos. I could barely make them out, but I got the gist. He had a family. Multiple photos were of him with an orange-eyed, burly man and a curly-haired toddler. One, in particular, had a blurry sign that said, *Love you, Daddy.* Years ago, this would have touched me. I might've felt bad for killing a family man. But not anymore.

I gathered sticks around the river and built a wood pile to burn the peasant. Once finished, I threw him on top, pulled out my flint stones, and ignited the mound.

The scent of burning flesh wafted in the air, and the crackling of fire drifted to my ears, along with a sneeze coming from a nearby bush.

Within seconds, I loomed behind it. Curled in a ball and shaking uncontrollably was Lila, my golden blonde bedwarmer. I yanked on her ruffled sleeve and pulled her up to face me. As her strawberry eyes locked onto my gaze, a sour taste filled my mouth. "What is this? You've been spying on me?" Inwardly, my veins blackened as my grip tightened on her forearm.

Her shoulders sagged, and the color drained from her face as she gripped the pendant on her necklace, a family heirloom she claimed protected her. I wanted to laugh. Nothing would save her now.

"No. After you left my chambers, I watched you leave and noticed he did, too." She half glanced at the peasant and jerked back. "It set me on edge, so I followed to make sure you were okay. I wanted to protect you, my love."

"Protect me?" A demonic laugh bubbled up my throat. "You moron. Now you need protection *from* me."

She dropped to her knees. "Please. Don't kill me."

"You've seen and heard too much. You know what I am now." In this realm, veins or eye colors revealed a creature's true identity. For me, it happened to be my veins, which were easy to conceal. But wanting her to see the truth for herself, I allowed my blackened veins to the surface and extended my arm, flaring my fingers in front of her.

A small gasp escaped her plump lips as she stared at my arms. "This doesn't change anything. My feelings are still the same. I love you, and I swear your family's secrets are safe with me. I would never tell a soul."

Words and promises meant nothing to me. People said anything to escape death. Everyone in this realm of element wielders and pixies grew up despising the seers and fearing the creatures of the night, especially the demons.

Even if, for some miraculous reason, she told the truth and intended to keep our secrets safe, if she ever accidentally slipped up and the realm found out, it would all be over. "I have no choice."

"Yes, you do, Tartarus. You can let me go." She gulped. "You care for me."

I snorted. "Care for you? Are you serious?" Besides Mother and Vilo, no one mattered to me. They hadn't in a long time.

"Yes, I'm serious. Be my hero! Save me." Tears rolled down her face, and I bit my lip.

"I can't," I said, tone flat. I wouldn't risk everything for some girl.

She shot up, grabbed my head, and smothered me with kisses. I dug deep into my soul and tried to find anything there for her—any reason to save her. She'd been my mistress for months. It shouldn't have been hard to find something. I should've cared about her.

But I didn't.

Not even a little.

It surprised me that she, or anyone, could still love me. They shouldn't.

She grabbed my ass, my turn-on spot. But I clenched my jaw tightly and held her away. Her lips trembled under my scrutiny, eyes pleading, as if there was some part of me that would care.

I sighed, shook my head, and snapped her neck. Her body sagged forward, and I heaved her up, then tossed her atop the burning pile like an old, dirty rag.

For a while, I watched the two bodies turn to ash. Though not an ounce of remorse formed, something raw and rampant burned deep inside, and my desire to break things magnified. Inflicting pain was the only thing that gave me some sense of life, that proved I was still alive. Otherwise, I would venture down an even darker path.

So, as the fire licked away, I gave in to my yearnings and destroyed the nucha trees nearby. I kicked and punched every trunk, branch, and root, ignoring the blood and sharp pain vibrating through my limbs and down my spine.

The poisonous sap dripping into my cuts, attempting to bypass my demon blood and eat away at my flesh, was a welcome burning torture, but not enough. Not this time. With those words echoing in my mind, *be my hero,* nothing could stop the memory of my previous attempt at being one— the reason I was dead inside.

Heat flashed through my body, and my muscles quivered.

I forced myself to watch the fire smolder instead of reliving my sacrifice.

Once it died down to a small flame, Lila's flower necklace glowed between two blackened branches. I snatched it up and stared at the tiny golden petals that once lay against her chest. I'd hoped Lila would break through my walls, but she couldn't. No one could. I flung the necklace back into the fire and turned away.

Back when I lived in Hellspace, many of the demons there had urged me not to make the sacrifice to the goddess Deesse. They had warned me I'd regret it, that being a foolish hero wasn't worth her demands. But at the time, I didn't believe them. Now it was clear they'd told the truth.

For the rest of my sad life, I'd never truly love anyone or care about those I killed.

It was impossible. I no longer had a heart. Deesse demanded it to seal the deal. Before I even had a chance to change my mind, she tore my heart from my chest and burned it to ash.

Two

From the mouths of frongflies, electronic dance music filled Madhushalla and soothed my soul. I swung my leg over the wooden stool at the end of the bar, took a seat, and held out my hand for my usual. After what had just transpired, I needed a thick, bubbly liquor. Nicols, the bartender with more hair than a horse, slid my drink down the floating fuchsia metal counter without spilling a drop. Just as I grasped the warm glass, a clammy hand encompassed mine.

What the hell? I glanced up, grinding my teeth, ready to kill a third person.

Demeatris, one of Mother's guards. He stood by my side, orange eyes taking me in, posture stiff. Not that he could slump while suited in all that golden armor. Above his ashen face, tufts of shaggy blond hair protruded from his metal helmet.

"Tartarus, sorry for interrupting your time off, but there is a heavy debate regarding your mother's safety that needs your attention." Demeatris leaned closer and lowered his voice to a whisper. "This is the only way I could pass along King Aris's message. He needs to see you. I swear you won't regret it. Please come." Demeatris turned, almost knocking over a tray of glitter bomb shots, and strode toward the exit.

One: How the hell did Aris corrupt our guard? Could we trust no one? Two: There was nothing Aris could say that I wanted to hear unless he was going to explain why he was spreading lies and accusing Mother of being a terror. But why would he share those things with me? He hated me as much as I hated him.

Demeatris's royal armor reflected the lights as he wove through the crowd, and a knot formed in my stomach. I stroked my freshly trimmed goatee before throwing my head back and sighing. I didn't want to disobey Mother's rule of not seeing the king, but this was the first time Aris had sought me out. I was the bastard. He wanted nothing to do with me. Now he did. And he'd be dead soon. I couldn't deny him.

I rushed after Demeatris as he opened the swinging door leading out into the sunny village. Nosey busybodies on their morning strolls mingled about, gossiping about Aris.

A fire-wielding mother bought *gasha* cakes from the dessert cart for her little one. As her palm blazed with fire, frying the child's pastry, she moved closer to the earth wielder covered in flowers who was whipping up another batch of cakes. "Bet King Aris will try to escape."

The pastry chef laughed. "He's a smart man. If anyone could do it, it'd be him."

Damn, if only I had the power to remove their tongues for irritating me with Aris's praise.

I placed my hand on Demeatris's shoulder. "How do you expect me to talk to Aris? He's locked up tight in the forbidden dungeon." Mother had established a law that anyone, other than guards on shift, who entered that section of the prison without her was to be immediately executed. She even removed the ability to portal into the area and the use of any powers, except demon magic, from working inside. But only Mother's most trusted guards knew that last bit.

Demeatris reached into his pocket and retrieved a metallic rainbow circle. The keys on it jingled in the wind. "Good thing my shift starts in thirty minutes."

"They'll question my being with you," I whispered as we passed several guards watching the villagers for any hint of an uprising to free their beloved fire king.

"Turn invisible." He raised a brow at me.

I jerked back. Invisibility was a power only certain demons possessed, and I'd always made sure no one saw me use it.

"The king knows more than you think."

His words knocked the wind right out of me. He knew. Holy shit. That wasn't possible. He would've done everything in his power to eliminate or torture me, just like his ancestors did to my kind. "Why hasn't he killed me, then?"

"That's a question for the king. Maybe you should hear him out."

Shit! Well, if I'd been on the fence about visiting Aris, Demeatris's words just demolished that fence. It was imperative I made sure this wasn't part of the rumors he was spreading. If it was, I had to make him stop.

I stepped between two brick buildings behind the open village market, out of view. After I inhaled deeply, my palm glowed onyx-black. I waved my hand down my body, a slight buzz drifting to my ears, and I faded into nothing.

When I trudged back out into the chaos, Demeatris was yards down the cobble path near the palace gates. I sprinted to catch up, completely forgetting my invisibility didn't hide my noisy footsteps or pained breath.

Damn my stupid curiosity.

Other than the rustling of cloth from those passing by, an eerie silence descended upon us as I followed him through the iron gates. My stomach dropped. This could be an ambush. Aris wanted to send a message to Mother. An eye for an eye.

At that realization, I should've walked away. It was the right thing to do. But I wasn't known for being logical.

Once inside the palace, I clenched my fists tight at my sides. Torches flickered over paintings of fire and earth element wielders on the walls. Annoying reminders of how corrupt this kingdom was, only allowing pixies and those two wielders. The realm's other half, The Kingdom of Ondin, wasn't any better. They only allowed the water and air wielders. Demons, witches, and any creatures of the night were banished to another realm if not wiped from existence like the seers were.

The closer we came to the dungeons, the more my lungs constricted.

In the center of the communal area, immediately before the prison, a case with spotlights displayed the treaty that had broken Climakru into separate realms and left this one with the two kingdoms—Astal and Ondin—forcing ultimate segregation. The thing Mother and I desperately wanted to repair.

My blood boiled as I scowled at the despicable contract. Before I could do anything rash, a cough echoed from the end of the hall and brought me back to the present.

We arrived in front of the prison. Demeatris spoke to the guards who stood stock-still in front of the massive wooden door. Parthenocissus vines climbed the walls, growing out and twirling near the hands of the two green-eyed guards. Fire flared from the sconces on each side of the door and covered the hands of the other two guards, the flickering flame reflected in their orange eyes. Each guard's palms glowed.

"Anything I should know before I start my shift?" Demeatris asked the guards.

"Nothing to report," one of the guards said.

Demeatris nodded, and the guards opened the door for him, releasing a cold gush of wind before revealing the long, dark hall lit by dim torches. He grabbed one and used his fire gift to brighten the flame. His palms glowed a bright orange, and his blond waves lightened a few shades. I followed him down the path, still invisible.

What did Aris want? My palms grew sweaty. Was he going to blackmail us? Our secret for his life? He had to be desperate. Mother had earned greater loyalty than him over the years. And once they found out about his betrayal, they'd never believe anything he said nor fight for him to stay alive.

Demeatris paused at an unmarked door, twisted the rainbow key until it glowed, and without ceremony, pushed it open and led us into the forbidden section. Warm air blasted the hair from my face, and the earthy scent of eucalyptus and balsam wafted forcefully into my nose. We crossed the threshold, and the stone walls, mixed with wet dirt, furthered the smell of petrichor. A few feet down, the marble floor ended, and rough stone blocks took their place down the path.

Past the main entrance, Demeatris turned right, and I trailed after him. A prisoner banged at his bars, yelling gibberish. Demeatris stopped at the cell and nudged his chin down the hall for me to continue in that direction.

At the end of the hall, a crossroads appeared. Both the middle and left halls looked identical with their red velvet tapestries of demons kneeling to the king's ancestors while being forced back to Delmore, the underworld.

I shivered and turned toward the right hall, which was completely bare, devoid of even grout lines between the stone. Two guards paced in a wide, circular opening near the door at the dead end. Their daggers gave off a rotten smell, and the poisonous olive-green sheen from the nucha trees coating the blades was impossible to miss.

If I weren't trying to remain hidden, I'd chuckle at the amount of effort Mother put into locking Aris away.

Silent as night, I slipped behind the first guard and tugged out an unconventional weapon—the enchanted chloroform handkerchief I kept at all times. Even though my magic worked here and I could easily kill them, I wasn't looking to anger Mother further when she discovered my disobedience.

The guard's lilac eyes rolled back as he fell to the stone floor with a loud thud. The second guard whirled in my direction. Sweat dripped down his neck. I stepped behind him and whistled. Might as well have some fun. The guard jumped, a wet spot forming on his pants.

A demonic cackle escaped my lips as I slapped the handkerchief to his face and directed his body toward the other guard. He collapsed in a heap on top of the first.

With both knocked out, I fumbled through their pockets and found the keys. Before unlocking the door, I hesitated, glancing over my shoulder. Finding no one, I turned the locks on the entrance and proceeded farther into the dungeon, waving one of the guard's swords in front of me as a precaution.

I only made it halfway down the hall before cringing from the stench of foul flesh and dried blood suddenly coating the inside of my nostrils. It came from a path blocked by a massive stone. This had to be where they were keeping Aris.

Scrunching my nose, I took a deep breath through my mouth and struggled with the weight of the stone, which finally moved after a few tries.

Aris's bare cell smelt like a mix of death and vomit, and I hunched over, gagging. The chains around Aris clinked as he lifted his head, crimson hair clinging to his forehead. Popped blood vessels highlighted his amber eyes, and his clothes hung loose on his body, torn in tatters.

I smirked. He deserved this.

He glanced around the room before his gaze settled on invisible me. Slowly, his dry, cracked lips curled up. "Tartarus?"

With all my strength, I pushed at the inside of the stone and attempted to roll it back as much as I could, and then waved my hand down my body. A faint buzz resonated before my magic vanished. This better be worth my disobedience.

Aris shook his head in disbelief, but his smile grew, almost touching his eyes. "Thank you for coming."

"Why did you want to speak with me, Aris?" If he didn't start confessing how the hell he knew about our bloodline or what he was planning to do with that information, he'd end up a little disfigured.

"You're the answer to saving the realms, yourself, and my child—"

"How dare you mention your treachery!" My breathing quickened. I wanted to kill him for his audacity. "You broke Mother's heart when she discovered you fathered a seer with the weak queen of Ondin." I paced the room, cracking my knuckles.

Several hundred years ago, the awful treaty that forced segregation was originally initiated to prevent two royal bloodlines from mixing and creating a seer. One reasonable decree inside the contract had ordered the execution of all seers. They were too dangerous to be allowed to live. We might've trusted their prophecies since they couldn't lie, but we didn't trust *them*.

Seers were incapable of love, and over time, lost their souls. Every past seer had let the darkness take over. They toppled empires, wiped out cities, and destroyed realms to the point some were unable to ever recover. And with their ability to see the future, they were extremely difficult to stop or kill, unlike demons.

"I'm sorry for breaking Queen Delilah's heart, but please put that aside and listen to me." He dropped to his knees.

"Why?" I rushed to him, wrapped my hand around his throat, and hoisted him up. "Unless it has something to do with why you hate demons so much and are turning people against Mother, I don't wanna hear it." My magic sizzled. "Better yet, even if it does, I don't care. Just get on with the *real* reason you sought me out. Since you know of our true heritage, I assume you want to broker a deal. Your life for our secret."

"N-n-nooo," he sputtered, waving his hands. I loosened my grip, and he coughed several times. "I've known both of your heritages for a long time and never said anything about it. I asked you here to tell you the truth. Your mother is fated to be a terror. You, on the other hand, have a different fate. Everything rests on your shoulders. Not only that. You have a chance to redeem yourself. But you'll have to save my child. Do the right thing. You don't have to be like those before you." Tears rushed down his cheeks.

Aris was loonier than I'd ever imagined. All the torture he'd endured over the last week since being in prison must've messed with his head. I released him, my body shaking. I disobeyed Mother for this. He just wanted a savior for his abomination. Thought he could convince me, a lost demonic soul. What a fool.

"Goodbye, Ar—"

"Wait. I'll share the full prophecy with you. The parts your mother doesn't know. The part confirming you're not too far gone." He knelt on the stone floor, hands pleading up at me.

The damn prophecy. The one claiming none of us would ever see peace as long as that abomination wasn't dealt with. Mother hadn't been able to rest, using almost all of her resources to find the child, ever since we discovered the prophecy a few months back.

Invisibly scouting out the palace, I'd overheard some of Aris's royal guards talking about a seer, Aris, and a treaty. I had shared it with Mother. She then searched his suite and found a stanza from the prophecy and letters between him and Queen Rosalida of Ondin, enough to warrant his execution. Mother had questioned Aris, but he had divulged nothing.

"You're lying!" I yelled, and Aris flinched. Saving his child meant the destruction of all existence, and I didn't believe any of this—especially the part about being saved since it was literally impossible. But if he knew the entire prophecy, I had to know what it was. That was probably how he found out we were demons and thought the way he did. "Is this why you think Mother is fated to be a terror?"

"That and because your mother's heart belongs to Lucifer, the King of Delmore."

"You speak blasphemy!" I fisted the collar of his shirt. My mother was a saint. She'd never align with the literal devil, the god of demons. "Besides, if you truly believed that, you wouldn't share the rest of the prophecy with me or even consider it has anything to do with me. I don't even have a heart."

"More reason to believe the prophecy is about you."

"My name isn't mentioned in it." I shook my head and shoved him away.

Aris stumbled on the cracked stone floor, then righted himself and took a deep breath.

> *"A time will come to be unified.*
> *First, the past must be rectified.*
> *The unknown seer has to be found,*
> *for the peace we live in is not sound."*

My jaw tightened. "I know this. It's the reason Mother's been searching for your child."

Torches along the wall bathed him in a flickering light, showing the clear agitation on his face. "Remember, there is more."

When I didn't move, he continued.

"Seers before have made life tragic
because of the one who woke their magic.
Today, we sway between two courses,
determined by the seer's finding forces.
A powerful—"

The stone behind me scraped against the uneven gravel, heeled shoes clacked on the floor, and the hairs on my arms rose as Mother screamed, "Tartarus! What are you doing here? Disobeying me?" She stepped in front of me, purple mist encompassing every part of her eyes, lilac curls swirling around her face.

It took all my willpower to command my legs to stay upright so that I wouldn't drop to my knees and beg for forgiveness. Behind her, Aris pressed his lips together in a taut line.

"I asked you a question." Mother dug her orchid-spiked nails into my arm. My stomach lurched into my throat. Someone had to have told Mother I was here. This was all a setup. I was such a fool.

Still holding on to me, she walked us out of Aris's dungeon into the hall. Three new guards rushed to her side. "Your Majesty, is everything okay?"

"No time to wait. The execution will be tonight. Prepare Aris and the kingdom."

The guards blinked back their confusion, and one by one, they nodded, then bowed before dashing off.

She turned to me, veins bulging in her neck. "How dare you? If you ever risk our lives again and disobey my orders,

I'll throw you back into Hellspace faster than you can blink."

The threat she'd never spoken of, but I always feared, was a reality. Holy Delmore. I had to watch myself. I'd rather die than ever return there.

Images of the tortuous place flooded my mind. I gulped as all feeling left my body, and Mother portaled us away.

Three

Once we arrived in my room, Mother released her tight grip on my arm and sat on my oak wood bed, the black comforter contrasting with her porcelain skin. Her fangs unsheathed as the mist leaked from her fingertips. It slammed into the marble floor, cracking it in several places. Paintings tore from the stone walls and flew in a whirlwind across the room. Vases, statues, and furniture split underneath the mist's claw-like tentacles.

My hands trembled, and I quickly hid them behind my back before she could see. Mother had plenty of full-blown tantrums before, even more after having her heart broken. But she had never destroyed my room, my things. But that didn't make her a terror. She'd never done anything like this before because I'd never disobeyed her.

"The audacity you had to defy me." She twisted her fingers, and the mist tore my pillow to shreds. Feathers fell everywhere. "You have always been so faithful. What did I do wrong that would make you visit the man who broke me, who killed our people? Unless ... you don't love me. You're trying to help him."

Black spots blurred my vision. "Mother—" The mist sealed my lips shut. Shit. I'd really hurt her. I never should've gone to see him, even if I was trying to help her. It sucks even more that the visit didn't amount to anything useful. Just a load of made-up stories and impossibilities.

Taking deep breaths, trying to calm the fear, sadness, and confusion, I leaned against the wall, now bare except for my speakers. The instrumental piano music slowly trickled into my thoughts. I focused on the minor keys, letting them soothe me and push the fears back down where they belonged as I waited for her to remove the mist or say something more. But that was a mistake. My freed mind gave Aris's words, words about Mother and Lucifer, room to dance inside. I'd never wondered how she had such advanced power or where the mist had come from. Neither half-demons nor vampires possessed that ability.

Both half-demons and vampires could portal, heal incredibly fast, and conjure some spells. But if we killed leaders of the underworld, we gained their powers. That was how I'd acquired invisibility and mind control—a relic from my time in Hellspace, the underworld's domain above ground on Climakru. Mother couldn't have aligned with Lucifer. She had to have killed a few leaders. One of them must've had mist abilities.

It made more sense.

Mother sat up, her breaths evening out. The mist ventured back toward her from all over the room and freed my mouth. Several things clattered to the floor with a bang as her veins glowed purple, absorbing the last of the mist.

"I'm ready to hear it. Why were you speaking to Aris?"

Think. *Think!* I couldn't tell Mother he searched for me or that he'd been keeping her in the dark about the prophecy until I knew its entirety. I had to ensure nothing upset her more or made her question my loyalty.

"On my stroll in the village, rumors reached me that Aris might escape. I wanted him to know what would happen if he tried." I fidgeted with Slinger, the deadly seven-pointed star dangling from my neck.

"Why didn't you tell me?" She bounded off the bed and approached.

"What if he was in the process of escaping? I didn't have time to come to you first." Did I just lie to her? What was wrong with me? I'd never done that before. My head ached. Any second, I'd hurl.

She lifted her hands, and it took all my strength not to step back. It didn't matter how much Mother loved me. Punishment was punishment, and we both enjoyed inflicting it on others, especially when they disrespected us.

Smiling, she caressed my cheeks as I flinched. "Thank you, my son."

Holy Delmore. My mouth dried, and the tension in my shoulders eased. The story really worked. She believed me.

Several thunks came from the marble tile just outside my door before I could respond.

"Come in," Mother said in her soothing voice.

A guard opened the door. "The execution platform should be ready soon." He bowed.

"Thank you for letting me know." Once the guard left, she turned back to me. "Time for Mama to get her rightful revenge."

Arm-in-arm, we strolled through the palace, venturing toward the execution platform outside. Mother remained silent, giving me more time to ponder this turn of events. She'd originally scheduled his execution for a week from now. What changed her mind? Did she fear I'd talk to him again?

Could she know more of the prophecy and want to keep it from me?

Impossible.

Aris was messing with my head with his talk of me saving myself. I trusted Mother with my life. She wouldn't keep me in the dark about anything—especially something like that. She probably figured he found out about her heritage and wanted to kill him before he shared it with more people.

Mother stopped outside the kitchen. "Want a cardamom roll? I know they're your favorite." She smiled and led me farther into the bright white room with shiny crystal countertops. The cooks backed into the wall, their hands folded in front of them, eyes gleaming with pride.

She opened the oven door, filling the room with crisp notes of camphor, and pulled out two rolls. I took one from her and smiled. Aris was wrong. A mother who spared time for her son wasn't one who aligned with Lucifer.

I bit into the roll, and a soft moan escaped my lips as I savored the sweet spice and enjoyed the warmth coating my throat. Once finished, I linked my free arm with hers. "All right, I'm ready."

The second we stepped outside onto the gallows, the chatter from the overpacked wooden pews silenced. Those gathered rose to their feet in respect as Mother and I strolled to her portable throne. The elegantly carved seat rested atop a stone platform directly between the palace and the black metal gates that opened into the eerie forest.

Mother squeezed my hand and took her seat. The sun shone on her face, brightening her lilac hair and dull stare. I rested my hand on the throne's bumpy armrest. Mother then took a deep breath, faced the cellar doors, and snapped her fingers at the guards. They nodded and signaled for the one holding Aris to bring him forward.

The chains around Aris's wrists rattled as the guard

dragged him onto the wooden square just below us. A guard next to the stone chopping block kicked Aris's knees and forced him to kneel. Another guard at the edge of the platform began chanting, a spell I didn't recognize, and a zoomed-in projection of Aris's bruised face hovered in the air. Several people in the pews gasped.

Wanting to know if anyone had reacted out of sympathy, I glanced over at the pews. No one shed a tear or protested with raised fists. Satisfied, I searched for Queen Rosalida's parents or those from Ondin, her side of Climakru. Somehow, they always made it to our executions, even when we planned one to happen within minutes. With this execution being *the king*, I doubted they'd miss it, especially when it involved Rosalida.

"What are you doing?" Mother placed her hand on mine.

"Seeing if anyone from The Kingdom of Ondin showed."

Mother's grip tightened.

"I don't see any." I smiled at her in an attempt to ease her worry. But we all knew they'd show at some point, just like we would if roles were reversed—always the unwanted guests on either side. The only difference, this time, I wanted them to show.

Since we didn't have authority over anyone in Ondin, we couldn't punish Rosalida or get involved in their politics. Instead, we'd have to rely on gossip spreading about today and hoping that would start a riot in Ondin and turn more to our side.

"Let's just get this over with." Mother glided off the throne and into the center of the platform. "Today, I, Delilah, the Queen of Astal, charge King Aris of Astal with breaking the treaty set forth by our ancestors and plotting against the royal throne. Citizens of Astal, seventeen years ago, your king mated with Queen Rosalida. They had a child, a seer."

People cried out, dropping to their knees.

Mother waited for silence before she continued, but it

took forever. They just kept wailing. A part of me loved that they understood the gravity of Aris's treachery, but another part wished they didn't care this much. Their incessant sobs made my head throb.

"Not only are their two bloodlines forbidden to have offspring together since they do more than just threaten the safety of our kingdom, but they also kept it a secret from you and let the child live. They hid the disgrace from us. I know this warrants his execution. But ..." Tears streamed down her face. "... I recently discovered something realm-changing hidden in a 300-year-old prophecy."

Several tilted their heads and gripped the edge of their seats as a deeper silence fell around us. Mother definitely knew how to capture the crowd's attention.

"This prophecy claims our peace is not sound while the child remains hidden. If we want peace, we must find this child and execute it. Every day it gets older, is a day closer to it gaining more power and destroying us all. It's biding its time, waiting to strike. Let's not give it one second more."

Cheers echoed around us and bounced off the white sandstone castle walls. Their eagerness for death eliminated some of my desire to shut them up. I glanced at Aris. He remained stone cold. For someone about to die, his blank expression surprised me.

"Because we must find the child, I'm going to give the king the chance to live if he shares the child's whereabouts. Does anyone have an objection?"

The air crackled with tension, but no one spoke.

"Proceed with the interrogation, Tartarus."

What the hell? She had moved his execution to tonight after I had talked to him, and now she wanted to let him live and have *me* be the interrogator.

I shook my head to erase the thoughts and stepped off Mother's platform onto the wooden square. Aris wouldn't share his child's location. He'd die protecting it, and with it, the impossible secrets of how I could save myself. Good thing I didn't believe him.

A few feet from Aris, I grabbed the dagger off the planks next to the guard and then towered in front of Aris. "Want to share?"

He shook his head as I'd figured he would.

"No last words before you die?" I spat at him and gave him a minute to react, but he continued to peer at me with a hint of desperation, his torn, bare skin exposed for all to see. Since Aris wouldn't acknowledge his discomfort, I pulled up my sleeves, kicked him to the floor, and stepped on his back, flattening him against the scratchy, uneven wood.

Before we'd talked in the dungeon, I'd longed to torture him for what his ancestors had done to my kind. I tried holding onto that feeling instead of concentrating on the lump forming in my throat. I couldn't let a deranged man get to me and ruin what I had with Mother. His pain was payment for speaking ill of her, risking my life, and making me question things. I pressed him harder against the planks.

He still didn't say a thing, but now his face held an arrogant grin as he gazed up at Mother. The veins on my forehead bulged. There was no way she missed that blatant insult, not with the huge projection showing every minuscule detail.

Gasps filled the air as shock spread amongst the witnesses in the pews. They saw. Mother and I should've cut his head off immediately. But I couldn't act too soon. Dead men tell no tales.

"Don't you want to live? Tell me where your child is. Look, if you don't tell me, when we find the child ..." I leaned down, grabbed a chunk of his hair, and pulled him up before speaking the last part quietly so that no one could hear. "... Mother will make its suffering even worse."

His stupid smirk disappeared, and he paled. A second

later, his eyes widened. His face said everything. He slipped. Though he tried to hide it, the veil had dropped, and there was no way to undo it. He just confessed to all who witnessed that he had, in fact, broken the treaty. Although he'd told me in the dungeons, Mother only suspected, and the witnesses could've doubted her.

With his unspoken confession, my lungs turned to stone.

"I knew it! How dare you betray the kingdom, our people!" Mother jumped from her throne and whacked Aris across the face, the scent of iron filling the air.

Aris's broken body stumbled, and he could barely keep his eyes open. But somehow, he mustered enough strength to glare at her and speak. "I'll neither confirm nor deny having a child, and you'll never torture me into telling you." He spat a wad of thick blood at her feet.

Bold. I flexed my fingers, ready to tear him apart. But then I glanced into his eyes, and the unspoken secret that lay there taunted me. My diaphragm compressed. I couldn't breathe.

Anger. Anger. Hold on to anger.

Mother's face blazed red as she slashed him again with her long, spiked nails, but nothing she could do would get a reaction out of him. He wouldn't apologize, beg, scream, or tell us where the wretched thing was. Still, she continued to try.

As Mother's fist swung back for another go, several from Ondin walked in, and I interrupted her.

"My Queen, is this necessary?" Although Mother and I loved making others pay for what they did, The Kingdoms—especially Ondin—couldn't know that. Plus, he needed to die before he confessed our true identities or the rest of the prophecy. It didn't matter that Aris and I never finished our conversation. I'd rather he take his delusions of my fate to the grave than have Mother discover the whole thing.

Mother wouldn't hesitate to get rid of me if she thought I'd mess with her mission of uniting the realms. Besides loving her, I owed her for bringing me out of Hellspace. She'd sent all of her wicked demon children and most of her demon servants there to live among the other riffraff once she believed they had no hope of living in society anymore. She sent me at the age of five, and I was the only one ever released. If I caused any problems with the mission, I'd wind up back there. She'd already threatened it if I disobeyed again.

Mother seethed. "Necessary? Everything *I* do is necessary because *I* am the queen."

"No disrespect meant, Mot—"

She slapped my cheek. The spikes from her rings drew blood. Tension in the air grew thick, the crowd dead silent. Only the glowing critters in the wind dared to move.

"My Queen." I bowed. "You know he won't tell you anything. No amount of torture will change that. Finish him." My voice shifted to a whisper. "Other witnesses from Ondin just walked in." I wiped my clammy hands on my satin tunic. "Get this over with." I moved to the throne, fidgeting with Slinger and keeping an eye on Aris.

"King Aris, you have neither confirmed nor denied these accusations. Without confirmation in either direction, the kingdom's rule is that such a person is admitting to the accused crime, and the punishment is death."

Mother's mist slithered around her hands. Shit. Did she want rumors to spread or a coup to start? She'd never been this bad at hiding her magic. I was usually more at risk than her.

Beads of sweat trickled down my forehead as I stepped before her again, grabbing her hands to hide the mist. "Let me take the burden off you, Your Majesty. I shall make it quick. Why don't you return to the throne? I'm sure your people will understand." I kissed her hands.

Straight away, the mist evaporated. I hated how we both had to hide our demon magic.

With a sigh, Mother glided back to her throne. Of course,

she wanted to make the killing blow, but all that really mattered was his death. With that, she'd finally receive revenge, payment for Aris destroying her heart. She'd also gain his throne. A position in which only the death of a royal spouse, by treachery, would relinquish the claim to a non-heir.

Mother would assume I did the honorable thing and was fulfilling my role as her bodyguard by helping her hide the mist that proved our true heritage, but I did it so I could seek vengeance and squash the questions he had provoked in me.

I plunged my dagger deep into Aris's chest. With my ear close to his lips, he choked out a pitiful whisper, "Historians know the truth."

I twisted the dagger in farther. He screamed, a heart-wrenching cry, and his body grew limp. Mother gasped while sobbing hysterics came from the pews. But I didn't pay attention to any of it. I was too intent on trying to understand his hidden message. Aris clearly wanted to use his last breath to ensure I learned the rest of the prophecy. Damn it, it'd worked.

Killing him didn't kill the questions.

This wasn't over. Not by a long shot.

Four

Critters chirped in the distance while several hundred people watched my every move, including Mother. I didn't have time to dawdle or stand here frozen by Aris's words. Not unless I wanted to create suspicions. Or worse, have people think I regretted it.

"The betrayer is dead, Your Majesty." I bowed. She tilted her head in acknowledgment, and I waved over the nearest guards. "Take this man's body and burn it. For the rest of you, your queen has had a rough day. She appreciates your condolences. Nevertheless, out of respect, we ask you to return home so your queen may mourn privately." My stern voice ricocheted through the air.

The witnesses rushed out, trampling over one another. Good.

Mother turned to me. "Meet me in my room tonight. We need to discuss our plans."

"Why not now?" I didn't want to be left alone with Aris's words bouncing around in my head.

"I need to feed. With all this stress, I haven't quenched my thirst in a while."

I thought her sunken eyes and the bones protruding from her body were due to the heartbreak, not lack of feeding. But it made sense. "Go!" I squeezed her hand, and she sped off, leaving me to relive the last few moments alone.

Historians? None existed in the palace anymore. And the moment Mother became queen, not just Aris's concubine, she burned every history book throughout Astal. She informed everyone she hated the inequality and didn't want any reminders of the war 300 years ago. No one questioned her. But now I did. If she truly wanted to rid the kingdom of any reminders, she should've also taken down the paintings, tapestries, and sculptures on the way to the dungeons.

I moved toward the back entrance of the palace. I had to visit the library to see if I could find anything the guards missed when clearing it out. But before I reached the door, someone tapped my shoulder. My magic stirred. I didn't want to be disturbed. "Go away before—"

"You want a distraction?" Darcy purred and bit my left ear.

I shivered. I hadn't smelt the potent mix of musky jasmine or heard that voice since leaving Hellspace two years ago. "How did you manage to find your way out?" No one escaped. It was impossible. Although I never thought it likely, somehow, she must've done something good to warrant Mother's attention and permit her removal.

"Queen Delilah let the leaders out to watch the king's execution. She said it'd be a test to see if we could behave." She turned me to face her, and I surveyed her juicy red lips, pink cheeks, and blood-red hair.

"Wait, leaders? You're a leader?"

"Jeroboam took over after you left. He made me his queen to spite you and convinced Saullis to rule with us, though

Jeroboam still holds the ultimate authority." She rolled her eyes.

A chill ran down my spine. Besides Mother and me, the three strongest demons now ruled Hellspace.

"She ordered us to return at dawn. So come on, how about one last night together before I leave?" She tugged on my belt and drew me closer.

"Won't Jeroboam get jealous or punish you for seeking me out?" I raised my eyebrows.

"Oh, trust me, he will. He has a vendetta against you and anyone associated with you besides Queen Delilah. But it'll be worth it. What do you say?" She bit her plump lower lip.

I groaned as my magic sizzled and urged me to take her up on the offer. Back in Hellspace, she was obsessed with me, and I took her as my concubine. I didn't care for her like she did me, though. But I loved her demon side and attitude. Plus, she was a force in bed. I shook my head to dispel the memories. "As much as I'd love to, there's something I have to do."

"Your loss." She brushed her hair off her shoulder and sauntered off.

I gawked after her, admiring her butt cheeks swinging from left to right below her oversized tunic. She had always found bottoms burdensome.

Once she disappeared, I continued on my mission to the library.

With the halls ten times quieter than usual, my shoes made an audible squeak. But it didn't bother me. I wasn't doing anything wrong. I was allowed to visit the library.

About to walk in, I stepped back as the picture frame next to the door caught my eye. I approached the painting and studied it. Mother posed next to a small window in a beautiful ivory gown. Her hair flowed down her left side with an olive ribbon loosely securing it. A bird rested in her hand, and she had the most joyous smile. It was the happiest I'd ever seen her.

But it wasn't the serenity of the photo that had caught my attention—it was the location.

The picture showed a smaller room inside her chambers. It was supposed to be for a pet, but Mother feared an animal living that close would stink up her area, so she locked the room and forbade anyone from entering, even me. On rare occasions, though, I'd witnessed guards carrying artifacts and concealed items into the place. I started calling it her private vault.

I grinned. If I knew Mother as well as I thought, she wouldn't completely destroy anything. The sealed area could have something about the Historians. It could have the banned items. But it was locked tight, and I was already on thin ice.

I weighed out my options. One: learn how to possibly save myself and risk Mother sending me back to Hellspace, as well as disappoint her. Two: drop this. My body ached at the mere thought of giving up.

My palm sparked onyx-black, and I waved my hand over my body. I vanished into thin air and headed outside. Guards watched her chambers at all times. I couldn't portal there either. I had tried before, but she sealed it against any magic other than her own. But the window was a different story. As an occasional assassin, I had learned how to pry open almost anything.

By the time I reached the vault's small sash window, my sweaty clothes clung to my back. I snapped Slinger off my chain, and he almost slipped out of my clammy hands. My lungs tightened, and I wiped my palms on my navy tights before using Slinger. I maneuvered one of his razor-sharp tips into the window's corner and picked at it.

After several scrapes to the side of my hand, Slinger snapped in place. I pushed the window up and created a big enough opening for me to creep through.

Pictures, lamps, jewelry, and other trinkets covered almost every inch of the floor, but I found a small, untouched spot and stepped inside. Next to me stood a Victorian lamp. I pulled the switch, and the room brightened.

A rustic bookcase concealed the wall behind me.

Thick dust covered the shelves like winter's first snow. Staring at it, I rubbed the back of my neck, contemplating whether to turn back. It'd be impossible not to leave a fingerprint or evidence that I'd been there if I stayed. And once Mother found out, she'd kill me.

But if I didn't discover the truth of Aris's words, I might let her.

I searched the titles of the leather-bound books. *History of the Gods. The Beginning. Forever Alive.* My shoulders slumped. None of these looked useful, but I kept skimming.

One section near the bottom displayed books whose titles were almost unreadable. I squinted. *Past or Future. Historians.*

Yes! My face broke into a grin, and I grabbed the book, but several others came with it. I reached out and tried to catch them, but there were too many. They fell to the floor with a succession of loud bangs.

Holy Delmore. My body tensed. Any chance I had of Mother not knowing had just disappeared.

Boots stomped on the other side of the door. I placed the book underneath my arm, shut off the light, and rushed out the window. Just as the pane clicked shut, the door flung open.

The guards searched the room, and after finding no one, they shook their heads and left.

I let out a painful breath. Shit. Though they hadn't seen me, they'd still report the disturbance to Mother. And when, not if, she asked me about it, I had no idea what I'd do. Could I lie to her again? I was supposed to be her favorite, not her disobedient, lying son. I'd lost all sense.

After my breathing calmed, my palm glowed onyx-black, and I rubbed my thumb and forefinger together. A light charcoal mist swirled around me as I portaled to my chamber. I slumped on the floor, back against the bed, and fidgeted with Slinger.

If I knew what was good for me, I wouldn't open the book. I'd let Aris's words vanish from my mind. But as I stared at the grungy leather cover, a magnetic pull called to me. I couldn't resist.

I opened the book.

A few pages in, a passage caught my eye.

When Sorcieres, the witch god, opened the gateway between realms, Historians used that opportunity to gather information about the other places. Historians might have received their title because they didn't have much magic, but their ability to remember everything they saw made them plenty magical. We wouldn't know the amount we did without them.

Well, that answered a question I had always wondered about, but it didn't help me with my current dilemma. I continued reading.

Stuffed between the pages in the middle of the book was a picture. I pulled it free. It was an image of a huge, gray-bricked building in the shape of an L, with orange benches and tulip patches in the central yard. In the middle was an archway with hefty bold letters above it reading, *Olivia Hall.*

I scrunched my eyebrows. Why had someone put this here? I flipped the image. On the back, someone had scrawled *The best hidden gem on Earth. My favorite library in all the realms.* It was written in cursive gold script with hearts for the dots above every I.

Oh, my gods! I shot up. This was Vilo's handwriting. Aris had meant her, my maiden, and his old Historian. When

Mother had asked the remaining Historians to leave the palace two years ago, Vilo's frail skin and wrinkled body had bothered me. She could've died out there in the dank villages. So, I had begged Mother to let her stay as my maiden. After all, she had been my nanny when I was little.

I couldn't believe it had taken me this long to piece it together. In minutes, I might know not only the rest of the prophecy but also how to possibly save myself. My breathing became shallow. What if she had forgotten? What if Aris was wrong? He couldn't be, could he?

I rubbed my fingers together and portaled to Vilo's room. She had to remember, or the risks I'd taken had been for nothing.

Five

The scent of rosemary hit my nose before I even fully portaled through. Vilo lounged at the head of her bed, leaning against the sidewall, legs crossed, the lamp shining a light on her perfect white hair and honey-colored skin. She had a book in hand, just like always.

"Ahem," I coughed.

She peered up from the pages and smiled. "What's troubling you?" She tossed her book aside and scooted to the edge of the bed.

"Vilo." I slumped into the chair beside the open window, the cold breeze kissing my cheeks. "This is hard for me to say, to even think." I stared into her sea-green eyes.

"Tartarus, you're scaring me. Your body is shaking, and is that sweat?" She lifted her hand to my forehead and wiped the dampness away. "I don't think I've ever seen you sweat."

"I think Aris gave me a message to speak with you before he died. Do you know why?" I grabbed her hand and squeezed. Vilo was like a second mother to me. I trusted her.

Her face paled, and her gaze drifted to the door.

Uncomfortable seconds ticked by, but I didn't interrupt her silence or thought process. I learned long ago that if I rushed her, she'd shut down.

Finally, she nodded, lips curling in, as she pulled her hand free from mine.

I gulped. "Does this have to do with the 300-year-old prophecy?"

"Yes." She took a deep breath and leaned against the wall.

Uh-oh. This couldn't be good.

"Do I have a place in this prophecy?" I hunched down and peered over at her.

"Yes." She kept her eyes averted.

"Please tell me. What is the rest of the prophecy? Aris was cut off after mentioning the seer's finding forces." I glided my hands over the scratchy comforter.

Vilo's head shot up, eyes turning a lime green as she whispered,

"If the dark soul cloaked in lies
convinces the seer to make ties..."

Her body shook. I placed my hands on her shoulders, but the shaking only worsened.

"...then we'll be under strict tyranny
without unification or harmony."

"Aris thinks this is Mother? That's part of why he was convinced she'd be a terror." My throat tightened. There was no way. Mother might have harsh methods for discipline, but they weren't any worse than those of Hellspace. She wasn't a bad person.

"Yes." She bit her lip. "As do I."

I shuffled backward as if she had slapped me, slammed

into the desk, and slid down on my backside. If it weren't for my love for Vilo, I'd have punished her for talking badly about Mother. Instead, I clutched handfuls of the shaggy rug. "How could you? Mother let you stay in the palace. She loves you."

"Only because of you."

The veins in my neck throbbed. "How does Mother capturing the seer and doing what Aris and Queen Rosalida should've done make her into a dark soul? She wants to kill her, not make ties." I glared at Vilo. She couldn't lie to me. If she did, the color of her irises dulled, giving her away.

"Your mother wants the seer for her own gain. She wants to control all the realms: Climakru, Trikru, Strikru, Skylight, Delmore, Earth, and the Gateways." Her eyes brightened.

"No, she wants to combine them. Unite everyone." I ground my teeth, trying to keep my anger from brewing further and doing something I'd regret.

"Tartarus, she wants to *control* them. She wants to be a god."

"You're lying." I jumped up and fisted her shirt. Her lips trembled under my heated gaze. I took a deep breath and dropped my hands. I wouldn't hurt her.

"Look into my eyes. Do you really think I'd lie to you? You're like the son I never had." They hadn't dulled. She wasn't lying. And deep down, my gut knew that. "Tartarus, don't forget there is more. The part about your fate. The reason Aris sought you out and you then came to me. Out of everything the prophecy shares, this is the part I care most about."

I shook my head, scared to hear it.

> *"A powerful warrior without a heart*
> *will bond with the seer at the start.*
> *A heart will form as theories are believed,*
> *then unification under love will be achieved."*

She placed her chilly hands on my cheeks. "Tartarus, this warrior is you. This prophecy is proof you can rebuild your heart and become the loving, caring boy I know is still inside you."

"I have no idea how you or Aris knew I didn't have a heart. But both of you are delusional. It's impossible for it to return." I couldn't believe in this prophecy. At least, I couldn't believe my supposed role in it. I couldn't allow myself to have hope. I took a deep breath, the earthy, sweet notes from the outside filling my lungs.

"We know a lot. Our knowledge goes even further back to when you were born. Aris saw the black in your veins and didn't see any color to represent an element wielder in your eyes. With Aris being a direct descendant of the fire god and seeing nothing inside you to resemble the fire element, he knew you weren't his."

"Mother pretended I was Aris's son?" Even I knew that was impossible.

"For months, she tried convincing him. He grew very suspicious and followed her for weeks. One day, he found her speaking to Lucifer. The god of demons was in front of her, caressing her, and she demanded more power from him. She wanted more than a son from him. He imparted some of his powers to her, including the mist she doesn't believe anyone notices. That's why it's so powerful. It's a part of him. Everything he can do, it can do, but to a lesser extent."

My breath caught in my throat. Vilo shook me, but I didn't move. I was the devil's son. I always wondered who my father was. I figured a demon. But *the* demon? That had never crossed my mind. My mother and Lucifer, an item? No way.

"If I'm Lucifer's son, how come I don't have powers like him? Or the mist?"

"After your mother had you, and before Aris found out about her partnering with Lucifer, he searched for answers on what your mother was." Vilo grabbed my hand. "Turns out she was human. One year, when Sorcieres opened the space between realms, hoping the witches would come home, Delilah followed behind one of her witch friends."

My clothing itched my skin. It felt like sandpaper scratching every inch of me. I yanked at my tunic to keep it from irritating me. But it didn't help. I clutched my chest. This couldn't be real. Humans were weak. I wasn't weak. "I'm human and the son of Lucifer." The words sounded strange on my tongue.

"Don't forget that your mother is a vampire, and her blood runs through you."

I observed my veins in a new light. Blood still flowed through them despite not having the necessary organ. I'd always figured the vampire gene had passed me or Mother turned after having me because being born a vampire should be impossible.

"It won't activate unless you're close to death."

I shivered. That explained why I didn't crave blood like Mother, but still, it wasn't possible.

"Tartarus, you're also my favorite person in the universe. Your human side is what keeps you anchored and from becoming fully demonic despite not having a heart." She hugged me tight and squeezed harder until I reciprocated. As her rosemary scent engulfed me, tears flowed down my cheeks, soaking her clothes and the gray comforter.

"But knowing my past and that Lucifer is my father, how can you still think I'm the prophecy hero? And that my heart will form again? You and Aris are dreaming of the impossible." Trying to give hope to someone who learned never to hope in the unseen.

"Because both of us witnessed you growing up before you left for Hellspace. Though your mother kept you secluded in that beaten down shack, I was still your nanny. Sometimes,

Aris checked in on you while I was there." She brushed my black hair from my forehead, her touch sending warmth down my spine. "You were such a joyful little kid. You tried to save several injured insects with your healing powers. It didn't work because it only works on you, but boy, did you try. You had such an outstanding heart."

"The keyword being *had*." I pulled away from her and stared out the window into the moonless night.

"Tartarus, Aris's child will bring back your heart, and I can't wait for that day. It's the only reason I care about the prophecy. It's the reason you should care." She squeezed my shoulders. "Since prophecies can always change, I never take stock in them. But this one I have faith in because I want your joyous spirit back. I want to see you happy before I die."

"Aren't seers supposed to be worse than demons? Destroyers of realms and all that? Not capable of love either?" More problems with their theory.

"That's because every seer ever born crossed over to the dark side, either by corruption or by getting lost in the greed of predicting the future for their own gain. They never had a chance to love."

"And this one won't be that way?"

"This one, like the prophecy implies, doesn't believe in anything magical. They don't know they're a seer. But with your love for them, you'll awaken them to the truth and their magic. You'll then guide them into the positive light, warning them of the dangers." She tipped my chin up to look at her. "Together, the two of you will bring out the best in each other and unite the realms under the incredible love you share."

Pain vibrated through me. "Vilo, I wish you were right. I want my heart back, to truly love someone, but not at the expense of Mother. Like you said yourself, prophecies *change*. They aren't set in stone, and what it's suggesting is impossible for me. I'm not the warrior. Besides, I'll never betray Mother.

The only sure way the realms will unite and find peace is with the seer's death. Mother wants to do what's right for this kingdom. I'll prove it." I squeezed her hand and turned to leave.

"Tarus."

Uh oh. She used my nickname. I faced her again, and her lips trembled.

"Don't give up your future to serve someone who doesn't love you. Who is lying."

"You're wrong about her. Mother loves us. That is why I live to serve her. It's my pride and joy."

"No!" She leaped up. "That's the ridiculous slogan she made you rehearse. She's brainwashed you."

"Stop." I couldn't handle more negative talk about Mother or confusion about all of this. "You're going too far. Why can't you accept my heart is never returning?" I stormed out, not waiting for her to reply.

But as the door banged shut, Vilo's last words drifted to my ears. "Things can change, along with your heart."

My fists clenched at my side. After making the sacrifice to Deesse several had tormented me with the fact my heart would never return. I accepted that fate. There was no point in believing anything different now. An impossible theory to a prophecy wouldn't change that. Besides, if I ever had to choose between love and Mother, I'd choose Mother every time, without hesitation.

Six

Every time I approached Mother's apartment in the south wing, I couldn't help but smirk. No one knew what lay on the other side of the doors. They didn't know our secrets, our true heritage, the blood that mixed in our veins, or our dark pleasures.

They only saw the outside chamber, which was beautiful with its pink ribbons, rose gold frames, fruit decorations engraved into the wood, and the ceiling elegantly painted with the goddess of love and virtue.

I pounded on Mother's door—where only her most trusted elite entered—with our quick pound, kick, pound signature. The mist granted me entrance inside her bedroom, where it was anything but serene.

Darkness covered every wall, the only light emanating from the flickering candles. Chains hung from the top right corner. They had spikes inside the metal cuffs with skin crusted to them. Blood stained the wall and soaked the floor beneath the chains. But the worst accumulation of blood seeped through her sheets, dripping to the floor. She really was hungry, in more ways than one.

"Sit. We have much to discuss." Mother dismissed the guards and concubines with a wave. Once everyone disappeared, she spoke again. "Someone entered my private sanctuary."

My muscles tensed.

"The guards swear they didn't see anything. They believe it could've been a coincidence, but the window seams were messed with, and they don't know about your invisibility. Was it you?"

Holy Delmore. I knew she'd know. "What would I need in that room? Isn't it vacant?"

She glared at me. "That's what I'm trying to figure out."

I stayed silent and fidgeted with Slinger.

"If I discover it was you, I'll ensure the punishment they inflict when you return to Hellspace makes your last time seem like child's play." Her purple mist swirled dangerously and lifted the hairs on my arm. "You understand me?"

I nodded.

"Now, about Aris. You saw his face. I was right about everything."

"Mother, though I've always believed you, his accidental confession doesn't get us any closer. It doesn't change anything besides knowing you're not foolish." I tried to keep my feet from tapping.

"I am not foolish!" Veins bulged on her forehead, and the mist wrapped around my throat. I gagged. She closed the space between us while my consciousness faded. My stomach turned rock hard, and I almost lost control of my bladder.

Mother was good. She wasn't in cahoots with Lucifer. Mother was good. She was only doing this because I disrespected her.

"Speak." The chains rattled from the magnitude of her voice.

To keep up with appearances as one who didn't know fear, I smirked and slowly, with all the energy I had left, gestured to my throat. She clenched her jaw and removed the mist. I dropped to the floor, coughing, the cold marble surface stinging my palms. Once I gained my composure, I glanced up at her. "I didn't say you were. In fact, I said his confession confirmed you weren't."

"Fine, but, Tartarus, you better watch yourself. Now, what are we to do?" She pulled at her hair. "How can I unite the realms now?" Mother paced around the room, and the mist followed her. She mumbled her plans, mapping each one on her hand.

It was the same thing she did every time we had this conversation. Only this time, something clicked. Something in the framework had changed. "Mother, the only option is for *you* to put everything into finding the child since you announced in front of the masses today that he had one."

She stopped pacing and glared at me.

My stomach dropped. "Though the majority of the kingdom is on your side and loves you, several from Ondin were there, and who knows how many in the pews were loyal to Aris? If several were, they might start searching for the child. This secret hunt has now become an open chase."

Besides Aris and Vilo's assumption of Mother and my role in the prophecy, I believed the prophecy itself could be real. And if it was, we needed to find the child before the real dark soul it mentioned did.

Mother grabbed a fruit from the table in the corner of the room and squished it. The hot pink juices flowed down her arm. "Agreed." She turned to face me. "But our entire realm learned the same teaching about seers. We all know they're the most dangerous creatures. Even those loyal to Aris wouldn't dare protect the child, even if they wanted to keep his lineage on the throne and take me out. The more searching for the child, the better."

"What if there are people out there who believe the seer could be good?" I should've shared what Vilo had revealed, but telling her that would've led to too many questions. Questions I didn't know how to answer. Not yet.

My knowledge of the full prophecy had me walking a slippery slope. "What harm would there be in you finding the child? Only good could come from it, whether others are searching or not. It's in your best interest." I rose and leaned against the wall. "If you found it, you could even learn more from it before killing it."

"You have a good point." She cupped my chin in one hand and stroked my cheek with the other. "You know how much I hate when others tell me what to do, even if it's my own son." She smirked. The mist swirled around her wrists. "Plus, you took my kill today. You know how long I've wanted to pay him back for crushing my heart, yet you took that gratification from me. I can't leave your disrespect unpunished."

My legs trembled. This couldn't be good. I stared at the ground.

Hot liquid flowed from my cheek where her nails dug in as she tried to force my head up. Pain ricocheted through my body, but I refused to squirm or show any sign of weakness. She didn't do this because she was dark. This was punishment. I did something wrong.

I ground my teeth and peered up.

"Very good. Now, seeing as I have your attention, you'll find the offspring and bring it to me to question before we kill it."

I couldn't have heard her right. She'd send me to find a child. Not only was that beneath me, but I couldn't. My hope. Ugh. This stupid prophecy. Wait. What if, on the very slim chance, my role *was* true? That didn't mean her role was, too. I could be opening the seer to greatness, helping Mother, and then maybe she wouldn't have to kill it.

But even if I was okay with finding the child, the probability of me doing so was unlikely. When I returned without it, I could only imagine what torment would await me. My nerves skyrocketed, and I concentrated hard not to shake. "Me? Don't *you* want to find the child?"

"Of course. But I can't leave the kingdom without a ruler. And out of all my subjects, you're the only one who'll have the motivation to return quicker. Plus, you're the only one I trust. Can't you see I need you?" She pouted and dropped my chin.

Warmth traveled through me at Mother's confession. "What makes the others' motivation not as good as mine?"

She sat behind her wooden desk. "First, it makes sense that we couldn't find the despicable thing here in Climakru with all the spells we've tried, especially the bloodline trace. His offspring isn't in this realm, nor any holding magical folk. They must've hidden the child amongst the humans in the non-magical realm, Earth, and probably bound its magic."

Before she could say any more, I dared to interrupt. "Again, why does this make my motivation different?"

"Dear son." She sweetened her voice and patted the desk for me to come closer. "You're accustomed to torturing those who annoy you. On Earth, you can't do that. They'll kill you or throw you in prison. You could use magic to break free, but you'll be on the run and unable to find the seer. So, when anyone annoys you, you'll find it difficult to ... *not* punish them."

See, I was evil. How could Aris or Vilo think any different?

"I'm also giving you a time frame, and every day you spend outside of it will be one year back in Hellspace."

No! I almost screamed. Veins in my eyes exploded, blurring my vision.

Mother smirked. "Since Jeroboam spent a year rebuilding the place after you demolished it, rumor has spread that he's after vengeance. They say when any enemy faces him, their blood turns to acid, and their bones crumble to ash. And you, Tartarus, are enemy number one."

Sweat dripped down my forehead. She couldn't really suggest throwing me back there for not finding the seer in her time frame, could she? This was beyond punishment. No. No. I couldn't think like this. "What is my time frame?"

"From the moment you step on Earth, you have four weeks." She smiled and tapped my knee. "You can do it, Tartarus. I believe in you."

About a month to find a child in an extensive realm? That wasn't possible. "How do you plan on getting me to Earth? We can only portal inside the realm we're in."

Mother walked to her nightstand and pulled out an old, worn book. She waved for me to approach her. I did, and she opened the book to a page on realm travel.

"For the last few weeks, I've wondered if they hid it outside of Climakru. If they did, we'd have to find a way to travel there. I found this." She pointed to the picture on the left.

A metal vault door that led underground, with symbols of the five elements, a cauldron, fangs, and horns circling it. "I don't understand. We're using a tunnel?"

"You've heard rumors about the Gateway?"

I nodded. Long ago, that was what Sorcieres had opened once a year for the witches. But if Mother was human and had followed one, she already knew this existed.

"This is how it's accessed. You must stand in the center and confess to the guardian who you are, where your heart lies, and your allegiances."

"Umm." I stroked my goatee. "I don't have a heart. It won't work for me."

"I worried about that. Which is why I found something else." She flipped through the pages. "This way is trickier and requires a lot of work." She pointed at a picture on the right.

A pixie flew with a wand touching a shimmering barrier. Beside the pixie lay a cauldron. I read the passage underneath it.

The space between realms will only open if the seeker burns a treasure in sacrifice during a ritual requiring an old spell that only a pixie knows. But beware, a Delmore beast might still attack.

I took a step back. "We could die this way!"

"Accessing the Gateway, you can die, too. If you don't say the right things, the guardian kills you. This option gives you a fighting chance." Closing the book, she smiled and grabbed my shoulders. "I wouldn't ask you to do this if I didn't think you'd survive."

"I'm not sure the pixie will see it that way or if I'll be able to protect it."

"Who cares? This is for their queen and their realm. They'll do it. But just in case they won't, trap one and force it to." She dropped her arms and glided back to her desk.

"Oh, that'll really get it to cooperate." Mother's plan was crap.

"Better get going. You have until tomorrow at midnight." Her mist opened the door again.

"Where do I even find a pixie? You forced them out of the palace. Or this treasure?" I held tight to the doorframe. My body struggled against the mist.

"Those are your problems to figure out." She waved her hand in my direction, increasing the strength of the mist. "Tick tock."

It was past midnight when I left Mother's chambers. Instead of searching for the pixie and the treasure, I trekked to my chambers, needing to come up with a plan. But the second my head hit the pillow, the instrumental music vibrating from the speakers and the burning essence from the diffuser lulled me into a deep nightmare.

Fire from Hellspace burned me and two children. They screamed in my ears, yelling to the leader that they'd comply. They'd kill for him. He didn't care. He kept them anchored to the burning wall and used his whip to make them beg for mercy. He made me watch their torture while I was chained by scalding links that I couldn't break, no matter my strength. I flailed around, kicking the hot stone behind me.

Pain seared through my body. Raw, burnt flesh scents rose to my nose and woke me from my sleep. I shot out of bed and gripped Slinger tightly. The cold metal against my skin helped calm my nerves. It was just a nightmare. I ran my hand down the smooth silk sheets. I was in my room, not in Hellspace.

Holy Delmore. I could never return to that torturous

place. Mother was right. I had every motivation to find the child as soon as possible. I also had every motivation to believe obtaining the seer would only help Mother unite the realms in peace, proving to Vilo and dead Aris that she wasn't evil. If I believed anything else, then I was dead or back in Hellspace. And though I didn't want to die, if I returned to that awful place, I might reweigh the idea of death.

No more wasting time. No more sleeping. My palms sparked with their onyx-black glow. I was ready to find the pixie, but before rubbing my fingers, I froze. Where should I portal to?

Sweat formed above my lip, and I yanked at my hair. Strands came loose with my tight grip. As I lowered my hand, it dawned on me. Before Mother sent the pixies away for being no-good gossipers, they were the hair stylists. If they kept with their profession outside of the palace, they'd be working at a salon.

At least ten salons bordered the kingdom, but Mother sent her maidens to only one.

It didn't open until ten in the morning. I'd have to wait. But I had to keep myself busy. I couldn't give my mind time to think about Hellspace.

There were two things I wanted to know more about: Earth and the seer. I could search the library for anything about Earth, or I could tear through Aris's chambers in the hope of finding something about the child. Option two sounded better. I was already familiar with some things about Earth from previous studies, and anything I didn't know, I could easily figure it out. But I needed as much information about the seer as possible.

I waved my hand over my body and became invisible. Before the glow in my palm disappeared, I rubbed my fingers and portaled inside Aris's bed chamber. I didn't have any other choice. Too many guarded the outside, and his windows were so high that unless I could magically jump, there was no way of reaching them.

Sconces on the wall held embers inside, barely lighting the room. The guards must've recently left. Since Aris wound up in the prison a week ago, they'd been in and out of the room, clearing it. But, to my luck, they hadn't gotten further than boxing things up.

Boxes spread across his wooden floor. The walls were empty. No tapestries, frames, or artwork from the citizens. The bed had been stripped to the frame. A wooden desk stood in the corner, and in the chair beside it sat a sleeping guard.

My body froze. Mother must've placed more security around the palace after I broke into her private sanctuary. Shit. At least he was asleep. I could still pull this off as long as I stayed quiet.

Once over the shock of him being in the room, I suppressed a laugh. This guard was lucky that I was trying not to be seen. Otherwise, I would've killed him for sleeping on the job. What a terrible guard, but an awesome one for me, at this moment.

I tiptoed over to the desk and searched it.

Every few seconds, I shot my gaze back and forth from the door to the guard, making sure neither moved.

Drawer after drawer was empty. On the top lay a map of Climakru. No use to me.

As I headed to the bookcase on the left wall, a snort came from the guard. I gulped and glanced at him. His head had rolled onto his shoulder. Pathetic. Shaking my head, I returned to the picturesque bookcase. Most of the carved shelves stood empty and full of dust, but a few books remained. I picked them up and read their covers. *History of Climakru. The Split. Witches.* More unhelpful things.

Box after box contained nothing of worth either. My chest

tightened. Aris was useless. How could he not have any information about his child?

A warm breeze drifted in from the open window far above. The sun's rays glared off the shiny walls. It was already seven in the morning, and I had found nothing. Jeroboam's wicked laugh filled my memory. My knees wobbled, and I collapsed onto the chair near the bookcase. I couldn't end up back in Hellspace. I leaned the chair onto its back legs, scrutinized the sleeping guard, and dug Slinger's sharp tips into my palm to focus on pain instead of Hellspace.

But it didn't help. Images of my skin melting and reforming repeated in my mind. I jabbed Slinger harder into my palm. Blood dripped through the creases in my fingers. I continued. Physical pain beat even the memory of Hellspace.

A soft voice came from the other side of the door. I halted my rocking and brought the chair back onto all four legs. The wood creaked underneath me, and my eyes widened. But before dropping to the floor to investigate, I pricked up my ears. Two guards whispered outside the door, but it didn't seem like either was coming in. Regardless, I needed to hurry.

I dropped to all fours, pushed the chair out of the way, and glided my hands along the wood. Nothing felt off. I squinted, dropping my gaze lower. Two planks had a wider gap between them. I put Slinger to work and picked at it. The wood screeched as it popped open. I gulped and glanced at the guard. He hadn't moved. Phew.

Underneath the two boards was a shabby brown book. My mouth gaped open. Could this hold my answers? This had to be about his child. Perhaps Aris was useful after all.

Leaning against the wall, I opened the book. Page after page spoke about his love for Queen Rosalida. I wanted to gag at his romantic words and stop reading, but I couldn't. Not when he might've written about the seer.

Five entries later, Aris spoke of his desire for a child. Here it was. Yes!

I couldn't believe my luck.

Several pages later, big, bold letters declared, *she's pregnant.* I straightened, and my grip tightened on the leather book as I kept reading. A few passages beneath that read:

We're fighting over a name. Rosalida wants Elliot if a boy and Shyla if a girl. I won't even consider it's a boy. By how she carries herself, I know it's a girl, and her name will be Sierra. It means saw. With her abilities and the prophecy, it fits perfectly since she'll make sure everyone is seen.

I shook my head. Aris had been incredibly delusional even then.

Tattered seams appeared after I flipped the page. Someone had torn out paper from the journal. Did they get here before me, or was it Aris himself? I released a ragged breath and continued reading. There had to be more.

Each of the following pages spoke about his loneliness. Nothing mentioned Queen Rosalida or the child. I almost gave up. At least I had names to guide my search. But since it was only nine o'clock, I continued to read more.

On the last page, I hit the jackpot. Bold letters at the top said, *June 2008: To Sierra.* Below, it said, *I miss you. In honor of your one-year birthday, I started a summer celebration in the kingdom. You'd love it.* He went on and on about the celebration, but I had read enough. Her name was Sierra. She was seventeen and had been born in June.

I portaled the book to my room and hid it underneath the mattress. I didn't know why I was being so secretive. Of course, Mother freaked about the break-in at her chambers, but there were no rules about Aris's rooms. Yet something deep inside my soul told me this information needed to stay private, at least until I could prove the prophecy wrong or Mother good.

Eight

Sure enough, once I ventured into the salon, I hit another jackpot. One of the hairdressers was a pixie. She had pink hair, and glitter flowed around her as she moved. She wore a gray, colorless tunic. The lack of color, silk fabrics, and ruffles signified her low rank. I watched her work a braid into the earth wielder's hair. From the looks of it, she had just started. I'd have to wait.

I leaned against the white tile wall and faced her dragon-print chair. The two gossiped about the palace. If I hadn't needed the pixie, I would've killed her. I pictured myself slitting her throat, the blood coating my hand, when a butterfly landed on my shoulder. I picked it up and placed it in my palm. Its wings were a beautiful gold, and the left one had a small hole at the top.

Napkins rested amongst the coffee supplies on the table at the back of the room. I ripped a small piece off one and molded it into a ball. Taking extra care, I placed it inside the hole in the butterfly's wing and smiled. The butterfly flapped its wings and flew away just as the pixie spun the wielder in the chair.

"All finished." The pixie unwrapped the cape from around the wielder.

The wielder stood and hugged her. "Thank you. See you in a few weeks." She dashed to the front counter.

The pixie strolled into an employee-only room in the back, so I followed her. She flopped into a chair at the round table. I snuck behind her, gripped her throat, and portaled us to my chamber.

Her face turned blue, and I released my grip as I threw her against the bed.

"Demon!" she screamed at the top of her lungs, and I yanked her right back up, squeezing her throat tight and closing off her vocal cords.

"You know?" Well, that was a dumb question. Of course, she knew. I just portaled her.

The pixie nodded, frantically clawing at my hand around her throat.

"You better not say anything, and if you scream again, I'll kill you." I arched my eyebrows, daring her to tempt me or think I wouldn't do it.

She nodded and slowly gulped. Sweat dripped down her forehead, and her eyes scanned the room. Fool. She wouldn't escape this. I rolled my eyes, dropped her, and stepped back.

Body shaking, she righted herself onto the floor and choked out. "Please don't kill me. Please. I have a family."

Like I'd care about that. "You're not here for me to kill." Not yet, at least.

"Then why? What do you plan to do with me? Punish me? What did I do wrong?" She scooted herself against the wall. The glow from the torch above her reflected off the tears dripping down her face.

"Besides exist?" I laughed. "You've done nothing wrong. I just need your help to realm travel."

The remaining color drained from her face, and she clutched at her chest. "We'll die."

"Not unless I find some treasure." I twirled Slinger between my fingers.

She dropped her head into her hands. "We're doomed."

With Hellspace as my alternative, I refused to believe that. So far, I'd had great luck gathering what I needed. It wasn't about to end with some stupid treasure. Vilo could provide answers. I left the pixie and ventured to Vilo's room.

Scant scents of rosemary hit my nose. She wasn't here. I pressed my lips together, about to head to the kitchen, her second favorite place, when a gush of wind flew in from the open window, and a piece of paper fluttered off the desk. I bent down to pick it up.

Tarus. I gulped. The note was addressed to me, and again, Vilo used my nickname.

You need to know others support Aris, and you should know the last part of the prophecy.

'If the worst-case scenario arrives,
the ancestral secret revives
by the one who saw the times ahead
and will help restore the realms instead.'

This proves you'll have help if only you look for it. Please give your role in this prophecy a chance.
Meet her first.

An ancestral secret? Someone, who wasn't a seer, had seen the times ahead? Gods, they were nuts. I crumpled the note and stuffed it in my pocket. Vilo was as bad as Aris with her love-sick beliefs and positivity. Even if I did give my role in this prophecy a chance, it didn't mean Mother was bad. Nor did it mean someone would help me. No one ever helped me.

I shook off those thoughts and portaled back to the pixie. She knelt beside a floor vent, her wand in her closed, bleeding hands. So, she had tried to escape? Good thing my room had entrapments around all exits. No one could leave unless I allowed it.

Assuming the mumbling, freaked-out pixie knew the rest of the spell, I approached her to demand that she tell me. As I got closer, her gibberish became clear. She was praying. Holy Delmore. Realm travel couldn't be that bad. She had to be freaking out over nothing. A demonic laugh escaped my lips.

She turned to me, and her nostrils flared.

"Do you know what the treasure is?" I hovered in front of her.

"Not exactly."

I grabbed the front of her tunic and lifted her off the ground.

"Whoever seeks the opening needs to sacrifice their favorite object." She gulped, her body vibrating underneath my hand.

My breathing slowed. I patted my chest where Slinger dangled and barred my teeth. Everyone demanded things from me. Why did I always have to go without, have to sacrifice, in order to save others? This was the last thing that truly belonged to me.

Slinger used to hang around the neck of the Hellspace leader I'd killed. He was my only reminder that though my attempt to be a hero failed, I still became the leader of Hellspace and got my revenge. Plus the artifact itself was beyond magical. With the right activation, branding it on someone's skin could kill them. But I didn't know how to activate it.

Before I had more time to think about it, Mother portaled

into my room, centimeters from my face. Her peppermint breath, mixed with her wicked grin, sent chills down my spine.

She was ready.

Nine

"Time to open a seam and start your clock." Mother grabbed my shoulders. "You ready?"

"Of course." I straightened, face impassive, hiding my fear and sadness over Slinger. I'd rather take that to my grave.

"You have four weeks to find this child and bring it to me." She squeezed my shoulder. "I believe in you. You're my son."

My cheeks warmed. This was the Mother I knew. A woman who cared about me. A woman who encouraged me. A woman who loved me. Aris and Vilo were wrong.

"Go grab a cauldron from the kitchen. I'll take the pixie." She turned to the trembling thing now cowering in a ball against the wall. Being nosy, I stayed to see how she'd handle this.

Mother pulled her up by the hair, and the pixie screamed.

Once she'd risen and Mother had let her go, the pixie spoke. "Please reconsider. This isn't going to end well."

"You're right," I said through gritted teeth. "This won't end well for you if—"

"What are you still doing here?" Mother asked. "You heard me. Go!" Tendrils of her mist swarmed forward, latching on painfully before throwing me to the door.

My anger built inside, my nails biting into my palm to mask the pain of her using the mist on me. I hadn't done anything wrong. This side of her had me second-guessing my last thought.

"Where should we meet?" My hand shook on the doorknob.

"The River of La Mont." Mother rubbed her wrists, and she disappeared with the pixie. Smoke lingered where they'd stood.

My lungs constricted. This was really happening.

Once I opened the door, I dashed to the kitchen. I couldn't portal in there for fear a chef might see and realize Mother and I were demons.

By the time I made it to the kitchen, sweat had formed in every crevice of my body. No one was there. I let out my breath and grabbed the decorative rose gold cauldron near the refrigerator. I dumped out the contents. Clinks sounded off the counter much louder than I expected it to. Before anyone barged in and noticed me, I portaled to the meeting spot, the cauldron in hand.

At The River of La Mont, the sound of rushing water filled the space, along with the smell of fresh leaves and wet bark. I slumped on the bench, giving myself a second to calm my nerves.

Why weren't Mother and the pixie here yet?

A few minutes later, Mother portaled in with the pixie and threw her at my feet. "Sorry for the delay. Issues arose from Hellspace." She glanced at the pixie. "If you don't open a seam and ensure he gets through, I'll kill you." Tears streamed down the pixie's cheeks. Mother chuckled and kissed my forehead. "I must take care of the Hellspace problem. You got this."

The mixed emotions from Mother were jacking with my head. Mother rarely showed this type of affection. It must be because I was doing something so great for her. She was proud of me. Finding Sierra for her would make me her hero. I bet she'd finally let me call her *mother* in public. I smiled at the thought, directing it toward her right before she disappeared, her touch lingering.

I unsnapped Slinger and placed him against the pixie's neck. "Activate the cauldron and open the tear for me, or *I'll* kill you."

She paled. "If I do this for you, I'm as good as dead anyway."

"I acquired the treasure. You're safe as long as you get me through." I shoved the cauldron at her chest.

Her body shook as she took it from me. "And the treasure?"

With one last glance at Slinger, I dropped him into the cauldron.

She stumbled upward and pulled out her wand. "Gather a tulip, twigs, and a handful of dry mud."

My lips curled up. This pixie was ordering me around. Again, if I didn't need her help, I would've killed her. But since I couldn't, I collected what she demanded and added them to the bowl.

In an ancient language I'd never heard, the pixie spoke over the bowl as she mixed the materials. Smoke materialized and lifted the items into a whirlwind above the cauldron.

"Being a demon, you can cast minor spells, correct?" Her eyebrows raised.

I nodded.

"Place your hands above the river. On the count of three, you must say *'colqua esbarke debna'* and pull. Imagine you're creating an opening to a world full of beauty on the other side. Keep picturing your gorgeous new world as I chant."

I did as she said, but it was hard to picture the world she imagined. Instead, I pictured Olivia Hall. If my luck continued, I'd land there. It was the best place for me to start since I needed a database to search for Aris's child.

"Tartarus, are you listening?" The pixie's eyes blazed hot pink.

I ground my teeth and faced her. "Watch yourself."

She shook. "Once we finish the spell, the opening will appear. You'll have seconds to jump through before it closes. On the count of three. One. Two. Three."

"*Colqua esbarke debna,*" we both chanted, and as an opening appeared, a supernatural, dark blue surge of wind broke through it. The wind formed a sphere around us and sucked the air from our space, blasting it outward with a sharp hiss.

I glanced between the seam's translucent glow and Slinger. Pain slithered through me at seeing him swirling above the cauldron. The star was special. I couldn't leave him behind, possibly destroyed by a spell or used by the pixie.

Unable to help myself, I dashed over to the cauldron, grabbed Slinger, and ran back to the opening.

Once I touched the seam, the pixie screamed, and a strong pink force turned me around to face her. I tried to move, but whatever the pixie was doing had me frozen solid. I glared at her, unable to say anything.

Veins popped in her neck, arms, and forehead. Her hair stood in spikes, and she pointed her wand in my direction. "Tartarus, you're a wicked soul. I curse you and the seer. You'll be unable to perform or utter a word about magic in the seer's waking presence. They must believe on their own without any help from outsiders to aw—"

A laugh bubbled up in my throat at her loss of words until fire blew straight at my face and singed the hair on my arm. Before I wrapped my brain around where it had come from, the sound of swooshing wings and gigantic thuds ricocheted off the sphere. Dragon wings closed around the pixie as the Delmore beast opened its mouth with saw-like teeth and swallowed the burned pixie whole. The pink force field holding me captive disappeared as the nasty thing turned to me. My eyes widened. It was going to kill me.

As it lunged forward, its wings spread open and hit me in the stomach. I flew to the side, a few feet from the seam, whose glistening ripples were slowly disappearing. Shit. I didn't have time to scream in pain or panic. I had to get through that seam before it vanished.

Just as the Delmore beast opened its mouth, its rotten stench filling my nose and its breath warming my back, I took a huge leap and dove through the opening.

Ten

The opening zapped shut with a loud bang as I landed face down in a thick pile of mud.

I sat up and wiped the gunk from my face, gagging. Our mud smelt of a rich, earthy substance. Theirs stunk like manure. Spitting out the nasty bit in my mouth, I looked around. Silver rays shone through the small, dark openings between the thick trees and gave enough light for me to register my surroundings. I'd landed inside a forest with high grass, no flowers, and crickets chirping atop the layers of branches.

Had the pixie's curse worked, and was that why I hadn't landed where I'd imagined? No. She'd cursed me *and* the seer. Her curse had nothing to do with my magic as a whole. Plus, the Delmore beast killed her before she could finish it. There was no way it worked now. Good thing, too. If I didn't have my magic, I'd never find her, and I'd wind up back in Hellspace.

Images of demon claws ripping my skin apart sent my body into a full-on shiver, so I threw the picture of Olivia Hall into my mind to block it. I had to stay on task. I couldn't think about what awaited me if I failed.

Staring at my palm, I conjured my magic. An onyx-black glow appeared.

Yes. My magic still works. Take that, pixie.

Before I rubbed my fingers together to portal, I waved my hand down my body and turned invisible. I closed my eyes to picture myself inside Olivia Hall.

Within seconds, a crisp warmth touched my skin, and the screeching of chairs on a sleek floor reached my ears. I opened my eyes and cringed.

The place was stuffy. The people next to me smelt odd, a mixture of sweat and sweet fragrances. They also dressed differently than Climakru's royalty: no gowns, tuxes, and tunics of rich fabrics and vibrant colors. They didn't even come close to the villagers' attire of less elegant dresses and trousers in dull shades. Almost no one here wore dresses. Their shoulders showed, and their colors were gloomier than those of peasants.

As for the library, on the left was a semi-open room with white bulky contraptions on top of desks. A long spiral staircase stood next to me, and rows of bookshelves filled the area behind me. Sliding doors opened at the front where people shuffled in and scanned something at a wooden desk. A restroom sign hung near the back. Needing to be visible, I trudged toward it.

Reaching for the doorknob, I jumped back when it swung open, and an older gentleman stepped out. As he grazed past me, the thin fabric of his tunic touched my arm. I froze, but he didn't seem to notice. I let out a breath, slipped through the closing door, and gagged.

Inside carried an even fouler odor than the manure dirt.

With one hand I covered my nose and mouth and waved

the other down my body, becoming visible, before stepping back out to find their electronic machines.

I headed to the front desk, chin up. This should be easy.

Along the way, people surveyed me. I winked at a scrawny male closest to me. He scrunched his lip in disgust. Weird. I wasn't used to this type of reaction. Whatever. I walked up to the oddly sequined person behind the wooden desk who was sorting a stack of books. His tunic sparkled with his every move.

"Could you please point me in the direction of your electronic machines?" I leaned on the counter and batted my eyelashes.

He blinked several times and shot his hand to his mouth, covering his laugh.

What the hell?

"Are you being serious?" He bit his pen.

"No. I'm trying to crack a joke and waste everyone's time."

"Dude. You don't have to be rude." He banged the book shut. "The *electronic machines*..." He air quoted. "...are right there." His thin, multi-ringed finger pointed to the awful bulky things.

I cringed and trudged over to them as "Sequin" said something about me being impolite. I didn't acknowledge him, nor did I care about his pathetic feelings.

I sat by an ugly contraption in the corner, away from the others.

It had a screen, just like at home. *Easy.*

I searched for the headset that brought it to life, but there wasn't one. Maybe they didn't need them. "Find databases," I whispered. The screen stayed blank. "Find Sierras." Still nothing.

Why didn't it work? Was it because I didn't have the headset? At home, they knew what I was thinking, and projections appeared of what I wanted. Ugh. How dare

"Sequin" not give me the material I needed. He must have a death wish.

I shot up, and my hand brushed across an oval gadget. The machine turned to life, with a blue screen and small folders scattered throughout. Okay. So, this oval thing made it work, but what did I do now?

Several people sat at the electronic machines around me. They had no headset and didn't look to be having any issues with making it do what they wanted. I crept toward the bathroom, observing them. They typed on the device in front of them, and the screen obeyed.

Perhaps I had to tell it what I thought.

With a sense of understanding, I returned to the screen. I used the oval object and clicked on the icons. Each folder revealed more things to click. I sighed but kept hitting them. A colorful circle brought a search engine to life. Yes! I typed in databases. It listened, giving me a list of different search engines. Okay, I could do this.

After several minutes of trying to figure out which site to use, I landed on the perfect one. On the top, it read, *Just discovered a family member and need to find them? Or did you lose someone? Look no further.* I placed Sierra's name in the top box and seventeen for the age criteria. Thousands of Sierras popped up. My muscles tightened.

With my fist only seconds away from breaking the screen, a thought came to me. She was born in June. I hit several keys till a toolbox appeared. It had a search button. I typed in June. Five hundred and seven matches. I sagged into the chair. How was I supposed to search through that many in such a short time?

By starting.

I had no other choice, and I wouldn't admit defeat now, or ever.

After I'd knocked out two hundred and seven Sierras, the

facility called a ten-minute warning before it closed. Shit. Where was I to stay?

An attractive woman sat three spots down, so I tapped her on the shoulder. She swiveled her chair and burst into hysterics. What the literal hell? I turned away just as she spoke. "Sorry, your attire is hilarious. Is there a Renaissance fair in town?"

Renaissance? "Umm. I'm not sure what you mean."

She waved her hand. "Never mind. How can I help you?" She glanced at my eyes, and her body melted into the chair.

"I'm new to this area and need a good place to sleep." I dropped my gaze to her over-exposed chest, and at seeing where my eyes lingered, she bit her lip.

"You can stay with me," she purred.

"That sounds delightful, but I'm on a time crunch." If I wasn't worried about my life, I would've taken up her offer. "I need like a personal chamber."

She chuckled. "A hotel?"

"Yeah, that."

She typed into the machine, *Hotels in London.* That explained where I was. A list popped up. She hit the print button, walked off, and returned in less than ten seconds. She placed the paper on the counter, circled one with a green highlighter, added some numbers, and shoved it against my chest.

"The circled one is my favorite. I have my family stay there. I've also included my number in case that time crunch finishes." She smiled.

"Got it." I returned to my screen to print the list of Sierras.

While waiting for the paper, I reviewed the hotel she'd circled. Hillshite, near Russell Square. It looked fancy. It would do. I grabbed the papers, hid in an empty aisle, and portaled to it.

An outdoor shopping area stood on either side of me. They reminded me of the villages at home, but everything here belonged to one building with lots of entrances. Hundreds of people walked everywhere. Behind me, cars blasted their horns, and several buildings were crushed together, all in different boring-colored bricks: maroons, browns, and grays.

Ahead of me, a hotel sign read, *The Hillshite.*

I walked inside, where people in tuxedos greeted me. I nodded and approached the receptionist.

"May I help you?" a lady in a black silk dress asked from behind the desk.

"I'd like a room."

She gawked at me, her lips twitching. What was with these people looking at me funny? Did they want me to lather them with pleasantries or something?

"Please." I clenched my jaw.

"I need to see identification. What is your name?"

Holy Delmore. I didn't have any identification. I leaned over the gray countertop and touched her tan, freckled hand. She looked at our connection and then at me. Her name tag read *Helga*. Onyx-black glowed through the gap between our hands, sure to match my eyes. She stared back, her mouth agape. I locked onto her gaze and dug deep until I hit the nerve controlling her mind.

"You've seen my identification. My name is Taran. A suite has been purchased for me for an infinite amount of time. You won't question me and will provide sufficient answers for anyone who does." I removed myself from her mind and eased my hand away.

"Taran, your room will be right this way." After grabbing a thick ring of keys, she walked around the counter and escorted me to the sixth floor, droning on about the amenities. Once at room 666, she scanned a key card on the gadget near the doorknob and handed it to me. "Enjoy your stay."

I opened the door and stepped inside.

Oranges and coffee ground fragrances wafted over. Not

bad. The suite had two tiny rooms. A small living space was furnished with a cotton-brown couch and a black table at the end. In front of me stood a little window with white curtains. I peered out. A park filled with tulips sat directly below.

I turned and looked at the rest of the room. To the right of me, and left of the couch, stood an entertainment system and a small desk with a little lamp on it. In the bedroom, a white blanket covered a medium-sized bed. I ran my hand down it. Stiff but comfortable.

The room would do.

After showering and letting the water scorch my skin, I couldn't sleep. Every time I closed my eyes, Hellspace filled my mind. So, I sat on the couch and sifted through the papers.

By the time morning arrived, I had narrowed the Sierras to 108. Unfortunately, their locations spread far across the realm, with ten in London. But I had twenty-seven days, and I could portal. I'd visit four girls a day. Of course, if she ended up being one of the last ones, I'd lose my opportunity to honor Vilo's request and get to know her.

I wasn't admitting I believed my role in the prophecy, but if it was real, I'd know when I saw her. Wouldn't I? So, then getting to know her shouldn't matter.

Eleven

Since I was already bored of London, the first girl I checked lived in Bangkok. Her name was Sierra Amarin. Each morning, before school, she worked at a dentist's office on the west bank of the Chao Phraya River as an intern.

On the paper with her information was a picture of the beautiful iconic temple, Wat Arun. I portaled there.

With the sun rising on the horizon and the light pinks and blues in the background, the temple marveled a bright gold, stopping several tourists. After admiring the famous structure, I ventured to her dentist's office, a fancy glass-windowed building in between two tall skyscrapers. A big sign above the revolving door said, *Dr. Krung International Dentistry*.

I slicked my hair back and strolled into the building. Antiseptics with a bitter soap fragrance perfumed the room in thick layers. The walls were white apart from the front one with the desk. It was yellow, the color of urine. With the combination of colors and odors, I did my best not to gag or wrinkle my nose.

Two women with dark, pinned up hair worked behind the

counter with their heads down. I approached them and rang the bell. They looked up.

The one on the left with a name tag that read, *Chi,* spoke. *"ฉันช่วยคุณได้มากแค่ไหน."*

I didn't answer. I had no idea what she had said. Instead, I glanced at the other girl's name tag. Sierra. My stomach turned as my gaze drifted up, and a small flutter built inside, making me come alive at the prospect. Was this her, the girl who'd change everything for me? Whether she'd put an end to my Hellspace dilemma or maybe rebuild my heart, confirming Aris and Vilo's theory, I didn't know.

But when I glanced into her umber eyes with no vibrant color to match those of Climakru, the flutter disappeared.

This wasn't the right Sierra.

I waved and dashed off before portaling back to Hillshite. I grabbed the glass of water on the TV stand and crushed it. This was going to take a heavier toll on me than I'd thought. More confirmation, not only of my fear of Hellspace but possibly of how much I wanted my heart back.

After destroying pillows, frames, and many other things in the room, I fell to the floor, clutching Slinger. I couldn't fall apart. There were still 107 girls to check.

I stood, grabbed the first three papers in the stack, stuffed two in my pocket, and read the third. Sierra Honeycutt, Ontario, Canada. I portaled there. Same thing. An empty feeling engulfed me when I stared into her sapphire eyes.

This continued for a week. I had no luck finding the correct Sierra. I ventured to Alaska, Hong Kong, Texas, New Zealand, and Florida. During the day, searching the different girls distracted me from Hellspace but not from the prophecy. After each failure, pain built inside my chest. It felt like a thorn bush was growing inside of me, and with each wrong girl, those tiny barbs sharpened. At night, Hellspace and the fact I was Lucifer's child wouldn't leave my mind. It added double-edged blades to the thorn bush.

Each time I laid my head to rest, the blades poked through my skin. I couldn't sleep with the discomfort. Even if I managed to, nightmares of Hellspace consumed me. I'd wake up drenched in sweat and screaming bloody murder.

Eventually, I stopped going to bed. I couldn't spend another moment in Hellspace, even if only in nightmares. Instead, I kept searching for the girls, seeking out more than eight a day. With each name I crossed off the list, I couldn't help but doubt my ability to ever find the seer.

This morning, at the start of the third week, it was harder than the rest. I sat on the couch, examining the last few girls, when Jeroboam appeared in my mind without me even closing my eyes. One second, I was reading, and the next, he ripped my clothes with his claws and poured lava down my body. Saullis watched while using the magic he'd acquired to manipulate the skies and shoot lightning at me.

I collapsed on the floor, both hands clutching Slinger and screaming.

There was a knock on the door, and my awareness jolted back to the present. "Bad nightmare," I murmured, sweat beading on my forehead and neck. There was no way I'd open that door.

"Are you sure? Do you need anything?"

Holy Delmore, humans were nosy. "Yes. No, I don't need anything."

Seconds later, his footsteps faded as they squeaked down the hallway.

My breathing slowed. I had to find this girl. I dressed quickly and took another glance at the papers to see the girls' locations. One of the Sierras said London. With all the stress, I guess I missed one here.

I headed toward her first. Her name was Sierra Mills. A

few days after her birth, a family from Texas had adopted her. By the time this Sierra had turned fifteen, her adoptive parents had passed. She now lived with her best friend in their private school dorm at Elite Boarding Academy.

Their school was a mini palace within a tiny village. One two-story, brown brick building with twenty-plus windows on both sides of the central wooden front doors. On both sides of the school were smaller, identical buildings with only three windows across. The lawn was freshly mowed and had tulip patches. Brown benches, surrounded by trees, lined each gravel path.

Four-story burnt-red brick structures formed a ring around this village. Students ventured out of them wearing burgundy coats with blue trims and a pocket with a handkerchief. They also had button-down white shirts. Boys wore slacks or trousers, and girls wore skirts or slacks.

Prep school.

A loud engine purred behind me, and I turned toward the noise. One yellow bus pulled in next to the black metal gate. Only a few students hopped off, with a lanky boy bringing up the rear. He took his precious time as he carried a bulky easel.

"Hey man, you need some help?" I grabbed the easel and his hand. He stared into my eyes as I entered his mind. I dug deep, bypassing the awkward thoughts he carried about his paintings and puberty, straight to the nerve I needed. "Head to the office. Request to see the senior's schedules. Tell them an auditor needs them."

He placed his stuff down and did as I'd ordered.

Within minutes, the boy returned with the schedules. After skimming through the names, I found Sierra's schedule and a map of the school. I took them out and handed the rest back to him. When our hands touched, I broke into his mind again. "Forget this conversation or ever seeing me."

The second I let go, I ventured to her first class.

Not a single soul was there. The bell chimed, signaling the start of class, and still no one showed. My body heated. How could an entire class be missing?

I approached the bulletin board on the back wall for any clues about where they might be. Several different flyers of activities were tacked to it. I read each one, coming up with nothing until one in the middle caught my eye. *Student observation day.* One student paired with a mentor and three psychology patients from 6:30 a.m. to 1:15 p.m.

That explained where the class had gone. I looked back at her schedule. At 1:05 p.m., her French class started. I'd return then. In the meantime, I searched for two more girls in Tokyo and Egypt. By the time I found the second one and learned she wasn't the right girl, my ghadee vibrated. A projection popped up that read *1:30.* I portaled to her French class.

The class was located in one of the side buildings away from the main campus.

Invisible, I knelt near the open window, peering inside and waiting for someone to call out her name. From what I could see, there were nine students. Either no one liked French, or the professor was as obnoxious as she appeared with her top lip curled up and her rough voice judging them with disapproval. Her highly strung attitude matched well with her white hair, long nose, and the way that she wore her glasses perched on the tip of her snout.

"Oui, Sierra?" The professor's words snagged me out of my thoughts. I followed the teacher's glare.

"J'ai une question por vous," one of the students said. She spoke just as I caught sight of her.

My stomach dropped, and a tingling sensation traveled down my spine. Magic danced inside my veins, palms glowing bright, urging me to portal next to her. I didn't even have to fully see her face to know this was Aris's daughter.

I slid down and rested my forehead against the brick to try

and calm my breathing before I passed out. It was her. But why the hell did my body react this way? It had to be because now I wouldn't be going to Hellspace, and Mother would reunite the realms. No other reason unless this reaction was because my role in the prophecy was real. It was *the bond forming at the start.*

This girl could be my mate, bond with me, and rebuild my heart.

I really could have another chance.

Images of me killing her father appeared in my head. She'd hate me when she found out, and it'd change the prophecy, making my part not come to fruition. There was no point in having hope now or believing it anymore. I just needed to stick with the plan and bring her to Mother.

I rose and looked inside, just in time to find Sierra glancing out the window. She had a small upturned nose, big, gorgeous chestnut-brown eyes, and thick eyebrows like her father. Her hair was a honey brown with red streaks, again matching her father. My magic went on the fritz again.

Yes. Now that I knew this was the right girl, all I had to do was wait until class finished and kidnap her. No big deal.

I crouched next to the window, waiting for the bell and replaying past events.

Something that had eaten at me for the past four years was how I could make the sacrifice to Deesse despite the warnings it would destroy me. Now, knowing I was Lucifer's son, making the sacrifice to be the leader of Hellspace made sense. I had kingship in my blood, literally. But part of the reason why I wanted to be the leader made no sense. Besides seeking revenge, I desperately wanted to be a hero and save the kids who'd suffered torture at the hands of the current "king."

Why would I care about them if I was Lucifer's son? Was that because I was half-human, like Vilo said? Even now, without my heart, I still cared about Mother and didn't want to betray her. That must be the human part of me. My conscience, my soul, something.

Ding! The bell chimed, and students shuffled out of the classrooms.

I shot up and looked through the window again. Sierra pivoted on her heels next to the front desk, deep in conversation with the professor. Better for me. She'd be the last to exit, and it'd be the perfect opportunity to snatch her.

As she headed away from the professor a minute later, I ran to the door. She pushed it open and stepped out. I went to grab her, but my body froze, and pain shot down my spine. What the hell?

My hands remained outstretched, frozen in place. I tried to pull them back, but they wouldn't budge. I tried to move my feet, but more pain sparked through them, electrocuting every nerve.

Sierra was almost out of sight, and I was going to miss my opportunity. I pushed harder, but my body wouldn't move.

Once Sierra disappeared, it was like a switch flipped. My body unfroze, and my arms fell.

Oh, my gods. A lump lodged in my throat.

The pixie! She had cursed me from performing magic in Sierra's waking presence. It worked even without her finishing the spell.

Holy Delmore.

Not being able to use my magic with her was going to put a damper on my plans.

Twelve

Without using magic in Sierra's waking presence, I'd have to seize her when she was alone and use chloroform as I had with the guards, except this one would be a nonmagical version, or I'd have to drug her unconscious.

Though both options sucked, they were something.

Somehow, tomorrow, I'd have her, and this entire thing would be over. I'd stop fighting the struggle of having hope in something utterly impossible.

Even now, having a plan, finding the right girl, and still having thirteen days left, my body wouldn't rest. The sheets grew uncomfortable against my sweaty, bare skin. Jeroboam's voice whispered in my mind and informed me of his doubts that I'd accomplish this mission.

Unable to sleep, I ventured to the hotel gym.

Once sweat dripped into my eyes and blurred my vision, I wiped it away and glanced at the clock. 11:30 a.m. Her lunch had started. Shit. I headed to the shower and dressed in record time before turning invisible and portaling to the beige double doors outside of the cafeteria.

Heaters warmed my back. Scents of vanilla, sticky syrup, and fried food wafted through the air. My nose scrunched. The smells didn't mix well with me. I missed the elegance of home food. We had filth in our realm, too, but I never partook in eating anything so disturbing.

I tried to enter the cafeteria, but my body froze. Aw hell, the stupid curse. I couldn't stay invisible. But going in, not wearing a uniform, I'd stick out like a sore thumb.

Groaning, I shook my body and peeked through the open doors. I wanted to find her before I turned visible, to see if I could hide behind something.

A monstrous oak tree grew in the middle of the room. Branches extended out from it, covering the ceiling. Lanterns hung from the branches and split the room into six sections of long, rectangular wooden tables.

Over a hundred people mingled about. My breathing turned shallow, and my eyes darted around the room. What if I couldn't find her?

Almost as soon as the thought came, I spotted her sitting at a table against the left wall, elbows resting on top, and a half-eaten sandwich on the tray in front of her. My magic danced.

Instead of dissecting my body's weird reaction, I observed her. Brown waves framed her face, chestnut eyes sparkled, and her smile grew as she spoke to her friend across the table. She looked serene. Happy. Too bad her life would be over soon.

While I tried thinking of a plan, a couple strode through the doors, trays in hand. I tripped the male closest to me. As his companion helped him, I caught his tray, waved my hand down my body, and became visible.

With the fully loaded tray covering my face, I ventured toward Sierra. That way, I'd know when she left, follow her, and find the perfect opportunity to snatch her.

"Emma, come on!" Sierra pounded the table.

"AJ will be out of robotics soon. I promised to meet him. It's been a hot minute since we had time alone." Emma brushed her black locks off her shoulder. Her spiked choker and skull handkerchief were now visible. Her outfit had a serious demonic flair. I liked her. She'd fit in our realm. "Why can't you wait till the weekend to get Choco Nits?" She raised her eyebrows, emphasizing her thick black liner and golden eyes.

Choco Nits?

Sierra pouted and snagged her books. "You're right. I should buy another coffee instead. History class is supposed to be brutal today."

"Snag me one, too?"

"Would I ever forget you?" Sierra twirled out of her seat and bumped into me. Electricity spread through my hand. Every nerve spiked. And inside my body, I could physically see my magic glow bright and illuminate an onyx-black vein from my palm to the vacant spot in my chest. I couldn't breathe.

"I'm so—" Sierra started.

But I panicked and dashed out of the room without letting her finish or checking back. Once alone, I portaled to Hillshite.

Hunched over, with my head on the itchy cotton couch, I clutched Slinger and counted to one hundred multiple times.

What was wrong with me? All we'd done was graze past each other. She hadn't really seen me. The tray had covered my face. This couldn't be the prophecy coming to fruition. But at the same time, how could it not be? Vilo still thought I played a role in the prophecy after I killed Aris. Perhaps that meant Sierra would understand when I eventually told her. So then, if this prophecy truly was real, including me being the warrior, and that hadn't changed, what the hell was I going to do about it?

As of now, there was only one thing I could do—get closer

to Sierra. If the interaction wasn't an anomaly, then when I tried to snatch her, it would spark again.

With an idea in place, I examined my ghadee. They had two minutes left of lunch, so the cafeteria wouldn't be my opportunity to test things. But I still had the last half of the day.

Whilst invisible, I portaled to the outskirts of the cafeteria, found a bathroom, and turned visible before venturing to the doors to wait for her.

The bell chimed, and students rushed out en masse, making it hard to keep my eyes on Sierra. But I needn't have worried. My body tingled the minute she passed me. A few feet away, she hugged her friend and turned the corner. I hid behind a group of students and followed her.

She turned down the next corridor. Her hair swayed and sent a strong scent of lavender into the air. I ran to catch up before I lost her and skidded on the vinyl, centimeters from her back. This close, the lavender scent intensified, along with the aroma of salt water and crisp fire—her parents' elements. She had to have them, too. But then that didn't explain why her eyes weren't amber like her father or sapphire like her mom.

I shook my head, trying not to think about those things. They didn't matter.

Two doors down the corridor, she walked into a room with several desks, each with four chairs. Weapons, flags, wars, and battleship posters covered the walls. So, their history was just like ours—minus the magic.

Sierra sat at a desk near the center, and the professor stood by the door. I tapped his shoulder and ushered him to the side. He stared at me with his eyebrows scrunched. Before he could say anything, I placed my hand on him, made direct eye contact, and dove deep into his mind. "You will tell S-S ..." I cleared my throat. "Si ..." Her name wouldn't form. What the hell! How far did this pixie's curse go? "Forget you saw me." I exited his mind and slumped to the floor in the hall. Once everyone had ventured inside, I turned invisible and waited.

Throughout class, I squeezed my knees to my body. I wanted to explode. Mother's face glared at me, full of disappointment. Saullis's lightning singed the hairs on my body.

On the cusp of hyperventilation, I jerked free of my morbid thoughts when Sierra's voice brought me back to the present.

"I did an extra credit project. Do you mind if I get it? I left it in my locker."

"Of course, Sierra." The professor grabbed an orange board and handed it over.

Yes! Perfect opportunity.

I hid in the adjacent hallway, out of view, before she walked out and turned to the right. Visible again, I crept after her, hiding between each batch of lockers. Several feet from the classroom, but before her locker, I hit an open locker door, slamming it closed with a bang. She froze in her tracks and turned. My stomach lodged in my throat, and I beelined into the nearest hall.

Seconds later, her shoes continued their squeaking and faded into the distance. I peeked out of my hiding spot. She had reached her locker. I released my breath, pulled the handkerchief out of my pocket, and snuck up behind her as she opened the locker.

With one hand, I tugged her close. As she screamed, I placed my other hand over her nose and mouth with the handkerchief. She fought against me, and my magic painfully zapped my insides. The agony was more unbearable than anything I'd ever experienced. I tried to portal with her, but nothing happened. She wasn't unconscious yet. Holy Delmore. This curse was becoming a rather big inconvenience.

Sharp pinpricks stabbed my spine. My knees wobbled, and

Sierra used my moment of weakness to bite my finger. The pain, plus the shock, made me drop the handkerchief. She ran off, but before she glanced back, I dashed behind a set of lockers.

Once she was out of sight, I portaled back to Hillshite, clutching Slinger and collapsing on my bed.

Being cursed sucked. If the pixie hadn't died, I would've killed her.

Evil to the core.

Now, I'd have to wait until tonight. When Sierra was in her dorm room, I'd knock her out. If she saw me, who cared? It wasn't like she could do anything before she became unconscious.

Thirteen

Invisible next to the woman's dormitory, I grabbed a girl who obviously was in the middle of the walk of shame. She screamed against my hand, but no sounds escaped. I dragged her into the bushes a few yards away.

Still holding on to her, I flashed visible. Her brown eyes expanded as our gazes locked. Before she could do anything, I jumped into her mind. "Don't freak out. Once you walk away, you'll forget ever seeing me. Please tell me what room is Si-Si ..." I shook my head and tried again. "... Emma's?"

Her mouth hung open, but she didn't say anything. I rummaged through her mind. It was disorderly. Thoughts of me kidnapping her, being hot, what her guy from last night would think, and who on earth Emma was. Shit.

"The gothic chick?" I clarified.

"Yeah." She beamed. "406."

"Thank you. You can go now." I dropped my hand and escaped her mind.

She walked away, stumbled a few times, and used her keycard to get in.

I followed her into the building and headed to dorm 406.

Once I made it to the door, my sweaty palms made the knob slippery to the touch. I wiped them on my tights before taking a deep breath, trying again, and sneaking inside.

No noise except for the rustling of trees from the open window met my ears. I glanced around the room. Neither girl was there. That explained why my magic still worked, and no pain ricocheted through my body. Both beds had their sheets tucked in. If it weren't for a giant photo of her and Emma dressed in princess costumes hanging on the back wall, I would've thought I'd mistaken her room for a child's.

Candles hung from the ceiling, and colorfully painted galaxies covered the walls on one side of the room. On that side, a planet wardrobe rested at the end of the bed, and the predominant colors were neon. The other side of the room had no decorations, but the walls and furniture were light blue and pink. A classy wooden vanity stood in the corner, underneath the window, next to a light pink desk.

I ran my hands down my face. It was Thursday night. She could be out late.

I could either wait for her to return or figure out where she'd ventured.

I decided on the latter. The sooner this was over, the better.

Not sure where she'd be, I searched every inch of the room for a clue. Everything I found was either unhelpful or lacking information. No journals, calendar, or anything gave me any insight. All I found was an album of photos.

Nostrils flaring, I slammed the photo album shut and shoved it back into the bookcase. Just as I turned to leave, a yellow sticky note blew off Emma's pillow and landed at my feet.

Hey, Emma. Be back around nine. I'm going to check if Zadina's Dreamspace is getting into the Halloween spirit and get my Choco Nits. Bring you back one. —Love, Sierra

Zadina's Dreamspace? What was that? She must really be obsessed with these Choco Nits. My new opportunity to kidnap her had arrived. I just needed to make sure only one *nit thing* remained wherever she was. That way, we'd both reach for it at the same time. I'd then charm her and convince her to let me escort her home. Along the way, I'd lead us into an alley, place the chloroform over her nose, and portal us to the hotel once she passed out. There, I could figure out how to signal Mother that I'd completed the mission unless another spark happened. Then, I'd have to reconsider my plan.

In the end, though, I'd have to bring her straight to Mother and not waste time because the chance of another spark happening, the chance of my role in the prophecy being real, was slim.

Still invisible, I portaled to the library to learn about Zadina's Dreamspace and Choco Nits. After discovering everything I could, I ventured there visible.

All my senses magnified as I stepped into the gigantic, repulsive toy store and arcade. Kids' laughter deafened me. The blasting of the pulleys on the video games and the ruckus from the carousel made me cringe. The lights were like a rave party gone mad. I wanted out of there, but I had a mission.

The internet said Choco Nits were multi-neon sprinkled mini chocolate-covered crunch candies from a movie called Stripped Galaxy. It also said they were near the register on the first floor.

Turning, I found the register to my right.

A teen boy, a few years younger than me, had his hand on one of the many Choco Nits. I walked over to him and tapped his shoulder.

The minute our eyes connected, I placed my hand on his arm and slipped into his mind. "Buy all of these but one. If you do this, you won't need to die. When I leave your mind, forget about me."

He shuddered as I slipped out.

He purchased all but one, and I waited near the register to ward off anyone who dared to try and buy it.

After an hour of waiting and fighting off three frightened children and two angry dads, Sierra finally noticed the last bag. Once she reached for it, I nonchalantly grabbed the packet. As my palm rested on the crinkled plastic and hers on top of mine, warmth radiated from our connection, and electricity traveled through my arm.

I glanced down at the top of Sierra's head, waiting for her to gaze up and say some sly words about needing the candy, my offer to trade ready on my lips. But the second her brown eyes, with a hint of blue, locked with mine, I realized fate or whatever had different ideas.

Holy Delmore. I was in trouble.

Although I begged my eyes to stop gawking at her, they wouldn't listen. My body froze out of its own volition. I couldn't move, couldn't breathe. Where the onyx-black vein brightened earlier today, it turned iridescent and formed an outline of a heart.

This couldn't be happening. My role in the prophecy *was* real. I could no longer deny it.

Though not a bond, my heart was forming. It was starting. A flutter filled inside of me.

My hope sparked.

As we continued staring, not letting go of the bag, my outlined heart sped up, and a slight flush crept into her cheeks. She, too, seemed entranced by this bizarre connection. What did she think while looking at me? For the first time, I felt self-conscious.

My physique rarely bothered me. I knew how attractive I was—especially my eyes. They were my best feature. Onyx-black. Many claimed they sparkled when the light hit just right.

Eyes that sparkled appeared to be the thing that made the ladies swoon. No one had ever denied me, and I'd never thought any would. But now, in this crisis, I worried whether Sierra might.

My behavior terrified me. The prophecy's words circled in my head: *A heart will form as theories are believed, then unification under love will be achieved.*

My outlined heart started thickening. I had to scram. I couldn't handle the pressure and the pain of feeling something that hadn't existed in four years. Back at the hotel, I could figure out what the hell I'd do now. But Sierra didn't move, and I couldn't bolt without saying something, nor did I want to. I wanted to learn more. How was she making me feel so alive, and how could I make it continue?

"Hey, Sierra!" Some guy appeared and broke our connection. I dropped my hand, my blood boiling as she turned to face him. I wanted to kill him. "I'm glad I ran into you. When I got back to the dorm, I was going to ask if you'd mind helping me study."

She looked between me, the guy, and the Choco Nits. "Umm ..."

"Please! I need your help."

And I need you to die. A fast but excruciating death.

"Sure. I'd be happy to help." She pursed her lips and glanced back at me. "You can have the candy. I'll buy another one tomorrow."

"No, it's okay." My voice cracked. Holy Delmore. She made me nervous. "Please, you must have it." I waved and rushed out of her sight before portaling to Hillshite.

Back in my room, I dropped to my knees and covered my head with my hands.

The conversation I had in secret with Aris and Vilo kept replaying in my mind. The last prophecy said a bond would form from the start. A bond hadn't formed. Why? Because I didn't have a heart. Or perhaps it meant a bond, as in a connection, not love.

Though that could be true, I refused to rule out Sierra being my mated pair, my one true love. If she were, it'd make sense she could break through my hard shell and form my heart.

But at the same time, who was I kidding?

I was the devil's son. I shouldn't be allowed to mate with anyone.

If this were true, that she was my mate despite who I was and my past—especially how it included me killing her father —it still didn't mean Mother was the dark soul. I had to be helping Mother because there was literally no way I could act against her. If I did, my life would be in question. Mother's wrath would be tenfold, and Sierra and I would be walking targets. Regardless of whether others supported Aris's theory or whether the prophecy claimed someone would help me if I went against Mother, we wouldn't last long.

Curious about the iridescent vein, I pushed my thoughts aside and looked deep inside my palm. My stomach dropped. It had vanished, replaced by black-onyx veins. Velvet black also covered the space in my chest. The outline of a heart had disappeared.

I yanked at my hair. I knew I shouldn't have gotten my hopes up.

But ... what if it only formed around Sierra?

The prophecy did say that together we'd unite the realms in love. Mother also gave me four weeks. I still had twelve days left.

Vilo had made me promise to investigate first, and the possibility of rebuilding my heart was worth trying to experience more and prolonging the inevitable. Maybe in twelve days, I could learn whether Sierra was like her reputation or someone worth saving. If I could just prove she wasn't bad nor the destroyer of realms, I could convince Mother to protect Sierra. She had kept Vilo for me—she'd do the same for Sierra. I believed this deep in my gut because Mother was good. She had to be.

New plan: get to know Sierra and see how much the prophecy was true. During that time, I'd figure out how to tell Mother, ensure Sierra lived after bringing her to Climakru, and tell Sierra about her father. At least with the latter point, I had time. I couldn't tell her without explaining magic.

But in order to do all that, I had to spend the remaining twelve days I had left with her. So, tomorrow, I was going to become a student at Elite Boarding Academy.

After switching out my white silk tunic, dragon-skinned leather belt, and black tights for the uncomfortable uniform I'd purchased at the shop, I approached the lady at the Academy's front office, who looked quite friendly. Some might even say she looked thirsty with all the makeup she'd caked on and her shirt slit super low, showing a little too much of her chest. But for me, this worked to my advantage.

I unbuttoned the last two pins from my shirt, popped my burgundy collar, and slicked back my black hair as I approached her with a grin. "Ms. ..." I peered at her name tag. "... Esmeralda, I'm a new student, and I'm lost."

She glanced up from the computer and smacked her bubble gum until her eyes locked with mine. "How can I help you?" She started to purr towards the end but immediately shifted gears and coughed.

I placed my hand over hers and slid into her mind.

Lonely. Sex. Hates job. Several of her thoughts lurched into my head, and I cringed.

Once in the correct spot, I struck. "Please hand me the

student enrollment papers." She did as I asked. While keeping one hand over hers, I filled out the paperwork with the name Taran Flyer. For parents' consent, I forged their signatures and then handed the papers back. "You'll take this information as accurate. You don't need to meet my parents or see any documentation. I'm a senior with whatever classes you choose, but make sixth period French." I smirked. "Please give me my schedule and forget that I spoke in your mind. Act like I'm a family friend." I pulled myself from her mind.

Her body relaxed into a slouch. "How's your sister?" She handed me my schedule.

"Great." I grabbed the papers. They slipped from her hands, and she yelped. Blood tinged the air from a fresh cut on her finger. A demonic cackle escaped my lips. "Have a good day."

Away from the office, I skimmed through my schedule—sixth period French. Perfect. What now? I glanced at the clock ticking on the wall. 11:25 a.m. Lunch.

I headed to the cafeteria without using my magic. Mundane and boring. Along the way, I pulled at my collar to show more chest hair. All young people my age had a one-track mind, and I wanted to know if Sierra did, too.

Not caring to eat, I leaned against the tree in the middle of the cafeteria. It was a perfect spot to view her and Emma. My goal was to appear unapproachable. That way, no one would distract me from catching Sierra's expression when she noticed the man from Zadina's Dreamspace was at her school. Would she show despair, fear, or longing?

But the unapproachable attitude backfired and made the students flock to me. Everyone tried something flirtatious to catch my attention. I practically growled at their unwanted pursuits, wanting to pluck my eyes out at their vanity.

Plus, they blocked my view of Sierra.

One green-eyed girl, attractive as can be, tall, with blond hair and a sexy-as-hell smile, sauntered up to me.

"Hello there, handsome," she purred.

My body told me one thing as I smirked at her, but my mind told me something else—nothing excited my magic, my every nerve, like Sierra did.

I kicked my leg up against the tree and messed with my sleeve, ignoring her until she took the hint and stomped off. The moment she was out of view, I faced Sierra's table again. Our eyes connected, and I froze before the next girl tried to make a pass at me.

As Sierra gawked, my nerves skyrocketed, my magic danced deep inside, and sweat dripped down my neck.

Needing more of Sierra, I pushed away from the tree and glided toward her. But before I made it there, Emma spoke, stopping me in my tracks.

"Girl, snap out of it. Look at me. Tell me why you look like you just saw a ghost."

With that, Sierra turned her face away.

Ghost? What? I took her intense stare to mean she wanted to see me, not that she didn't.

Shaking my head, confused by what had just happened, I needed air. I strode toward the door, tugging my arm free from the grip of some stupid girl trying to talk to me. She cursed at my rudeness, but I just laughed.

This couldn't be happening. Besides not wanting Mother to be evil, part of me feared Sierra awakening my heart, even if it was to help Mother. If Sierra didn't kill me after finding out I'd murdered her father, then the feelings that rushed at me from the past might. The flashbacks of gray engulfing the little scarlet eyes as Manny, the old leader of Hellspace, drove his demon spirit into the three-year-old's nostrils was too much for me to handle. But a small part of me thought reliving those moments was worth it if I could feel love once more, no matter how brief it may be. The thought that Sierra hadn't felt butterflies at seeing me stung.

I pushed open the school's door, one hand clutching Slinger, and leaned over the railings. Seconds from throwing up, I faltered as a blurry black figure moved in the distance. Black orbs stared back, and musky jasmine filled the air.

My mind had to be playing tricks on me. Mother would never have sent Darcy to Earth.

Fifteen

To keep myself distracted from my fear of someone lurking in the shadows—especially Darcy—I headed to the school library instead of fifth period. As I opened the doors to a modern yellow and blue brick library filled with books of all genres and a small section of textbooks, an idea struck me. Sierra would share her book with me if I didn't have one.

I waved my hand over my body, fading into nothing, and whisked around the room until I found the French section. Sixteen books for the class. That wouldn't do. I grabbed them all and headed outside. A green dumpster with a heavy rotten stench stood a few feet away.

I tossed them inside and rubbed my hands together. Deed done.

Seconds later, the bell chimed, and exuberance bubbled inside me. I dashed straight to my sixth period class with a mile-wide grin. Sierra had already taken her seat at the back of the room, alone. Buried deep in her French book, she was unaware of my entrance.

Oblivious to the professor or anyone else in the class, I

crept toward her, counting my breaths. If only I could control my nerves. I was shaking uncontrollably. But I finally made it to her and placed one hand on the corner of her desk to steady myself.

The bell rang, and Sierra still hadn't glanced up from her textbook to notice me. As I waited for her to acknowledge me, the atmosphere in the room shifted, the heat amped up to near scorching, and sweat beaded from every pore I had. My mouth dried. Words wouldn't form. Shit.

The professor spoke something inaudible in French. Sierra glanced up. Her face flashed from smiling to downright confused as her brows knitted inward and her nose crinkled. I shuffled beside her, my shoes creaking on the glossy floor. Her body stiffened, and I smirked.

"Pardon me, my name is Taran, but I go by Tarus. I'm sorry to disturb you, but would you mind sharing your book with me?"

Her chest rose a few times before she turned and glanced up at me. My breathing accelerated in response, the electricity sparking once again. Her beautiful, plump lips captivated me whilst also making me nervous. I couldn't stop fidgeting with my fingers. How could she not automatically agree? Anyone else in the room would have.

So, what was taking her so long?

The French teacher must've been annoyed because she said something that grabbed everyone's attention. Chairs screeched against the floor as several students turned to face the professor. Not only had she taken everyone's attention, but she'd also given Sierra a chance to break our contact. With her eyes glued to the floor, she shifted in her seat but remained silent.

Interesting.

Giving up on suckering her into helping me, I considered other ways to stay near to her when she spoke. "You should've already picked up your textbooks from the library. I'm surprised no one has taken you to get them."

I hadn't gone to any classes for anyone to have tried. But even if they had, I wouldn't have let them. I was there for one person and one person only.

Her.

"The library didn't have one for French. So, is that a no to sharing?" I pouted and tried to portray the most innocent boy I could. I plastered on a slight smile, and tears formed behind my eyelids to help with the *poor-misfortunate-soul* look.

"Sorry, yes. You can share." She pushed the book closer to me and her chair farther away. Not what I'd expected, but I'd take it. I sat and scooted my seat nearer to her, shrinking the distance that she had tried to create between us.

"My greatest thanks to you." I grabbed a pencil from my bag and brushed my knee against hers. Both our bodies tensed, and the iridescent vein reappeared. It lit all the way to the void spot in my chest and disappeared the second I moved away.

The teacher pointed to the board as she spoke in French, but I couldn't focus on her. Sierra's expression distracted me. She bit her pencil, eyebrows scrunched. I inched closer. Heat radiated from her, and her lavender scent filled my lungs. "Are you okay?"

As she crunched down on the pencil, breaking it, a snap resonated around the room between the professor's words. "Umm. I can't shake the feeling that we met yesterday."

"Man. Here, I was thinking I met the girl over there." I nudged my chin to the right.

She crossed her arms. "Never mind."

Oops. I reached out for her hand to get her attention so I could tell her I was kidding, but she pulled it away. That stupid, painful thorn bush began growing inside again and stabbed my chest deep. I stared at her, blinking. How could I fix this?

A few seconds after she slumped in her chair, I spoke again. "At Zadina's Dreamspace, we both went for the last Choco Nits. I'd never forget a face like yours."

Her cheeks turned strawberry pink, but she didn't glance over or acknowledge what I'd said. Shit.

While the professor droned on, my body ached. It wanted to touch her, to hold her, and I had to fight the urge to do just that. I wanted these feelings to last for the next twelve days, not to end now with me trying to touch her without her consent or after that one stupid remark that had bothered her.

I squeezed my jaw tight to create pain and focus on anything other than Sierra.

But I couldn't resist the urge to talk to her. I couldn't help it. Plus, I needed to fix whatever I'd just messed up.

"I'm new in town. Could you show me around?" I asked, head forward but peeking at her from the corner of my eye. She stiffened, and her breathing stopped. My head jerked back. That wasn't a typical reaction.

"Sorry, I'm busy."

If my head hadn't already wrenched back, it would've popped. I couldn't help but blink. What the hell? No one ever said no to me. Most girls would drop whatever they were doing to hang with me. She had to be lying. Guess without her believing in magic, the part about seers not being able to lie didn't apply. Well, then, I'd just have to find a way to prove she was lying. Prove that she wanted me.

"Sierra, Vas-tu te joinder Moi et r ponder la question?" the professor asked, and everyone turned to face us.

Sierra swallowed. But before she could respond, the bell rang. I collected my things and bit my cheek as the professor approached Sierra.

"I'll expect better from you next time you're in class. Please be attentive, or I'll have to correct the distraction and move one of you to a different period," the professor said, her glasses slipping down her nose.

Cheeks crimson, Sierra mustered several apologies. My toes curled.

Once the professor stepped away, I stumbled out of my chair, ending inches from Sierra. My lips grazed her ear, and my focus blurred this close to her. Magic zapped like crazy in my veins. It was hard for me to stay on task. Part of me wanted to bite her ear and feel her reaction.

But before my body responded any further, I said, "Sorry if I've contributed to any of your distractions today."

She stiffened, her breathing growing shallow.

"See you, Sierra." I purred her name in the most sensual way possible.

Without looking at her, I glided toward the exit. Once through the door and out of sight, I placed my hand on the doorframe and peeked back inside. She sulked after me, her mouth hanging ajar, just as I'd hoped. I winked and continued on my way.

Once school ended, I'd prove she wanted me.

Sixteen

Bells chimed for the end of seventh period, and I lurked near the door of Sierra's math class, waiting for her to leave. But she stayed behind, yet again, to talk with her professor.

"Sierra, I've filled out a teacher recommendation for you." He handed her a paper and added, "I've also placed your name in the candidate pull for Dartmouth. Since your mom went there, I thought you might want to give it a shot."

Sierra's eyes watered. "Thank you, sir." She scurried out and headed to the right, tears streaming down her face.

The sight made my insides ache. I wanted to wipe away her sadness. Besides Mother and Vilo, no one had made me care this much since Deesse had destroyed my heart. It scared me, but at the same time, intrigued me. I couldn't believe my heart was returning. It was surreal. But I still didn't know how to ensure Mother wasn't the dark soul, no one would hurt Sierra, and how to get Sierra to forgive me.

She leaned against her locker and slid to the floor. Since her emotions seemed all over the place, it didn't feel like the right time to approach. Instead, I waited down the hallway.

After a while, she rose, jammed her textbooks in the locker, and shuffled away.

I followed, hiding behind whatever I could.

We wound up in the school library. She strode past the blue-blocked desk, waved at the brunette receptionist, and trudged to the far back corner. The receptionist yelled something after me. My stomach jumped into my throat. Had she given me away? But Sierra was too distracted by her emotions to notice.

I flashed my ID badge at the receptionist, and she shut up.

In the clear, I tiptoed behind Sierra again. I expected she'd venture to a dark section with witchy stuff, but she didn't. Instead, she chose the brightest area where the sun's orange hues shone in through the floor-to-ceiling windows.

A royal blue tufted couch faced the windows. On either side of it sat two comfy yellow chairs. A side table stood next to each one with a yellow-shaded lamp on top. A Middle-Grade Fantasy sign hung above the shelves behind the furniture. I hid on the other side and pulled out several books, making a gap large enough to watch her through.

She placed her backpack on the floor and slumped on the couch. Unsure how to handle the fact she'd lied about being busy, the despair on her face, or to explain how I'd wound up here, I debated leaving until she grabbed a small notebook and pen from her bag, sparking my curiosity.

I snuck behind her and peeked over the couch to read as she wrote.

Hey, Mom & Dad,

    Today, Mom's best friend put my name in for Dartmouth. I got teary-eyed, and I bet he expected it was from my gratitude and from missing you guys. But

A teardrop fell onto her paper. She used her sleeve to dab the drop dry and returned to her writing.

it's because I don't want to disappoint either of your legacies. I graduate in nine months and have no idea what I want to do. Will I do something that'll make you both proud?

She sniffled, slammed the journal shut, and brought her knees to her chest.

As she rocked, two people passing by pointed in my direction. My eyes widened, and I dashed away.

After I was sure they'd left, I returned to the gap in the bookshelves, wishing I could comfort her. With every swipe of her sleeve to her eyes, the thorns on that aggravating bush stabbed my chest. Everything inside me ached, dying to take this terrible pain away from her.

The part of the prophecy about me was real. I couldn't deny that. But it didn't make sense that Sierra had lied to me and hadn't seemed interested. It said that our love *together* would reunite the realms. That meant she needed to love me back. Someone who liked the other wouldn't lie to them. Would they? Damn it. Why couldn't her powers be active? Then she couldn't lie to me, and I'd know the truth.

Once she returned to the journal, I tiptoed behind her again. Scents of the ocean, embers, and lavender intensified as I hovered over her shoulder. Just as I took my next inaudible breath, she turned and gasped. "What are you doing?"

"Trying to figure out what made you so busy that you'd miss a chance to hang out with me." I yanked at my tunic's collar. Before seventh period had ended, I'd changed out of the itchy uniform and back into my comfortable, rich tunic with ruffled sleeves and cashmere tights.

She sized me up. "Aren't you rather conceited?"

"Aren't you a great liar?" I stuck my hand out. "Nice to meet you."

Her cheeks turned rosy, and she pushed my hand away. "I didn't lie."

I plopped down on the mahogany side table. "Explain how it wasn't a lie, then."

"I don't have to explain myself to you." She crossed her arms and sunk deeper into the couch.

The thorn bush tore at my insides. Shit. "What if I asked kindly?" It had seemed to work on others who, soon after, followed my every bidding.

"You can try. But I don't think it'll work." She smirked.

"Will you please explain why you won't spend time with me?" I pouted. "Anybody else would've jumped at the opportunity."

She rolled her eyes. "Great. Go ask them and stop bothering me."

I was about to respond when the librarian appeared, a finger to her lips. "Students are complaining about the noise. Please keep it down."

"Yes, ma'am. Sorry," Sierra said.

My toes curled. She was a princess, for crying out loud. She should bow down to no one.

As the librarian walked off, I headed to the middle-grade section. Sierra's smile grew.

If I wasn't so mesmerized by her beauty, I'd have laughed at her for counting this a victory so soon. I picked up a book with a witch on a broom, ventured back, and plopped onto the opposite side of the soft couch.

She groaned but didn't say anything. I winked, and her lips thinned.

Despite my urge to laugh or talk to her, I refrained and read the book.

Several times, I peeked at her, and each time, I found her

doing the same. Her abhorrence with me made no sense. Sierra acted as if she didn't want to give me the time of day, but I'd say she wanted to give me much more. Eager to prove it and see if the iridescent vein would appear again, I inched closer to her.

By the time the room darkened from the setting sun, my forearm touched her thigh. The vein glowed. Both of us gasped. Yes! I was getting to her.

I continued touching her, letting the vein rise to my chest. I couldn't breathe. Not only was this everything I'd dreamt of for years, but this girl was better than I could've ever imagined. I liked her spunk, bluntness, and her ability to say no to me.

With my thoughts consumed by her, the pages no longer captured my attention. I felt a sense of peace in her presence. A peace I hadn't felt in years.

A few minutes later, her look of wonder crumbled, and she jumped up. She gathered her things together without saying anything and sauntered off while I stared after her.

What the hell had just happened?

Before she completely vanished, common sense struck me, and I followed after her into the noisy streets of London. I managed to get ahead of her and held my hands out. "Please forgive me. I didn't mean to bother you."

"You're forgiven." She walked past me. "Have a good night, Tarus."

My blood sizzled. Gods, I loved this girl's audacity to ignore me. "Are you dismissing me?"

"I'm trying to." She kept walking, but being over a foot taller than her, I managed to keep up.

"But why?" I clutched my chest.

She stopped in front of a fancy steakhouse. Someone opened the door, and a strong fragrance of garlic drifted out, along with a warm breeze. "You keep asking me questions. How about you answer one for me?"

"Anything." As long as the curse let me answer, I'd tell her my whole life story if that meant I could spend one more second with her.

"Why are you so eager to get my attention?" She glanced down at the wet cobblestone walkway, her reflection rippling in a puddle.

"B-because ..." I stuttered, and not because of the curse, but because of my nerves. I didn't know what to say. I wasn't used to putting so much effort into wooing girls. "Sierra." I inched closer, and despite the chilly autumn, the temperature rose. "You're the most fascinating person I've ever met. I want to know you better. Is that so wrong?"

Her face flushed. "No."

"Good." I brushed my lips against her ear. She straightened, and the iridescent vein vibrated, the thorn bush vanishing. "Because I'm determined to find out every little thing about you, Sierra," I purred. "The things that make you tick and that please you." The vein formed the outline of a heart, and it beat so hard it pulled me away from her.

"Though it might not be wrong, that doesn't mean I'll let you." She winked and bolted into the steakhouse.

I hunched over, hands on my knees, and burst out laughing—something I hadn't done in years. I couldn't stop. She made so much come alive.

Once calmed down, I debated what to do next. My entire purpose for being on Earth was to find her. Now, I either needed to return to Astal with her and align the realms or stay for the remaining time and do as Vilo had suggested.

For once, I wasn't ready to get this over with. I was choosing the latter option.

I had to feel more of this.

But for the next two days, there was no school. I wouldn't be able to see her or know where she'd gone. Better I stayed outside her dorm where, hopefully, my magic would still work, and I could keep an eye on her, as well as find an opportunity to talk to her.

Since I didn't know how long Sierra would take at the restaurant, I ate at a burger joint nearby. After I scarfed down the scrumptious food, I left the restaurant, hid in an alley, turned invisible, and portaled a hall away from her dorm. The second I reached her door, a strong beat from inside soothed my nerves. I imagined her dancing to it, and my mind started to drift to sleep until Emma approached with a strong scent of musky jasmine surrounding her.

My body went into overdrive. Pins and needles poked my spine. This was the second time I'd smelt Darcy. That couldn't be a coincidence. She was close. I jumped up and dashed after her scent.

I searched the entire perimeter of the dorm but couldn't find her. The last I knew, she didn't have invisibility powers. She shouldn't be able to hide from me, but somehow, she'd managed. Unless, of course, this was just my crazy nerves. Someone else could obviously have that same scent. It didn't belong just to her. Nonetheless, I'd search every crevice of this school to find her or the other two demon leaders.

After hours of nonstop searching, trying to pick up the scent, I chalked it up to Emma wearing jasmine perfume. I balled my hands into fists. With the emotions Darcy and the Hellspace leaders had rekindled, I was in need of breaking something. I portaled back to Hillshite and froze.

Darcy lay on my bed underneath the covers.

Seventeen

Jaw clenched, I glared at Darcy.

She stood, and the comforter slid to the floor, revealing her naked body. My pants grew uncomfortable.

I gulped as she approached me.

"What are you doing here, Darcy? Why haven't you returned to Hellspace?"

"Problems arose. Queen Delilah thinks it best I stay out for now." Her cold hand caressed my cheek, and I managed to suppress a shiver. After feeling the things Sierra had awakened, Darcy's touch felt like a torch burning my skin.

I blinked several times, my body tensing. "Does she know you're here?"

"She sent me after I told her you might need help searching this vast realm."

My stomach dropped. Mother knew she was here. Darcy was supposed to be helping me, and the fact I'd caught her scent all day, especially near Emma, meant she already knew I'd found the seer.

"Well, I have eleven more days and nine women left to

search. I've got it covered. You can leave." I pushed her hand from my face.

She ground her teeth, and her dark irises grew, covering the whites. For several seconds, she stared at me before slamming her lips on mine.

"What the hell, Darcy?" I portaled to the back wall.

"Don't you want me? You used to beg for me multiple times a day." She portaled in front of me, her hand now at my crotch.

I stiffened. Damn. Out of everyone I'd ever slept with, Darcy topped them all by thousands. Back then, seeing her naked would drop me to my knees, but now, all I wanted to do was cover her with the comforter. Her touch didn't just burn. It was detestable on my skin.

"That was two years ago. Things have changed." I shimmied away and portaled next to the open window. The cold breeze was a comfort to the blistering pain.

"Your body says different." She slammed me against the wall, her chest against mine.

"Darcy! I don't care what my body says. I don't want you anymore!" I screamed and shoved her off. She fell on her butt, fingers curling into the rough carpet beneath her.

"You're lying. We're mated!"

Holy Delmore. I'd forgotten she'd mated with me before I'd left Hellspace. In our realm, one can mate without the other. To be recognized as a mating pair, both had to form a bond in their hearts. But it didn't happen often. When it did, the bond crystallized, and the pair could communicate by speaking in each other's minds, no matter how far apart. They could also share powers.

"You mated me. I never mated you, Darcy. I never will. I don't have feelings for you in that way. Not now. Not ever." Especially not after meeting Sierra.

Demon claws sprang from Darcy's hands as she tore apart

the brown carpet beneath her. She bounded up and sliced at my face. I clenched my fists but remained silent.

"You have some balls talking to me like that." Her black magic glowed in her palm.

My eyes widened. I did have balls. I shouldn't have talked to her that way. Not when she knew about Sierra, and I wasn't ready to bring her to Mother.

"Sierra Mills. She's seventeen. She looks a lot like Aris, don't you think?" She scraped her finger from my ear to my chin, drawing blood.

I shook my head.

"I think she does." She smirked. "I should take her to Queen Delilah."

"No!" Pain shot through every nerve ending. My vision tunneled, and a ringing echoed in my ears.

"Why not? Are you not the queen's most loyal servant? Her bodyguard and assassin? Oh, and don't forget, her *beloved son*?"

"Yes, but I need time. I need to make sure it's the king's child and learn about her ways before I give her to Mother." Darcy knew me too well. She had to know I was lying.

"Huh. I saw the way you looked at her today. How cutely human of you." Darcy sucked her claw, her tongue darting out to taste every last drop of my blood she'd drawn.

"I only looked at her one way, like I found my ticket out of Hellspace." I bit my lip.

"So, you have no feelings for her, then?"

"How did you even make it here to Earth? Did Mother kill another pixie to get you across? What item did you sacrifice? You treasure nothing."

"Why are you changing the subject?"

"It just crossed my mind." I fidgeted with Slinger.

"You have feelings for that chick. That's why you won't sleep with me."

"No, I don't have feelings for her." I wanted to say more, but I couldn't with the threat hanging over me.

She crushed her lips against mine, and instantly, a rain cloud formed above the thorn bush that randomly appeared after starting this quest to find the king's daughter, the girl who brought my non-existent heart to life. Now, under Darcy's lips, a sense of betrayal squeezed my chest tight.

I cupped her cheeks and pushed her face away. Veins bulged on her forehead, her eyes throwing daggers back. With my hands still on her, I took the opportunity to dive into her mind. Death, torment, and blood swarmed her thoughts. I dug through the images, searching for the nerve I needed, the one that cast a rainbow hue in everyone's mind.

Just as I found it, she shoved me against the wall and ejected me from her mind. Holy Delmore. She must've recently killed a leader somewhere. No one had ever been able to force me out before. "How dare you try to control me." Her hand snaked out quickly, punching me square on the nose.

Before she could portal away, I fisted her silky red hair and yanked her back. "Stop."

"Why? Afraid of what I might do to your precious Sierra?" she purred her name with venom, spit flying from her mouth.

"What are you going to do to me? With Queen Delilah?" I might have questions about Sierra and this prophecy, but one thing remained—I cared about myself, first and foremost. Nobody who'd ever discovered or suspected I had a mind-controlling ability had lived to talk about it.

Even without a heart, I was aware of the immense danger mind control could be. I'd seen the last leader, Manny, make others into machines. I'd never wanted to do that—it also took too much energy. And, although Mother was an angel, if she knew I had that ability, she wouldn't be able to stop herself from begging me to control those who hated us. And I'd do it for her if she asked. So, I needed to keep it hidden.

Darcy must've known how dangerous it could be, too. She used to be Manny's concubine and knew of his gift, which meant she must've figured I had it. But she'd never mentioned it, especially to Mother. I couldn't help but internally tremble at the possibility that Darcy might change that now out of anger.

"Make you beg." She smirked.

"Please, don't say anything to Mother about my gifts or the seer. Let me go at my own pace. I'll bring her to Mother. Just not yet." I dropped to my knees. "There is a reason you haven't already confessed to her about both things. I'm not sure why you haven't told her about my abilities, but the reason you haven't told her about Sierra is because you like being out of Hellspace. If you share Sierra with her now, you'll end up back there." She had to hate the place as much as I did. I had to be right about this. It was the only string I had to pull.

"If I give her Sierra, I'll be her new personal bodyguard. She'll kick you to the curb." She patted my head, and it took all of me not to fight her.

"Mother didn't choose you two years ago and won't choose you now. She'll take Saullis before you."

A demonic cackle escaped her lips. "You know what?"

I gulped. This couldn't be good.

"I've always found making you squirm a great hoot. The more you stress, the more your temper escapes, and you destroy things. It's sexy as hell. Plus, you deserve the torment after what you've said to me."

"What's that supposed to mean?" My stomach launched into my throat. I couldn't breathe.

"Better keep one eye open when you sleep." She knelt beside me and scraped my chest with her claws. "Better yet, you probably don't want to sleep." At those words, she portaled away, her scent lingering in her wake.

Before I fell apart, I turned invisible and portaled to the hall outside Sierra's dorm. As laughter came from within her room, I let out a breath and slid to the ground, my back against the smooth wooden door. This prophecy, Sierra, Vilo ... they were all getting to me, changing me.

I groaned, burying my hands in my hair as my head rested on my knees.

This path wouldn't lead to a happy ending like Aris and Vilo had hoped. Not now. Not when Darcy held my life in her hands.

Eighteen

Water droplets smacked the glass window in a rhythmic pattern, lulling me to sleep. Suddenly, Emma screamed. Adrenaline shot through me, and I jumped. Nobody was staring at me or even near me. I looked down. I was still invisible.

"Thank you." Emma smiled and took something from a girl at the doorway. She turned to look inside her dorm. "Sierra, you might have another opportunity to see your handsome friend." The door shut behind her with a loud thud.

What the hell? I glanced at the young girl in front of Sierra's dorm, dressed in a weird costume and holding papers in her hand. As she passed me, I grabbed one.

With her eyebrows scrunched, she searched the area, but after two turns, she shrugged and continued as if nothing had happened.

No longer distracted by her, I read the flyer.

Plans just got interesting. It seemed I now had an extra credit event to attend. Going would give me a chance to hang out with Sierra, one that didn't seem too creepy. And, from the way Emma had reacted, I was confident she'd convince Sierra to go.

With time to kill, I walked to the library to learn about bowling.

I searched through several unhelpful books before moving on to the bulky machine. Videos upon videos appeared, showing every little detail that I might need. After the tenth clip, I practically groaned, my brain ready to combust, so I returned to Hillshite.

After taking a shower, I slicked back my hair and shrugged into my black tights and silk tunic. Ready, I portaled a few blocks from the bowling alley.

A small backstreet was nestled between the venue and a coffee shop. I turned into it and waved my hand, shifting to visible. As I waited for others to pass by, my thoughts ran rampant. What if Sierra avoided me again? Worst of all, what if I wasn't the *handsome friend*? Emma had said *friend*. Sierra and I only spoke yesterday, after I'd forced it.

We couldn't be considered friends.

Once in the clear, I shimmied out of the secluded area and breezed into the bowling alley. There were several lanes for bowling, a small desk with red and white shoes behind it, a medium-sized cafeteria, and a descending stairwell. Colorful disco balls hung from the ceiling and lit the area. A few groups huddled beside the lanes, but none of them looked like Elite Academy students, and no sign suggested that it was them. I headed down to the basement level.

Pop music blared and the scent of grease and pepperoni wafted up as I descended the last few steps. Turning from the staircase, I found a room full of students and faculty. Signs hung from the ceiling, announcing the extra credit assignment and displaying the school's name. They must've booked the entire room for the event.

Girls left their groups and dashed toward me. I cringed, ignoring them, searching over their heads for Sierra instead.

Seconds later, I spotted her at a bowling lane near the back with Emma and two boys. Sweat beaded on my forehead. She hadn't been talking about me after all. But who cared? I'd make her talk about me by the end of tonight. I'd be the one on her mind. No one else.

Puffing out my chest, I ran my hand through my hair and headed straight for Sierra.

I maneuvered between the two boys to be in front of her. With them out of the way, I leaned against the ball return. "Nice seeing you here." I smirked.

She glanced at Emma, raising her eyebrows. Emma

shrugged, and Sierra returned her gaze to me, arms folded across her chest. "Excuse you. I was in the middle of a conversation."

This girl had no trouble lying to me, avoiding me, confusing me, and talking to me however she wanted. I wasn't used to this. I stood there frozen, unsure of what to do. She shoved past me. Our arms touched, and she stopped. The iridescent vein appeared in my hand and rushed to my chest. But it didn't make it as far as to form an outline of a heart before Sierra gasped and continued to walk away.

This was the second time she'd reacted to our connection. There was no way she could continue to deny the spark between us. I just needed her to admit it, to stop avoiding me, and to have a one-on-one conversation. Not because I forced it, but because she wanted to.

I tapped her shoulder with my quivering hand. She turned around and sighed. "Yes?"

"I'm sorry." I bit my lip. Why did I keep apologizing to her? That wasn't me. I made fun of those who apologized.

"Don't let it happen again." She focused back on the boys.

Unsure what to do, I trudged over to a table full of pizzas and munched on a slice. Two pizzas later, I still didn't have a single idea. But for once, Sierra stood alone by the ball return, playing a solo game. I made my way over as she picked up a ball and rolled it down the lane. Strike. She picked up her next ball. Strike again. Damn, she had skills. An idea sparked.

She walked off the platform and stopped when she saw me standing by the machine.

"Sierra, I really am sorry."

Her lips curled up.

"That was an impressive roll. Would you mind helping me?" I placed my hands together and moved closer. "Please."

She shook her head. "You can't be that bad."

"Wanna see?"

She gestured toward the lane.

I threw the ball. It bounced down the lane and slid into the gutter, not even halfway along. Sierra burst out laughing, and I whipped around just as she covered her mouth. "Don't laugh." I pouted.

"Sorry. I couldn't help it." She tightened her lips, a hint of a smirk tugging at one corner.

"Teach me how?" I smiled. "Please."

"It'd be cruel if I didn't." She laughed again and approached the shelf of balls. "Do you know what size you are?"

Blood rushed to my bottom half. The front of my pants tightened, and I had to take a deep breath. "Excuse me?"

"Come here." She ushered me over. Holding a ball in her arms, she studied me, biting her lip. "See the holes? There's a size between them. Depending on the weight you can manage and the size of your fingers, it determines the ball you can use."

"What makes you think I don't know this?" I leaned against the shelf. She was right, but dang, what a way to make me feel stupid. I saw the holes. I just didn't use them. My fingers couldn't fit.

"You used Emma's ball. Her fingers are smaller than mine. From looking at your build, I can only imagine your fingers aren't that small." She raised her hand. I blinked at her. "I'm not going to bite. Let me see your fingers." She chuckled. Her laugh resonated like piano music, soothing my soul. I could listen to it all day.

I lifted my hand to hers. She pressed our fingers together. Electricity spread down my spine, shooting my nerves with adrenaline. The iridescent vein shifted into solid lavender. I gasped, pulled my hand away, and massaged it with the other.

Sierra stared at her hand, blinking. "Sorry. I must've touched something charged with static. I didn't mean to zap us." Static? She seriously thought that was static. That was *chemistry*. That was the prophecy. *She doesn't believe*, I reminded myself. She didn't know about magic.

She rubbed her hands along her strapless cream dress. "Wanna try again?" She raised her hand.

Of course. I wanted nothing more than to touch her. I raised my hand, and hers collided with mine. Sparks flew, but I kept my gasp inside, scared she'd pull away again.

She used her other hand to compare the lengths of our two fingers together. "Your fingers are massive," she said in a pant. Dang, this had to be doing something to her. But what? I could slip into her mind and find out. But as I tried, pain ricocheted through my body. The curse. I'd forgotten already. I couldn't creep into her mind. My magic didn't function around her.

"I bet an extra-large size sixteen ball would work." She let go of my hand and grabbed a blue and black marbled ball. "Come with me."

She stepped onto the platform, and I followed her, still trying to calm my nerves.

"Watch my stance." She held the ball with her right hand at waist height. Her right foot moved back. "This is how you start. You'll walk up to the line and your right leg should be in front, bent. Your left leg back, heel lifted." She did as she described. "If you want more control, use both hands to hold the ball and then release it." She tossed my ball, and even though its weight exceeded hers, she rolled a strike.

She turned around and twirled. The bottom half of her dress whirled around her legs. Her lavender scent wafted under my nose. I smiled and gave her a high five, adapting to her world's customs. "Girl, you're good."

She shrugged, cheeks blushing. "Your turn."

Once the ball had returned to the machine, I grabbed it and followed her instructions. But still, it landed in the gutter.

She chuckled and approached me with her yellow marbled ball.

"Stand behind me."

I complied but left a large gap between us. But why? Was I really afraid of what the closeness would do? She stepped backward until she leaned against my chest. I couldn't breathe. Heat radiated from her, and butterflies fluttered inside my stomach. The lavender vein spread to my chest and formed a newfound iridescent heart. I almost stepped back out of shock and excitement, but I didn't want to move away from her, causing it to fade.

"Place your hand on mine. Feel how the ball moves with me," she said, each breath heavy and deep.

I placed my hand on hers and immediately bit my lip from the electricity zapping through every muscle. She tossed the ball, and it landed in the gutter. I laughed, trying to think about anything other than the way she felt this close to me. She turned around. Our chests touched, her face inches from mine, and time froze. Nothing existed but her.

She bit her bottom lip at a slow, agonizing pace. My body reacted, dying to bite it, dying to taste her.

"I'm wiped. Wanna talk?" She broke away and headed toward the pizzas.

Wherever this girl went, I'd follow, no question, at least for the next eleven days. In that time, I needed to find out why the mating bond hadn't formed and why everything disappeared if we weren't touching. Plus, I still hadn't figured out what to say to Mother.

So far, the best option was to tell her the full prophecy, minus the bit about her being the dark soul. Maybe, if Mother knew we'd achieve her mission and that Sierra was meant to be a good seer, she'd let her live. If we formed the bond, it'd be easier to convince Mother. It was against the law to kill another's mate alone. A mated pair had to die together.

"You okay?" Sierra steered me to a high-top black table and sat down.

"Yeah. Sorry." I sat next to her. "So, is it time to learn more about you?"

She rocked her head back, eyebrows lowered. "Do we have to?"

"It'd be the highlight of my day." I propped my elbows on the table, tilted my head, and studied her.

For the rest of the evening, Sierra talked about her adoptive parents and Emma's family. She talked about her classes and her plans for college, which, as of now, she had none. She talked about her hobbies, books, and dancing. The entire time, I listened. A few times, she'd ask about me, but I'd turn it back to her.

My nightmares and worries evaporated as I listened to her. For the first time, a heat radiated through me in a good way. I loved the way she made me feel.

"Sierra, the assignment's over." Emma pulled at Sierra's arm. "Your date is waiting."

My lungs combusted. Date? She had a date? Who the hell did I need to kill?

Nineteen

Unable to breathe, I stared after her as she walked away with Emma. For this prophecy to work, or at least to save her from Mother, I needed to be her only date. No one else.

I'd follow her and kill the man after he left Sierra's presence. My stomach twisted at the thought. Okay, fine. I'd *make* him forget her. A little mind control went a long way. No big deal.

Once they disappeared through the doors, I counted to ten to ensure enough time had passed before following them.

Sierra and Emma walked arm-in-arm a few blocks down. Pedestrians shuffled all around the dark London streets and provided enough noise to mask my footsteps as I rushed down the sidewalk toward them.

A few feet away from them, their conversation reached my ears. I stopped running and used the shadows to hide.

"Emma, I still don't understand." Sierra grabbed Emma's arm, pulling her to a stop, and I lunged behind a nasty dumpster. "Aren't you the one who said you wanted me to find a soulmate? Why pull me away?"

"Yes, but not with him. He was rude."

Her words slammed into me like a heavy boulder crushing my chest. I clutched Slinger and took several deep breaths to calm the overwhelming hurt flowing through me.

"There's something you're not telling me." They continued on, and I waited until they made it a few yards away before following. "We already knew he was arrogant, but I can't explain the connection I have to him." She twirled, hands in her pockets. "He's like a magnet that pulls me to him. He energizes every nerve in my body."

She did feel something for me. I was the handsome friend. But what about this date?

"Did you know he has a girlfriend?" Emma stopped them this time, and I crouched down to tie my shoes, half hidden by the bus stop.

I didn't have a girlfriend. Why the hell would she think that?

Out of the corner of my eye, I watched them. Sierra's eyebrows raised, her hand clutching her chest. "No. He couldn't. He just moved here. When would he have time to find someone when he's always chasing me? Plus, there's the way he talks to me and gives me his undivided attention. He wouldn't do that if he had a girlfriend."

"She cornered me at the bowling alley."

What the hell? I clenched my fists. My nails dug into my skin. Darcy!

"She warned me that he was bad news. That he just came out of rehab. Rehab, Sierra, and a girlfriend! He's bad news. A manwhore."

I sucked in a deep breath. Rehab? Girlfriend? What the hell did Darcy say to her?

From the red tinge in Sierra's eyes to the clenching of her jaw, it was obvious Sierra wasn't happy. How could I fix this?

How could I stop Darcy? Even if I wished to throttle Darcy and watch the life drain from her body, I couldn't. If I knew her as well as I thought, she would've already warned someone else. So, if I killed Darcy, the person she warned would kill Sierra.

"Everyone is allowed an explanation and a second chance, Emma. Maybe she's a jealous ex, and he's changed. Rehab could've helped him." Sierra broke apart from Emma and strolled in front of her. "You should've talked to me about it first instead of lying to him. What if he thinks I'm two-timing him?"

"You can't two-time someone you're not with, and who cares if he's already two-timing you?" Emma ran to catch up with Sierra, almost bumping into a pedestrian glued to their phone. "Whatever. I didn't lie. You do have a date."

Sierra glared at her.

"With your books. Like you do every Saturday." Emma smiled. "If you really believe he's innocent and want to see where things go with him, maybe it'll bring out his jealousy?"

Sierra shook her head, and both girls laughed.

A lightness filled my chest, but it didn't erase the unease of Darcy's words. Since Sierra seemed okay, wanted to give me the benefit of the doubt, and wasn't going on a date with some guy, I dashed off in search of Darcy. I needed to handle her before she messed things up for me.

Hours later, after finding no sign of Darcy, I turned invisible and ventured back to the hall outside Sierra's room. If this could be over at any moment, I needed to spend all my time near Sierra to try and form the bond. It was my only chance of saving her.

No music blared from behind the door. I pushed my ear up to it but couldn't hear anything. Veins stood out in my neck. If she was in the room, my magic wouldn't let me portal inside. What better way to check than to see if the curse reacted?

My palm glowed its onyx black as I rubbed my fingers and portaled into her room. It worked. She wasn't there. Adrenaline shot through my system. Where the hell was she?

Just about to portal out to search for her, something shiny snagged my attention. Resting on an unwrinkled, light blue comforter lay Sierra's journal. I picked it up, curious to see if she'd written anything about our encounters. Though I might not be allowed to break into her mind, nothing could keep me away from her journal.

I started at the beginning, wanting to learn as much as I could about her.

Besides, when the professor spoke to her about her mom, she always had a smile on her face, a pep to her step. But this journal represented something more than what the world saw.

Every entry tugged at me, from the devastation haunting each word. My body stung with every turn of the page. And once upon a time, her tears most certainly drenched each note, and I had to hold mine back from joining them.

Mom, I miss you, started almost every page.

The career counselor brought me to the office today. She droned on about how amazing you were. She kept saying she knew my future would heal hundreds, just like you had. Mom, what if it doesn't? I don't know what I want to be. Part of me wants to be an event planner. But how will that live up to you? I'm a failure.

A few pages later, she wrote another heartbreaking entry.

On days like today, when Emma has a birthday and family comes to celebrate her, I miss you and Dad. I'm thankful for the Hutchinsons, but they aren't you guys. AJ's gift also brought tears to my eyes. He bought her a promise ring. Emma's certain they'll marry after high school. Will I ever find anything like that? Like those two, or you and Dad? Every person I've ever dated has tried to change me. Dancing in the streets, embarrassing. Singing in my room, uncomfortable. Skipping in the halls, absurd. Am I that awful, that childlike? Should I change? Is that the only way to have what you guys had? I wish you could give me advice. Tell me if you changed for Dad.

Holy Delmore. This girl hurt.
Another page stuck out a few entries later.

Dad's organization is throwing another gala. Mom, why did he never take me to them? I begged, night after night. Was he ashamed of me? It still kills me wondering what made him never take me when I'd dreamed of going since I was four.

That was rough. Why hadn't he taken her? What was a gala? Later, I'd have to visit the library. I was building a list of things I needed to check out.

Once I reached the entry about when we met at Zadina's Dreamspace, both of us going for the last Choco Nits, my body shivered.

Mom, I met a boy

Keys jangled outside the door, and my magic began to boil me alive. Rubbing my fingers together to portal before they opened the door, the voice on the other side of the door froze me in place. Darcy was here.

As the door swung open, I portaled to the end of the hallway. Darcy stood behind Emma and Sierra, wearing a skin-tight black suit showing off all her curves. She waved goodbye to them as Emma shut the door, and I hustled toward Darcy, lunging for her arm. But before I connected, Darcy portaled away, winking.

Twenty

Until Monday afternoon, I had spent every waking moment searching for Darcy, if not checking on Sierra, but nothing came to fruition. To make matters worse, every second I was away from Sierra, Hellspace preoccupied my mind.

By French class, I was in desperate need to *feel* Sierra. I also wanted to murder every person who flocked my way. At least ten people stopped me on my way to class, handing over their numbers or flirting with me.

But their attempts were wasted. None of them sparked a vein or made me come alive. Instead, they annoyed me, and my thoughts dipped close to murderous until I stepped into class and couldn't find Sierra in her usual spot. Thoughts of death and violence vanished, replaced by panic.

Where was she?

I scanned the room, unable to breathe, until I landed on her familiar silhouette at the front.

What made her change seats? Holy Delmore. It had to be because of what Emma had told her. She must be mad or scared of me. Knots formed everywhere in my body. I couldn't fix this without her finding out that I knew. But that wasn't an option.

"Excuse me. The librarian informed me she still didn't have a French book. It seems I need to share again. Since you were so kind to me the other day, I hoped you wouldn't object." My mouth dried as she remained silent.

I shuffled my feet on the floor, and killed Darcy in my head, as I waited for a response. Sierra pivoted in her chair to face me. On cue, my body warmed, and my magic stirred.

"This will be two days in a row. How about we make a trade? I'll share my book with you for an answer to a question?" She batted her eyelashes.

All the knots inside of me instantly vanished, and I couldn't help but choke back a laugh. She wanted to play a game. I loved games, and she definitely didn't make things boring with her audacity to challenge me. "What's the question?"

"Should I stay away from you?" Sierra bit her lip, her gaze flitting across my face.

Woah, what? I didn't expect her to ask that. I loved her boldness. Hell, she turned me on. I didn't want her to stay away. But should she? Mother wanted to kill her. My father was the devil, and I'd killed hers.

"Yes." I sighed. My legs grew weak, and I would've collapsed to the floor had I not grabbed the corner of the table at the last second. Once I had steadied myself, I glanced at Sierra. Her breathing had stopped. "I don't want you to. But I'm not the good guy." Why did I confess?

Before I could turn away, she grabbed my arm. The lavender vein appeared and rushed to my chest. "Maybe I'm tired of the good guys."

Her words electrocuted me from the inside out. She was everything I'd ever dreamed of. But she had no idea what she was heading into, and I really shouldn't let her run in blind.

Deesse, I don't pray to you, not anymore, not after you took my heart. But I need your help. So now, I'm praying. Please let my role in the prophecy be true, and it be a mating bond that forms so I can convince Mother to keep her alive. And once she learns about magic and I tell her about her father, please help her to forgive me.

After a moment of silence—with some stares and added commentary to "get a room" and "I'm better"—she coughed.

"You going to sit and share the book with me or not?" This woman was either immune to me or had a volcano's worth of fire brewing inside of her.

I suspected the latter.

With a wink, I sat down, placed my bag between us, and brushed my lips against her ear as I bent down to gather my things. Warmth radiated from her. Loving the way she made me feel, I hovered near her ear longer than necessary.

The second I straightened, Sierra released a ragged breath. Impossible not to hear.

In an attempt to save her from any more embarrassment, I faced the professor, who glared our way.

For the rest of the class, we couldn't continue our game or talk because the seats were in a terrible location, and the professor kept asking us questions.

Once the bell chimed, I placed my hand on Sierra's. "Wanna get some coffee with me?"

"I can't." She curled her lips and swiveled out of her seat and my touch.

She just said she was tired of the good guys and had shared her book with me, but she wouldn't get coffee with me. Why?

After seventh period, I followed her. She took the bus to a small cemetery that had unkempt grass, no lights, and tombstones squished together. Why on earth did she choose a graveyard over me? There was no way that it was because she was dark, like the other seers.

Sierra knelt beside a gravesite and placed a letter between two stones. I hid between some eerie trees and an angel statue to read the tombstones.

Melissa Joy Mills: beloved mother, founder of Families Supporting Families. - January 19th 1983 – October 21st, 2022.

John Damien Mills: beloved father, founder of the Cranial Foundation. - August 26th 1982 – October 21st 2022.

My hand shot up, muffling the gasp. Her parents had died two years ago today. No wonder she looked sad and had refused to go for coffee with me.

Tears rushed down her cheeks. I wanted to comfort her. I needed to comfort her.

As if a magnetic force, or the prophecy, pulled me to her, I crept out of the shadows. But before I freaked her out, my sense of reality hit, and I crouched behind a tombstone. It wouldn't end well if she saw me here.

In an attempt to calm my nerves, I took my eyes off Sierra and fidgeted with Slinger as I counted to fifty. At forty-nine, leaves crunched beside me, and Sierra yelled, "What the hell are you doing here?"

Twenty One

My throat constricted.

Sierra stood over me, her arms crossed, nostrils flared. Owls hooted from the trees, providing some noise in the awful quiet. The moon shone in the velvet sky, casting a spotlight on the veins bulging in her forehead. The tension and silence grew between us.

"I asked you a question." Sierra tapped her foot.

"In class, I noticed something was up." I stood. "I wanted to ensure you were okay."

"So, you followed me like a stalker?" She threw her arms down.

"I'm sorry." I didn't know what else to say.

"I'm not dealing with this, or you, today."

She stormed off, and I trailed after her. I seriously had a death wish. She headed to the underground tube station. I nearly choked as the lingering scents of sweat, marijuana, and beer wafted over us as we stepped into the train's cramped space.

Several people bumped into me as I followed after her. If it wasn't for her proximity, I might've killed a few people whose awful, sticky bodies touched me.

Once I reached her, she moved farther along the tube. "Sierra, please talk to me."

"Please leave me alone." She groaned and leaned against the tube's wall.

"But ..."

A buff female jumped in front of me. "You heard her, pal. Leave her alone."

I clenched Slinger, dying to use him. But I couldn't. Not in front of Sierra. Instead, I crossed my arms and watched her, waiting for her to disembark.

A few stops later, Sierra exited at King's Cross Station, and I chased after her.

"Tarus, stop following me." She charged up the steps and out into the dark night.

"Not until you talk to me. Your parents died on this day. You shouldn't be alone."

She sighed, shaking her head, but didn't say anything more. We continued to wherever we were going in silence, her glancing at me with narrowed eyes every so often. I didn't mind. I'd take anger over her telling me to stop following her. Hopefully, it meant she accepted me tagging along.

Having arrived outside a brownish-red brick building, Sierra slumped her shoulders and let out a deep breath before continuing to the entrance with a smile spread across her face.

I squinted at the bright lights inside and rubbed my eyes before looking around. A desk with *British Library* engraved on the white concrete wall stood before us.

"Good evening, Sierra. The kids are going to be happy to see you." the male at the front desk said.

"Happy to see them, too. I hope they need a leader in the fantasy section tonight." Sierra scanned her white card. "He's with me."

So, she was going to let me stay. Yes!

We took the elevator to the fourth floor. Once we stepped off, an obnoxious sign caught my attention: *Teaching Kids Literacy*. Center stage in the picture was Sierra, standing behind a podium, with different aged children holding books around her.

"What's this?"

"Something I did in honor of my mom," Sierra said as she headed into the children's section, where someone checked her bags and waved us through.

We ventured down a dimly lit hall toward double glass doors at the end. As she opened them, the leader on the wooden platform stopped talking, and several kids sitting on the bare floor turned in Sierra's direction. Their faces lit up with excitement.

They must love her.

"Sierra! What are you doing here, of all days?" the lady in the front asked.

Tears trickled down Sierra's face, and she sniffled. "Being with kids and reading them fantasy stories is exactly what I need." She smiled. "Am I too late to take over?"

"No! We'd all love that." The lady jumped off the platform, rushed to Sierra, and embraced her in an all-encompassing hug. While the lady led Sierra to the stage and filled her in on what they were reading, I zoned out and glanced at the flyers on the back table.

It turned out it was a literary program for kids started by Sierra and her mother.

Once the lady situated herself amongst the children and everyone silenced, Sierra grabbed the book off the stool and began reading. As she read, her eyes sparkled, and she changed her voice with every character. The kids tilted their heads up, enamored. My smile spread. It was amazing watching her.

A few feet away, a kid read along with her. I glanced at the title at the top of the page. *Life Twists II.* A picture on the page showed a boy in servant's clothing talking with a girl in a royal dress. An idea sprung into my mind, and I bent down. "May I see your book? Please." I handed him five pounds, and he obliged.

I skimmed through it, trying to see what she'd enact next. The upcoming chapter had a dance scene. My adrenaline spiked. This was perfect.

After taking a deep breath, I walked onto the platform and stood inches from Sierra. She stopped mid-sentence, mouth agape, then shook her head and continued reading.

A sentence before she read, *Garner took her hand, spinning her,* I shot my hand out toward her and read his line. *"May I accompany you to the dance floor?"*

The kids screamed their excitement, and Sierra jerked her head toward me, eyes wide. I repeated the question.

Shaking her head, she took my hand. Electricity surged up my arm, and the lavender vein reappeared, outlining a lavender heart. I spun her into my chest and held her tight. She glanced up, our eyes locked, time froze, and my heart rumbled. I spun her back out. *"When will you see you're so much more than the king's daughter?"* I read the following line.

"When will you see that none of that matters?" She slumped to the floor, arms crossed.

I knelt beside her. *"Tell me why your dreams are meaningless?"*

"Because they're the dreams of a foolish child. I have one purpose, and that's to serve after my father. Raise the kingdom's people to glory, like he does." A lone tear trickled down her cheek. I wiped it away, my hand trembling, and the outline of my heart solidifying.

We both took deep breaths before I tilted her chin to face me. *"Why can't you have both?"*

"You think I could be a dragon rider 'and' a princess? Are you serious?" She laughed.

"You can be whatever you set your mind to." I bit my lip and pulled her up. *"You're stronger than you give yourself credit for. Show the world, and me, what you're truly capable of."* Damn, this book suited our lives perfectly.

"If I promise to consider it, will you just dance with me?" She batted her eyelashes, and my heart melted. I'd do whatever she asked. The kids in the audience hollered, swooned, and yelled at us to dance.

"Nothing would make me happier." I clutched her right hand in my left and began to waltz. Every second her skin touched mine, my lavender heart beat. It was incredible.

Sierra and I continued enacting lines from the book until the event ended an hour later. Several kids hugged Sierra and offered their condolences for a few minutes. After the last kid left, Sierra turned her attention to me.

"Why did you do that? How did you know the book I was reading so well? And why did you stay?" She crossed her arms and leaned against the stool.

I laughed. Damn, she had a lot of questions. "I told you I want to know everything about you. I'll do whatever it takes to prove it." I shrugged.

She shook her head. "You don't give up, do you?"

"Not when I want something. No." I grinned.

"You know, I don't see you as an MG fantasy reader."

What was MG? My mouth dried for a split second before I came up with a clever retort. "You know, I don't see you walking home alone." I smirked.

She did a once-over on me. "Is this your attempt at offering to be my escort?"

"No. I'm letting you know that I *will* be your escort." I closed the distance between us. Her breathing accelerated, and she gulped. I mimicked the action. Being this close to her warmed my body, her lavender scent filling my lungs.

"What if I don't want you to be?" She stepped back, and this time, I swallowed first.

"Aren't you tired of the good guys? Good guys would ask permission and care what you think. Bad guys don't." Although, this bad boy sure as hell cared.

"Well,..." She laughed. "...what are you waiting for, then? You going to start walking, or what?" She jumped off the platform and grabbed her backpack.

This girl and her mouth.

I hopped off the platform and held out my hand. "May I take your bag?"

"Isn't that a *good guy* thing?"

"It's a Tarus thing." I shrugged as she handed me her bag, and I slung it over my shoulder.

We ventured out of the library to the underground tube and took the long way back to her dorm, deep in conversation the whole way. She spoke about Teaching Kids Literacy and her favorite students. I chimed in, every so often, to share my opinion of the event and how much I loved watching her face shine with joy.

Once we reached her dorm, I leaned against the doorpost. Her eyes sparkled in the moonlight. The crickets chirped in the silence. And my desire for her grew. I placed my fingers in the pockets of her tight jeans and pulled her close. My pants bulged against her thigh, and her breath hitched.

"May I ask you a question?" She placed her hands on my chest. I bit my lip, and she clutched my shirt. The lavender vein vibrated.

"Shoot."

"Do you want to kiss me?" She licked her lips and leaned a smidge closer.

"What kind of question is that? What do you think?" I pulled her tighter, chest against chest.

"That I'm confused. I don't understand why you'd want to if you have a girlfriend." She pushed her hands against me and shoved herself away.

I blinked several times before responding. I couldn't believe she'd asked or still thought I could have one after I'd spent all this time with her and the obvious chemistry we had. "Would you believe me if I said I never had one?"

She laughed and grabbed the key card from her pocket.

Holy Delmore. What could I say to make her believe me? It was the truth. I never had a girlfriend. Concubines, one-night stands, yeah, sure. A relationship, no. But Darcy was good at many things and excelled at lying. Who wouldn't believe her?

"Before coming here, I was talking to someone. We slept together a couple of times. But she's in the past. I promise you. She's nothing to worry about." I cupped her cheek.

The tension left her body, and she leaned farther into my hand. "Promise?"

"Cross my heart." I bit my bottom lip.

"Okay, good." She kissed my cheek, and the outlined heart solidified once again. Butterflies fluttered in my stomach as my body melted. Before I could respond or kiss her back, she used her card and darted into the building.

"Well, well. Thought you said you didn't like her?" Darcy appeared out of nowhere, the moon's glow shining on her blood-red hair.

Pain surged through me.

Not now.

I stood silently.

Her claws came out, and she raked them across the back of my head, grabbing a clump of my hair in her fist. "She's dead the minute she steps into Climakru. Everyone wants her gone. She's an abomination."

We were the abominations. Those of us who lived in Hell-space. Sierra was good, and not *everyone* wanted her dead. But I couldn't tell Darcy that. Not when she could twist my words and tell Mother before I had the chance.

"Then I guess it doesn't matter what my feelings are for her."

Darcy ground her teeth.

"What is your plan? What are you trying to do?" I needed to try again to mind control her, but she was smart. Every time I attempted to touch her, she moved out of my grasp.

"To make you suffer. To shatter your heart, like you did mine. But it can't happen yet. You need to fall more for her first."

My eyebrows rose. What the hell? Darcy made no sense.

Before I could ask her what she'd meant, Sierra pulled the door of her building open and yelled, "Tarus!"

Darcy's cold, hard lips smashed against mine.

Sierra gasped and then coughed. With a wicked grin, Darcy broke away. "Hey, Sierra. Can I help you?"

"Sierra, I can—"

"May I have my backpack?" Sierra's tone was devoid of emotion as she held out her shaking hand.

I handed it to her but kept my grip on the strap. "Sierra, please—"

"Don't wanna hear it." She spoke through clenched teeth. A lone tear escaped as she turned and shot back into the building.

The door slammed shut behind her. At the same time, Darcy portaled away.

The vein, which only appeared when touching Sierra, blinked twice, transformed into thorns, and then vanished.

Holy Delmore. What the hell did that mean? This couldn't be over.

Twenty Two

Every second leading up to French class, my mind wouldn't erase Sierra's pained expression, and Darcy's thrilled one. I couldn't eat, sleep, or function. Everything inside hurt like hell. What would Mother do in my situation? Or Vilo? Mother would destroy Darcy. Vilo would confess, sit me down, and explain.

Vilo's option was the only one that had a chance. I'd make Sierra listen to me.

Numb, unable to feel my skin, I trudged into class. Sierra had returned to the seat at the back. Thank the gods.

"Sierra, can we talk?"

She turned the music on her phone up louder and ignored me. I tilted my head back, sighing, and stood there frozen.

"Take your seats!" the professor roared.

Not wanting to irritate Sierra but wanting to convince her to talk, I plopped down next to her. She stiffened and removed her headphones but still refused to acknowledge me.

Throughout the class, I kept trying to talk to her, but even sitting farther from the professor, she still asked us enough questions that I couldn't get a complete sentence in with Sierra.

I stayed after class and used mind control to manipulate the professor into dedicating the final ten minutes of class for the rest of the month to group study.

After seventh period, Sierra headed to her dorm. I dashed in front of her and leaned against the doorpost. "How about a coffee today so we can talk? Please."

"No." She attempted to push me out of the way, but I was too strong.

"What if..." I pulled out a surprise which I'd bought after French. "...I gave you my Choco Nits? They're your favorite."

She shook her head, her lavender scent flowing everywhere, and bit her lip to prevent herself from smiling. "Are you going to keep asking until I say yes and talk to you?"

"Haven't we already established that I don't give up when I want something?"

She laughed, as I had hoped.

"Wait here. I'll be back." She grabbed the two Choco Nit packages from me and used her key card to let herself into the dorm. I paced outside. Would she really return?

Less than ten minutes later, she stepped back outside dressed in a flowing skirt that lifted just above the knee and a pink tank top. I shifted my hips to hide my arousal and counted to a hundred as Sierra spoke of whatever coffee place we should try.

Once Sierra started walking off, I focused on her instead of the bulge between my legs. "Why won't you stop bothering me if you have a girlfriend, Tarus?"

"Sierra," I said, and she twisted to face me. "Darcy was the girl I was sleeping with. She wanted more. I didn't. We ended things a long time ago, but she still wants me."

"You expect me to believe that?" She crossed her arms.

"Darcy's never seen me show interest in anyone. Now that

she has, she's trying everything she can to stop it." I stepped closer to Sierra. "She's not who I want. Not now. Not ever. She knows it, too. So, she wants to ruin whatever it is we have." I grabbed her hand, electricity shooting through me. "Don't let her mess up what we're building. Please."

"You're the bad boy, remember? This is typical *bad boy* behavior." Sierra didn't move.

I rubbed her arm, and her hair rose, her body shaking under my fingertips. "Good thing you're tired of good guys, then. Darcy is nothing. If you don't believe me or don't want to see where things go, walk away." I dropped my hand and took five steps back. Sweat poured down my neck, my body turning stiff. What the hell had I just done? And what the hell would she choose to do?

She twirled around and sauntered off, away from her dorm and me. A knot twisted in my gut, and I almost fell to my knees until she placed her hand on her hip and did a once-over on me with hungry, curious eyes. "Your legs stop working?"

My smile rose, and I caught up to her.

"So, what made you come to Elite?" Sierra stared straight ahead.

"Family suggested I attend." Truth, in a way. "Why did you?"

"My caregiver owns the school."

"Good reason." We wandered through a park with a stunning tulip patch. I picked a red one and placed it behind her ear, my fingers lingering in her hair. She stepped closer, our bodies touching, and the lavender vein throbbed against my chest. "You're beautiful."

She blushed. "You're a flirt."

"Can you blame me?"

She shook her head. "We're almost at the coffeehouse. It's just at that corner." She pointed down the street and skipped to the shop. Her journal entry came to mind. People always asked her to stop skipping. What would happen if I did the opposite?

I skipped next to her. "You might beat me at bowling, but I can beat you at skipping. The last one there buys the coffee." She liked games. Plus, I had no money on me and couldn't control a single mind in front of her, so why not try this?

Her smile rose to her eyes, which sparkled with different hues of blue and amber. She dashed off, skipping at full speed.

I chuckled when I passed her and made it to the coffee shop first.

Out of breath, she gave me a high five. "Change of plan."

I stopped breathing.

"Let's take the coffee to go. I'd rather sit in the park."

"Sounds great."

She purchased pumpkin spice lattes, and we backtracked to the park we'd passed along the way. Once inside the gates, Sierra found a tree facing the pond, where several ducks swam, and leaned against it. I stood next to her, my side pressed against the rough bark.

"Wanna feed the ducks?" She pulled out a loaf of bread from her bag. My eyebrows rose. "Don't tell me you've never fed them."

"Okay. I won't." I winked.

She grabbed my hand and led us to the edge of the lake. The vein brightened.

Ducks swam toward us, and Sierra knelt. She broke off chunks of the loaf and held it out to them. As they pecked at her palm, she beamed. "Join me." She handed me a piece of bread. Staring at it, then at her, I smiled and dropped down beside her.

A duck moved closer and nudged my palm open. I cringed, and Sierra fell backward as she burst out laughing. I gave the bread to the bird and joined her on the soft grass. The glaring sun provided warmth against the chilly wind.

For hours, we talked about anything and everything. As the day got away from us, we sat in silence, watching the sun disappear and the moon take its place.

Nearby, crickets chirped, their songs accented by owls hooting in the distance. They were harmonizing, singing a soft melody. One so full of love that it gave me the courage to be bold. I shifted onto my side, facing her, and she copied me, her hair falling in front of her face. I brushed it away and scooted closer.

Her breath hitched as I leaned in, and the vein dulled. Why the hell did it not brighten? I shook my head. Was this my imagination? Was Lucifer trying to get to me, showing me that I wasn't allowed to be happy? I puckered my lips. She did the same. Centimeters from touching, the tension intensified, but a frisbee landed between us, and she leaned back.

I almost destroyed the thing ... and the man who ran up to us apologizing. Sierra hopped to her feet and handed the frisbee back. "It's probably time we headed back. I'll see you tomorrow." She dashed off, flushed.

The scent of lavender disappeared, and musky jasmine took its place. My insides twisted. I glanced around, searching for Darcy, but couldn't find her like usual. She only showed herself when she wanted. But this time, a note rested where Sierra and I had laid moments ago.

Shivering, I picked it up.

The urge to tell Queen Delilah is getting stronger. You only have a few days left, though. I wonder how you'll spend them. Better yet, I wonder how I'll spend them. Sierra smells nice. Bet her blood tastes even sweeter than honey silk.

Twenty Three

Waiting for the study break in French, I fidgeted with Slinger. If only she'd kiss me, then maybe my heart would form permanently, the bond would activate, and she'd be safe from death.

The only tricky part of this situation was getting Sierra to kiss me. I couldn't explain why, but after the vein dulled yesterday, something in my gut told me it had to be her who initiated the kiss.

"Students, the last ten minutes are for group studying. Be productive," the professor said.

Sierra turned toward me, eyebrows raised.

"Yes?" I moved to face her.

"She's never offered this before." Sierra toyed with her notebook. "Wanna study?"

"Do you? Or would you like to do something else?" I bit my lip.

"Perhaps. But I don't think it's appropriate for a classroom," Sierra murmured, and I laughed as my body grew feverish. She wanted to kiss me. Music to my soul.

"Who cares what's appropriate? Remember, I'm the bad

boy. You're the *straight-A* student. I'm sure you could do whatever you wanted." I waggled my brows.

She shook her head, and a flush of red crept up her neck. "If only it were that simple." She sighed and added, "What's your favorite food?"

Random, but okay, I'd play along. "Steak." I rubbed my belly.

For the next ten minutes, we talked about our favorite foods and songs. Even though she kept her hands to herself, I was captivated by the way she focused on me.

Once the bell rang, Sierra smiled and rushed out of the classroom. I stood frozen until I remembered Darcy was some-where nearby and had upped the stakes. I couldn't leave Sierra alone, nor did I want to.

I sprinted after her. "Wanna skip seventh?"

"What do you have in mind?" She grinned, leaning against the lockers.

"River?" I shrugged as she grabbed my hand, and the lavender vein sparked.

We almost made it to the doors when a gentleman called her name. She whirled around, eyebrows scrunched.

"Sierra, Dartmouth accepted you in early admissions. Janine and I want to pull you and Emma from class and head up there. You'll miss school tomorrow, but your teachers are okay with it." The man looked like Emma, with the same nose and brown hair. The only thing missing was the gothic clothing.

Sierra turned her gaze back to me. "Sorry, Tarus. I'll see you Friday?"

I squeezed her hand, and she dashed off.

On Friday, I'd need to up my game. I'd get the kiss out of her. But until then, I'd follow her at a safe distance. I had to ensure Darcy stayed away.

Sierra wasn't safe.

Friday morning arrived, and I was ready to get the show on the road. Today would be fun. While following them around in the shadows over the last several hours, two things had become apparent. One: she really loved games. Two: she loved the theater.

Thursday night, after they'd arrived home, I prepared a gift that I was about to surprise her with.

"Good afternoon, Sierra," I purred her name, and she bit her lower lip. "Turns out the French book won't arrive till Monday. Mind sharing with the beggar one more day? I've already come up with a bargain for you."

She peered at me, eyebrows knitting together.

I pulled out my side of the bargain—a light pink and blue wrapped box to represent the colors of her room. She smiled as she marveled at the box, but she refused to budge.

The fact she could stay quiet fascinated me.

"I assume you're forcing me to spell it out. I'm curious as to why you don't want to play the game. I thought it'd be right up your alley unless you lied about loving games." I waited for her to say something. Again, only silence followed. She was seriously making me work for her. I couldn't tell if it turned me on or frustrated me.

"This bargain is based on chance. There could be nothing in the box, or it could be something you'd enjoy. But you won't know until the end of the day because I'd like you to wait to open the box until you're in your dorm with Emma." I smiled, but inside, my body quivered.

Dimples appeared on both of her cheeks. "Bargain struck. Should we shake on it?" She held out her hand.

Electricity spread throughout my entire body as our hands clasped. The lavender vein filled in a complete heart in my chest. My skin became clammy, and she gasped but kept holding tight until the professor spoke. Her voice shattered the moment and forced Sierra to drop her hand.

During our ten-minute study break, Sierra's face lingered close to mine. Everything about her pulled my lips to hers like a magnet. Centimeters from her mouth, I jumped as the bell rang and then stood to leave. But my heart and lower body didn't want to comply. Instead, I grabbed the box off the table and bent down to place it in her bag.

Once I straightened, I made sure to be a hair's breadth away from her face, my lips dangerously close to hers. If she dared to move a smidge, either our foreheads would collide, or she'd brush a kiss against my lips.

She seemed dazed and frozen. Afraid I wouldn't be able to stop myself if she kissed me, I backed away. "I'll wait to hear your opinion of the gift. Hold strong. No opening till you're in your dorm with Emma." I winked, walked out of the room, and headed to Hillshite.

Because of Darcy, I only stayed away for a split second to control my libido in the freezing shower. After calming down, I portaled to a hall near her seventh period classroom.

The minute class finished and she made it back to her dorm, I was at a crossroads. I didn't want to know her reaction to the gift. I wanted the game to play out. But at the same time, I needed to keep an eye on her, just in case Darcy showed. So, I sat, invisible, outside their door, like always, my senses on high alert.

Ten minutes after Emma arrived, I imagined them reading the letter I'd written.

Hello, Beautiful. While you were away, I couldn't stop thinking about our first meeting over the Choco Nits. The movie Stripped Galaxy, which the Choco Nits are from, has a theater performance in town. I'd love for both of you to join me at it tomorrow. Please wear the clothes provided. For the way of answering, use the method you use when communicating with each other. Suppose I receive a no, then I'll go to the dorm's communal kitchen to eat my sorrows in ice cream. If I receive a yes, I'll be so happy, I'll go to the rooftop and shout my joy to the world. I trust this is a big enough clue for you. One more thing: if Emma wishes to bring AJ, there is a suit waiting for him at his dorm.

Many things in my note hinted at me knowing more than I should. For instance, I shouldn't know Emma's boyfriend's dorm room or their personal way of communicating.

When I first wrote the letter, I contemplated burning it. Anger exploded out of me for providing so many hints. But after much consideration, I felt it was the right thing to do. This way, I gave her an out. She'd walk away if she was as intelligent as her *straight-As* suggested. Perhaps that was what I needed? Even if I didn't want it, everything in me knew it was for the best.

Without Mother and my mission or my part in the prophecy, she should still run far away from me. I *was* the bad guy. Not only was I heartless, but I was Lucifer's son. My life, my kingdom, my role, everything about me screamed danger. Part of my job was to kill people. How did that not spell trouble? Adding eleven years of my life in Hellspace to the mix screamed even more trouble. What I did and what they did to me had damaged me beyond repair, no matter what Aris or Vilo thought.

Somehow, if she could see how dangerous I was without me telling her, maybe she'd run and hide. I'd find a way to erase Darcy's mind. That way, she couldn't disprove my lie when I told Mother the girl had vanished. Of course, this would land me back in Hellspace, regardless of Darcy's confession, but at least Sierra would be safe.

Deep in thought, Sierra's doorknob clunked, and my blood boiled. Before it opened, I portaled to the end of the hall, hiding around the corner. She and Emma strolled out in a fit of giggles. I wanted to follow them, but I figured they were answering my question.

Deesse, I'm coming to you again, which is still kind of weird to think about. But please protect Emma and Sierra from Darcy while they answer my note.

By midnight, I couldn't wait any longer to see her response.

My first stop was the freezer, the place I'd go to drown my sorrows. A minuscule part of me figured I headed there in hopes Sierra had run from me.

With trembling hands, I opened the freezer door, and my stomach dropped. There was a note. Though my vision misted, I couldn't help but be happy that Sierra had chosen to walk away. Not wanting to read her sticky note, I almost ripped it before returning to Hillshite. But my fingers had a mind of their own.

Never... (flip) ... Would I ever turn this down ... or would I? Guess you must go to the rooftop to find out.

Aside from knowing she was foolish for continuing these games with me, I couldn't help but become a little giddy.

On the rooftop, one of the three balloons I'd placed up there earlier had vanished. It didn't take a genius to know why. Two of the balloons were typical colors—one white and one gray. But the third, and missing balloon, was onyx-black, with glitter inside and on the top—a perfect resemblance to my eyes.

Attached to the white balloon was her note.

Without another second of time wasted, I tore it open.

Yeah, this is a terrible idea... (flip) ... to... Oops. Look for the other card to find your definitive answer. To give you a hint, Notre professeur pourrait ne pas tre heureux de trouver celui-ci.

I doubled over in laughter for her creativity and boldness and because it was a pleasant and wonderful thing to do. This girl did such odd things to me.

I darted to French, eager to read the next note.

Plastered onto the chalkboard was her third and hopefully final clue.

Now, what to do with my hair? I'm sure a headband won't match the elegance of this beautiful dress. Thank you!

I flipped the note over multiple times and searched every little crevice, but she hadn't written "yes" or "no."

Did this mean her answer was yes? Or was it yes, only if I found something to do with her hair? Of course, I didn't mind her wearing a headband. They were cute and her signature. But if she'd say no to box seats for one of her favorite movies based on wearing a headband, I needed to fix the issue.

In the morning, I'd mind-control a hairdresser to go to their dorm and style their hair. She'd already gone this far that I wouldn't have her say no just because of her hair, even if this provided her an excellent opportunity to walk away.

I cursed myself for getting in so deep. Even if I was the prophecy's hero, if a mating bond didn't form before Mother's time frame ended, how would I save her from a grim fate?

Twenty Four

At her door, waiting for the stylists to finish, I grew antsy. Every muscle in my body kept twitching. Today would be the day we kissed, and if the bond didn't form, I didn't know what would happen. I didn't want her to die, and ever since she accepted the invitation, images swarmed my mind of Saullis and Darcy ripping her apart. They didn't fade away until I came up with another game.

She'd said yes to coming to the four-hour show, but what about alone time during the forty-five-minute intermission? The small break could be another opportunity to convince her to back out. One more chance to show her something was very wrong. Even though I should've walked away and done the right thing, at this point, it was impossible. It needed to be her who walked away.

So, instead of being in the limo or waiting for her outside her dorm, I'd have another present waiting to keep her wondering.

Finished with the note, I left it in the limo and portaled outside the theater.

"Please, let Darcy stay away," I prayed to Deesse before dipping my shoe into a water puddle, sending ripples across the surface. With the sun hidden by the tall buildings, the cold chill in the air spread goosebumps along my arms.

Not wanting to go into the theater without her and needing a distraction from the freezing air, I reread the letter in my head.

Hello, Beautiful. All this is for you. I hope you like it. During the interlude, if I'm so lucky, I'd love to spend that time alone with you. I'll provide accommodations for your friends. If you agree, ask the chauffeur for the package labeled "yes" when you leave the limo. If you disagree, ask for the package labeled "too much."

With minutes left before the limo was due to arrive, I stopped rehearsing the letter and stared at my reflection in the puddle. A splash of black glitter accentuated my sapphire tuxedo collar, and my bow tie was shaped like fluorescent wings with a hint of black. The addition of the black added an element to how the rainbow bounced off it in the light. Even by my standards, the magnificence of it was breathtaking. I knew Sierra would approve and be fascinated by my choice, just as she'd captivate me with her attire.

Satisfied with my appearance, I walked the few steps to the huge *Stripped Galaxy* sign. I arrived in perfect time, to Sierra asking the chauffeur for the *yes* package. Emma and AJ stood beside her, both peeking over Sierra's shoulders.

I couldn't drag my gaze away from Sierra as she opened the box. Her profile was ... Wow! An elegant leg peeked out from the slit of her pearl-white, floor-length dress. Her calf muscles tightened under the straps of her diamond silver heels, which curved up her legs in the shape and style of wings. It made her calves look even stronger, more appealing.

It wasn't even a full view, and yet my mouth was already watering.

Throughout all the realms, paintings, and imaginations, my mind had never beheld such beauty as when Sierra turned and our eyes met.

I admired the rest of her as she sauntered closer. A sexy, red-lipped smile pulled at the corners, almost reaching those beautiful brown eyes. The lipstick emphasized her porcelain skin, bringing attention to her braided wing hairdo with a scarlet ribbon laced throughout.

The dress's bodice was a thin mesh that extended to her neck. Diamonds flowed throughout it. It showed off more of her figure than I'd expected. She was also more filled out than I'd thought, so the dress was tighter than it was supposed to be. But I wasn't complaining. My magic longed to undress her right then and there.

Unable to listen to the magic humming in my veins or the parts of my brain begging to whisk her back into the limo, I bit my lip. Sierra shivered, and my forehead beaded with sweat.

Although I didn't want to, I broke eye contact, bowed slightly, and held my arm out. "May I escort you to our seats?"

"Why, of course. I'd be delighted." She gave a small curtsy, which did wonders in the dress, and my pants grew tight.

The second our arms entwined and the lavender vein formed a heart, it soared, and my hands grew clammy. Being a gentleman would be hard, but still, that gut-wrenching feeling warned me that she had to kiss me. But at least it didn't stop me from tempting her with my touch.

Box seats made the situation tricky. My chair couldn't move, so I settled on the edge of my cushion. To any onlooker, I must've looked like a crazed fan trying to get as close as possible to the stage. But Sierra wasn't an onlooker. She must've guessed what I was doing.

Almost slipping off the edge of my red velvet seat, I had

just enough room to stretch and lean my legs against hers. From the moment we touched, a constant stream of heat radiated from our connection, and the lavender vein pulsed. It brightened off and on. The sensations fogged my brain, and I couldn't focus on the theater. Instead, I fixated on the way the shadows danced on her face and how the small lights running along the railing emphasized her glittery blush.

Questions about why she wouldn't hold my hand or try anything consumed my mind. Beyond being eager for her to try, I occasionally scratched my goatee or slid a hand through my hair. Each time, I watched her reaction to see if she'd reach over the armrest and grab my hand or if she'd at least noticed every movement I'd made like I monitored hers. But nothing provoked even the slightest reaction in her.

I frowned at not being able to entice her with my charm. What if Sierra wasn't that interested? Every time the thought crossed my mind, my breathing slowed, and my legs began to shake.

By accident, my shaking grew so intense that my legs broke the connection with hers, and the next time they came back in contact, my knee brushed her bare skin. Her body tensed. Yes. I smirked.

My arms might not have caused a reaction, but my legs sure had. Excited by that information, I couldn't help but be cruel. The time for my bottom half to sit still was done. Instead, I grazed her leg over and over, sparking my magic each time.

She held firm throughout the first half, though the minute the instrumental interlude began, she darted out of her seat. I gulped and glanced at Emma.

She shrugged and sprinted after Sierra.

"Girls and touch-ups," AJ said with a dramatic eye roll.

"Yeah," I said, short and simple.

AJ and I made small talk outside the box while we waited

for the girls to return. He was totally at ease, though I was anything but. I couldn't help but claw at my skin.

The moment they stepped out of the restroom, a thickness grew in my throat. Sierra was going to leave. She'd taken the hints and was mad at me for tempting her.

Biting my lip, I tried not to look down. Sierra met my gaze, and her smile eased my tension. She wasn't leaving.

"As you took the box agreeing to *alone time* during the interlude, it's time for us to split. I've provided AJ with money to take Emma out. Meanwhile, I have a surprise for my beautiful lady. We'll meet outside the box at half-past six." Sierra beamed and locked arms with me. Electricity shot down my spine, and my breathing hitched.

Emma and AJ waved us off and headed out.

Their silhouettes faded into the distance, and the heat between Sierra and me increased tenfold. Sweat formed in every orifice of my body, and Sierra shook beside me.

The game was on. I'd get her to kiss me by the time the interlude ended.

I cupped her face to ensure she focused on me, and the lavender vein brightened. Good guy or not, I wanted to see how far I could take it. I bit my bottom lip in a very sexual way. Her skin instantly warmed underneath my hands.

The way she looked at me made my knees wobble. Holy Delmore. I'd kiss her. It was probably me being weird, thinking it had to be her that initiated it. I leaned in closer, and the lavender vein grew spikes. It tore everything it touched and burst my blood vessels. I almost screamed bloody murder if it wasn't for the fact I didn't want to scare Sierra. I backed away, biting my lip, and the vein smoothed. Sierra's breathing turned raspy as the tension between us grew.

That gut-wrenching feeling was more than a feeling. It was a warning.

It was okay, though. I wouldn't freak out. I'd get her to kiss me.

I attempted another tactic.

Smiling wistfully, I leaned toward her again. Our foreheads touched, and I tilted my head to close the distance to her lips while remaining free from touching them. Pain traveled down my spine, but before I pulled away, in the most sexual voice, I drew out her name, "Sierra."

Her knees wobbled.

With my free hand, I braced her back to steady her and pull her in closer.

She continued to resist.

"Earlier, I asked the theater to arrange our section into a small dining area. I had your favorite café cater snacks and coffee." I took her arm and guided her back to the box.

Her face changed, going from a megawatt smile to lips thinning when she saw her favorite Spanish latte from Dulcie's and parmesan fries from Kinkers. "This is beautiful, and of course, I love everything, but how did you know about AJ's room, and how did you know these clothes would fit us? I've never shared that stuff with you. You're observant. You know a lot about me, but I don't know much about you." Her shoulders slumped.

Instead of running away after seeing how insane and terrifying it was that I knew all this information, Sierra asked me about it. At least a part of her saw how I knew too much and the oddness of it, but I wished she wasn't so calm about everything, giving me a chance to lie or skirt the question.

She continued to watch me.

"How about we fix this disadvantage?" I guided her to the chairs around the small table. "What would you care to know?" I said with a coy smile. I'd try to answer any question she asked if it brought me one step closer to gaining her trust and a kiss. Time was running thin. I needed the bond to form.

Her brows narrowed, and she scrunched up her nose, aware of my diversion. For a second, she glanced away and nibbled on the fries. "Do you have brothers or sisters? Do you have plans after graduation? The list can go on. But one question keeps pressing, tormenting me."

"Now it's tormenting me, too. I have to know." Woah. Way to go, me, for egging her on.

She fidgeted with her drink, keeping her gaze averted. "Did you ever go to rehab?"

Shit. I'd forgotten all about Darcy adding that to her conversation with Emma. Sierra's boldness in asking turned me on. If it wasn't for my magic keeping us apart and forcing her to act first, I would've jumped across the table and ripped her clothes off. It had been weeks since I slept with anyone. I was thirsty, especially for her.

She took a sip of her latte and walked over to me. I watched her, unable to tear my eyes away. She knelt and placed her hands on my cheeks. "I'm not sorry for asking, but I'm sorry if I hurt you. You don't have to share the answer with me. It's none of my business, and it doesn't change anything. I still want to know you."

Sierra wasn't evil. The way she spoke to me, the way I heard her speaking with others, this girl didn't have a cruel bone in her body. The Historians had to be wrong about all seers being worse than demons. Or perhaps that was another thing that further proved Vilo's theory about the prophecy. Seers could be good if the ones guiding them with their magic were. But I wasn't good, so how could I make sure I directed her along the right path?

"My past is clouded with a lot of darkness." I grabbed her hands, and she stood. "Getting over the past, I got addicted to some things." Good thing I checked in the library about what rehab was.

"I'm sorry to hear about your past. How are you now?" She leaned against the table and took a few more bites of the fries. So did I. Their savory flavor ignited my tastebuds in a way I wished Sierra would.

"Amazing. When I'm with you, I forget about my past." I

rose from my chair and stepped closer. Her breath hitched, and I grinned.

"Where did you live before here?"

"A—" A burning sensation ran through my veins as I spoke, reminding me of the curse. Even if I wanted to, I couldn't say anything about the magic realm. "Australia."

"You don't have an accent."

Damn. This girl was good.

I gave her free rein to ask me whatever she wanted, but the curse prevented me from answering certain things. So, we needed to steer clear of topics I couldn't answer without speaking about magic unless I didn't mind my body's betrayal as it boiled me alive. "Is there not something else you wish to ask me? You do have free rein."

Most girls wanted to talk about love and where the relationship was headed. She needed to do the same. One look at her and it was clear a battle raged inside. I slowly bit my lower lip.

She gripped the table, gulped deeply, and watched my mouth. "If you have a hunch there is something I want to ask, why don't you tell me what it is?"

Bold. She was utterly ingenious with that mouth. Though she wasn't wicked, she was clever, and her comment made this game even more fun.

I smirked and closed the distance between us—placing her left leg amidst mine.

Brushing my lips against her ear, I said, "There are actually two questions you want to know. The first answer will have to wait until you ask. The second answer is *not yet*. All good things come to those who wait." I straightened and winked.

My response batted a thousand. Without accessing her mind, there was no guarantee I'd know what she wanted to ask. So instead, I thought about what I wanted to know. Why did she choose me, and why wouldn't she kiss me?

At first, I wondered if my vague responses had given my bluff away, but once I winked, her expression said it all.

She seethed, breathing hard. If those weren't signs enough, her face turned beet-red. Not the embarrassed flush of reddish pink, but a deep fire engine red. It was adorable. Everything she did was, even the way she flared her nostrils when something agitated her. I wanted to tell her, but I didn't dare. At the current moment, I feared her biting my head off.

"If you have a problem with it, or might I say, if you're that eager, why not do something about it?" I moved my face centimeters from hers. All she had to do was lift her chin.

My hands clenched as she slid off the table and back into her chair. Her willpower to resist astonished me. The harder she pushed away, the harder I pressed toward her.

People often said opposites attract.

"Maybe I read this wrong." I took a sip of coffee and slumped back into the chair. Multiple feelings crowded in. My stomach hardened at not getting my way, and a dull ache pressed at my chest.

While brewing in my emotions, building a land of a different sort of misery in my head, she spoke. "I'm not saying you read them right or wrong. But I refuse to one, make the first move, and two, to be eager." Sierra spoke with sass and folded her arms across her chest.

I couldn't help but laugh. My mind tormented me with thoughts of not being adequate, or worse, something being wrong with me. Me, the perfect man people dreamt of being with. In the meantime, she was complicating my life because she refused to make the first move.

Somehow, she had to see the only way anything would happen was if she initiated it. Otherwise, we'd stay in a stalemate, and time would run out. "Why is it you can't make the first move? Are we not in the twenty-first century?"

"Okay, granted. Regardless, when a gentleman goes out of

his way and does this…" She gestured around the room. "…Should he not be the one to make the first move? Wouldn't all these elegant gestures mean he was into her? So, he should start it." Confidence radiated from her at an extreme level. If only she had her magic, would her skin glow?

Without meaning to, I laughed from deep within my throat. "Point made. But I can make two additional arguments. Number one. I agree these gestures signify the gentleman is into you. Therefore, what fear can you have for not making the first move? It's not as if you'll face rejection. Number two. What better way is there for you to show your gratitude?" My lips curled into a wicked grin. I had her.

Her body eased forward. This was it. She was finally going to kiss me. My eyes closed until a noise from my left had me groaning.

The ushers had impeccable timing. Too soon, reality forced me to give up on the giant leap I'd made when they informed us that we needed to step out. Both of them cringed at the killer expression on my face, and the younger one looked like he had pissed his pants. They should think themselves lucky we weren't in Climakru and that I'd turned a new leaf. Otherwise, I would've destroyed them.

Sierra grabbed her latte and moved toward the door. I pulled my head away from the dark thoughts and followed her lead.

Outside the box, her friends were all over each other. A perfect way to rub it in. All the romantic gestures and over-the-top gifts were supposed to put Sierra and me in that embrace.

Not them.

Holy Delmore. Was I *jealous*?

The theater over, Sierra led us outside and headed straight for the limo. Emma placed her hand on Sierra's elbow as she stepped in and pulled her aside. "After tonight, I thought you might want some more *alone time* with him, so AJ has already called a cab. We're going to give you both that time on the way back." Emma squeezed Sierra's shoulder.

Yes! That helped. Throughout the second half of the performance, I'd been racking my brain, trying to come up with a plan to get Sierra alone again, to try and get that kiss. We'd been so close during the interlude I was sure I'd end up with one tonight. I had to. I only had three days left.

They hugged, and Emma added, "I'll be waiting in the dorm. Don't stay out too late, and please don't do anything I wouldn't." She winked and giggled as if what she'd said was a joke. But I hoped it meant things might get a little spicy.

I rushed over to stand beside Sierra. She didn't say anything or glance my way until she was inside the limo. Once seated, she winked. My blood sizzled in a good way, and my palms grew damp.

Greedy, and in starving need of more from her, I followed her into the limo, not caring to check my libido at the door.

The wicked smirk plastered on her face matched mine. The game was on.

With reluctance, I sat across from her, and my grin grew bigger. *Your* move, darling.

She shifted her gaze, taking me all in, every bit of me, and my body sizzled under her stare.

Uh oh, I might've played into her plan.

She crossed her legs ever so slowly, and the slit in her dress reached centimeters away from her hip. Though her leg covered her intimate parts, the dress did a poor job of covering anything else. Our space shrunk, and every aspect of my body reacted to her.

My magic held me back. The lavender vein appeared without touching her, but spikes came with it, reminding me if I moved any closer, it'd slice me open from the inside out. Her legs taunted me, and my shaft rubbed against my pants. I wanted to glide my hands over every single part of her bare skin.

I'd been wrong about her.

She did have a cruel bone in her body.

She bent down in that perfect way to expose her chest and took off her shoes. I couldn't help it. I groaned and bit my lower lip, hard. This must've been a weakness for her because she leaned into me. I lifted my brows, wondering if this was the breaking point.

She leaned over just enough that our body heat mingled, keeping her eyes on mine and catching every single time my gaze traveled across her exposed skin. We barely moved an inch as I squeezed the seat.

We remained like this even after we arrived at her dorm. I'd met my match in stubbornness. The conversation in the box had only upped her game. She was trying to entice me into checkmate rather than surrendering her queen and ending this stalemate.

Tensions were high, silence ongoing, no end in sight, and time ticked by.

She leaned back, and her coy smile spread. Her beauty deeply mesmerized me, so much so that I missed her next move. One second, her hands rested in her lap, and the next, she was squeezing my thigh. I glanced down at her hand, and again, she upped the game when I didn't think it was possible.

Her hand moved to the inner part of my knee, and with a slow crawl, she slid it up my thigh and stopped a hair's breadth away from my bulge. She leaned in, lips hovering at my ear. With every brush of air, my body melted into her. Just when the torture reached an arousing peak, Sierra glided her hand back down my thigh.

As my body tensed and moved forward in the seat, she said, "Not yet." She winked and eased out of the limo.

With my shaft in agony and my mouth left open, I watched her like a dumbfounded fool who was now on the receiving end of his own hand. When the limo driver pulled away, I asked him to stall the car, waiting for her to turn around. But she never looked back.

With my shirt shredded to tethers in my grasp, I squeezed the bundle tight and cursed. I'd woken to yet another horrible nightmare. This time, Mother didn't just send me back to Hellspace, she made me bring Sierra and forced me to watch the mist's tendrils rip her apart and tear out her humanity.

It took me a long while to get the images out of my head and to regain function.

With an annoying chime from the school's tower, I glanced at the clock and flinched. 1:00 p.m. Sierra was already in fifth period, and I couldn't miss seeing her today, not after that nightmare. And a church event had kept us apart yesterday.

I was having Sierra withdrawals.

I portaled to the bathroom nearest the French classroom before turning visible and walking into class.

My feet squeaked on the vinyl floor seconds after the bell had rung. All eyes darted toward me and my rude entrance, but I didn't care. I cared that Sierra was in one piece in the back of the room, like nothing was amiss.

"Are you impressed by what you see? You must be because you haven't taken your eyes off me." I took my seat beside her, and her face grew crimson. My chest tingled, and I added, "You don't need to answer. Your face already did." I winked and flashed my dimpled grin at her.

"Who says it's because I'm impressed? Your haughtiness never ceases to amaze me." Sierra twirled her pencil and did a once-over on me.

"Apologies for misinterpreting the rosy-red cheeks." I raised my eyebrows.

"Anger can cause cheeks to flame red from the heat. Also, one's eyes tend to travel toward any intrusion or noise, no matter who they come from. We're creatures of curiosity."

Angry? Was she mad at me? My smile dropped in fear until she laughed.

"So, no part of you finds my appearance absolutely ravishing?" I waggled my brows and brushed her side. Tingling sensations shot through my body.

"I ..." She was at a loss for words.

"Ladies and gentlemen, today we have a pop quiz," the professor said, interrupting Sierra's retort.

An eerie silence hung in the room after the quiz had finished. Lost in my thoughts of failure, and the misery that came with it, I barely registered the ten-minute break until Sierra poked my shoulder.

"What are your plans this evening?"

"You asking me on a date?"

"You wish." She chuckled. "The seniors are going to Covent Garden to watch some play. I wondered if you'd be joining them?"

"Will you?"

"Haven't decided." She shrugged as the professor approached us.

"Do you mind helping me mark the quiz?" the professor asked Sierra, and I slumped in my chair as she nodded.

Before the bell rang, Sierra returned to the desk and grabbed her things. A folded piece of paper fell out of her book. She picked it up and blushed again.

"I love making you blush," I said with all the arrogance I could muster.

Her face scrunched up, making her look even more adorable. "Wish I knew how to return the favor, but I don't. Though it did remind me, I have conditions before our next soiree." She handed me the paper and walked away. Just like Saturday night, she didn't glance back to see my reaction.

My mind raced again. What had I done this time? Unable to handle the shift in emotions and fumbling with the letter, I barely got away from public view before portaling to Hillshite.

I took a deep breath and tore into the letter.

Dear Tarus,

It was an honor to be the lady on your arm, accompanying you the other night. I look forward to many more adventures with you. But I must tell you, my escorting you is under a strict stipulation. You see, there is something I no longer can stand to let go any further. My side continues to have an unfair disadvantage. The balance beam between us is slanted dangerously low in favor of your side. We must make the pendulum swing to the middle before I agree to accompany you again.

I have compiled a list to help with the balance. Feel free to answer at your earliest convenience and by any method. At least one must have an answer, with the promise of the rest to follow. One is the ticket for me to accompany you, and the rest is the ticket for any questions answered by me about myself. I think this is a reasonable request. Below are the questions. I await your answers.

1) Is Taran your nickname? I thought it was Tarus. What is your real name?

2) Will this be the only method you plan to communicate with? Back to the golden ages, or do you have another much more accessible, more modern option?

3) Are you so blessed you can afford to live off-campus?

4) Why don't you like talking about yourself?

PS If you keep me waiting too long, I'm going to assume you're not interested, or worse, you have something to hide. Dun dun dun. Just kidding. :)

There were so many things in her letter to dissect. First, I could breathe again. This letter proved she was interested. Even if she had tried to tempt me, succeeded at resisting me, and made me feel like she wasn't interested, I now had a letter proving otherwise.

Second, this girl never stopped blowing my mind. She wasn't scared of me. She saw unfair disadvantages and wanted them corrected, whether or not that meant losing me.

Third, I loved how she enjoyed playing games. Our mutual respect for a *playful* match made whatever we were, whatever we were heading to, more entertaining.

Fourth, as for her questions, she knew more than she let on to herself and me. From those explicit questions, it was obvious she knew there were things amiss, but either she didn't care or couldn't stay away because of the prophecy.

How did she know I didn't live on campus? I'd mind-controlled everyone who knew.

With pencil and paper ready, I debated for a long while about what to write, unaware of anything other than how I could make it the most fun. A fit of laughter escaped me as I came up with the perfect solution.

Before writing back, I printed her name on the front like one of her favorite book titles on her bedside table. The most challenging part was drawing the *I* with blood dripping from it. Having to make sure it was nothing short of perfection, I picked it up and placed it under the light above my head to examine my work.

One second, I was studying the angle of the *S*, and the next, the paper had vanished.

"Brother, brother." A slithering voice echoed off the wall. "Whatever would our dear queen think if she saw you spending your time drawing instead of capturing the girl?" With one hip leaning against the desk, Saullis stretched his hand toward me, magic glowing a velvet black in his palm. My jaw clenched as he read the note, his face morphing into a wicked sneer.

My body trembled. I already knew Darcy was here, but Saullis, too? He must've been her backup plan. I was in deeper shit than I'd realized.

"Look at this. The perfect bodyguard and confidant of the queen was writing a love letter—a rather devilish one." He held the letter out to someone. Darcy's musky jasmine hit me as she appeared from behind and took it. Had she told Mother also, or just Saullis?

Saullis picked Sierra's letter off the desk, and I reached out to grab it from him, my palms drenched in sweat.

"Stlatka!" Saullis screamed, and invisible chains pinned my arms against the chair with incredible force. They sliced my wrists. I jerked, trying to breathe through the pain and break free. I needed that letter.

Teeth grinding, I screamed and yanked myself free from the chains. Blood poured down my wrists before my healing kicked in.

I jumped on top of Saullis and started beating him senseless. His head swung from left to right, blood dripping from his nose and mouth before crusting over from his own demonic healing. Fighting a full demon was hard when it came to fists, but that didn't stop me from ripping into his skin.

He looked nothing like his true self. Where his body usually held gray, slithery skin, he now had dark human flesh. His usual long, pointy claws were now human hands. And the oddest part, where he usually wore no clothing, he now wore tight jeans and a white top. Darcy always changed her appearance. She never looked like her true self. But Saullis and Jeroboam loved embracing their full demon. Darcy must've forced him to blend in.

"Get off him!" Darcy screamed loud enough that my ears bled, but I didn't stop. If I left him alive, I was as good as dead.

On my next brutal swing, Darcy yelled, "Stlatka," the same words Saullis had used.

I should've seen that coming. The chains shackled my wrists to the ground. I struggled, yanking at the cuffs to break free. Saullis used my momentary distraction to kneel, his knees pinning my chest down. With his physical strength plus Darcy's spelled chains, I wasn't budging.

"Saullis, we already know he's found the child. Haven't you, Tartarus? Though I wonder how long it has been since you first knew she was the *princess*," Darcy said, hatred coating her words. I locked eyes with her, trying to understand her aim. She knew.

Darcy winked. So, she hadn't told Saullis everything. Why?

"I don't know what you're talking about," I choked out.

"Don't be daft. We found the king's journal under your mattress and knew it was either a girl named Sierra or a boy named Elijah. Your note is to a Sierra. What sort of coincidence would that be?" Darcy knelt and licked my ear, my soft spot.

My libido rose, but my chest ached. I didn't care how long it had been or how great Darcy once was. I only wanted Sierra.

"Plus, we saw you together three days ago. Your interactions with her were like those of people who knew each other quite well. Whatever will the queen think about your lies and betrayal?" Saullis punched me in the chest.

Darcy continued taunting me and biting at my ear.

Pain ricocheted down my spine, and I spat in her face.

Her demon claws slipped free, and she smacked me across the cheek, drawing blood.

"Our roles are reversed. I'd be careful if I was you. Plus, I know your body is craving me, or at least, craving *something*. Your little princess doesn't put out." Darcy spat back in my face.

Brave. Or was it actually showing how cowardly she was? If we were in Hellspace, and I was still her acting leader, I would've beaten her for a week for the way she'd spoken to me. But things were different. She was right. My position was in question, and they outmatched me.

"Darcy, you can torture him later. Let's portal him back to the Gateway before the queen decides we're betrayers, too." Saullis grabbed her wrist.

She dug the nails of her other hand into my bicep, her grip firm. If I dared to move or portal away at the same time they did, I'd be one Tartarus without a bicep. My magic was strong, but I couldn't heal fast enough to regrow a body part. I'd bleed out in less than ten minutes.

All I could do was growl as they transported me into a dark forest, still on Earth, the trees blocking the moon. Owls hooted in the shadows, and the wind blew through the branches.

Leaves crackled underneath my body as they threw me at Mother's feet. I swallowed. My face turned white, and my bowels loosened.

Mother would never forgive me for this.

Twenty Eight

The hair lifted on my arms. I didn't dare move. Instead, I stayed face down, eating the wet dirt beneath me. I still didn't know whether to tell Mother about the rest of the prophecy, not when the mating bond hadn't formed. Without telling her, it wouldn't explain why I hadn't found a way to bring Sierra to her the second I'd located her.

"Look at your queen, now!" The ground shook beneath me as Mother's screech pierced my ears. She used her purple mist to force my head up. "Did you not hear me, you insolent dimwit?"

Less white showed in her eyes than before, and the mist swirling around her had thickened. I shivered. Had she gotten stronger? If she had, I only prayed my instincts about her were right, and she wasn't the dark soul.

Her mist shifted around my throat. She squeezed tight and cut off any airflow. She knew more than I suspected. Perhaps Darcy had told her? Maybe, while I was away, she'd learned the rest of the prophecy, and this was my death?

Never in a million years would I have imagined Mother

giving someone a clean end, especially her own son. My bones snapped, and the world around me blurred. I wouldn't question how she killed me. I'd welcome this end versus returning to Hellspace or any other torturous deaths I'd witnessed her commit over the years.

Images of a laughing Sierra danced around in my brain. Then, all too quickly, they disappeared. Delmore must not allow any pleasure into its realm, and I most certainly was in Delmore after all I'd done. Besides, I was the prince. There was no way Skylight, our realm's heaven, would ever let me in. Not even if I confessed or did a million charitable deeds.

"I'll have so much fun watching you get everything you deserve. What pleasure it'll be to be the one who tortures you." Darcy yanked my head back, and pain rippled in waves down my spine. Mother's mist vanished so Darcy could have her way. I gasped and tried to cough, but Darcy pulled harder and bit my ear. "Only when you beg for mercy, will I ease up. But if you agree to bond with me, your punishment will be quicker."

Blood dripped from my ear, and I cursed, a slew of profanity filling my head. This wasn't Delmore. I couldn't be that fortunate. No, I was still alive, on Earth, and kneeling before Mother near the Gateway vault. It wasn't good that we were meeting here. Mother said I could die accessing the Gateway. If I lied in my confession, the guardian would kill me. My insides knotted into a ball.

"I see you've noticed where we are. What would make your face lose all color unless you're hiding something from me? Is there more you're trying to keep secret? Besides the seer Your Majesty sent you to retrieve? The girl you failed to bring to me the minute you found her? Regardless of the number of days you had left?" Mother fisted my shirt and yanked me to my feet. Her tendrils of mist returned, swirling around me.

Sweat dripped from my forehead and into my eyes. I could barely see her.

With every drop, I wondered if it'd be the last.

She tossed me onto the Gateway's circular floor door leading to the underground as if I was as light as a feather. Dread filled my body, and seconds later, I remembered one of the things I had to confess was where my allegiance and my heart lay.

Two months ago, this wouldn't have bothered me.

I'd have laughed at anyone who ever reckoned me anything but heartless. But now, after meeting Sierra, I couldn't help but wonder if I might no longer be. I already believed that my role in the prophecy was true. My legs trembled. At least my allegiance remained with Mother, but I feared it might be with Sierra as well.

"Tartarus, are you still loyal to me, your queen?" She hovered inches from my face without stepping into the circle. Tears streaked down her cheeks. Even with me hiding Sierra from her, she still loved me. She wasn't evil.

"Yes." I choked out the word and scooted to the door's outer edge. My fingers touched the rim, and several invisible hands grabbed me and forced me back into the center. I gripped hold of Slinger, and my jaw clenched.

I was trapped.

"Don't lie to me!" she screamed and threw her mist at me, but it slammed into a force field around the circle's perimeter. Well, at least Mother couldn't hurt me.

"You're my queen, Mother, the reason for my existence. There is no other reason to live or breathe except to serve you." I recited our memorized quote that she had made me repeat every day after removing me from Hellspace. She practically carved the phrase into my forehead.

"Let us see if it's still true. Get us in the Gateway unless you'd rather die." Did she not understand she wasn't giving me much incentive? Either way, this ended with me dead.

"Do you not suspect I would have someone out there watching Sierra? Look around you. Darcy and Saullis are here, but where is their third? Do you see Jeroboam? Or did you forget he took your place as leader of the trio when you became my bodyguard?" Her words froze me. She'd sent the vilest one of us to follow Sierra.

Mother would've chosen him to be her bodyguard and assassin because she loved how vicious he was. She had several demons and her half-demon spawn compete for the position. I only won because the cruelty didn't shape me to the point nothing else could, leaving her room to develop me into whoever she wanted.

Everyone else quickly became too consumed with their need for torture. They sometimes chose it first, over her, and she couldn't have that. If Mother could estimate the difference between the love each demon or spawn carried for her versus the darkness, the darkness would outmatch her every time, especially with Jeroboam. Torture was a drug, and drugs were addictive.

I fell to my knees as images of Jeroboam touching Sierra flooded my brain. My eyes watered before I remembered whose presence I was in. Thankfully, my face was pressed against the cold metal vault, and she couldn't see. Otherwise, it would've made things worse.

"Open the Gateway now. Show me where your heart and allegiance lie, or I'll unleash Jeroboam."

I hesitated. Jeroboam was difficult to tame. He had prob-ably already tortured her.

"You must believe me. I'm in control of Jeroboam. Even if I wasn't ..." She drummed her fingers on her chin. "... why would it matter, Tartarus? You know she's going to die in the end."

I took a barely noticeable breath to disguise my emotions before rising to my feet. "Nothing matters except for my queen's happiness." Another phrase I'd learned to repeat.

"Show me now," she demanded, as the others watched with hungry eyes.

Shit. I didn't want to, but I really didn't have a choice. Maybe the fact she hadn't brought Sierra here but had left her guarded instead was because Mother questioned why I hadn't brought Sierra to her yet. She trusted me and might be worried something had kept me from bringing Sierra to her, something that could affect her mission. Since she cared so much about uniting the realms, she wouldn't force anything if she had any doubt or suspicion that something might go awry.

This was a good thing. I could work with this.

Twenty Nine

On the verge of hyperventilation, I turned to the front of the circle. A small tear escaped. I wiped it away without being obvious as I snapped Slinger off my necklace and sliced my left palm. I squeezed and went counterclockwise around the vault perimeter.

Drop by drop, my blood trickled onto the symbol of three waves representing the water wielders. Freshwater scents sprung to my nose. Next, I dripped blood onto the figure holding flames that represented the fire wielders. Smoke rose from the carving. Darcy gasped, and I moved on to the next symbol. Two women blew clouds representing the wind wielders. A breeze lifted my hair. Last, I smeared my hand onto the tulips growing from an earth wielder. Flower fragrances filled the air.

Nothing else happened.

I searched around the perimeter to see if I'd missed anything.

Wedged in the middle of the metal door knocker was a carved purple bird in flight, representing the spirit element—

Rosalida's bloodline. I placed my bloody hand over the bird. Soft music drifted into the air, and the perimeter of the vault glowed lavender.

Holy Delmore. No wonder my vein chose that color.

"Please state your name, your position, your allegiance, and where your heart lies. Remember to speak the truth. You have two attempts before death claims you," a raspy, sinister female voice said out of nowhere. No physical form accompanied the voice.

An empty feeling grew in the pit of my stomach. This had to be the guardian.

I swallowed my nerves and said, "My name is Tartarus Obsidian of Astal. I am the queen's personal bodyguard. My allegiance is to the queen, and I am heartless." My blood on the symbols sizzled, mimicking the blood inside me. I fell in agony and screamed at the top of my lungs.

Behind me, Mother gasped, Darcy whined, and Saullis snickered.

The Gateway was burning me alive, and there was nothing I could do about it.

"Two attempts are all you get. You wasted your first one by admitting half the truth. Fifty-fifty chance you might get the second and last try right," the voice said, and my blood stopped boiling. No longer screaming, I sat on my knees and clutched my chest. "I will give you sixty seconds."

A fuchsia cloud in the form of a clock appeared in the circle and began ticking down the seconds. There was no time for me to wonder what inference Mother drew. I had to figure out what the female voice meant. For some reason, she'd given me a clue.

One truth is false. One truth is false.

The time slipped away, and my body quivered. If the confession required three things, but she referred to it in halves, she must not care about the job portion, which would make sense. That wasn't really a confession. So, it had to be allegiance or heart. As of now, even if I felt allegiance to both, I still had it for Mother. But when I touched Sierra, the lavender heart formed. I must've lied about being heartless. I glanced up at the clock. Ten seconds left.

"Heartless," I blurted out.

"Was the lie or truth? If I were you, I'd begin again," the female voice said.

"My name is Tartarus Obsidian of Astal. I am the queen's personal bodyguard. My allegiance is to the queen. Where once I used to be heartless, I can no longer claim this," I said, not daring to peek at Mother. The anger radiated from her in a wave of heat, her breath hitching. If the female voice wasn't boiling me from the inside, Mother was from the outside.

"Count yourself lucky. What you speak is the truth … for now," the female voice said.

Despite wanting to know if I'd soon be heartless again and why, I stayed silent, waiting for the vault to open. I wasn't in the place to ask questions.

"Would Tartarus wish to make a request or gain entry into the Gateway?"

"Entry," I said.

"Very well." Several tons of metal moved around below, and a thousand locks unlatched, click after click, a labyrinth of coils. It was spectacular how secure the Gateway was.

Silence only lasted a millisecond before the glow disappeared, and Mother's tendrils gripped me. They forced my arms behind my back, tightened around my throat, and chained my legs, only leaving me enough room to walk.

"Saullis, open the door. Tartarus, follow behind him. And Darcy, fetch the pixie and earth wielder."

The pixie answered how they'd entered the realm and planned to leave if things hadn't worked out with me, but what was the earth wielder's importance?

Following Saullis, I tried to escape the mist. Each time I fidgeted or attempted to use my magic to break free, the misty tendrils shoved themselves deeper within me. Inside my skin, they grew spikes and dug around. A trail of blood followed them as they shifted to a new spot. Pain slithered in their wake. My knees wobbled. Mother's punishment was never child's play. Thickness lodged in my throat. I hated causing her this much torment. I shouldn't have withheld Sierra from her. I shouldn't have been selfish in trying to awaken my heart.

Torches hanging on the stone walls erupted with bright flames as Saullis stepped off the final wooden step onto the limestone floor. Besides the light that they cast and the shadows dancing around the cave, it was dark and cold.

There was no sound besides that made by the four of us, and it smelt of salt water. The area looked like any other cave: stone walls, one massive opening to whatever realm we wished, three moderately sized curved regions, and stairs that we had just come down. The opening above closed behind Mother.

"I need time to process everything and to decide what to do next. More than anything, I wish to punish you for being such a huge disappointment. But you're my son. There must be some rationale as to why you did this. A reason why Sierra can't come to our realm yet. I'm just not ready to hear it." Mother used the mist to rub her temples.

"Earth wielder, you're to sit here and keep this space from closing." Mother shoved him underneath the other opening. "Do not let the cave build itself back over this space unless you want your airways to follow suit. Before I leave, I shall cast a spell removing your need to eat, sleep, or relieve yourself. Then, nothing shall prevent you from using your full focus to keep the space open. As the Gateway allows you to navigate, no Delmore beast will come after you."

He cried when the mist released him, and blood dripped from the spots that they'd occupied. I didn't empathize with him or even care that he'd wound up in this situation. All I cared about was what I'd say to Mother when she returned. Could I blame the curse for all of this?

"Darcy, chain him to the cave. And Saullis, watch her. Return to the throne at midnight." Mother turned back to the earth wielder, cupped his face, and cast a spell. With her final word, she slithered through the opening.

"Guess I grew bored watching you woo Sierra." Darcy circled me. "Saullis, bring me the chains." Out of nowhere, metal links fell into Saullis's arms. He dropped them with a thud at Darcy's feet before gliding to the earth wielder to play with his *soon-to-be meal*. Saullis enjoyed drinking blood, but he wasn't a vampire. Just evil.

Once I saw the awful chains with spiked loops covered in silver magic, my bowels loosened. These weren't just any chains. They belonged to the leader of Hellspace, and magic didn't affect them. I couldn't heal while wearing the chains, nor could I break them. Nothing except the key could unlock them.

As Darcy bent to find the end of the chain and Saullis was preoccupied with his meal, I took my chance. I snapped the chains around me and attacked Darcy. I pushed her against the wall and strangled her. She gasped, calling for Saullis, but he was too fixated on the earth wielder. Her claws pushed through her hands, and she raked them across my arms.

I clenched my jaw and refused to scream. Instead, I banged her head against the stone wall.

With one hand pinning her to the wall, I used the other to chain her.

A few moments later, I had her arms and legs secured, and her mouth gagged. I turned toward the opening. Only the earth wielder sat below it. Saullis had disappeared, but to where? I couldn't focus on that. Hell knows how long I had to get out of there.

I rubbed my fingers and tried portaling out, but it didn't work. I gulped and ran toward the opening. A foot below it, I cried with pain as something hard shattered on the back of my head, and I fell forward. Saullis stabbed my hand with one of his sharp, enchanted daggers that left the victim helpless, and he used every bit of magic he had to keep me pinned to the ground. I tried to fight back, but with the blade still lodged in my hand, he was stronger than me.

With fast work, he held me up against the wall and wrapped the chains around my legs so tightly that it restricted my circulation. Next, he jammed the links into the wall and shackled my hands in a Y, high enough that only my toes touched the ground. Testing the chains on my arms, Saullis yanked down on them, ripping my shoulders out of their sockets as I screamed.

My vision clouded with red, my insides thundering in protest. Being held captive like this brought me back to my days in Hellspace, and my fear grew. While I tried to breathe through a panic attack, Saullis removed the blade from my hand and broke Darcy's chains.

Darcy turned, the fierce stare of a lioness in her eyes. And I was her prey, a mouse trapped in a snare. She approached and snatched Slinger from my neck. "I have always told you that one of these days, I'd make you beg, though I didn't quite picture it this way." She slid one of Slinger's tips down my cheek and drew blood. The smell of iron wafted to my nose.

"My lord." She spat in my face. "I'm worse than death, even worse than the death of Sierra." She slashed the star across my shoulders as I squirmed, the bite of the blade burning deep.

"You always looked better with your clothes off." Darcy sliced Slinger down my tunic, ripping it off, and tore my tights as best she could. With the breeze on my bare skin, I bit my tongue against the sting.

I squinted, and sweat drenched my back. As Darcy dropped Slinger and placed her hands on my chest, I jerked back. She dug her claws deep into my flesh and crept her hands downwards. Her talons took chunks of my skin with them. My body betrayed me, and I screamed. Pain, especially *my* pain, curved her lips into a vicious smile.

Without losing eye contact, she removed her hand from my body and licked her talons.

I cringed in revulsion.

She sucked the last bit of blood from her finger. "I think ten lashes from the leader's thistle should do." I jerked against the chains as she pulled out the awful weapon that had a multitude of shining hot fangs at the tip of the whip. They'd slice straight through whatever blocked their path, burning soft tissue as they went.

She swung the whip with all her might.

The thistle fangs latched onto four spots on my chest. They burned my skin as they searched for a bone to singe. I roared so loudly at the onslaught of pain the Gateway rattled.

After the fifth blow reached my skin and sizzled, cooking my insides, I lost control of my bladder. Ammonia filled the cave as she took her sweet-ass time with the remaining five lashes. She'd say something between each blow, but I couldn't hear her words over my bloody screams echoing off the cave walls.

Once Darcy had finished, she smiled wickedly and bit my lower lip.

"Darcy, let's go. Leave our lord alive. The queen will destroy you if you harm him in any way that makes him dysfunctional," Saullis said.

"You go. There's something I need to do. I won't hurt him physically again." She winked, and my breathing hitched.

"Fine, I'll go have my own fun without you, then." Saullis waggled his brows before disappearing.

Sick laughter filled the cave as Darcy picked Slinger up and twirled him in her hands. "Nihuke." She spoke to the star and grabbed two of his points. "My punishment for you is killing something you love, like you did my heart." As Slinger glowed, she crushed the star between her hands, shattering him.

My stomach dropped, and I screamed louder than when she'd tortured me. This was worse than any torment. Right then, right there, she'd destroyed a part of me. I couldn't hold back the flood of tears, nor did I care if she thought me weak.

Once my voice grew raspy and I couldn't scream anymore, she bit my ear. Heat rushed from my face to between my legs. She grabbed the bulge. "You love it rough."

My manhood grew tighter. It ached against her touch.

She caressed her hand up and down until the point I'd soon explode. "I want to hate you, but my heart can't stop loving you." She sat on the floor and for a few minutes, remained quiet. "Torturing you is the next best thing. Especially when it reminds me of the nights we spent together in Hellspace." Darcy stood. "You begged for more, for it to be rougher, and when I obliged ..." She groaned and portaled to the opening.

Until I met Sierra, all I wanted to experience was pain. It was the only way to live with what I'd done. But I didn't feel that way anymore.

Just before Darcy fully disappeared, she turned her fierce glare on me, her grin widening. "Saullis's fun involves Sierra."

Thirty

"Holy Delmore. What is he going to do to her? Darcy, you come back here and tell me!" I screamed, my throat raw, coughs wracking my body with the strain. "You're lying. Mother wouldn't allow him to touch her." But what if she didn't know?

Tears streamed, stinging as they fell into the wounds Darcy had created.

For hours, as my body healed at a slower-than-usual rate, I didn't stop yelling at the cave full of shadows dancing beneath the semi-lit torches. The only response I received was the echo of my own voice.

He wouldn't harm Sierra, nor even touch her. But if he did, he at least wouldn't kill her. Not yet. Somehow, I needed to save her before he or anyone else did. I had to free her from this, and be the prophecy's hero, at least for her.

The only way I had a chance was to trust that Mother had left Sierra alone for now, wanting to hear my reason first to ensure nothing could mess with her plans. If so, I could manipulate this situation in my favor. But who was I kidding? It couldn't be that easy. Demons didn't get happy endings. Darcy and Saullis proved that when they destroyed my favorite blade, threatened to do something to Sierra, and left me chained to this place.

It was over for me. And most likely Sierra, too.

With those thoughts haunting me, I thrashed against the chains, attempting to break free. Raw skin surfaced from underneath the chains. My voice grew hoarse from screaming, and my face swelled from crying.

What felt like hours, maybe even days, later, when my voice was almost gone, a nasty cough came out of nowhere, halting me.

A tingling sensation traveled throughout my body. I glanced at the earth wielder standing stock-still, arms raised to the opening, stars glowing within his red-veined eyes. It couldn't have come from him. He was in a trance.

I scanned the small cave. Not one thing was different. Just dark stone with nine torches spread a few feet apart from each other.

The torture was getting to me. I shook my head when the raspy voice of the guardian echoed off the walls. "Tartarus, your yelling keeps upsetting my sleep."

What the hell? I growled. "So, you have a problem with me yelling for answers? Where were you when they tore my body apart? Do you prefer that type of scream? Aren't you sick and twisted? Go figure."

"When the one who is yelling is daft, then yes."

"I'm daft? How dare you say such things." My skin boiled for a split second, reminding me of the pain I'd experienced at the vault door. This guardian was powerful.

"Earlier today, I learned something. Would you like to know what?"

She wanted to tell me a story. This guardian, whoever she

was, was being ridiculous. I rolled my eyes and stared at the glow on the earth wielder. Could he hear us?

"You're going to tell me either way." Again, my skin sizzled, and the torches rattled against the stone. I needed to learn to shut my mouth.

"True, but only because it means I'll receive peace from your nagging voice."

"What could you tell me that I'd actually care about?" I winced. I hadn't meant to say that aloud.

"The pixie you used to cross realms was amongst royalty of her kind. After the queen took two more this week, they grouped together in defiance. Not a pixie can be found. Even if they could, they took a blood-binding oath to never create an opening between realms, except for one person: Sierra."

"Oaths can be broken." I'd know.

"Pixie blood oaths are strong. With their oaths, they only need one person from every bloodline to make it, and every pixie with their blood, whether they want to or not, is bound by it."

"Great. Realm travel can't happen anymore without the Gateways. Mother has access to you, and there are several other Gateways out there. So why does the pixie stuff matter?" I must've lost too much blood because whatever this ominous voice said made no sense.

"All the sphinxes guarding the Gateways decided to hide. Without them, there is no getting to the other realms."

"So, you're a sphinx? Where is your body? And why didn't *you* hide?" She had gaps in her story. I didn't really care to fill them, but I figured she wouldn't leave me alone until I understood her tale.

"Since the war 300 years ago, I've been cursed to live inside the cave wall. To be only a voice. As for this curse, my body is the cave. But this isn't about me. This is about you whining."

I groaned. No wonder she was cursed. She was rude.

"Earlier today, I learned something that made *me* not afraid for this Sierra you care about. The only thing able to get near her at present is Jeroboam, but he is under tight control. She remains blissfully unaware. I promise."

Promises meant shit to me, but it made sense why she'd shared everything with me. She wanted me to know Sierra was safe. But why? What was her angle in all this?

"By the way, my name is Lukita. Now that I've shared two important things with you …" Her voice turned sweet, the caveat I'd been waiting for. "… would you answer a question for me?"

I stayed silent. I never asked her to share.

"Don't ignore me."

My blood boiled again, and my veins turned to spikes. "What?"

"Why do you still trust your mother?"

I tilted my head back. What the hell?

"Because she is my mother. She loves me. She wants to reunite the realms. Many reasons. Why?"

"You yelled that Mother wouldn't allow Jeroboam to touch Sierra. I wanted to know why you felt that way. She'd most certainly allow it."

Not this again? Not more people against Mother? They didn't know her like I did. More reason to prove the prophecy wrong. The next time I saw her, I'd share my part of it. No more questioning whether I should. "You're wrong. I'm going to prove it."

"I wish you wouldn't."

"Why?" I rolled my eyes.

The sphinx responded with silence.

"You don't even know what I'm going to do."

Still more silence.

What the hell? Telling Mother was the smartest option.

Now that the torment of wondering about what was happening to Sierra had vanished, I thought about Lukita.

What had I learned about sphinxes? They told riddles. She didn't, but she did, sort of, at the entrance to the vault. Oh my! The second-best thing to seers' magical gifts was sphinxes. They couldn't tell prophecies, but they could catch glimpses of the future and understand what others thought.

She was reading my mind. She knew I'd share the prophecy. So, she wished I wouldn't. Even more reason to do so. I needed to prove Mother was good, to prove the future wasn't set in stone, and whatever she'd seen had to have been wrong.

Thirty One

Sounds of footsteps came from above the sunny gap the earth wielder held open, and the wind blew a cold breeze against my torn skin.

Mother walked into the cave with tears rushing down her cheeks. "Tartarus, you're my favorite son. My world. I still don't know what to do with you. But please tell me you kept Sierra from me for a good reason, that something would change with the mission if you brought her to our realm."

This was my chance. "Mother, there is something you don't know about the prophecy."

Her mist swirled around the cave, extinguishing the torches. The temperature rose several degrees, and sweat dripped from the back of my neck. Mother closed the distance between us. Her navy eyes were full black now, with mist sparkling in and out of them.

"Lies! You're covering for yourself." Her mist encircled my throat.

"No, Mother, listen," I choked out. "Before I left for Earth, someone shared more of it with me. They said:

'Seers before have made life tragic
because of the one who woke their magic.
Today we sway between two courses
determined by the seer's finding forces.'"

"Why does that matter to me?" She seethed.

"There's more." She stayed silent.

I continued.

"A powerful warrior without a heart
Will bond with the seer at the start.
A heart will form as theories are believed
Then unification under love will be achieved."

The mist loosened around my throat. "You said you wanted to unite the realms. I believe I'm the way to do that. But it's taking time to get her to fall for me. Things are happening in reverse. My heart is starting to build, but a bond hasn't formed yet."

"Why did you keep this from me?" She placed a dagger at my throat. "Don't lie."

"I didn't believe it at first. I don't know. I was foolish to keep it from you. I'm sorry." My body trembled as she held tighter to the blade, her knuckles turning white.

"Tartarus, you've left me with a lot to think about. I'm disappointed in you even more now. We're supposed to trust each other. Nothing excuses you from not sharing this with me." She tucked the dagger away and rushed out of the Gateway.

I didn't have a chance to respond.

"You foolish kid," Lukita said.

Tears streamed down my face. I couldn't help but scream and thrash in my chains. I'd destroyed everything. I'd hurt

Mother. Sierra probably hated me for disappearing. If she didn't already hate me, she would if Mother captured her. My knees wobbled. I hated having feelings. I hated all of this.

"Tartarus, I need to share something with you," Lukita said several minutes later.

"Why share anything with me? I don't deserve to know a single thing."

"Just watch."

In front of me, a shimmering window appeared, smoke forming the perimeter. Waves rippled across the mirror-like surface. They tumbled faster and transformed into a transparent screen.

Mother appeared in the window. I couldn't see her face, but I knew it was her by the lilac curls and the dark purple mist flowing around her. She strolled through the palace halls with a sense of purpose, Saullis at her heels.

"Why—?"

"Just watch," Lukita repeated.

A few seconds later, Mother appeared at a small wooden door. She blasted it open with a powerful force from her hands. I'd never seen that magic from her before. The door swung open to reveal Vilo reading a book on her bed. My insides twisted.

Vilo sprang up, her eyebrows scrunched. "May I help you, Your Majesty?"

Mother's mist twisted around Vilo's neck. She gagged, reaching for her throat and trying to pull the mist away. My body jerked in the chains. I tried rubbing my fingers together and portaling to her, but nothing happened. I remained in the Gateway. Chained. Helpless.

"What did you tell Tartarus?" Mother screamed so loud the window shattered.

Vilo gulped, her body convulsing.

"I asked you a question." Mother seethed and tightened the mist further as Saullis rubbed his hands together.

"That people aren't what they came from."

That wasn't what she'd said.

Mother squeezed tighter, and the veins in Vilo's eyes burst. She glanced to the left of the room and winked. She sensed me. Somehow, Vilo knew I was watching.

"Proof," Vilo said as Mother approached her. Mother unsheathed her ruby sword and sliced Vilo's head off. It fell to the floor with a sickening thud.

My breath hitched, and I let out the most wretched scream. I thrashed against the chains. I needed out. I needed Vilo. I couldn't handle these feelings. First, Darcy destroyed my favorite possession, then threatened the torture of Sierra, and now this. If it weren't for the chains holding me up, I'd have crumbled to the floor.

Black spots swarmed my vision.

Mother *was* evil. Vilo, Aris, Lukita, they'd all been right.

She was the dark soul the prophecy spoke of.

She'd killed the kindest woman I'd ever met. I'd never forgive her for this. I could no longer look past the truth staring me straight in the face. Mother might've loved me, but only because I killed for her. I was an asset. She didn't love me like Vilo or Sierra might.

Sierra. My chest tightened, and the lavender vein blinked into existence, torn in several places. *No.* I had to save her from Mother. There had to be a way.

The window disappeared, and Lukita coughed.

"Are you going to tell me you told me so?" I asked to distract my mind from all the truths surging around it. The minute I let them consume me, I'd fall apart, and I didn't know if I'd get back up. Not this time.

"No," she said gently. "I can't blame you for thinking it

might help. But now I must ask. Do you still trust your mother?"

"What do you think?" I screamed.

"What are you going to do?" Her question sounded sincere.

"I want to save Sierra, but I don't know how. You saw the power Mother possesses. Sierra doesn't have magic. We couldn't survive against her." The energy drained from me, and my head spun.

"Seers are more powerful than demons. She can defeat your mother if her magic manifests."

Defeat Mother? I hated her. Worse, I was mad at myself for believing her deceptions. But did I want to defeat her? I shook my head. I couldn't think about this. Not yet. "I'm chained here. How do you expect me to help her magic awaken?"

"That's a problem for later. Right now, you need to convince your mother that you must return and help fulfill the prophecy."

"But what do I do when Sierra's magic comes alive? She'll need training. The prophecy says I have to make her believe. I'm assuming that means believing she's the savior." I bit my lip. We were doomed.

"If you awaken her magic, you can train her here."

I shook my head, not seeing how this helped. "Mother knows where you are. How will that save us?"

"I can hide. I just haven't yet. It wasn't the right time. Now it is. But I can only protect us for so long. Sierra will need to fight back, and soon."

"What do you gain in all of this? In protecting Sierra and defying the queen?"

"Sierra will know how to break me free from my curse."

Enough said.

But what the hell would happen if I couldn't convince Mother? She'd kill Sierra like she did Vilo. And like Darcy had destroyed Slinger. Everything and everyone I had ever loved died. There was no point in having hope. No point in believing I could convince the dark soul to let me go. We were dead. All of us.

Thirty Two

For hours, I thrashed against my restraints. The chains bit into my skin, drawing blood. I welcomed the pain. I needed it. Otherwise, my emotions would destroy me.

By the time Mother returned, my voice was raw. I'd screamed through every minuscule minute since realizing we were doomed.

"Tartarus, for lying to me ..." The moon shone through the opening and highlighted the water forming in her eyes. I wanted to scream that I knew her tears were fake, that she didn't care about me. "... I'm sending you to Hellspace for a year. After that, we'll see if you'll return to my side."

No! A heavy weight crushed down on my chest. This couldn't be happening. I couldn't go back there. Plus, I couldn't admit defeat. I had to put up a fight and try to save Sierra. *I* had to turn the tide.

"Wait! Mother, I promise I'm doing this for you. Let me get her to fall in love with me and awaken her magic."

Mother's mist circled, squeezing me tight. "I don't care about her magic anymore. I want her dead."

"No, you don't. You want the answers she has first." My voice strained against the mist that was choking me.

"I needed the answers to unite the realms, but it's not worth it anymore. Someone else can have that task. I'm in control of Climakru. I can unite the two kingdoms. That's enough. So again, I ask, why do I need her? Seers are dangerous."

Shit. My breathing became shallow. She didn't mean it. Mother knew her importance. I had to exploit that. "Because … you, my queen, will never be satisfied if you know you could've done more."

"At the risk of having my son betray me and losing the realm I've already acquired? The loss most certainly isn't worth it. It's best that the girl dies." She smiled and leaned against the cave wall.

"Give me one more chance to make your dreams come true. Even add a time limit to it. Let me get her to fall in love with me and believe in magic. You know it's worth it," I answered.

Silence surrounded us until her lips twitched, and a demonic laugh erupted from her throat. "You're right. Uniting the realms is my dream. But you can't go unpunished, and what if you're trying to betray me with her?"

"I'd never. You're my mother. You love me more than anyone ever could. I put you above all else, and that'll never change." I'd say whatever I could to make her believe me. I had to get out of these chains and back to Sierra. "When the Gateway opened, it asked me who I was loyal to and where my allegiance lay. I said you. It was the truth and opened the cave. That hasn't changed."

Mother paced the cave, circling the earth wielder several times. I couldn't breathe, waiting for her to decide her verdict.

"My rules, my way. Because you've lied to me already, I can't take another chance on you. At least for a while." She fastened a bracelet around my wrist. "Ilkeoya Neklta," she murmured.

A bright red and black light flashed along the clasp and then disappeared.

"Infused in the bracelet is part of my mist. There is also a demon trapped inside who is now part of the mist and me. He will report to me and show me all. He can't possess your mind, but with my mist, he can control the arm where the bracelet is attached." She paused. "You have two days, until an hour past midnight on the night after what the humans call Halloween, to make her fall in love with you and for her to accept magic. Then you're to bring her to me, here. My mist will kill her with your hand or drag her here if you don't. Do you understand?" Her mist pierced my skin and drew blood. A metallic taste formed on my lips, and I groaned.

Dumbstruck by the turn of events, I blinked several times. Never in a million years would I have thought she'd find a way to entrap one of her demons, especially forcing them onto someone else without possessing them entirely.

Even though I worried about my task and the demon, relief washed over me. Mother hadn't initiated full possession. If she ever did, I'd wish my death followed suit. Death, even Hellspace, was better than full possession. There was no coming back from it. I'd heard the soul remained at first but died while watching the demon take over.

"Saullis, unchain him, give him food, and let's go."

Mother waited while Saullis removed my chains and pushed food onto my lap. "Remember, I see everything through the link. You no longer have any privacy." At her words, she and Saullis vanished, and what little hope I had for Sierra disappeared with them.

I fell onto the cold stone and pounded the ground. My situation sucked. It was clear I needed to get Sierra to kiss me. But in two days? That was impossible. In almost two weeks, I hadn't got her to budge. If and when I did, how would I free her from Mother and bring her to the Gateway to train in secret? Mother now had eyes on me.

This was hopeless.

I wanted to curl into a ball and wail, but I had to try. Otherwise, Mother would kill us both. There was no question about that. And I wanted to do everything in my power to ensure Sierra lived. If that meant groveling, I was going to grovel.

Pushing myself over and leaning against the wall, I ate as my body healed at its usual rate. With every bite I took, I told myself I could do this. I could save her.

Tartarus. A soft voice sounded inside my head. Most forms of telepathy had died after the multi-realm separation, other than through mating bonds. Manny was thousands of years old and had mind control telepathy, and I took that ability when I killed him.

Oh yeah, Lukita was a sphinx. They had a type of communication telepathy.

"Y—"

Shh! Act as if everything is normal.

I flinched. "O—"

It's not normal to talk to the air.

Why are you in my head? She sounded different. This voice was beautiful, sweet, and ancient.

Rude, I'm not ancient. But thank you for the compliment.

You're in my head, so you know every thought. Don't you? I had always wondered what it'd be like to be on the receiving end, and this was a typical question one would ask. Because whether or not I might trust this guardian, no one knew I had mind manipulation abilities besides Darcy.

Only the ones you're currently thinking. Unless I want to explore, but we don't have time for that. Lukita spoke in an annoyed tone.

So why are you in my head? You've never done it before, and you spoke many times aloud. I took another bite of my food.

Because now we have an audience. The queen can't use the mist to possess you inwardly, and the bracelet can only possess the object it's attached to. In this case, it happens to be your arm. Your thoughts are free.

That made sense. *What do you need to tell me that she can't hear?*

We must follow the same rules as before for you to gain access to Earth. Since I'm opening the Gateway, I'll accept the answers you gave before. But I'm going to ask for an extra payment because of how tough realm travel is right now. Regarding that extra, I tell you now, there is always a deeper meaning behind requests. Look for them.

On the wall to my right, the circular vault door flickered a metallic silver. Huh. I shrugged. I'd never noticed it before. As if it were second nature, I sliced my hand with a piece of Slinger and spread the blood on the five symbols. I repeated the same words from when I'd entered before.

"Tartarus, what would be your request, or would you like access to another realm?" Lukita's raspy voice had returned.

"I desire safe passage to Earth—to Sierra's dorm." Even though I knew Sierra was safe for now, I needed to see her, to ensure no harm had come to her.

"A request to Earth at this time will require extra. As I assume you'll be coming back, because this is the only way to gain access to Climakru, my request will be to return with a gift."

"Whatever you truly long for, I shall provide as long as I'm capable."

"Bring me a freshly severed hand the next time you appear. Fresh, but at least a few minutes old. I don't like them too ripe." Lukita laughed and opened the seam into Sierra's dorm.

I recoiled at the thought of a severed hand. But before I could overthink her odd request, my body began to vanish, and she spoke inside my head again. *May the gods grant you favor, Tartarus. Remember, you aren't who you come from.*

Neither Sierra nor Emma were in the room. The hair on my arms rose until the clock on the wall chimed. It was noon. They were at school. Though I ached to see her, I had an hour to kill until French, and I needed to spend that time finding a way to ensure we kissed.

I used Sierra's computer to help come up with a plan. One thing I was sure of—I needed to pull at her heartstrings, somehow nudging Sierra into showing a little gratitude, hopefully with a kiss. From reading her journals, I knew both her parents had worked in global charity organizations, and she longed to do something similar. So, what better way to pull at a few strings than by setting up a date involving some charity work?

If only I could find something dealing with her dad's organization, I'd be set. But I'd settle for anything similar or perhaps even a gala. I picked up her journal and flipped through the pages for the gala entry. Perhaps it had a date.

Yes! Not only had I stumbled upon the date, which happened to be Halloween, but after I'd turned to the last page, a picture glared back, giving me an idea for the costumes. I didn't know what the picture was, but I had a computer in front of me.

The picture was of a younger Sierra in pajamas with a bowl of popcorn in her lap. A woman stood behind her, playing with her hair. The woman's face was blurry, so I couldn't make her out, besides having a darker skin tone.

Underneath the picture was a drawn TV and the words *Ever After*.

I looked up *Ever After TV*, and my spine tingled. This would be a perfect costume.

Putting the plan in motion, I portaled to various places, making the arrangements. While doing so, I came up with another game to spark Sierra's interest.

I finished decorating her present and then portaled a hall away from her French class. Once there, I waved my hand over my body and walked into the room. Sierra wasn't there yet.

My nerves skyrocketed as I half-way sat atop my desk. I needed to see her.

The blood drained from my face as Sierra finally appeared at the entrance. Her downcast expression almost had me abandoning my plan and running straight toward her, forcing her to tell me why the hell she was so upset and whom I needed to hurt. Instead, I gripped the edge of the desk, knuckles blanching white, as she shuffled to her chair, unaware.

Sierra rubbed her eyes when she got close enough to see what awaited her on the desk. She slouched and gasped as she peered back at me. Damn. She was beautiful, real, and in front of me. I hadn't lost my opportunity to see her again. Tears burned my eyes, but I blinked them away and took her in.

Sierra's skin was clear. No bruises, no scruffs, nothing. Jeroboam hadn't touched her.

"Hello there. Miss me?" I winked.

Sierra's nostrils flared. I didn't know what I'd expected, but it definitely wasn't this.

"I'm sorry I haven't been to class. I've answered two of your questions. They're in the note on the box. I've also added a few other things you might like. Hopefully, it'll make up for me dashing off without a word." Not just hopefully, it had to.

"Where have you been?" Anger tinged her voice. Sierra glared at me, her arms crossed.

Shit. I had to stop focusing on my relief that nothing was wrong with her and pay attention.

"Have you been sick? Are you okay? I was worried."

Worried. Sierra was concerned about me. My nonexistent heart fluttered. I wanted to whisk her away, hide her from my mother, and embrace her in an all-encompassing hug.

After she sat down at her desk, silence followed. I owed her an explanation, but I didn't know what to say, especially having been cursed not to mention magic.

"I had to take care of something at home. My mom needed me." I ran my hand through my hair. "When she calls, I have to come. There's no time to say goodbye. I'm blown away that she let me return. I was afraid she wouldn't, and I wouldn't get another chance to see you or explain."

Sierra seemed to consider what I'd told her. Perhaps she could see there was so much I hadn't said and my many hidden messages. "Well, you're back now. I'm glad you're not sick."

Me too. And I was glad we were both still alive, and no harm had come to her. Every hour in the cave had been torturous, not knowing if Jeroboam had done something to her.

The bell rang, and we both jumped. Sierra's body went rigid as she pivoted toward the front of the classroom. My gaze followed. Everyone faced us, and the professor ground her teeth.

"Do I need to give you another essay, Sierra? Or, Taran, would you like your first one on the importance of paying attention in my class?" the professor asked.

Everyone except me cringed at her tone. Class had just started. There was nothing to pay attention to. Whatever, I rolled my eyes and bounced off the desk to sit in my chair. I moved it as close to Sierra as possible. Both our bodies stiffened as heat radiated from our touch.

A millisecond after the professor had turned her attention to the class, Sierra attacked the letter. I eased over, lips close to her ear, and placed my hand over hers. I blew into her ear, watching how her body reacted.

She straightened in her seat and focused dead ahead. I wanted to continue tempting her more, but I only had seconds. "I'd wait if I were you. Don't open it until you're ready to be distracted for the rest of the day or until you see me again." I smirked.

Sierra's body went into overdrive. Her chest rose and fell so fast.

Until our ten-minute break arrived, I faced forward while I kept glancing her way, desperate to know what Sierra thought the note said. Desperate to know what she thought the box held inside. And even more desperate to feel her touch. I'd almost lost this chance. Almost lost her. Gods, I had to save her. These attempts had to work.

"Do you think your mom will ask for you to go back again?" Sierra swiveled in her chair to face me.

"Eventually, but until then, I plan to spend every free moment with you." I placed my hand on her knee. My lavender vein illuminated and vibrated.

"Don't you worry that I might get bored of you if you're always there?" She shrugged.

I laughed. I loved how she spoke to me. "Impossible."

She shook her head and pivoted back in her chair. She picked up her textbook and started quizzing me.

Once the bell rang, she stayed in her chair, though she didn't speak.

"You don't want to hurry off? The sooner the class ends, the sooner you learn what the box and note are about." I glanced over, daring her to answer what I couldn't stop wondering. Did she not want to leave me?

Instead of saying anything, she batted her eyelashes. I almost laughed at her attempt to appear innocent. She knew what I wanted her to say.

Fine, if she wouldn't say it, I would. "I'd rather stay with you all day, but we have class. Afterward, we'll have time together."

"I'm glad you returned," she said aloud, but in a whisper, she added, "I missed you."

Thirty Four

Walking away from Sierra, I couldn't handle the exhilarating emotions flooding my system. She liked me, and the way my throat tightened in reaction made it hard for me to breathe. I was used to these emotions in a negative way, not this, not in this wonderful way. What was I supposed to do with these feelings? Unsure of the answer, I dashed off to the bathroom and portaled back to Hillshite.

I threw myself on the couch and rubbed my temples.

Without Sierra believing and her magic igniting, I had no place to hide us. Mother would find us, kill Sierra, and send me to Hellspace.

I shivered as images of my skin shredding and rebuilding multiple times flashed in my mind, the horror of it engulfing me. Hell, I still didn't know what Lukita had meant about a severed hand, or how I'd accomplish hiding us with Mother's demon bracelet spying on me.

Not needing my past to beat me down, I replaced those terrible images of Hellspace with those of my own—the note

I'd written to Sierra. I reread it several times until my worries began to fade away.

My darling lady,

These last two days have been torturous. Not seeing your beautiful smile or looking into those gorgeous eyes pained me. Even worse, it killed me to think you could be pondering all the worst things about why I left. I hate to think I could have caused you any pain.

I assure you it had nothing to do with what you DID.

To show you just how sorry I am and how interested I am in you is where the box comes in. You may open it now or read on for not just one of your answers, but two. I'm feeling generous and believe it's the least I can do.

#1 Am I blessed to live off-campus?

Well, yes, I am. Little curious to learn how you came to know this. It's not public knowledge or something the admissions board wanted to get out.

My family was able to pay excessive amounts to help fund the school. In return, we requested my accommodation be in a quiet, off-campus place. After agreeing to the stipulations and rules, they were more than happy to oblige.

#2 In what ways do you plan to communicate?

This one was tough, and I thought it over thoroughly and came up with an answer I thought would be incredibly fun. The answer is in the box, with another note explaining.

The second time through the letter, memories of Hell-space had faded into nothing. Thoughts of Sierra's lovely right-sided dimple replaced them.

With fear no longer crippling me, I portaled to her dorm room and hid under her bed five minutes before she got out of school. The sheer light pink skirt kept me well covered.

By the time the bell rang, my palms had grown clammy.

The cold breeze from the open window sent chills down my spine.

The door creaked open with a giddy Sierra already unraveling the bow on the box. My mouth dried. What if I'd got it wrong, and she didn't like it?

Once she opened the box, my thoughts of failure crumbled away. Her smile brightened the room more than the glare from the sun did. I could lose myself staring at her.

All too soon, her face changed. She looked confused, blinked several times, and picked up the second note. With the note in her hand, she slumped on the bed. I sighed.

Unable to see her now, I reread the letter in my head.

To my dearest lady,

I hope you enjoy the present. After spending several days with you, I hope I didn't get one thing wrong about you—your joyous, childlike spirit. Hence, I thought these would be the perfect way to communicate. If you must insist on the normal way, then I'll give you my number next time you ask. But I hope I was right about the childlike spirit and you prefer the other method.

My signature was at the bottom, and I'd added a winking smiley face with wings behind it. I thought it would be a cute way to design the note. I imagined her smiling with her one-sided dimple. My heart fluttered. I couldn't wait to hear her thoughts on the gift.

Static sounded from the walkie-talkie as she clicked the button. My throat constricted. Shit. Why hadn't I expected her to use it?

"You ..." She spoke into the walkie, and it echoed from my pants pocket. She stopped speaking, probably due to hearing her own voice speak back. Holy Delmore. This wasn't good.

Crushed underneath the bed, unable to breathe from

nerves, I squirmed around, trying to reach the walkie to turn it off before she spoke again.

"You ..." She paused, her voice hesitant. "We ..." Before she could finish the sentence, I grasped the knob of the walkie-talkie and twisted it off, releasing a silent breath.

"... quite right. Guess you must know me well enough. I do enjoy this," she said as she paced around the room, moving curtains back, searching for me or the reason why her voice had echoed. I rammed myself farther back, trying to make myself as small as possible. I wanted to be excited that I'd guessed her right, but instead, I was sweating over the fear of being caught.

"Are you not going to answer me?" The bed creaked again.

I cringed. *Nope. Not until I free myself from this blasted place.*

"Fine. Leave it up to mystery." She sighed. "But if I wear the wrong thing to wherever you're taking me today, it's your fault." Inside, I chuckled. Gods, she was awesome. And her concern was premature.

On cue, someone knocked on the door.

Sierra jumped off the bed and walked toward the door. "Well ..." She froze upon finding another person behind the knock in lieu of me. Awkwardly standing there was an older gentleman that I'd mind-controlled earlier.

"Umm, Miss. Tarus informed me you'd need this. May I place it in your room, or would you like to take it from here?" the gentleman asked.

Tongue-tied, she opened the door wider. The mail carrier went straight to the vanity, placed the package down, bowed to her as instructed, and left. Thank gods it was on the vanity and not the bed. Now, I could see her expression in the mirror.

Sierra stood frozen for a minute before she moved toward the package and opened it.

With a glazed expression, her body trembling, she lifted

my present out of the box. It was the white and gold fairy-tale dress the character Danielle wore in the 1998 film *Ever After*. Underneath it were the fluorescent wings.

Once she picked up the wings, she noticed the note. Again, I recalled the letter from memory.

This outfit isn't for this evening, I'm afraid. The outfit is for tomorrow, Halloween. I hoped you'd accompany me to a party and wear this. You'll find your outfit for this evening's event where the note was. Hope it fits and you say yes to tomorrow.

A black outfit lay underneath the note: a black shirt and leather pants.

Sierra lifted her shirt over her head to change, and everything in me went on high alert, my pants tightening like crazy. The lavender vein appeared with spikes on it and ripped at my skin. I shook, trying to erase the awful feeling, but it didn't vanish. I closed my eyes, and the vein suddenly disappeared, as did the pain.

Holy Delmore. So unfair.

I kept my eyes shut until the bathroom door closed. Once out of her waking presence, I turned invisible and portaled outside.

After gaining control of my libido, I returned to Sierra's and knocked on the door.

When she opened it, I couldn't help but admire every inch of her. Her figure in the outfit teased the hell out of me. The leather clothes did wonders for the imagination: from the outline of her calves to the curve of her hips to the swell of her breasts. My libido fought with me again, and I suppressed a moan. "I'm glad the outfit fits."

"Me too. Although it's tighter than the usual things I wear, I do like it. Thank you."

I'd hope so because if we somehow made it through everything, she'd receive an order of every color of shirt and pants in leather.

"I'm curious—what event needs this attire? And what shoes shall match this soiree?" She slowly bit her lower lip.

"You may wear any shoes for now. The ones you'll need are in the car."

For a brief second, I wished we were going somewhere different because her boldness to grab heels turned me on. I imagined her wearing them at the surprise charity event, and I couldn't help but chuckle, which forced Sierra's bold expression to flicker to one of uncertainty.

My cheeks burned. "Please don't fret. I laughed because where we're going is the farthest thing from heel attire. If you could pull it off, I'd be impressed. Regardless, you look stunning."

Even with my words, her sadness remained. I tipped her chin up to gaze into her eyes. "You wear your emotions, thoughts, and feelings on your face. I'm sorry for any sadness my chuckle caused, but I promise, you're the most beautiful woman."

Captivated by her eyes—the hidden specks of blue, green, and white—I sank deeper into them. When she accepted her true identity, what would it do to those beautiful colors? A brief glint of amber sparked within that kaleidoscope of color, a tiny hint that her father was in there. Were parts of her magic trying to burst through? If I could pull at that, it'd make this easier. I hoped.

Back to the present, I dropped my hands and held my arm out. "Ready to be my escort?"

"Why, of course," she said, linking arms.

Thirty Five

When we reached the venue, I handed her a pair of boots, the soles fashioned like tennis shoes. A salesperson at the store had sworn they were *fancy running boots*.

We stepped out of the limo once Sierra had pulled them on, and her head shook as she took in her surroundings.

Doubt forming, I fidgeted with my black leather jacket, taking slow breaths to calm my nerves. Before I changed my mind and took us somewhere else, I said, "Do you not like it?"

"Oh my gosh. I love it. Now I understand why the heels wouldn't work." Her dimples deepened.

"Good." I smiled, and my muscles relaxed. "This event ..." I gestured at the scene and saw how obnoxious, but fun, it looked. "... is a run for colors." Strung between two of the enormous trees lining the wide, red-rocked pathway was a huge banner reading, *RUN FOR COLORS, RUN FOR YOUR CHOICE*. Each person was dressed all in black and had a neon-colored number hanging around their neck.

She leaned against the limo and folded her arms. The

midday sun glistened against her brown hair, accentuating her juicy, pink, pouting lips. "I don't run."

"I know." I smiled and grabbed her hand. The lavender vein solidified for the first time since returning. "It's not a race. Instead, you're running for the most solid colors."

"I'm still hearing the word run."

"You can go at whatever speed your heart desires. The winner isn't who passes the finish line first. Again, it's about the colors."

"How long is it?" She scrunched her nose.

"Two laps around the park, equivalent to a 5K. Not too long." I squeezed her hand, and electricity shot through my body.

"What made you think I'd like this?"

"Cause you like games and because of the prize."

"I'm intrigued." Again, a dimple appeared.

"Throughout the run, or in your case, brisk walk, buckets will drop paint on people, but they'll drip the color before dumping. Volunteers hidden around the course will also shoot paint at people as they pass by. Before they fire, they're supposed to scream the color."

"Sounds fun. Do I get to shoot people?" Her eyebrows raised in question, a hint of innocent wickedness sparkling within her eyes. Okay, she definitely had a mean streak. I loved it.

"No. Your purpose is to maintain only one color throughout the entire race. The person with the most single color will win."

"Are there rules?"

"Participants must wear all black, hence the reason for your outfit. You can't stand in one position for longer than five seconds, track backward, sideways, or anything not continuously moving forward."

"Doable. I guess it's not too bad." She smirked.

I escorted her to the ticket booth to get our numbers. Hers was 777, a number honored in our realm. I'd mind-controlled the ticketer to give her this special number. Mine happened to be 666, the cursed number in our realm. Either the ticketer had tried to be clever by giving the two opposing numbers, or someone knew we were there. A ripple of alarm had my hair standing on end. Jeroboam was still in this realm, trapped.

Keen to not let speculation about Jeroboam ruin the night, I placed my hand on Sierra's back. Touching her always took away the fear and horrible memories.

Once calmed, I guided her toward the starting line. Sierra had a question on the tip of her tongue, but just as her mouth opened, the gigantic gong resonated. Organized chaos erupted throughout the group. People on the sidelines danced, participants screamed their battle cries, and others launched into the run, dodging obstacles.

We followed the mayhem, but before we crossed the starting line, I stopped. With an apologetic smile, I turned toward Sierra. "I forgot to tell you another rule. You can push people into the line of fire or underneath a bucket."

Her jaw fell, mouth popping open.

"Chin up, beautiful." I winked and sprinted off.

To run for pure enjoyment versus running for my life was beyond freeing. Not having to care who'd attack next or if I'd make it another step, I ran, full of joy, like a wild horse.

Colors splashed on me from out of nowhere. I looked down. Green and red spots dotted my black shirt and leather jacket sleeves. I kept running. Two steps farther, someone sprung out from under the bench and shot me with yellow. Well, I wouldn't be winning any solid-color prize.

Thick, slimy darkness crowded in, swallowing the air.

I pulled up my jacket sleeve and glared at Mother's *pet*.

Nothing radiated or pulsed from the bracelet.

I froze, still as stone. *Jeroboam* was nearby.

His signature darkness crept over me.

Whenever he was near, he had the ability to suck the life out of anything present, draining its will to exist. And that was exactly how I felt.

Veins stood out in my neck, and I jerked my head from left to right, searching for Sierra. She was nowhere near me, and I was confident she didn't run. This left me with one terrifying conclusion.

She must be *way* behind me.

I was a fool not to watch her back.

I didn't know how long it'd take her to catch up. Going back or waiting here would disqualify me. Not an option I could take. I needed to be in this race to protect her from Jeroboam. Tiptoeing wasn't against the rules, but surely the speed would annoy the judges.

As runners jogged past, my unease grew. Sierra was taking too long, and I couldn't handle waiting to ensure she was okay. The constant slow pace, glancing over my shoulder, and my energy draining—replaced by sheer adrenaline—continued until I made it between the halfway mark and the three-quarter mark. With each step, I groaned internally. It felt like elephant-sized weights strapped around each of my ankles. And it didn't help that I wanted to murder everyone who kept shooting me with colors.

I peeked over my shoulder again, and behind me, mist had formed in the distance. Five figures on the outskirts of the track glided away in the opposite direction, and all wore white masks, their hands dancing to a rhythm. I squinted to get a better view. As they strode forward, they chanted.

Sierra was back there, somewhere. What the hell were they about to do to her? And what had happened to Jeroboam's leash or my time frame? I gritted my teeth. I didn't have time to think about those things. I needed to protect her.

In the seconds it took to wonder what was happening,

they'd formed a circle, and a soul-wrenching scream coming from their direction pierced the air.

Sierra.

Anger pulsed through me—fire and heat, building from the inside out—and something happened that I didn't even know was possible.

I froze everything.

Thirty Six

Crisp silence engulfed me as the sound of chanting came to a halt, and Jeroboam turned his black orbs my way, the dark mist snaking out of him.

Both my strength and willpower drained as the storm of darkness hurtled in my direction. It hovered around me, yet Jeroboam refrained from any torture. Wow! That was a first.

"The queen's lacquey appears," Jeroboam said with a hiss, his forked tongue slithering out with every word, as two of his minions appeared on either side of him.

"What are you doing to her?" I yelled. "Let her be. I have more than a day left."

"The queen wanted to see if we could help. Promise we're not hurting a tiny hair on her oh-so-lovely body, brother."

At his words, I snarled and ran at him.

Mother's mist formed a shield around him. "Brother, brother, calm down. We're all on the same side unless you're changing?" He circled me.

"Jeroboam, are you so afraid of me that you have to keep

the shield up? Take it down, and let's battle for the girl. Or leave and give me my time." I taunted his pride but was careful. The others were now circling Sierra, putting me slightly at their mercy.

"Like I said, we were here to help. We wanted to wake Sierra's magic. Unfortunately, her parents have spelled it better than I can figure out. There's no need to fight. She is yours ... for now!" He grabbed my wrist with one hand and twirled the bracelet with the other.

My nostrils flared. He needed to get his slimy fingers off me before I killed him.

"Iskla," Jeroboam hissed, and the bracelet burned my wrist.

What the hell?

"We're leaving now." He snapped his fingers at his minions. As each faded into nothingness, Jeroboam uttered, "I spelled a tracker onto the bracelet in case you get any funny ideas."

I folded in on myself, crumbling downward, and pounded the ground until my knuckles bled. How would I save us now? Not only did I have the stress of the kiss and the demon spy bracelet, but now I also had to worry about this.

Taking a deep breath, I turned to Sierra. She looked lifeless, lying in the grass.

I stared into her beautiful, wide-open eyes. My hand shook as I searched for a pulse. When I couldn't find one, my breath lodged in my throat. I wanted to unleash my wrath and destroy everything in this park, and more, but I tried to remain calm.

She couldn't be dead.

Mother wouldn't let her die, *yet*. Not until she had obtained the information she wanted.

I cried onto her chest, squeezed her cold, lifeless hands,

and screamed, but nothing changed. So I begged. "Deesse, save her! As you allowed Sorcieres to open the Gateway for the witches, I can only imagine you want the realms to reunite. That won't happen if you kill the savior!" I brushed her brown hair off her face. "Unfreeze her!"

Snap! How could I have been so stupid? Though I had no idea how, *I* had frozen things. Had that affected her, even though it hadn't worked on Jeroboam and his minions?

My neck stiffened as I stared at her lifeless form. I grazed my lips along her forehead. The minute I connected with her skin, electricity surged through my body, and the lavender vein formed a perfect heart.

I picked her up, and everything unfroze.

Sierra's eyes fluttered.

She grimaced, then glanced up and smiled. "When did I get in your arms?"

Yes! She didn't remember. I could still play out this event.

"Why do you look like you've been crying?" Her eyebrows knitted together.

"You passed out, and it was the scariest moment of my life."

"I what?" She gulped.

"Someone must've knocked you over. But it's nothing to worry about. You're better now." I brushed a loose strand of hair behind her ear, my fingers tingling at the touch of her skin. "Although I could hold you forever, and then some, we must finish the run. Maybe after, we can return to this." I winked.

Part of me wondered if she'd protest. If she did, there was no feasible way I'd put her down. I'd forget the race and take her straight to my hotel. By all means, I wanted to.

Unfortunately for me, I had to take this at the right pace. I needed all the help I could get to convince Sierra to fall for me. This meant she needed to see the other reason I'd chosen the event. My lips dipped down as I eased her to her feet, but it quickly turned into a devilish grin when she pouted.

After a moment of silence, with Sierra glancing at her watch, her posture changed into that of a runner.

Out of habit, my arm stretched toward her to stop her before she ran from me. I couldn't have that. Not only because of the mission, but also because if she deserted me, I didn't expect I could continue this anymore, not a single bit of it. After having a taste of living, how could I go back to being dead?

But within seconds, I realized it was just my anxiety, and she wasn't leaving me. She was running to the finish line.

With my energy rejuvenated, I skipped past her.

As my feet crossed the line, I swirled around. She was yards behind, taking baby steps. Her outfit was still one hundred percent black, with not a drop of color on it. I glanced down at my clothing and raised a questioning brow. I looked like the rainbow had thrown up a child. If I didn't know about magic, I'd have wondered how all my colors hadn't ended up smeared onto her while I'd held her close.

Seconds from calling out to her that she'd lost, she moved underneath a bucket as it tipped. Hot neon pink poured over her, and my mouth flew open, but not because of her wicked cleverness. Tiny little pixies materialized out of nowhere. Their wands pointed at Sierra and shaped the paint around her as it fell.

One by one, as the four little pixies finished their master-piece, they turned to me, eyes narrowed and teeth visibly grinding. Once everyone had faced me, they flew off. Anyone who might have caught a glimpse of them would've seen small birds.

Pixies? Lukita had said they banded together and would only open the barrier for one reason: Sierra. But I'd figured that meant they knew the prophecy and would help us cross when the time was right if something happened to the Gateway. The prophecy had claimed someone would help me.

Was this their way of giving me a message? Confirming that they'd help? But then, why look at me with disdain? My mind raced with thoughts as Sierra crossed the finish line and stared at me with triumph.

Sierra's gorgeous smile drew me back to the present and the pixies' masterpiece. She looked incredible. When she'd embarked on the race, her hair had been in a messy bun, her outfit black with no slits, black boots, and no makeup.

Now, her outfit was similar, but neon pink. It looked like an outfit swap. The pixies had also added their own spice. A slit now started between her breasts, dropping dangerously low, ending centimeters above her belly button. My body warmed.

Highlights of neon pink raked through her long, flowing hair, which was no longer pinned up.

"Do you mind explaining why you and everyone else are staring at me?" she asked.

Words weren't enough to explain. Sierra needed to see for herself. "Let me show you."

I guided her toward the mirror near the stage. Her mouth instantly dropped to the floor. Obviously mystified, she smoothed her hand across her outfit and squinted at the mirror.

"How did this happen? I expected to look like a hot pink blob, a mess."

"It's …" But the words wouldn't come. I shook my head and continued. "We're all wondering the same thing."

Before she could ask anything more, a crowd formed, and an announcer took center stage.

"Time to reveal the winners!" Several loudspeakers boomed, and people rushed us to the center of the field. I gnashed my teeth. It took everything in me not to react when so many humans touched me. Unable to do it alone, I inhaled and placed my hand on Sierra's back to steady myself.

They brought us to a line of other people, each covered in different solid colors.

"Ladies and gentlemen, are you ready to meet your winners and to hear their choice?" The crowd hollered. "Our first winner, the lady of the neon lake. My dear, what would you like to say? Name and choice, please."

Sierra's eyebrows knitted together.

"My name is Sapphire. My choice is Wood Blue." Many howls filled the air, but oddly, some meows were out there, too. Humans were weird.

Sierra's face changed by the fourth person's announcement, her features glowing. She jumped a little, in her spot, at what the choices and the whole race were for.

As I had hoped, this was something she appreciated. A race for charity. Each winner got to choose where to donate their winnings.

"The girl who looks like she should be a model. The one I'm sure no one saw coming—I sure as hell didn't. The one and only lady of beautiful hot pink." More people than ever hollered, and Sierra blushed.

"My name is Sierra. My choice is CSW-Christian Solidarity Worldwide." The *howlers* continued.

"Last, but not least, we've decided to give one additional prize. And it goes to the person who looked like every color fought to be chosen by him. Gentleman of multicolor."

Busy admiring Sierra's beauty, I didn't even process the fact that the announcer had meant me. Sierra had to elbow me in my ribs and nod at the podium to make me understand.

"I'm Tarus. My choice is also CSW."

"Never have I had two people name the same organization, but I believe they came together. So let us ..."

With only one need in mind, to get Sierra alone, I placed my hand on her back and led her off the stage.

Sierra turned. "Thank you for tonight." Her eyes twinkled up at me.

Inside, I melted from the fire she'd lit. I glanced down at her hand—it called to me, and I needed skin-to-skin contact. Otherwise, my body would combust. I eased my hand down her arm, grazing the soft skin, and interlocked our fingers.

The second we touched, my body electrified, and the lavender vein thickened, forming a small hollow knot inside my heart. The bond. It was working. The prophecy was solidifying. I stumbled backward, and Sierra paused, waiting for me to catch my breath.

Once I got a grip on myself, we headed toward the limo.

On our ride home, we talked about the organization. I confessed to having chosen it because she had. I left out how I already knew what organization she'd choose and how this whole event had been based around it. She blushed when I told her and squeezed my hand tighter.

For the rest of the journey, Sierra told me everything about her mom. Enamored by her words and openness, I nodded as she spoke.

Outside the dorm, I gazed into her eyes and placed my hands on her cheeks. Her breath hitched, her gaze lingering on my lips. She wanted me to kiss her, but I couldn't. The kiss had to be of her volition, and I needed it to happen. Now. So, I tempted her by moving closer, staring deeply into her eyes, silently pleading with her to make a move.

Besides another intake of breath, she didn't move, and there was definitely no kiss involved. "Thank you for taking me out tonight and listening to my stories. Have a good night." She smiled. "I can't wait for tomorrow," she added, before turning away and climbing out of the limo.

My chest grew heavy, and I rubbed the area where my

heart should've been. Sierra was everything I never dared to dream about. Did I dare now? I shouldn't. Until I figured out how to save her from the all-seeing bracelet that was now tracking us, I remained the *bad boy* who would destroy her, the one who didn't deserve her. After all, I had killed her father.

Thirty Seven

The clock was ticking.

This was my last shot. My last chance. If she didn't kiss me after tonight's extravaganza, we were all doomed. Everyone in this realm, my realm, the entire universe, would be shit out of luck. It would be an apocalypse. A doomsday.

My breathing became raspy, and my throat constricted. I had to stop these thoughts. Sierra still had twenty minutes before I was supposed to pick her up, but I couldn't handle being out of her presence a second longer. I'd wait by her door, like usual.

The second I portaled to her door, still invisible, an older, unfamiliar female voice spoke from the other side. The hairs on my arms stood on end. Who was in there with her and why?

Before doing anything rash, I placed my ear against the door and listened.

They were discussing what they thought tonight's plans were. In between the date conversation, they mentioned their past adventures together. Whoever this person was, she'd known Sierra for a while. I released a breath. It wasn't one of Mother's minions.

Since she still had time before our date, I paced along the corridor.

At six twenty-nine, one minute before we were due to meet, I turned visible and walked to her door. Two minutes later, she hadn't stepped out. Still wanting to give her time with whoever she was with, I waited, even though every second set me more on edge. Thirteen minutes later, when she hadn't come to the door, my anxious thoughts took over, driving me mad, and my lungs froze.

What if she was backing out? I couldn't have that, so I pressed my ear to the door again.

This time, the unknown person talked about how proud she was of Sierra.

My lavender heart returned without me touching her. She was still going through with the evening. The hold-up seemed to be that they'd lost track of time and were having a heart-to-heart.

Not wanting to be rude, but knowing we were in a time crunch, I knocked.

When the door swung open, the unknown woman came into view. Her long blonde hair and brownish-yellow eyes brightened as she studied me. A hidden aura radiated from her, sending scents of roses into the air with a random gush of wind. It was like a summer breeze on a muggy day. It was magic. She was from Climakru—there was no way that she wasn't.

Everything inside me turned to stone. Our reactions mimicked each other. Recognition of who we were and where we came from had us narrowing our eyes, lips pressed flat, and jaws rigid. The tension in the room intensified, and the air vanished where I stood. A low, intense growl escaped my lips, but her expression didn't waver.

We threw silent threats at each other just as Sierra appeared, her eyebrows knitting together.

Even though I caught Sierra's expression from the corner of my eye, my focus didn't move from the unknown female. I'd seen her before. At first, that thought didn't bother me because I remembered her silhouette from Sierra's journal picture. This was her nanny. But a new memory came now after sensing her aura—this woman was in many photos with Sierra's birth mother, Queen Rosalida.

This woman meant something to Rosalida. Maybe they'd sent her with Sierra when they'd brought her here. They wanted to ensure someone from their kingdom watched over her. But if this woman had been here with Sierra for the last seventeen years, she shouldn't know who I was.

Based on her reaction, she either knew or could feel the magic around me and realized it contradicted her warm, cozy aura. Our showdown could go one of two ways: the woman could confess everything to Sierra and convince her to stay away, or she'd have to try another tactic.

Lucky for me, the former option was least likely because if what Vilo had said was true, if anyone forced her to believe, it could destroy her.

So, it'd be the latter.

Sierra screamed as she tripped on her petticoat. She reached for the wall, but she was too far away. Air became trapped within my lungs, and the tension in the room disappeared as the female and I kept Sierra from face-planting.

"Sorry, this is all my fault." My chin trembled. "I forgot not everyone wears petticoats and corsets."

"It's okay. Sometimes, I have two left feet and trip over myself. Thank you both for being my wonderful knights and catching me." Sierra smiled widely, and from how she looked at me made it hard to hold on to the negative feelings.

"Tarus, I presume. Would you mind waiting in the hall so

I may put Sierra in her gown and place the final additions on her? We won't take long." Her tone was super dismissive.

My insides twisted into knots as I quickly glanced at Sierra. "I shall wait for you." I bowed and walked out.

Deep down, I knew every word I spoke went far beyond this day. No matter what, I'd wait for Sierra. Unsure in what sense, but I'd wait until my last dying breath.

Her nanny held all the cards at this stage, and I didn't want to give her a reason to deal the deck against me. So, I took her hidden message and waited in the hall, far enough from the door that I wouldn't be tempted to listen in.

Thirty minutes passed, and my heart shattered. It was over. I was going to become the monster I dreaded. Tiny black sparks from the bracelet began to ignite on my wrist. Mother's mist stirred, her pet ready to take over, and there was nothing I could do about it.

Thirty Eight

Sweat drenched my suit, and my lungs constricted. Mother was truly watching us. The sparks were a reminder of that. Nothing else explained why the bracelet would react six hours ahead of schedule. With this blasted thing on me, the added tracker, and Mother's warning that I wasn't alone, there was no way we'd make it to Lukita. The blocks were piling high against us.

Unable to breathe, I yanked the collar away from my neck.

To top everything off, I'd found out Sierra's nanny was from Climakru. She knew something. No wonder she'd visited Sierra today, of all days.

Wrapped in thoughts of what that could mean, I barely heard the wooden door creak open.

"You both have fun tonight. Sierra, remember to stay safe and be careful ..." The rest of the nanny's words faded as if whispered.

I shook myself out of my trance the moment my eyes landed on Sierra, and the sparks slipped back into the bracelet.

The shattered bits of my heart fused back together, all the

glass shards connecting like puzzle pieces. Once it was complete, the light lavender bond formed without me even having to touch Sierra. It looked more magnificent than it ever had before.

My knees wobbled under the intensity of it all. Emotions I'd buried long ago surfaced. My chest ached as if being stabbed. To stop the guilt that was pushing through, I tucked a loose strand of hair behind Sierra's ear.

The instant our skin touched, my breathing leveled off.

Sierra blushed and gave me a quick once-over. My outfit was literally the exact one Prince Henry wore from *Ever After*: a white top with gold stitching and black bottoms.

Her outfit looked even more stunning than I'd expected. The dress fit her perfectly. Her hair was identical to how Danielle had worn hers. She braided it on the top, creating a crown. And her makeup was elegant with added glitter. Her face shone like a thousand diamonds. Behind her, the long translucent wings sparkled, and I couldn't help but imagine her as the true queen I hoped she might one day be. Sierra, the Queen of Climakru. She was too good to be true.

"You're the most breathtaking woman I've ever met. I'm honored to be escorting you tonight." I bowed low and held out my arm, ready for her.

She curtseyed and took it.

On the ride to the venue, Sierra's presence had me hypnotized, but in the back of my mind, something kept eating at me. I'd seen Sierra many times, observed her in extravagant outfits, even in winged attire the night of *Stripped Galaxy*. In those moments, the recently formed bond had never appeared without us touching.

Did it have something to do with her nanny being there and clearly having magic?

My mind kept shifting through every scenario to explain the reaction, but I had no idea what had changed. All I was certain about was that the nanny had a hand in it, because once we were in the limo, out of her vicinity, the bond had dulled and cracks had formed. Was that a sign? Would my plan fail, no matter what? Would I become a monster tonight?

Music from the venue thundered loudly, reverberating through the limo.

Ready to get the show on the road, I took her hand. "Close your eyes."

Without a second thought, she shut them. Her trust in me made the bond crack even further.

"Sierra, I hope you don't mind, but I researched your adopted family and learned about this event." I helped her out of the car and led her to the entrance. "From everything I learned about you, I thought this would be perfect. You may open your eyes."

Holding on to her made the lavender vein burn brightly, but when she looked at me first, the moon's glow shining on her face, a visible piece of my heart shattered. Even though a lot was happening in front of her, and her curiosity was overwhelming her, she chose to look at me before anything else. Shit. I wished that encouraged me, but with everything building, twisting deep inside my chest, my gut, and my head, I took it as a bad sign.

She smiled and turned to study our surroundings.

We stood in front of a beautiful three-story mansion, which stretched far to our left and right. Golden gates with angels mounted on them blocked the entrance.

Bewilderment clouded her features as she kept blinking.

When her smile spread wide, I knew she'd seen the banner, *American Craniofacial Association Halloween Gala*. The place

I'd chosen was none other than the organization her adoptive dad had co-founded. The organization was for kids born with facial anomalies and helped pay for the surgeries they needed.

This was the gala she had in her journal.

"How did you find out about this? The tickets must have cost a fortune. This is too much ... I can't believe it. I-I don't know what to say." Her brown eyes sparked all five of the elemental colors—red, green, blue, yellow, and purple—as she gazed up at me in awe.

I almost gasped. Could her magic be waking? Maybe all wasn't lost. Gods, my emotions were on a roller coaster.

"It sounds to me like you have a lot to say or at least, many questions," I joked, placing my arm out to escort her into the venue. She obliged and let the questions go.

As we made our way through the entrance, her heels clicking on the white marble floor, I could see why Sierra wanted to attend a gala. There were crystal chandeliers, a piano and violinist next to the stairs, and a dance floor in the right corner where people engaged in a waltz.

Ushers in different colored tuxes lined the walls, leading to the silver velvet carpeted stairs with gold spindles and rails. Sierra walked to them with a skip to her step, her smile growing wider.

Past the stairs, the ushers opened the tall, wooden, carved double doors into another room containing a bar, round tables, booths, and another dance floor, where an instrumental band played in the corner. I led her to one of the booths.

"I'll be back with some drinks." I smiled.

Sierra didn't drink alcohol, but she had said that some events would classify as an exception. Not knowing if this was one of them, I flirted with the bartender to give me one alcoholic beverage and one juice.

Two unambiguous identities so she could choose what glass flute to take.

No pressure from me.

I approached her, drinks held out, with my head cocked to the side. She chose the sparkling pink champagne. For several minutes, we drank and watched those around us.

Sierra's expression danced with admiration and wonder as she observed those in the center dancing the waltz. When she couldn't look away, I realized it was her turn. Maybe taking her out onto the dance floor would move me one step closer to the kiss we desperately needed to share.

Once the next song started, I placed my glass down and turned to her. I bowed low, one meant for a queen, and held my hand out to her. "May I have this dance?"

Just like a queen, she lightly placed her hand in mine.

I spun her onto the dance floor in one fluid movement.

She batted her eyelashes as I grasped her right hand and eased my other behind her back, below her wings. She jumped at my touch and gulped. I followed the other dancers, waltzing in circles around the perimeter. As the song finished, I spun her out, brought her back into my arms, and dipped her to the left. Her eyes flickered with different elemental colors, and my heart galloped.

The next song switched to a slower tempo. I pulled Sierra back in, the distance between our chests nonexistent. Her lavender scent wafted up, warming my body. She kept her eyes on me as we danced. The butterflies in my stomach fluttered in chaotic patterns, and everything else ceased to exist.

At the song's chorus, the beat picked up, and I flipped Sierra around, her back against my chest. She held my hands tighter and rested her head against me.

Once the song ended, she kissed my neck. Shivers spread down my spine, and I led her back to the booth. A piece of the bond crystalized into a bright lavender hue, something that only happened when the mated pair was forming one. It was true. Everything about the prophecy. I had a mate. Me. The devil's son. I wanted to scream, to dance, to kiss her.

"How do you know how to dance like this?" Sierra asked.

"Years and years of practice. All so I could dance with you." I beamed.

For the rest of the night, we rotated between dancing and talking in the booth.

"Is it time for me to learn the answers to the last two questions from my note?" She blushed again.

I bit my lip, unsure if I should answer or wait as planned. I took a moment to respond. "Not yet, but I'll tell you by the end of the night. The wait will be worth it. I'll get us another drink."

I kissed her hand and walked to the bar. The whole way to the counter, my lips tingled from the touch. Even more reason for a drink. This time, I needed alcohol. The bracelet was burning my wrist as we neared the night's end.

A few feet from the booth, a dark figure appeared next to our table, dressed in a slim-fitting, velvet-black slip. Darcy.

My chest tightened, and I glanced at my ghadee. We still had two hours. I ground my teeth and glared at her. Stupid bracelet tracker.

She winked and tapped at her ghadee as she mouthed, *tick tock*.

With an even greater sense of urgency, I touched Sierra's shoulder, pulling her attention away from the dancers. "Let us leave now because I have one more stop for us. I know you'll love it. We can't miss it," I said with forced excitement to mask my genuine fear and dread.

I chugged my drink for the courage I needed to continue.

"Lead the way, handsome." She grinned.

If only she knew what I was leading her to, she wouldn't be so eager. Where we were going, there'd be no turning back.

Her life would never be the same the minute we crossed this threshold, whether this went according to plan or not.

Thirty Nine

Before stepping out of the limo, I stared into her beautiful brown eyes and sent a silent prayer to Deesse. *Please let this work*. One foot on the grass, I held out my hand to her. "Will you trust me one more time?" She nodded, and I almost crumbled to the floor, knowing this might be the last time she ever agreed to trust me. "Close your eyes."

When our hands connected and she followed me onto the grass, the bond completely fractured, slamming into my chest. The fragments stung me in thousands of places.

I'd have fallen at the pain if it weren't for her hand in mine.

Without the kiss, this would destroy me, but no matter the end result, I had to continue. I had to believe she'd kiss me so I wouldn't have to drug her to use magic. I tapped my pocket with the vial inside. It jingled, and I cringed as a shock wave of pain blasted through every muscle. It seemed the curse didn't like the idea of me using it just as much as I despised the plan.

Instead of screaming, I focused on what I knew was true. The prophecy. The bond forming was proof. Which meant this was all in Sierra's hands now. Once she kissed me and her magic awakened, I could take her to the Gateway. A safer, better option than the one with Mother. Once at the Gateway, I'd have time to help her believe in herself and her role. Hopefully, she'd also learn how to keep us safe from Mother.

Leading her to the surprise, I said, "Ever since I met you, I've always wanted to do the typical cliché thing. To have a picnic, but in this case, dessert and champagne underneath the stars and to dance the night away. You may open your eyes."

Her jaw dropped as she took in the scene.

Earlier, I had prepared a perfect date in the park with a picnic basket filled with dessert and champagne on top of a red and white checkerboard blanket. On the left of the picnic basket, against the tree, sat an old-fashioned portable music box.

Right here, right now, would she realize she loved me, kiss me, and, in turn, change everything? My ultimate goal. Maybe once her magic awakened, the bond would form within her, completing the mating ritual. Specks of it had to be there since a piece of my bond to her had crystallized before the bond shattered.

She grabbed my hand and ran to the picnic blanket. Owls hooted a soft melody in the branches above, and the night sky, full of twinkling stars, created a perfect canopy.

"Thank you for everything you've done for me." She picked up a strawberry.

Her words melted my still heart. She was all I'd ever wanted. And man, did I want her. I glanced down at my wrist, where the suit covered the bracelet. If only life had dealt me different cards. "It's been my pleasure."

She brought the strawberry to her mouth, her luscious lips forming around it. My libido spiked, and my face flushed. I tightened my grip on the blanket, and she removed the strawberry. "Before we dance, I must have the last two answers." She batted her eyelashes. "Please."

"Fine." I groaned. I didn't want to talk—especially about sad things. I wanted to kiss. But if this made her connect with me and draw us closer to the goal, so be it. "One of your questions was: Why do you not like talking about yourself?"

She leaned against the tree.

"It's because I never cared to get to know anyone. Since I was five, no one taught me to love, care, or make friends. Instead, power was all anyone taught me. With this type of power, there was no room for love. Not in the world where I was raised. Having power and no love, I didn't have a reason to know anyone. When I met you, I felt things I'd never known before, most specifically guilt. Guilt about the things I had to do and about something I wish I didn't have to."

Instead of being bothered by my words and scooting away, she wrapped her arm around my shoulders. "If you don't want to do something, you don't have to." The lavender vein flickered. It, along with me, couldn't decide how to feel about her words. "You have free will."

"I wish that were true."

She raised her eyebrows.

"Enough about sad things. Your second question. My nickname is Taran." Truth, to a point. She smiled. "Now, tell me, what is your favorite part of the entire night?" I turned my head toward her, our faces centimeters apart, our breaths hitching in sync.

"Being with you, of course." Her cheeks flamed crimson.

Warmth spread through me. "Thank you for finally saying yes to me."

"Thank you for not giving up." She bit her lip and inched closer. This was it. "One more dance?" She pulled away.

Holy Delmore! We were so close.

"Of course." I stood and with forced footsteps, dragged

myself to the music box to play a perfect song for dancing. I poured our champagne into the glasses, and as I spiked hers with a sleeping potion, the pieces of my heart vanished.

It was gone.

A lone tear escaped, and I brushed it away as I turned and gave her the glass.

We clinked them, saying cheers. For once, with Sierra, my enthusiasm was fake.

Afterward, I pulled Sierra up to dance. The moonlight shone on her wings, and a rainbow bounced off the mesh fabric. It highlighted the colorful sparkle in her eyes.

Bravery must have hit her because she chugged her drink and squished herself against my body. The lavender vein formed all the way to my chest, but no outline of a heart reappeared, and the string had shredded pieces poking out.

She leaned closer, her lips centimeters from mine, but before she could do anything, the music changed to a sad ballroom melody. The piece didn't fit the mood.

She eased away to dance.

I couldn't lose the opportunity. This was supposed to be the mega event in the fairy tale, where the princess and the monster had true love's kiss, and all the power in the magical realm changed because of their love. I needed that to happen now. She was so close.

I glanced down, taking her in, and with my hand on her back, I pulled her toward me again. She stared up in awe, and I gulped. *Deesse, please let her kiss me, pl* ... Sierra's lips slammed against mine, and everything came alive inside of me.

Instead of the lavender vein attacking me, the shards repaired themselves. Pieces of my heart and the bond reappeared from hidden places, coming alive again. All the other veins in my body flashed in different colors as an electric charge blasted through me.

The kiss, a simple meeting of our lips, was nothing I'd ever dreamed of or imagined.

Nothing had ever tasted this sweet and felt so right. I needed more. I wanted more. My body demanded it. About to deepen the kiss, I smiled under her lips as she grabbed my collar, pulling me closer, and her lips parted, her tongue finding mine. I groaned, and her body shook.

This moment was perfect—we were perfect—and darkness no longer had a hold on me. Nothing was there but the two of us, like one person, and the lavender bond grew bigger and brighter, glowing at such an intensity, it hurt to peek at it.

Another second of this, and everything would be right in the world.

But before it could happen, the smell of musky jasmine wafted over, and Sierra slipped from my grasp and fell to the ground with a loud thud.

"You don't get to have a happy ending." Darcy wrapped her hands around Sierra's neck, and Sierra's normal, non-magical eyes widened.

Everything vanished—the bond, my heart, my happiness. Darcy was going to kill Sierra, and neither of us could stop her. Sierra's magic hadn't awoken. The prophecy wasn't real or Darcy's appearance here, breaking the kiss, had changed things.

Hands up in surrender, I approached Darcy. But that pissed her off, and she spat at Sierra.

Sierra screamed bloody murder, her torment and fear slicing me apart.

Darcy growled and covered Sierra's mouth with her free hand.

Sierra kicked at the ground and clawed at Darcy's arm, but she was too strong—especially when the drug was weakening Sierra. Shit.

My knees wobbled. "Do not hurt her. I swear to gods, Mother would never forgive you."

"She'd never know." Darcy tightened her grip around Sierra's throat, causing her to gag.

"Have you forgotten about the bracelet she spies through?" I pulled up my sleeve and showcased the ancient wristlet.

Sierra's eyes narrowed, and she bit Darcy.

Darcy screamed and threw Sierra against the tree. She hit it so hard that it broke in half, the top collapsing onto her. Blood gushed from a gash on her head as her eyes fluttered closed.

"What the hell did you do?"

"Punished her." Darcy shrugged.

My magic flamed alive. Sierra was unconscious. It'd work now. I portaled to Darcy and shoved her to the ground, my knee digging into her throat. "I should kill you."

"Go ahead, try." She choked as she raked her claws down my thigh. "But I'll kill you first." With a strength I never knew her capable of, she flipped us over, her hands now at my throat.

The bracelet burned my wrist, and I trembled underneath her.

Darcy's grip tightened, and an idea struck me. As she chuckled, I fluttered my eyelashes, attempting to give the appearance of passing out. The more my head wobbled, the more demonic her laugh became. I used that opportunity to slip past her defenses and find the vein I needed. She'd spot me in seconds, so I needed to make it quick. "Faint."

Her body went slack, her grip loosened, and her eyes shut as she toppled over.

Yes! I rushed to Sierra and flung the tree off her. Blood and dirt caked her face. I yanked off a piece of my shirt and rubbed it against her skin, cleaning away the dirt. A thick green bruise surrounded the deep gash leading from her forehead to her lip.

Her chest slowly rose, and her heartbeat grew fainter. Shit.

Tears streamed down my face. I needed to get her to Lukita. She'd heal her. She needed Sierra alive to break her curse.

I glanced at the bracelet, and Mother's *pet* stirred. She was watching and didn't seem thrilled. Thank the gods she couldn't reach this realm, or I'd be dead.

I checked the time. Midnight. Though I had one hour left, Mother could activate the bracelet at any second. I needed to hurry.

With Sierra in my arms, I portaled back to Hillshite. I placed her on the bed, ran to the desk, and took the hacksaw I'd bought earlier from the drawer. Every muscle trembled. Sweat dripped from every orifice, and a nasty stench filled the air.

I ripped a section of the sheet off the bed and stuffed it in my mouth. Unable to do anything noticeable that the mist, or Mother, might catch on to, I placed my hand on Sierra's, hoping they'd suspect I planned to do something to her.

They might be mad, but they wouldn't question me.

Holy Delmore. This was really happening.

I couldn't breathe.

I could barely focus.

But I managed and counted to three.

On three, I placed my hand on the nightstand next to Sierra and used my other to control the thin-bladed hacksaw. As the tool hacked through my skin, sawing through my bones, my mind fogged, and my deafening screams escaped the sheet bundled in my mouth.

People banged at my door, and a black mist swirled out of the bracelet. It tried to find places to sink into my skin. As the tendrils of mist pounced, and the humans said they were bringing in reinforcements, the saw blade finally hit wood.

My severed hand rolled off the nightstand and thumped onto the floor.

Pain and blood gushed from the stump.

I ripped off the bracelet and threw it in the drawer before wrapping my stump with the sheets. With Sierra tucked under my arm, my free hand holding Lukita's *present*, I portaled to the Gateway. Once there, I stepped into the circle.

Rushed, and not yet in the clear, I used my stump to rub blood on the five symbols. As I worked, I stumbled, eyes blurring, the loss of blood affecting me. My magic couldn't heal this.

Pressing my stump to my chest, I screamed, "I am Tartarus Obsidian of Astal! I am no longer the queen's bodyguard or in allegiance with her. My heart is shattered."

"Do you have the gift I demanded last time? If not, you were foolish to return." Lukita's voice roared in the dark, creepy forest. Branches swayed at the magnitude of her voice, and they grew closer to me like extensions of her.

"Yes." I tilted my head at my mutilated hand on the floor.

"The bracelet?"

"Not here."

"Good. You understood my clue. Now, Tartarus, I'd ask if you wanted passage to a realm or a request, but I already know you're here because of my offer. If I'm not mistaken, you didn't fulfill the requirement. So, why did you come, risking everything? Remember that your words must be true in this circle."

"I came to beg for your help. Sierra makes me come alive, and though my role in the prophecy might've changed, I know she's the realm's savior. After what you showed me, I believe that Mother is the dark soul in the prophecy. If Sierra ends up in Mother's hands, you and I both know chaos will erupt." My voice shook.

The core of the matter was that regardless of Sierra's feelings for me, and whether I was still the powerful warrior, I couldn't let Mother have her. Not after she had killed Vilo and I realized her true colors.

Mother wouldn't think twice about killing Sierra. She knew that Sierra was a weapon. Just not a weapon *for* her, but *against* her.

"You didn't awaken her magic. Maybe your kiss almost formed a bond, but it didn't awaken her, and I don't think it will anymore. Without her magic, she can't protect the Gateway. The queen eventually will find this place even if we move it. When she does, she'll figure out a way to break through. I can't provide safety for us—only Sierra can. If her magic isn't awake, Climakru will become worse once the queen finds her betrayer and the weapon you've denied her. So, what benefit is there for me to help you?"

Her words stung. Lukita was a sphinx. She saw glimpses of the future. Which meant it had to be true—Darcy had changed the prophecy. I was no longer the warrior, but that didn't mean I couldn't find other ways to awaken her magic. I could still help her and the realms.

"Give me time. There is a book in the palace with several spells I can use to awaken Sierra's magic. Just her being in here should help. This space has magic. Even with a spell hiding hers, magic speaks to magic—especially when it's in a space bursting with it. I'll also train her and help her become comfortable with it. We'll find a way, and I promise, somehow, her magic will ignite by the time she leaves this cave. But regardless of whether you help me, please heal Sierra. She is dying."

A gold mist swirled around Sierra for several seconds. Once it lifted, I gasped. Sierra's face was clear, and her breathing had returned to normal. I fell to my knees and clutched her tightly to my chest.

"Thank you, Lukita. Does this mean you'll help us?" My words slurred, my brain fogging from the loss of blood.

"Help me fix your hand before you die. Then, we shall continue this conversation." As she finished speaking, a complete set of surgeon's equipment appeared out of thin air, on a cloud of smoke, next to me. I gaped at the equipment and blinked. I didn't know what to do. "Place your hand on the stump. I'll mend it."

I did as she said. The moment I aligned the bones, magical invisible hands touched my skin and sewed the ligaments together. The odor of burned flesh assaulted my nose and pain radiated throughout. My mouth tasted foreign, my senses overloading as I concentrated on breathing to avoid passing out.

Once she finished, I wiggled my fingers on both hands. "Thank you."

An eerie silence followed. No birds chirped in the distance. The wind stood still, the branches unmoving. With each second that ticked by, I worried she might've changed her mind about possibly helping us.

"Hurry up and get in here. We have five minutes to hide this place before the queen arrives," Lukita said as the vault creaked open and the stairs appeared.

Forty One

From the moment I settled Sierra on the freezing floor, fear drove me. Lukita and I worked in a state of frenzy as we placed spells throughout the cave. She gave me the enchantment, and I worked the magic. I was happy she knew the incantations that would move us to an unknown area, even if we would only remain hidden for so long.

I cast the last spell, shaking uncontrollably.

Breathless and exhausted from all the effort, I leaned against the cold cave wall as Lukita spoke in a devastated, heart-wrenching tone. "Tartarus, because of the pixie's curse on you and Sierra, I can't speak with her. I'm only a voice until she breaks my curse. She won't understand a voice talking to her. Even if I could speak to her, my magic is under the same rules as whoever resides inside."

"How do I wake her, then?" I collapsed, knees landing heavily, and rested my head against the stone. Without an opening, the dark blue cave cast little illumination onto the shiny, smooth floor.

"Like you mentioned at the vault, you're going to have to

use a spell. You can still use my magic to help you without her knowing. Just like you used my magic to cast the spells, you can have me bring you any books you can remember that might help. But I can't make myself known to Sierra, perform any type of magic in front of her, or heal her again. That skirted the rules of the curse and has cost me. But it was something I don't regret."

Shit. I gulped. "How did it cost you?"

"It's not something I can share."

"I understand." I should've slit Darcy's throat for ruining things.

"Tartarus, while you're working for the love of all the realms and Sierra, I'll let you come and go freely. You can also make the cave grow in whatever way you want. Anything you desire regarding an object or a landscape, all you have to do is ask. The sky is the limit with this cave's magic, for the most part, and since I live inside the walls, I have unlimited access to it, unless it pertains to my freedom or breaking the rules of your curse."

"What about keeping Sierra unconscious while I look for spells? Can you do that?"

"Yes."

"Thank you."

Before I started on a plan, I spent a few precious moments trying to make Sierra comfortable, but it hadn't eased my guilt. No position or thing that I did changed the torment that raged inside me. I'd destroyed her life. I'd kidnapped her. I was evil. Why did I ever believe the stupid prophecy would come true? Vilo had said it could change, and Darcy ensured it had. Lucifer's son couldn't have happiness.

Now, the only way to wake her magic was through cheating, which could cause a disastrous ending for us all. Maybe Darcy had turned me into the dark soul. Tears rushed down my cheeks as I gripped the broken pieces of Slinger.

Lukita coughed. "Do you have a plan in mind? Is there anything you need?"

In my studies, there had been a spell I once learned about making hidden things seen. Starting there would be an excellent idea. After I told Lukita everything I needed, it appeared on a cloud of smoke.

To accommodate the amount of equipment I'd use, I needed another room. I passed this on to Lukita, and the cave moved, rocks shifted, dust blew everywhere, and things parted until another room emerged. The walls were glossy limestone, the room was about the size of a classroom, and in the middle was a rock raised high, the perfect height for Sierra to rest on while I worked over her. I asked Lukita to place Sierra on a mattress fitted with silk sheets, and she obliged.

She even constructed a thin wooden door between the two rooms, closing them off from one another. If it wasn't for the stress about waking Sierra's magic, and the fact I'd betrayed the only person I ever thought loved me, I'd have laughed. But tensions were high, and joy was nowhere close.

I made Sierra comfortable in the bed and brought everything into the room so I could work. Lukita placed white metal desks around the room, scattered with potions, tubes, and glasses. She even added a small bookshelf and a reclining chair in the corner for me.

With everything in place, I chalked a casting circle around the stone bed, then worked on a sleeping potion just in case she woke. Once finished, I moved on to the mixtures for the spell and the words I needed to chant.

Deep into the chant, and whilst stirring the mixture, a loud gasp sounded from behind me.

Not possible. Sierra shouldn't be awake.

The magic Lukita had cast on her was to keep her unconscious, unless her magic awoke or I woke her. Could her magic be that strong? Enough to overpower the Gateway's? I didn't have time to wrack my brain around it. I needed to put her back to sleep.

As I walked over to her, I kept repeating, "I am sorry." I uncapped the sleeping potion and blew it in her face. Her body went limp, and she collapsed into my arms.

After placing her back into a comfortable position, I returned to the spell. Once satisfied, I cast it on Sierra.

A scarlet force field grew, encircling Sierra's body. Several billion red lights buzzed and shifted around to keep the shield ablaze. Slowly, the lights faded into light pink until the force field vanished, and her veins appeared as if visible on her skin. They were every color important to Climakru, the five element wielders: red, blue, green, yellow, and purple. Where there was a connection of veins, rainbow hues shone. A dark mass twisted near her brain and heart. I couldn't see the veins where the black resided, only a sharp-edged blue and pink outline— possibly the hidden place of the original spell concealing her magic.

I took a deep breath. How could I remove those blocks?

While I committed the image to memory, everything returned to normal.

The spell had only lasted five minutes, but that was enough time. I now had something to work with.

Forty Two

For four days, I went back and forth to different libraries on Earth.

When I arrived back at the Gateway, I reclined in the chair near Sierra and read the books Lukita had summoned from Climakru's library. I read everything possible from both realms about the element wielders, spells, magic, and the great divide.

One rather ancient book had a spell that seemed important. It wouldn't help with Sierra's magic or beliefs, but it might prove useful in other ways. The incantation created a barrier around someone that magic couldn't penetrate. It required just a simple phrase and almost all of the caster's concentration. So, I memorized the phrase just in case.

Several other spells inside the ancient tome and other books looked beneficial to Sierra's predicament. I tried them, but none made the tiniest of breakthroughs. Sierra even woke up many times during this period, and each time, a bitter taste coated my tongue as I apologized and gave her juice before putting her under again.

When I finally stumbled upon something promising, a tingling sensation traveled down my spine. Over a thousand years ago, there had been a myth that two powerful royals feared a particular type of magic, so they bound it to a spell—the first recorded two-part incantation. One part tied the magic and hid it entirely, while the second part was for the magic to become visible. The creature under the spell had to not only believe, but also had to accept it.

Was this the reason why Sierra's magic hadn't awoken when we kissed? It wasn't because of Darcy. It was because Sierra also had to believe in it. Had Lukita known that, and was that why she'd said she didn't think a kiss would work? But if she'd caught a glimpse of us kissing and Sierra's magic not coming to life, she couldn't have known why.

If a kiss wouldn't work and Sierra had to believe in her magic, herself, and her role, that could pose a problem. It would take time and a lot of convincing for her to accept it, especially since the curse prevented Lukita and I from showing her. We didn't have time on our side. So, though this gave me hope that Darcy hadn't changed my role in the prophecy, the fact I'd continue to throw spells at Sierra to wake her magic could still turn me into the dark soul.

For the rest of the day, I searched for ways to break a two-part spell. It turned out that information was much harder to find because people rarely undertook the challenge. It required a wielder from each of the four main groups to cast the spell, and getting every element wielder to agree on something was difficult when they'd split in half and hadn't worked together since the great divide of Climakru.

By the night's end, I'd found a potential way to break the spell, which called for three things: a piece of someone with pure intentions to help, a sign of a union bonded or close to it, and the blood from a creature unseen since before the multi-realm war.

After a lot of debate on where they could come from, I only managed to figure out two. First, my heart had pure intentions to help, so I snipped off a few pieces of my hair, and for good measure, sliced off a piece of skin from my thigh. Second, Sierra had almost completed the mating bond, yet mine had formed, so I thought about a sign proving my loyalty.

The only option I could think of that had the least risk was to use the wings from her Halloween dress. While cutting away at the fabric, I found a note tucked into the fold between the wings. I placed it in my pocket for later and returned to the spell. The more important thing was waking her up—the letter could wait.

As for the final piece of the spell, I was stumped. I yanked at my hair, pulling it in fistfuls. I was so close. I threw the book, and it hit the wall with a loud thud.

"Ouch." Lukita chuckled.

"Now is not the time for jokes." I groaned.

"Stop being so daft, and maybe I wouldn't have to chime in."

"Daft? How dare—" My blood sizzled.

"Tartarus, what is Sierra?"

"A seer?" Why did this matter? I ground my teeth.

"When was the last time you've seen one besides her?"

They hadn't existed for years, since before the multi-realm war. Holy Delmore. I *was* daft. "Thanks, Lukita." I sliced Sierra's palm and squeezed her blood into the mixture.

As I walked in circles around her, I chanted. Each time I passed her, I chanted louder. I pushed everything I had into believing this spell would work.

Out of nowhere, an unbearable pain radiated from my manhood. Teary-eyed, I looked down. Sierra was awake, and her hand was squeezing tightly onto my balls. Agony filled my lungs, and I changed from chanting to screaming. She glared into my eyes, spat at me, dropped her hold, and sprinted to the wooden door.

I fell to the cold stone floor, hands cupped between my legs, trying to ease the pain. There was no need for me to go after her. Magical barriers would contain her within seconds.

She approached the outline of the casting circle, and the force field flung her backward. Once she was on the floor and my pain had dissipated some, I hobbled over, repeating, "I am sorry," before blowing the sleeping potion into her face. Within seconds, she passed out.

Fear crippled me as I flopped down beside her. Something was dangerously wrong. Her eyes hadn't shut this time, and staring back at me was a gaze of bright white orbs, like a pair of crystal quartz balls. Either I'd blinded her, or this was her true identity. If the latter, her eyes shouldn't be white, at least not permanently.

This turn of events might've meant the spell had gone wrong, or maybe when she'd intervened, it had changed the dynamics.

Over the next few hours, I spent every waking opportunity searching for ways to fix what had happened. I performed a few more spells, but Sierra's eyes didn't change.

I broke several of the potions on the desks surrounding her bed, threw the books against the stone cave walls, and screamed at the top of my lungs. If Sierra didn't already hate me for kidnapping her without an explanation, causing her to lose her eyesight would do the trick. With her hatred for me, I might not be able to break through her barrier and make her believe. She'd want to stay far away from me forever, and I wouldn't blame her.

"Tartarus, we keep moving the Gateway to different locations to hide from your mother. Soon, she's going to find us. We're running out of time. We need to wake Sierra, train her, and see if something will spark."

"What if it doesn't?" I dropped to the floor and leaned back against the wall. The cold rock bothered my skin. Instead of shivering like usual, it burned me and itched everywhere it touched. "What if she refuses to talk to me? Without telling her the truth, I don't have any good excuse as to why I kidnapped her."

"You're going to have to come up with an alternate plan."

"Like what? Without Sierra, there is no other plan."

"There might be …" Lukita's voice grew distant, almost inaudible.

Whatever this alternate plan could be, if it made Lukita quiet, I probably wouldn't like it. But the thought of Sierra dying or being corrupted into darkness was more than I could handle.

"You know your star? Slinger?"

"My *destroyed* favorite possession." I curled my lips.

"It's an ancestral weapon."

"Why does that matter?" I pulled out a piece of Slinger, twirling it.

"You heard the entire prophecy. At the end, it says:

If the worst-case scenario arrives,
the ancestral secret revives
by the one who's seen the times ahead
and will help restore the realms instead.

The ancestral secret is Slinger. It can destroy your mother."

"Destroy her in what sense?"

"Death, though you'll still have to decapitate her to make it permanent. Otherwise, she can, and will, find a way back to the surface."

A chill spread down my spine. I might hate my mother, but I couldn't kill her. "Say I agreed to this—which I haven't

—do you even know who's seen the times ahead and can revive Slinger? You?" I stared at Slinger's broken body, running my finger over the blade.

"Queen Rosalida knows how to fix it."

"How do you know this?"

"One: I'm a sphinx. Two: Queen Rosalida and the king used me to hide Sierra on Earth. They confided in me because I used to be close with Aatmaeeshvar."

I blinked several times. "You knew the spirit god? That would make you thousands of years old. No way."

"Just like your mother, I'm immortal. I'm not a full sphinx. So yes, I'm that old."

"Holy Delmore!"

"Queen Rosalida shared parts of the future with me that she'd seen from Sierra at her birth. But she didn't share how to repair the star. You'll have to speak to her."

"Speak to Queen Rosalida? You have to be joking." I cringed. Meet the mother of the girl I've kidnapped? That seemed smart. Oh, and the lover of the man I'd killed? What a fantastic plan.

"What other option do you have?"

"Sierra. Please release the magic holding her asleep." I stood.

"Tartarus, the sooner you talk to Queen Rosalida, the sooner the realms will be free from the threat of extreme darkness."

"I'm done talking about this. I'm not killing Mother or speaking with someone who'd rather see me dead."

While I waited for Sierra to wake, Lukita and I worked on transforming the cave in awkward silence. We made it into a massive labyrinth and placed three bodies of water and several rooms throughout the complex. Once Sierra woke, we wanted to give her areas to explore and spaces for each of us to call our own. Make it homier, despite the fact we knew she wouldn't feel anything close to homey.

With nothing more to do but wait, I paced near the waterfall Lukita had created. It was huge for a magically made cave. The stream fell from a stone mound about four car lengths in width and a three-story building in height. It emptied into a miniature lake of aqua-blue water. Near the perimeter, the lake shallowed so one could lie in peace.

I figured this place would be an excellent spot for Sierra to mull over things and, on occasion, for me to just get away from everything, like now. While watching her, I had tried to hold it together, but with all of the uncertainty barreling in, it took everything in my power not to crumble into pieces.

Lukita had silenced the instrumental music when lifting the magic from Sierra, so being by the waterfall, surrounded by its fresh scent, and listening to droplets hit the rocks, soothed me.

After several minutes of pacing, I leaned back against the waterfall, letting the water soak my shirt, and read the letter I had stuffed in my pocket many days ago. I hadn't read it yet for fear it might break me.

It was a love note from Sierra to me. My insides twisted, and pain shot through my veins.

About to read it a second time, I jumped at a noise in the distance.

"Tarus!" the scream echoed off the walls. It took me until her second shout to realize this was real.

Sierra was awake. Severely pissed, but awake.

Forty Three

Avoiding Sierra wouldn't prevent this encounter from occurring. I needed to talk to her. But because I needed time to prepare, I walked to her cave room instead of portaling near it. With every step, I braced myself, telling myself it'd be okay. Her eyes would return to brown. They had to.

Her door was already open, her blanket tossed on the floor, and her presence absent.

My throat constricted.

One hand stroking my goatee, the other braced against the cave wall, I called for her. "Sierra! Where are you?" I repeated my call until a faint echo of my name reached my ears.

"Sierra!"

"Tarus!"

This back-and-forth happened multiple times until we were a few meters apart.

Once I turned the corner to the narrow tunnel she was in, she sighed and leaned against the wall. The torches' flames cast a faint glow on her face as she crossed her arms, tears streaming down her bright red cheeks. Sounds of her teeth grinding bounced off the cave walls.

Not knowing where to begin, I remained silent but eased in front of her. She opened her eyes, and my stomach dropped. They were still shiny white crystals.

"Tarus, what on earth is happening?" Nostrils flaring, she slid to the floor and pulled her knees to her chest.

"Sierra, I am—"

"*No*! I don't want to hear 'I am sorry' again. I'm starting to hate those words. I need answers, Tarus. Now!" She scrunched her knees closer and rested her head between them.

"Okay, I won't apologize for now. But please let me explain and ..." I expected her to yell, but she stayed silent. "... I don't know where to start or how much I'll be able to share. Losing your sight was an accident. I'm unsure if the spell ..." I held my breath, waiting for the curse to attack me, but nothing happened. "... went wrong." I guess spells, perhaps even witch stuff, didn't count as magic since they existed on Earth, which made sense as to why the sleeping potion had worked. "... or maybe it could be a reaction to you trying to escape. But I'd have already fixed it if it were that. It must be something else."

"S-S-Spell?" Sierra choked out between sobs.

I waited for her to continue, but when she kept silent, I spoke again. "I went to the library to read more about y—" An aching pain raced through my veins. The curse was still there.

Thankfully, the pain didn't last long, and I was able to pick up from where I left off and change it a bit without her noticing. "...spells and see what I'd done wrong. But nothing helped. No one had ever heard of this. At least, no one had ever read or written about anything like this happening. This made me think someone else must have put a deep spell on you. I brought you here, hoping it'd help, but still nothing has changed. Everything is the same, apart from your eyes."

I gulped, ready for her to say the worst.

"Tarus, spells? You never once made me think you practiced witchcraft."

I shouldn't have been surprised she'd gone there, but this was Sierra, and she always left me in awe. Out of everything she could've asked, the thing she chose proved the Sierra I came to know was still there. "Witchcraft?"

"What did you do to me?" Sierra's voice rose five octaves.

"I wanted to wa—" A pain like no other slammed my lips shut. After a few seconds, I tried again, "I—"

"How long have I been unconscious if you had time to go to the library?" Sierra's lips trembled.

"Five days." I let it sink in and again waited for the yelling that never came. "You woke off and on. I was able to provide you with nutrition before you passed out again."

She rubbed her temples, rocking back and forth for a while. "How come no one has found me? Are they not looking for me?" She curled in on herself and clutched her chest tight. It was so odd. Sierra hadn't reacted harshly when she'd woken up blind, learned she'd been asleep for days, or realized I'd kidnapped her. Nope. But the anguish over her loved ones not finding her important enough to search for her had wrecked her.

"They are looking for you, but it's impossible for them to find you." She needed to know she was important.

"Tarus, please let me go home. My nanny has already lost my parents. Please, I beg you, don't let her lose me, too. I won't tell anyone you were involved or about your crazy ex trying to kill me. I'll ... I'll make up a story." More tears streamed down her face, every droplet a reminder of the waterfall, each making a pitter-patter sound when hitting the cold ground.

"Sierra, I want to, but—"

"What type of witchcraft were you messing with that made me lose my eyesight?"

"Sierra, I promise my intention was never to blind you. On the contrary, I only meant to help you. I could've said something wrong when you startled me. One word, one syllable, can change a spell drastically. The long pause between the chants could have even done it." I bit the inside of my cheek to hold back the tears.

"Explain to me how you said you've been to the library to study spells and ways to help me." She lifted her reflective crystal orbs to me, eyebrows scrunched.

How could I answer that without triggering the curse? "The library doesn't have information about how to help you, per se, only things that might be similar. Finding that information proved harder than you'd anticipate. The things I searched for hadn't existed in thousands of years. Almost every book out there is just full of stories."

She shook her head as if some lunatic told unrealistic tales. Though I knew she was skeptical, she was also curious, even if she didn't believe me.

"You are a S—" I arched back, hissing between my teeth. Pain like never before seared every nerve ending, rippling up my spine. It stabbed my insides and crushed them worse than Mother's tendrils ever had. I fell to my knees with a loud thump and screamed.

"Tarus? What's happening?" Sierra shouted.

Sierra kept screaming at me, but I couldn't answer her. The pain tied every muscle in knots, burning, stabbing, squeezing, all at once. *I'll stop trying to speak against the curse.* The pain eased, and I bit my lip.

"Tarus?" Sierra screamed again. She stumbled to her feet, back against the wall.

"Damn it! I'm trying, Sierra." I punched the wall, and my bones cracked in the silence.

"Trying?" she screamed.

"I can't explain." Ugh. I took a deep breath. How could I share what I needed to? Church. She loved church. Thank heavens I'd semi-paid attention when I followed her there. "Your bible mentions Elijah and Elisha helping the kings?"

Sierra blinked. "Yes? What does that have to do with anything?"

"Pretend for a second that you're like them." I gasped. The curse had let me speak the words. Elijah and Elisha were prophets ... seers. Maybe because I told her to *pretend*, I was letting her believe what she wanted to?

Without saying a word, she stomped off, her hands in front, reaching for the wall for guidance.

The revelation of her identity must've pushed her off the train. She no longer wanted to listen. It was too hard for her to believe, and her brain block must've made it easier to think me looney.

"Where are you going? You can't see," I yelled after her.

"Right now, I don't care. I'm just going anywhere you aren't." Sierra hummed to drown out any response I might've made.

As she disappeared, I rubbed my aching chest. She needed space. This had to be a lot, and she needed time to mourn her eyesight. Besides, if I tried talking to her now, it would fall on deaf ears. She'd come to me when she was ready.

I hoped.

Hours later, she still hadn't come back, and I was tired of waiting.

I checked her cave room first. She wasn't there, but Lukita had remodeled the space. The desks and potions were gone. A painting supply case had replaced the small bookshelf. Odd. Her rock bed turned into a real one, with a wooden frame and a soft comforter, and the rocking chair still sat in the corner, with a wardrobe to its right.

"Thanks, Lukita." I smiled before returning to the search, all the while panicking over where she could have gone. Lukita and I had enlarged the cave by hundreds of feet.

I took a deep breath and listened to the noises around me. A low snore sounded in the distance. I ran in that direction.

My knees threatened to give out as I stared at Sierra. She lay asleep, in the fetal position, on the ground between two cave walls. From the look of her wet arm and the growing damp patch on the ground, it was clear she'd been crying a fountain's worth of misery.

"There you are. I looked all over for you." I spoke loudly, hoping to wake her.

She turned her body toward the wall, angling away from me. A sharp pain pierced my chest. The woman of my dreams thought me a monster.

"Please, Sierra! We must talk more about this. Do you not want your sight back? I might have an idea about how we can restore it." Her curiosity and need for answers would get her to listen. Ever so slowly, she straightened her legs and eased over to face me.

I reached over and grazed my fingertips along her hand. She took it, and I almost jumped when the iridescent vein appeared in my palm. It didn't travel to my heart, and it lacked the lavender hue, but it was back. I wanted to think about what this might mean, but I had Sierra's attention and needed to focus on that first.

"I'm going to take you to a more comfortable area where there's some soup, and we can talk more about bringing your eyesight back."

Once in the room, she felt around, familiarizing herself with her environment. After she'd explored the area, she said, "Tarus, enough with the riddles and vague responses." The color drained from her face. "How do you figure you can return my sight?"

"First, I believe your mother must have cast such a strong spell to hide—" My veins boiled, and I bit my cheek hard. What the hell? I stuck with the rules. The word *hide* shouldn't have activated the curse. I let out a deep breath and started again. "A previous spell cast on you prevented my spell from working. Not only that, but I feel like your mother must've attached a condition to it. A way to ensure that if anyone ever tried to do what I did, it would backfire. Unless you believe, you—" Holy Delmore. I fell to my knees, pain ricocheting off every nerve. "Unless you believe, you'll stay stuck in limbo, or, in other words, blind." I sighed. This was going to be much harder than I'd thought.

"You're making no sense."

"I am—"

"Don't say sorry," Sierra screamed, and I cringed.

"I'm trying to say what I can."

"Sure." She curled her legs into her chest. "Where am I? The last thing I remember clearly is Darcy trying to kill me."

A tear escaped my eyes as I plopped down beside her. "Do you remember me saying it's hard to get to know others?"

"A little."

"I lived in a home with a lot of bad people. Those people are after us. I brought you here to protect you. I couldn't tell anyone you knew, like your nanny, because the people looking for us would kill them to find that information."

Sierra panted and fanned her face. "Why is someone after us?"

"It's hard to explain." I brushed the top of her hand, but she pulled away.

"Are you into witchcraft? Are you insane?" She ground her teeth, her hands clenching into fists at her side.

"No, to both. I hope."

She stayed silent for a while. I studied her face, her every expression, afraid to breathe or look away.

"Tarus, did you know my mother?"

"Your mother isn't important right now. What is important is we get your sight back."

Her jaw tightened, and she pinched her nose as if she had heard enough of the conversation. "How am I supposed to believe this, Tarus? I can't believe anything you say. I don't trust you anymore." Her words hit hard. They were agonizing to hear, even with my inability to blame her and my understanding of why.

"I know you no longer believe me or trust me. Those

things I understand. But somehow, find it in yourself to trust me on this. You are identical to Elijah and Elisha and must believe it if you ever wish to get your sight back." Desperation clung tight to every word because my life, her life, and the realms depended on her belief.

She needed time, so I gave her a while to ruminate over everything. Also, because of the curse, she had to guide this conversation.

"Tarus, was this all just a game to you? Was everything we had a ... lie?" She choked on the last word.

As the first lone tear clung to the tip of her nose, I closed the distance and brushed it away. Her body shuddered, but my iridescent vein grew.

I caressed her cheek, watching the vein rise to my chest, when she finally found the courage to speak. With it came a newfound rage. She shoved my hand away, her clouded eyes brightening, and she screamed, "Don't touch me! You lost the right!"

I frowned and dropped my hand into my lap. Her words wrecked me.

After her outburst, we sat in silence, our raspy breaths the only sound between us.

"I believe I should go. I'll return in a little while with some food." I sniffled and added, "And Sierra, what you made me feel, and how I felt for you, was never a lie. My feelings for you are impossible to fake. They were, and still are, real."

I trudged to the waterfall, alone with my thoughts.

Left to my imagination, I dissected our conversation. Our discussion wasn't as bad as it could've been. I didn't know what I'd expected, but I feared Sierra would completely ignore me. Worse, I figured she'd be so mad, if not heartbroken, that she wouldn't even be able to tolerate my presence. Instead, she remained calm, for the most part.

Out of everything she could've asked me, she wanted to

know if this was a game. This question, along with the fact the iridescent vein had returned, had to be a sign there was still something between us, even if I turned into the prophecy's dark soul.

Future possibilities with her were definitely something I wanted, and I could sit here for hours daydreaming about it. But this path would distract me. Eventually, I'd focus solely on gaining her love, which would take me away from training and preparing her. As Lukita had said, *we were running out of time.* I needed to either return to Sierra and wake her belief or visit Queen Rosalida. My body shuddered at the latter thought.

Sierra sat on the floor, back against the bed, her legs pulled up, her head resting between her knees. This must've been a soothing position for her, as she went to it an awful lot.

Her stomach growled. It was so loud that it resonated off the cave walls. If her nose hadn't identified what I'd brought in, her belly sure as hell had.

"I've brought you food," I said, a little too cheerfully, trying to change the mood. "I hoped some nice items from home might help you with your thought process."

"I'll eat, but as I do, please answer the question you avoided."

Please, oh, please, ask me about magic. I hated having to skirt around the topic. But I did give her props for bargaining with me.

"Was. This. A. Game?" she enunciated each word, one at a time. A sure sign that I wouldn't be avoiding the question a second time.

For a while, I held my tongue, not knowing how to answer

without triggering the curse. Instead, I munched on her fries, the salty tang pleasing at least one of my senses.

When her face dropped, and the brightness in her crystal orbs dimmed, I replied, "It was never a game. At least, not the kind of game you're talking about. But my mother had orchestrated our meeting."

Her unchanging expression gave me no insight into what the information did to her.

I gulped the coffee, the hot liquid scorching my throat, and took a deep breath.

She was in for quite a story.

Forty Five

I paced around Sierra's room. Several times, I opened my mouth to start explaining but then shut it in fear of the curse. I had no idea where to begin or how to phrase everything without triggering it.

After a while, I braced myself against the cold sting of the cave wall and prayed to Deesse. *Please help me explain using their Earth God so it'll make sense to Sierra.*

"In the Bible, Isaiah prophesied Jesus's coming and what would happen. Mother figured out something similar about you and how you'll help in an upcoming war." *Yes! Thanks, Deesse.* These words had to have come from her. I didn't know anything about Isaiah, but I hoped Sierra did.

"War? Prophecies? I'm not Jesus." Sierra sipped her latte and blindly gazed up at the ceiling. "You're making no sense."

"Just like the kings sought out Elisha before going to war to learn if God would be with them, my mother is searching for you. The only downside, people like Elisha aren't what they were once considered. They are now seen as dangerous, the worst type of people in all humanity."

"I'm not dangerous." Sierra slammed her latte on the floor. The lid burst open on impact the contents sloshing out everywhere. Scents of pumpkin spice and espresso beans filled the air.

"She, and the majority of my mother's people, believe you are. That's why she searched for you. She needed to find you first. But she didn't want you destroyed, at least not initially, because of the vast knowledge you could share."

"What knowledge?" Sierra fiddled with her fingers.

"From my understanding, you have the knowledge on how to unite people," I said the last word slowly and tensed, preparing for the inevitable pain. Nothing happened, and I sighed with relief.

She shook her head.

"She wants to unite everyone under her control." I grabbed the soft cloth Lukita had dropped in the room and cleaned up the sticky mess.

"Like, making her a queen?"

"Yeah, but a dark one."

Sierra gasped, and I took a seat next to her after mopping up the spill.

"Your mother's bad?"

"The worst." My chest tightened. It still hurt knowing how evil she was and how she'd fooled me.

"Why are you helping her?" She pushed the food away and curled up again.

"I'm not anymore." I reached for her hand, but she scooted farther away. "Until recently, I thought Mother was the kindest person I'd ever met. I'd have followed her through hell and back. She promised me she was finding you to unite everyone under love. She lied to me."

Sierra glanced over, her face devoid of color. "How did you find out she'd lied?"

"She killed my nanny." The fresh pain of it erupted again.

If I had a heart, it would've bled. I pulled my knees close to my chest, copying Sierra, and bawled.

I couldn't hold it back this time. Everything had been building up for weeks.

Some time into the hysterics, a soft, cold hand touched my arm, and the iridescent vein darted to my chest. I flinched and shifted my gaze toward Sierra. Her eyes were swollen, too.

I lifted my hand to hers and squeezed. The vein vibrated. Sierra gasped but didn't pull away. The vein outlined a heart again.

"How do you know I'm the one she's looking for?"

"I found a journal your father had written about what your name would be if you were a girl or a boy. He also threw a festival every year, near your birthday, for the last seventeen years. With the two clues, it narrowed my list. So, I searched almost all of them." I shrugged.

"And what makes you think I'm the right one?"

"Your eyes are like your mother's, your mouth like your father's, and your personality is a mixture of both. The inquisitiveness, talkativeness, and questions are just like your father. The joy, gratitude, childlike spirit, and friendliness are just like they described your mother." Also, my magic had sparked like crazy when I'd glanced into her eyes, and an iridescent vein appeared every time we touched. But I couldn't tell her that.

"You knew both my birth parents?" She pulled away and stood, her teeth grinding in the silence.

I jumped up and placed my hands on her shoulders. She squirmed, but I didn't let go. "Sort of. Not well. But I knew of them." I took a deep breath. "Sierra, one day you'll meet your mother, but first, we have to save you from mine."

"My birth mom is still alive?" Her shoulders sagged.

"Yes."

"What about my dad?"

I cringed, tugging at the collar of my shirt. She was talking to me again. I couldn't tell her about killing her father. I couldn't confess. Not now. She wasn't ready to hear it. Plus, I still held true to the fact it'd be easier to tell her once she believed in magic and fell for me. "Sierra, we're off topic."

"They left me. Gave me up for adoption. Why?" she screamed. "I thought they were dead."

One is.

"They needed to protect you. They knew my mother was evil and had to hide you from her." I squeezed her shoulders and guided her blind gaze to mine.

"That's no excuse." She shoved me away and paced around her bed, one hand keeping hold of the bedframe.

Breaths shallow, she spun toward my direction, her face crimson. "So, my parents didn't care for me. And neither did you. I must be repulsive."

I dashed over and wrapped her in a hug. She didn't reciprocate, but I didn't care. She needed it, and so did I.

"Sierra, you have no idea how much I care about you and how much your parents cared about you. That's why they sent you away. I betrayed my mother for you. I'm risking certain death, or worse, by hiding you. But I believe in you." I broke from the hug.

Her knees wobbled, and she fell to the floor, so I scooted in next to her. She stayed silent, breathing heavily. Had my answer been enough? Did it prove I wasn't a monster, and that I had her best intentions at heart?

The eerie silence built as she continued not speaking. I couldn't fathom what was taking her so long, and now, instead of pondering our conversation any further, my raspy breaths and full-body tremors returned. What if she didn't believe a thing I'd said and secluded herself? If she did, I wouldn't be able to wake her magic. Time was already running thin.

I could no longer sit there and watch.

"I've told you enough for tonight. I'll give you time to

unpack everything and formulate more questions. What did Emma call you? Queen of questions?" I chuckled, trying hard to break the tension, but it was to no avail. Nothing would snap her out of it unless I freed her, she began to believe she was a seer, or her eyesight returned.

Or ... An image popped into my mind. If she had the blood of the water goddess and the spirit god from her mother's side, and the blood of the fire god from her father's, then she had to have those abilities to some degree. Rumors spread that another reason why seers were powerful was because they possessed all five elements. I had already glimpsed specks of every color in her eyes. Maybe she possessed them all?

Affinities were like senses. When she reached for smell or hearing, it might make her fire or water elements react since plenty of torches and bodies of water were scattered throughout the cave. Of course, it was a long shot, but it was something. And despite the predictability of success, it was worth trying if it meant it could awaken her magic.

"Turns out I need to leave for a few hours. I have to do something. You should eat, and you'll need to hone all your senses. So, I'll leave food, items for bathing, and clothes throughout the cave. They'll be in various locations. To find them, you'll have to use your senses. When I return, I hope to see you've learned how to use them better." In the midst of the situation, I scooted closer and pressed my forehead against hers.

The temptation to kiss her forehead and wish her well was strong. Once I lifted my head and my lips came close, my breathing became jagged. What was I doing? I took several steps back, but it didn't help, so I dashed away.

The truth of the matter was, I had nowhere outside of this cave to be. Sierra didn't need to know my whereabouts, though. She just needed to think I'd left. I'd always lied to my subjugates and repeatedly to peasants, and I'd never once felt wrong for doing so.

Things felt very different, and out of the ordinary, when I lied to Sierra. Even with it being a half-truth, I wanted to hurl.

If the bond between us was real, this would make sense. Once Darcy had broken us apart and the bond had shattered, then I'd used spells to help awaken her magic, I'd given up all hope of believing I was the powerful warrior or that my heart would someday return. But since the iridescent vein reappeared when I touched her, I didn't know what to think. Maybe there was still something between us.

I shook my head. I couldn't think like this.

Besides, after all that happened, once she found out I'd killed her father, she'd refuse to mate with me, even if her heart wanted to. She'd never forgive me for my past. Not anymore.

Forty Six

For hours, while Sierra slept, Lukita and I filled two areas full of food and then placed bathing items near all three bodies of water within the cave. We wanted to ensure they were all prepared, not knowing which one she'd venture to. And in the hope of sparking the fire element, we scattered more torches throughout the tunnels.

Most element wielders could only manipulate the element of their birth. If the element wasn't in front of them or nearby, they couldn't do anything with it.

There was an exception to manipulating the elements without them being present: being a mix of Aggeeshvar, the fire god's bloodline, where her father belonged, and Panneeshvar, the water goddess's bloodline, where her mother belonged. But since the treaty prevented them from mixing, no one could ever prove if it were true.

A minor myth claimed that those from either Aggeeshvar or Panneeshvar's direct line were also the only ones known to manipulate a second element, but to a lesser extent. Another reason why Sierra could have at least two.

With Sierra using her senses, would she be able to feel the magic of the elements and maybe connect to them? It might not be strong, but perhaps if she felt a spark of magic, it'd make her curious enough to look deeper into herself.

After Lukita and I finished, I checked on Sierra. She cuddled into her pillow, snoring.

It ate at me, watching Sierra. In her sleep, she snarled every now and then, flared her nostrils, and squeezed her face tight. Even she had nightmares because of me. Though I was trying to do the right thing and keep her safe, why did I still feel like the villain?

As I tried to convince myself I wasn't a monster, Sierra stirred. She shot up, eyes shut, and hunched forward over the bed. At first, my muscles tensed, and I almost ran to her, but then she dry-heaved as she cupped her throat.

After nothing came out, she straightened and then flopped back in bed, lying as straight as a pencil. She pointed her toes and placed her arms down by her sides, hands tucked underneath her butt. She took three deep breaths.

The smell of lemons wafted into the air with such a strong force I scanned the room in search of the culprit. There was nothing, and Sierra remained frozen.

Before I had time to contemplate it, the sound of a stream rushed into my ears as if it were right underneath me. Water droplets smacked my face and dripped onto my lips. I jumped.

Sierra was calling to her senses.

Thus far, air and water had listened to her. I had no experience with seers and not much with element wielders, except for torturing them and masquerading as an earth wielder. So, was this normal?

Sierra bent down like a robot and took off her socks. With both hands outstretched, she rubbed her palms on the floor before standing.

Hands in front of her, she walked out of the room.

For a split second, she opened her eyes.

Perhaps she'd forgotten about the fact she couldn't see because she closed them soon afterward. They were open long enough, though, for me to pick out green, blue, and yellow, which shined in and out like stars throughout the white crystals.

The spark in her eyes after calling out to her senses had to mean she was starting to believe and that her powers were awakening. A flutter filled my stomach. Yes!

Curious to see the direction Sierra headed in and how vital the elements were, I crept behind her. Thirty minutes into the walk, she reached one of the tables with assorted food Lukita and I had placed for her. Her smile lifted, and her belly grumbled.

She took several bites of the cardamom roll, hash browns, and sausages before grabbing the pumpkin latte and stood still. She breathed in, and the stream's rushing water echoed around us.

It took her five minutes to reach it.

After she'd explored the perimeter twice, eventually finding the soap and change of clothing, she sank her feet into the water and splashed them around before lifting her shirt.

Though I shouldn't have stayed and watched, my legs wouldn't obey. But as her bra became visible, the iridescent vein appeared, its spikes cutting my insides, and my feet finally listened.

Instead of taking the quickest route to my room, I took the long way around in an attempt to lull my manhood back to sleep. With the amount of sexual frustration building inside me, even if I pleasured myself at this point, Sierra would hear me. So, I had to do it the old-fashioned way and imagine things from my past to dull my drive.

I conjured up my nightmares, all the misery I'd been

through, to help control my urges before slipping inside my room to speak with Lukita.

"Any glimpses of the future or Mother's progress on finding us?" I leaned my head against the bedframe and clutched the comforter. The soft silk kept me grounded. Hell-space didn't have such luxuries.

"No. But I peeked into her kingdom," Lukita said in a strained voice.

"And?"

"I think you need to see it."

The shimmering window appeared. The waves rolled and opened into a clear picture of The Kingdom of Astal. A black dome covered the palace and the immediate village on its outskirts. Another bigger dome encompassed the smaller one, but it had holes throughout. Electricity buzzed through it, and colors radiated in several spots. That wasn't good. It looked purely demonic.

The window's image zoomed to the inside of the dome. Six guards stood side-by-side, inches from the dome's shield, Demeatris amongst them.

Mother paced in front of them, her lilac hair flowing over her shoulders. She wore a black dress with a slit up both legs and another slit down the middle of her chest. The mist hovered around her frame, and her eyes were a sickening black with only a small perimeter of white. Since the last time I'd seen her, they had darkened. Her power was increasing.

I gulped.

"See this wall? It'll become your death if you don't find Tartarus! Search high and low. Find him. He's planning to destroy the kingdoms and make us answer to the Lord of Delmore."

Several gasped, including me, but not Demeatris.

Mother stalked over to him and clamped a hand around

his throat. "Are you not concerned?" She squeezed, and he thrashed about in her grip.

"Sorry, Your Majesty. I'm so concerned my body froze." He choked the words out, spittle flying from his lips.

"Good. You better be." She pitched him into the grass.

I released a breath. I didn't want another person to die, especially those who'd helped me learn the truth.

The window's image changed again to the outskirts of The Kingdom of Ondin. It zoomed in until it landed inside a pub called Waves. Several water and wind wielders mingled across a wooden table, bubblies in hand.

"They say Queen Delilah is trying to unite the realms and that Queen Rosalida is losing it," a wind wielder said, then chugged his beer.

"I'm not siding with Queen Delilah. It's not happening." A water wielder slammed his mug down, causing several of the others to jump.

"Almost everyone in both kingdoms are siding with her. Why won't you?"

"Give me a rational explanation for that dome of terror, and maybe I'll consider it." The water wielder stood.

I couldn't help but chuckle. That was a clever name.

"To protect those willing to fight with her. She's offering a lifetime pension and any job our heart desires." The wind wielder smiled.

The water wielder shook his head and stormed out of the pub.

As the image disappeared, I struggled to breathe. Damn, Mother was convincing. No wonder she fooled me for so long.

"Why did you show me all of this? Other than to reinforce how important it is that Sierra believes she's the savior."

"Not only are we rushing against time since they are searching for us, but once the white vanishes from your mother's eyes, she'll be gone. Lucifer gave your mother that mist, but that mist is a part of Lucifer, and he'll have gained full possession of her. So, it'll no longer be your mother controlling all the realms and bringing chaos ... it'll be your father."

Vilo and Aris had been right. Mother was in cahoots with Lucifer. After I'd watched her kill Vilo, I knew she was pure evil, but I'd still refused to believe she'd aligned with the King of Delmore. But now, it was impossible to deny.

I clutched my chest at the sudden pain. Unknowingly, Mother was ripping apart that piece of my soul belonging to her.

Not only did I have questions about what the hell Mother was thinking, but fear also gripped hold of me. Mother's eyes were almost black orbs. Only specks of white remained. Our time had always been short, but now there was no time. Shit.

I needed to wake Sierra's magic before Lucifer took over.

Rubbing my fingers together, I landed outside Sierra's room.

She lay asleep, and as her body stirred, her hair falling across her face, I moved closer. Seconds from brushing the loose strand away, I thought better of it. She hadn't forgiven me, and it might piss her off.

Sierra groaned and pushed the comforter off. I bit my lip,

wishing I'd caused her to make that noise. If only she still cared about me, it'd make everything easier.

She stretched on the bed, and her nightdress rose. The moment the bottom part of her light pink thong appeared, I licked my lips, almost moaning, but instead, I coughed. "Good morning, Sierra," I purred.

When I said her name in that manner, it always produced a response, and this time was no exception. Heat radiated from her. That, combined with the stretch she had most definitely done for me, made no sense. She should still hate me or at least be confused.

"Good morning, Tarus," she said with the slightest tinge of saltiness. Yep, still mad. "How was your time away?"

"Good. I'm hopeful I might've found help with bringing your sight back."

"What is this possible newfound help?" Eagerness seeped through her.

"All in due time. Good things come to those who wait." I tried saying our old phrase to see how she'd react.

Her jaw tightened a smidge, but enough for me to know she didn't like my choice of words.

"I know we aren't what we used to be, but I'm trying to help you. You'll see."

The torches flickered multiple times before she responded. "Yes, I know, and I'll take all the help I can get."

I sighed. "You look refreshed, and I don't hear your stomach growling. Am I right to assume you let your senses guide you to the feast table and the bathing stream?"

"As a matter of fact, I did. Would you like me to show you?" She smiled.

"I'd be delighted to see." Though I had already seen it, I didn't know how she called on the senses to make the elements manifest. Whatever it was, it might help in training.

"Okay. You can't interrupt. Also, no making fun of me."

My stomach fluttered. She was talking to me and didn't seem too mad. This was a good sign. "Deal." This time, I couldn't refrain from brushing the strand of hair behind her ear. She flinched, and the iridescent vein appeared, flashing lavender.

Wanting the string to turn solid lavender and loving the feel of her skin, I kept my hand in place. She lifted her own and placed it on mine.

"You going to watch or what?" she asked, out of breath, and dropped our hands.

"Yes." I groaned.

She went back to lying flat, took three deep breaths, removed her socks, and hopped off the bed. Within two minutes, she'd spoken with all four senses. Once she'd thanked them, unbeknownst to her, all the elements, except spirit, sprung to life around us.

She guided me to the feast table. I stayed silent and followed behind.

When we arrived, she munched on warm croissants while I remained mute.

"Tarus, you can talk now." I swear she rolled her crystal orbs at me.

"You reminded me of someone speaking to the elements. I wonder if elements and senses have any correlation." My mouth fell open in astonishment. Why had the curse allowed me to speak of the elements?

"Tarus, that's going way too far. You already want me to believe in prophecies and uniting people. Don't stretch it by talking magical nonsense."

I slumped. I had an opening. The curse wasn't shooting pain down my spine, but she'd flat-out shut the magical conversation down.

I couldn't make her believe in herself or train her if she

wouldn't even let us talk about it. Shit. My stomach turned rock hard. This wasn't good.

"Would you be willing to escort me on a walk?" she asked after the silence dragged on.

I almost jumped at the suggestion. This would mean us touching. She willingly approved of me touching her. My smile grew.

"Of course. I'd love to escort you. It's not much, but I can show you where another water source is. There are three in the cave."

She held out her arm, and I led her through various parts of the cave, the iridescent vein dancing.

Once we started talking, it felt like we were back to the times before all this happened.

When we arrived at the lake, I guided her around the water's perimeter so she could get a feel for the place. After the second lap, I led her to the lake's edge, where we could sit down with our feet in the water. For a while, only the sound of the rippling water filled the space.

Wanting to know how far she'd let me go, I laced my fingers with hers. She didn't move or show any sign of displeasure. The iridescent vein turned solid lavender, and my breathing accelerated.

A few minutes later, I scooted in closer until our sides touched. The lavender vein outlined my heart and the bond again. My eyes widened, and a lone tear escaped.

This wasn't over.

Perhaps I was still the powerful warrior.

Tartarus, I hate to be the bearer of bad news, but the clock is ticking. If you refuse to use Slinger, you need to wake her magic, not laze around, Lukita said, her tone fierce.

Inside, I groaned. This was the most peaceful I'd felt in days. I wanted it to continue and not return to reality.

Reality was a drag.

How do you expect me to do that without triggering her? It's too soon. Sweat formed under my armpits.

Connect with her. Do something basic?

Like?

That's your expertise, not mine.

Clenching my free fist, I tried to think of something that'd spark her elements without upsetting her. What would speak to her? What would bring her into the moment? Games?

That was it.

"Though I'd love to stay like this with you, we must prepare you for those coming, and I'd like to bring out your creative side by doing something fun. Give me thirty minutes, and I'll be back." On a spiked adrenaline high, I acted without thinking and kissed her forehead before scurrying off. My lips tingled.

Lukita and I prepared a game for her that included dancing. The entire time, I couldn't stop reliving the gentle kiss and the fact the curse had allowed it. About twenty minutes later, I returned to her, panting heavily.

"Your party of fun awaits." I held out my arm next to hers, ready for her to grasp. She took hold, but her shoulders slumped, and no smile appeared. Gods. I should've figured mentioning our predicament would ruin the mood.

Feet from the feast table, ballroom music bounced off the cave walls, and the aroma of coffee drifted in the air. Sierra took a deep sniff, her stomach grumbling.

Besides pumpkin spice coffee, Lukita had provided lamb, steak, wings, green beans, and chocolate truffles—all of Sierra's favorite items.

"Let's play an instructive game." I waved her hand over the long rectangular feast table near the entrance.

After she felt several of the foods and grabbed a truffle, I glided her onto the square vinyl area in the middle of the room. She remained silent, but her nose scrunched.

"We'll do some ballroom, waltz, and country dancing. You can't see my feet or my moves. Instead, you'll have to use your senses, your intuition. Let them guide you."

She nodded. My nerves calmed. Thank the gods she was willing to play, and I had again guessed the right way to connect with her.

"Challenge accepted, but what about the food?" she smirked.

"For every song you master, you'll try one of the delicacies."

"Umm. That could take all night." She gasped, and I grinned. That was exactly what I had planned.

"We have nothing but time."

She held out her hand. "So, let's start, because I don't know about you, but I'm hungry."

I laughed, deep and throaty. This was the Sierra I adored.

With one hand, I embraced her waist, and with the other, I clutched hers.

Lukita, please play a tango.

Lukita chuckled inside my mind, and the accompaniment rhythms of marcato and síncopa resounded off the walls.

As expected, Sierra was a disaster but a graceful and beautiful one. She stepped on my foot multiple times, almost fell, and ran into the wall.

When the song ended, I arched a brow. "Did you even try to use your senses?" It didn't seem like it. One: she kept messing up. Two: her eyes never sparked an elemental color. If she refused to use them, how could I come up with any other training for her?

She barred her teeth, stepped back, and massaged her forehead. Without looking in my direction, she rubbed her foot on the ground. "You're right. I didn't. Can we try again?"

Her ability to calm herself and admit her errors was definitely the behavior of royalty. She really was the perfect queen to combine our realms in love. Any of us would be honored to be led by someone with her qualities.

Lukita started the music again, and this time, she picked a waltz.

I guided Sierra while she spoke to her senses. Confidence radiated from her as she smirked, switched our hand positions, and took the lead. Like a good teacher, I let her have her way, regardless of whether we crashed into a wall or fell to the ground.

By the second chorus, I no longer noticed anything other than Sierra and the purple rim surrounding her eyes. I couldn't breathe, couldn't think, and barely noticed the wall we were about to smack into. My breath hitched as Sierra tensed. Just before we crashed, she glided us away in a smooth 180-degree turn.

When the song came to a finish, I guided her to the feast table and placed a piece of lamb in her mouth. Her body trembled with ecstasy as she bit into the juicy meat, and I bit my lip.

"How does it feel trusting your instincts?" I smirked.

"It felt weird. Like this thing inside of me warmed my veins, forcing me to pay attention. Once I focused on what they were saying, they protected me."

Our game continued for the entire day. Lukita or I would choose a song, and sometimes we'd increase the difficulty level. After each successful dance, we'd go to the buffet.

Near the end of the night, every elemental color glimmered in her eyes. They were all there, and I could easily create several training exercises that spoke to each of them. With the tide turning in favor of waking her magic, a lightness built inside my chest, and my courage soared. I closed the distance between us, needing to feel her.

Stomach against stomach, forehead against forehead, the heat rose several degrees. With both hands, I cradled Sierra's face and kissed her. I put every emotion into the kiss—passion, hurt, betrayal—and not that I meant for it to happen, but tears fell, slipping down each cheek. There was no doubt I loved her, even more than myself.

She stepped back and slapped the living daylights out of me. Or at least, she tried. She hissed through her teeth, shaking the beet-red hand she'd hit me with. My skin was too strong, and it had felt like an ant bite in terms of physical pain, but she'd scored a home run in terms of internal pain.

"Where do you get the audacity to presume it's okay to kiss me?" Her white crystal orbs burned scarlet.

"I ... uh." Where were the words when I needed them? "I just thought we were having a moment. We're connected, you and I. We're meant to be. Have you not wondered why it has been so easy to forget all the bad things and go back to normal? Have you wondered why you still love me? I know you do, as I still love you."

"Are you serious? How can I still love you after what you did, Tarus?" She threw her arms down, hands fisted.

"I ..." My heart ached, but I still held on to her shoulder, and the bond still held in my heart. "When we connect, our hearts beat on the same drum. You love me."

"Tarus!" she screamed and shoved my arms away. "Did you really think I'd forgiven you? This entire time, I've been playing you in hopes you'd slip up or let me out."

My knees wobbled, and I fell to the ground, clutching my chest. "No. You can't fake what your heart feels for me." If she would accept her magic, her nature, she wouldn't be able to fake anything. Not anymore. Not with her inability to lie.

"Tarus, even if my heart still loves you, I'll never listen to it. You're delusional and probably belong to some sadist cult that believes in magic and the impossible."

Her words hit another home run, and my vision blurred. If I didn't fix her belief or remind her about what she felt for me, I could really lose her for good. "But your note. You said you'd walk through hell or high water with me."

She turned to stone.

I pulled out the note, the paper crackling in the crisp air.

Forty Eight

"Dearest Love ..."

She rested a hand on her heart as if it had stopped beating, and I almost stopped reading, but I needed to do this.

> *If you have this letter, I expect I succeeded tonight. My goal was to make the first move. To finally kiss you and show you how much you mean to me. You see, I'd stay stubborn and not make the first move, even try to entice you to do it by making myself so irresistible you'd have a challenging time staying away from me. But last night, I realized the most incredible thing.*

Tears streaked down her face, mirroring mine. She knew where this was about to lead.

> *I love you, Tarus. My love for you is why I am fine with making the first move. I want you to know what you mean to me. This love's more extraordinary than anything I've ever felt. Greater than anything I've ever experienced. In fact, my*

love for you feels more profound than a typical crush, as it feels true. Dare I say, true love?

I don't know how to explain it or write it in words. Yet, I'll try. There is something inside me you awoke the first time we stared into each other's eyes. The first time you held my hand, I knew it was the only one I wanted to embrace for the rest of my life. You awoke something that literally comes alive every time you're near and feels complete when you're next to me.

That something can only be my heart. My heart is telling me it'll walk through hell or high water for you, will jump in front of a bullet for you. Wherever you go, I'll follow. I trust you with my life, Tarus. I don't even have to question it. You're my soulmate, and something tells me you feel the same, making me not scared to tell you this because I know it's recip-rocated.

PS I thought about saying it in person, but there's some-thing about a note and always getting to remember what I'd said (in this case, written) and how I felt.

Breathlessly, I refolded her letter. Sweat poured down my neck. I was desperate for her to remember how she'd felt. Desperate for her to mean the words again. Desperate to stay alive.

When I glanced her way, she was no longer on her feet. She had slumped down the cave wall, hugging her knees to her chest and her face was puffy.

I couldn't bear knowing that the note had done this to her, that *I* had done this to her. I'd caused this beautiful soul such tremendous agony, and it killed me. As I closed the distance, the space warmed.

At first, I figured the warmth came from the tension between us until an orange flame formed, surrounding her and forcing me backward by flashing in my face several times before it deconstructed. The fire element was awakening. But now wasn't the time to think about that, even if Lukita and time might disagree. I needed her to discuss the letter and feel something for me.

I attempted to tip her head up, but she wouldn't budge. Both her physical and mental strength impressed me.

"Was walking through hell or high water just a lie? Was it all a lie?" I clenched my fists to keep the anger contained, anger I had no right to carry.

"No," she answered in such a soft whisper that I could barely make it out.

"Then how can you not still love me?"

She lifted her head. "Tarus, it was before you did *this*." She waved her hands around the room and pointed at her eyes. "No soulmate, no true love, would do this."

"I had no choice. You have to believe me. More than anything, I want what is best for you. I'm trying to protect you, but I have limits. You have to open yourself up to believing the impossible." Damn this curse. I kicked the stone wall. Bones shattered, and I groaned.

She flinched. "Tarus, remember I don't believe anything you say anymore. You've still lost my trust."

My lips tipped up at the corners. Sierra's words gave me optimism. "But not your love? You still love me?"

"No, Tarus, I don't." She grimaced after saying those words.

My expression brightened. She was lying. Change of plans. Gain her trust back and then get her to accept us, that we still had a chance. From there, the rest would fall into place. Her belief in herself and in magic intertwined with her love for me.

"No, it's not true. I refuse to believe it. True love doesn't just stop. What we have, our connection, is destined, and you can't control destiny. Somehow, I'll find a way to prove it and gain your trust back." I paused to catch my breath, but before she could respond, I added, "Let me escort you back to your room and ensure you're okay before I go take care of something."

I reached for her hands, but she shoved me away. "Leave me. I'll figure it out by myself." Her voice was so harsh that I stumbled backward.

After a second, when she still didn't move, I plodded away. But before I was out of her earshot, I whispered, "One day, we'll be together, and everything will make sense. I promise." Unsure if I wanted her to hear, I let Lukita and her magic decide if she'd carry the words to her.

Lukita, I need your help.

With getting her back or waking her magic? It's getting hard to tell which path you're on.

I groaned. *They're one and the same. I need to make her trust me. It's the only way to wake her.*

Stop being so daft. Think outside of the box. Lukita's voice rose, shocking me.

I hate when you say that. I ground my teeth.

Boy, what's the most important thing we need to fix for everything else to fall into place?

Her believing.

We sat in silence for a minute before several ideas popped into my head: games, senses, and bringing something magical to the cave. But every idea I had, Lukita shot down or explained how the curse would prevent it.

After a while, I almost yelled at her for not coming up with any ideas when suddenly, an entirely different thought formed. It was dangerous, and I'd be playing with fire, most likely resulting in my death.

I jumped up. *Our answers are in The Kingdom of Ondin.*

I like what you're thinking.

You and I are cursed from sharing or showing Sierra anything to do with magic, but what if others aren't? I need to find someone who knows the prophecy and doesn't want to destroy Sierra for being a seer. I paced around my bed, shoes squeaking against the shiny floor.

You still need to prepare for an alternative option if Sierra won't believe you. That alternative option requires Queen Rosalida. Why don't you kill two birds with one stone? Ask Queen Rosalida for her help with both. I'm positive she'll assist.

My stomach tightened. *She'll take Sierra away from me, and I'm still not okay with killing my mother.*

She can't take Sierra away, she can't portal, and she has no idea where we are. Talk to her. If anything feels off, portal back.

I must've had a death wish. She was gonna kill me. My hands grew clammy, and I hadn't even faced her yet. I clutched my chest and hunched over.

So, you're going to see her?

Yes. I groaned.

Forty Nine

I waved my hand over my body and turned invisible before portaling into Queen Rosalida's throne room, inside her half of Climakru. Even though she was no longer my enemy, I still expected to feel some hatred for her. I'd grown up loathing her.

But, as I stood before her beauty, taking in a throne room full of life, color, and equality for all element wielders, a fluttering feeling built within my chest. No images of her or this kingdom had prepared me for this.

Her wooden throne, and the two chairs next to it, had carvings of birds on them, and they leaned against a wall with a huge banner reading, *Kingdom's pillars: faith, love, and hope. Greatest of all, love.* Vines and fire flowers covered the rest of the wall. A delicate flower only capable of growing amongst fire wielders. Not only did they thrive here, but the queen had several interlaced through her light blue, silky braid dangling over her right shoulder.

She spoke to three buff men and two warrior women. All five gazed over at her from a stone bench attached to a massive water fountain in the middle of the room. A fresh scent swirled around the room, and beautifully carved windmills hanging from the ceiling produced a sweet musical melody with every sweep of their elegant blades.

"I'm sorry. What did you say?" Queen Rosalida asked in a smooth, velvet voice.

"Do you think she killed her?" one male asked.

Killed her? Sierra?

Instead of answering him, the queen remained silent, her sapphire eyes drifting in my direction. The hair on the back of my neck stood on end. I was invisible. She shouldn't know I was there.

"Delegates, please excuse me. I need a moment alone. I'll meet you in the Commons soon." Queen Rosalida stepped down from her throne and strolled over to a vase of tulips resting on a cabinet beneath a window, mere inches from me. She eased the burgundy curtain aside and gazed out.

The same male stood abruptly. "But, Queen Rosalida ..."

Distracted by the paintings of playful children covering the wall behind him, I almost missed the sweat dripping from his shaggy blond hair and how his dark blue eyes brightened several shades.

"Kaito, I understand Panha is your mother." She returned to him and placed her hand on his shoulder. "I love you."

Whoa, did she just tell someone she loved them? That would've never happened with Mother.

"Let me think about how to save her. I promise that the next time we meet, I might have a solution."

"Yes, ma'am." He squeezed her hand, and the five warriors left the room.

"Everyone else, please follow suit. I don't need any protection right now." Several guards bowed to her and stepped out.

Once the double doors shut, she faced me and clasped her hands together. "I know you're there."

A buzz appeared as my palm glowed and I turned visible. "How?"

"A mother knows her daughter's scent, and it clings to you." She smiled.

Okay, first off, I knew Sierra had a scent, but why would it be on me? Second, where was the anger? The punishment? Anything to show how much she hated me?

"Come sit with me?" She sat at the fountain and patted the section of the bench at her side, not covered by her white skirt.

"I'm okay with standing." I gulped.

"I'm not going to hurt you." She patted the bench again.

I obliged. "Why not?"

"For a hundred reasons." She curled her lips up. "I understand why you did what you did. Sierra will, too. You had no choice, and your mother tainted you. All that matters now is that you're doing the right thing. Besides, why would I kill the prophecy hero who is meant to work with my daughter to unite the realms, regardless of what he's done in his past?"

Tears stung my eyes. "You consider me kidnapping Sierra and keeping her hidden is the right thing?"

"I'd consider that someone who took my daughter, and who killed my bonded mate, yet still came to me, may mean he's doing the right thing. So, why did you come?" Her eyes brightened to a different shade of purple. Her spirit element. It guided this conversation and must be telling her to trust me or at least to hear me out.

"Lukita."

Queen Rosalida's smile widened. She didn't look surprised.

"She told me to seek you out. I need help with an alternate plan in case Sierra won't believe in herself and her magic won't awaken. Lukita said you'd help." My nerves started going crazy, my fight-or-flight response activating. What if she couldn't help or refused?

"She still doesn't believe? Even with you performing magic in front of her?"

My shoulders slumped. "Before crossing to Earth, a pixie cursed me from being able to use magic or even mention it in Sierra's waking presence."

Queen Rosalida nodded. "I can see why it'd be hard to convince Sierra, then. So, you want someone to return with you to help her? Someone who can possibly mention these things to her?"

"Yes."

"Say that still doesn't wake her. What's your alternate plan?"

I pulled out the pieces of Slinger. Her breath hitched, and she lifted her hand to touch him but pulled back.

"You know the weapon?"

"The gods that both Aris and I descended from formed it together to send Lucifer to Delmore. Until the war 300 years ago, it remained around the necks of the queens in my bloodline. In almost every picture, you'd see them wearing it."

"Lukita says you can fix it."

"I can. But why do you want me to?"

I took a deep breath and let the sounds of the rushing wind mixing with the waterfall soothe me before I mentioned the plan I hated. The one I hoped it didn't come to. "If Sierra's magic doesn't awaken, branding my mother with it is the only way to save your daughter and the realms."

"Since the weapon was meant for Lucifer, and not her, you know she'll be sent to Delmore, where she can eventually escape, unless you behead her. The two things, together, will prevent her from ever resurrecting in any way."

"I know." I dropped my gaze to the mosaic floor, unable to look at her.

"And you wonder why I don't want to harm you?" She placed her hand over mine. My body tingled underneath her touch, but warmth also radiated from our hands. The scent of cinnamon drifted from her.

"Will you please help me?" I choked out.

"The weapon requires two *pieces* to unite, which must then mix with my blood. I have one of the pieces." She pulled her necklace out from under her clothes. A beautiful crystal glass orb with an ember of fire flaming alive inside dangled from the chain. "If you get me the other one, I can fuse them together. It'll both awaken the star and fix it."

"And you trust me, just like that? Where's the catch?"

"No catch. But ..."

There it was. There always had to be a catch.

"The other *piece* is with Panha, my lady-in-waiting. She happens to be in your mother's forbidden dungeon."

My mouth slackened. "It can't be done. I can't enter that place. Plus, with the dome she's built, I doubt I can even get into her kingdom."

"My delegates, the five you saw here with me, want to break in and free her."

I sprang up and paced. "Are they delusional? She'll kill them."

"If you go before them, it can be done. Only problem. They can't know you're there."

"Why? They aren't as forgiving as you?" I tilted my head.

"Panha is Kaito's mother. I don't think he'll understand you taking her."

"Taking her? I'm just helping rescue her."

"You need someone to help with waking Sierra's magic. Steal Panha from them, bring her to me to revive Slinger, and then take her back with you."

"So you will know where we are hiding, and you can take Sierra for yourself?"

"It has to be you that wakes her. None of us can intervene. We can only help."

Pain coursed through me. "It might not be. We didn't form—"

"Tartarus." She stood and grasped both of my hands.

"I'm—"

A knock came on the door. "One second," she yelled and squeezed my hands. "You need to portal back. Return in a few hours. That way, I can let the delegates know the plan, and you can check on your mother's kingdom."

Check her kingdom? So, not only did they want me to sneak into her palace and steal someone, but they also wanted me to venture in beforehand. Were they sentencing me to my death?

I'd be a fool to even consider this.

But I had to. I needed to give Sierra the best chance of survival.

Fifty

"You came back alive!" Lukita screamed, her voice bouncing off the walls.

"You didn't think I would?" I crossed my arms. "Lukita!"

"I'm just kidding. What's the plan?" She chuckled.

"In order to repair Slinger, I need something her lady-in-waiting has."

"Easy." She made a clucking sound.

I laughed and threw myself onto my bed. The tension in my body lessened as I tightened my fingers around the soft down comforter. If only it were that easy.

"Not easy?"

"No. She's in the forbidden dungeons."

Lukita gasped.

"My thoughts exactly. She wants me to follow her five delegates there. She says, together, we can rescue her." I shook my head. This plan was impossible.

"So, after you rescue her, she'll fix Slinger?"

"Yes." I sighed.

"And what about helping to awaken Sierra's magic?"

"She says after I rescue Panha and she revives Slinger, I can bring her here."

"Perfect. What do we do now?"

"I head to Mother's kingdom and figure out what we're up against." I eased up and killed the fire flickering in one of the torches, smoke spiraling upwards. I inhaled the wonderful fragrance and changed into my tight leathers.

Just about to leave, I hesitated, a thought bothering me. I had to ask before I risked my life. "Lukita, something's eating at me."

"What?"

"Why were you so sure that Queen Rosalida was the help the prophecy spoke of? What is the future that she saw? And why was she so kind to me after everything I've done?"

"For many reasons, I'm sure. Probably because she sees how hard you're trying."

"She doesn't know how hard I'm trying. It has to be because she's seen the times ahead. Why won't you tell me what she saw?"

"Fine." She groaned, and the torches on the wall flickered. "Sierra had a prophecy when she was first born. Only, it wasn't *exactly* a prophecy. It was two future images."

I bit my lip. "Of what?"

"One was of Slinger branding Queen Delilah. The other was of you two marrying."

The lavender vein reappeared, spread all the way to my chest, and formed the heart and bond. It vibrated with a bright light before disappearing. I was still the powerful warrior. It was me. Darcy hadn't ruined it, nor had I. My heart ... it was going to return permanently. When Sierra's magic awakened, she was going to mate with me. Holy shit. Holy shit!

A smile spread across my face as I wiped happy tears away. Sierra would forgive me.

Now, it made sense why Queen Rosalida had been so kind. One day, I'd be her son-in-law.

This was surreal. It made venturing to Mother's kingdom worth it.

Invisible, I portaled to the sea-green River of La Mont, which divided the two kingdoms. But this time, I ventured to the opposite side from where Mother and I used to have our one-on-ones. In the past, this river had contained the happiest of memories for me. It didn't anymore.

An uncomfortable silence surrounded the river. Birds no longer chirped, glowing critters didn't flap above me, and the wind had ceased to exist. I cringed.

The shimmery domes Lukita had shown me stood on the other side. They now encircled her entire half of Climakru. I could see through the first layer of the black shield. Multiple cracks existed, meaning it was either incomplete or Mother's magic was faltering. We'd soon find out.

A second solid black sheet ran up on all sides of the shield to meet at the top. In various spots, savage electricity sparked with life. I gulped. Her dome was more dangerous than a standard defense.

I studied it, along with my old domain. Even with the sun at its full height, its golden rays cast no light on her side. It had darkened. Colors no longer existed. All the flower petals next to the barricade had wilted, drooping toward the ground.

After taking several walks along the riverbank, studying the structure of the domes and the guards around the outer layer, the salty tang of the river's water and my sweat clung to my skin and dried my mouth. I'd spent too much time observing this area. It was time I did more.

A fissure in the dome, located between two oak trees, was big enough for me and the delegates to fit through, so I explored the area. There were two guards nearby. Mother must've known openings existed.

She'd positioned the guards about five meters from the opening, one on either side. If two were all she needed, it either meant her power had grown, or she expected the shield to do its job.

With a deep breath, I stepped through the fissure. I needed to see whether my magic would work once across, and whether I could still portal inside her kingdom, just not out of it or into the forbidden dungeon.

An ear-piercing alarm sounded the minute my feet crunched on the dead grass. Guards swarmed in from everywhere. They looked around and arched their eyebrows.

Sweat dripped from every orifice as I glanced down.

Yes! I was still invisible.

They already knew someone had breached their defenses, so why not have some fun?

Concerned by the alarm, yet not seeing any intruders, the guards gathered closer to the fissure. I examined the eyes of the guard closest to me. Solid black orbs. Demon. So, I shoved him against the shield, curious to see what would happen if someone touched the dome.

Black currents shot from the covering and wrapped themselves around the guard. His body convulsed, his hair fried, and I covered my ears against his demonic wails. All the other guards watched with horror, and some of them smiled wickedly.

None helped.

Once the guy had burned to a crisp, murmurs traveled around the dome about whether he'd fallen, whether one of them had pushed him, or whether the intruder had. Guards turned on one another. Their palms sparked their signature black color.

They couldn't pass up a fight, even if it was against one another, and since they couldn't find me, they'd settle for attacking their comrades.

Fact one: Touch the dome and die. Good to know. Fact two: My magic still worked.

Before the first guard could launch his attack, Mother's chariot bells echoed amongst the outskirts of the kingdom, and the guards stiffened and retook their positions.

Not wanting to see Mother or hear whatever she was about to tell her guards, I attempted to portal to the forbidden dungeons.

Nothing happened.

I tried again, but still nothing. I portaled a few feet away. It worked. I attempted to portal out of the dome. It didn't work.

Fact three: Just like always, my portaling worked within the kingdom, but it couldn't get me inside the forbidden dungeon or out of the kingdom. Looked like I'd definitely be relying on Queen Rosalida's unaware delegates to get Panha.

For a few hours, I stayed inside The Kingdom of Astal, working out the kinks in my plan to make sure it went down without a hitch tomorrow. My strategy was risky, and there were numerous ways it could fail, especially when I didn't know the delegates' plan. But I had to trust our efforts would succeed. If it didn't, there was a ninety-nine percent chance we'd all die.

After I'd finished observing Mother's palace and learning all I could, I returned to Queen Rosalida.

She wandered around the room. Every few feet, she stopped to shake hands with one of the children or to give them a fire flower from her hair.

It was a beautiful scene to behold. Sierra would fit right in.

Since we were on a time crunch, I crept behind Queen Rosalida. Her body stiffened as she sniffed the air, a smile tugging at the side of her mouth.

"Follow me," she whispered.

She headed to the wooden doors. Guards wearing dark blue uniforms opened them, and once in the hallway, she turned to the left, following it until we reached a kitchen. Sweet chocolate filled the air. My stomach grumbled. Queen Rosalida turned, her eyebrows raised, but a smile still rested on her lips. She walked into the pantry, on the left, and shut the door.

"They're in a basement beneath the pub called Make Waves, on the outskirts of The Kingdom of Ondin." She held up a picture of a dark stone room. It had a bar top in the background, kegs littered throughout, no windows, and one long wooden staircase. "I didn't know if you needed to see a picture to portal there."

"Just the name." I shrugged. "Thank you, though."

"Help where you see fit, but whatever you do, make sure you end up with Panha. Portal her to my bed chambers once you know my delegates are safe. Do you understand?"

I nodded. "I'll do my best." That wasn't a lie. I'd do anything to protect Sierra and to awaken her magic. She was the only hope any of us had—especially me.

She squeezed my shoulders. "May the gods grant you favor."

Once she dropped her hands, I portaled to Make Waves.

The tension in the place was so thick it was hard to think. Everyone was on edge, standing with stiff postures, their feet tapping in the silence, possibly waiting for the five delegates to arrive. Since they weren't here yet, I yearned to portal back to Sierra to make sure she was okay, but I refrained. I didn't want to miss something important.

A couple of minutes later, they appeared, armed for battle. Each wore a breastplate the color of their element and had different weapons strapped across their backs.

"Kylie came a few minutes ago to inform us what we needed and what she expected. She did so to save time. Kylie, would you now like to share with everyone else what Lilli told you?" Kaito spoke with a calm demeanor, eyes focused straight ahead.

A small pixie with rainbow-colored hair braided past her knees flew to the center of the room, next to the delegates. "The forbidden dungeon is two levels below her palace on the east side, nearest the river, which is to our delegate's advantage. Another advantage that we know is something, or someone, tried to break through yesterday, and alarms blared. So, whoever was foolish enough to venture past her shields, into her kingdom, let us know that it triggers an alarm."

I chuckled to myself. I wasn't foolish. I was collecting information for us.

"But that's where the advantages end. Panha is in an isolated dungeon where stationed guards are always on watch. Every four hours at the half-quarter mark, the guards change. They do so, one at a time, in a zigzag rotation. The only way in is to get through during a rotation change, if you can manage it." She flew across the room, back to the empty corner. I touched her arm and placed my hand over her mouth.

As I whirled her around to face me, I flickered visible for a second to stare into her eyes and slip into her mind. Once inside, I turned invisible again before anyone noticed. Instead of taking over, I used my telepathy to communicate.

Please don't let me alarm you. I won't hurt you. I want to help you with this mission. You have someone on the inside, spying for you? It was the only way they could know what they did about the guards.

She stayed silent, but images of fire raged in her mind.

I want to help. I'm the one who set off the alarm.

Pictures of another pixie with dark black hair and pink streaks appeared.

Who is that?

She groaned. *My wife, Lilli. She's our spy.*

Holy shit. They really did have one.

Tell the delegates Lilli learned that the guard near Panha's dungeon changes at half-past one and messes with his uniform. He won't pay attention to the entrance for the first five seconds. Make it count. I escaped her mind, not wanting to invade any longer.

She hesitated, her body shaking as she repeated what I'd told her. "I know it sounds too good to be true, but apparently, the guard has no brains," she added, with no help from me.

For the next thirty minutes, the crowd discussed their suggestions about how to escape afterward, until another delegate stood and silenced the room. "If we need to be near the entrance at half-past one, we must head out now. Send positive energy and prayers that we find a way out. We must have faith that we'll escape."

"Thank you, ladies and gents. We'll meet again tomorrow, hopefully with the good news of our lady-in-waiting," Kaito said, and the five delegates, along with Kylie, walked out of the basement. Invisible, I followed three yards behind them.

They traveled to Queen Rosalida's side of the river with hushed voices.

Since I had broken through the dome, some of the fissures had closed. Electricity hummed through the shield at a greater voltage, too. If I thought this was bad, how bad could it get if Lucifer took over? I shivered.

Neither of them could ever get a hold of Sierra.

One of the delegates said, "No wonder it's called the Darkened Kingdom now. Each day, the wall is getting worse."

The group murmured their agreement.

Two of the delegates, who must've been earth wielders, started digging. They built a tunnel many feet below the surface so we could pass underneath the river of death. One by one, the delegates slipped inside, with me following.

Kylie's wand shone a light in the dark tunnel. The pungent odor of fresh soil reached my nose the farther we ventured. That, combined with the wet ground seeping through my shoes, made me want to gag. I understood using the tunnel to break into Mother's side of the river, but how would they know when they were under Panha's cell?

"Kylie, you're sure you'll be able to feel where the entrance is?" Kaito asked.

"My wife left something buried for us. My wand will feel it." That was the only answer she gave. We continued in silence, though my mind was anything but silent. Horrid images of Lucifer sucking the life out of Sierra kept flooding in.

A few minutes later, we passed beneath the river and traveled onward until Kylie stopped.

She twirled her wand in the air above her head, eyes narrowed, searching for whatever her wife had buried. Something the size of a toothpick flew into her outstretched hand. She kissed it, and the tip turned orange. "We're here. This is where I part ways with you. I wish you *all* the best of luck. Stay safe."

When Kylie disappeared, Kaito glanced at his ghadee. "Perfect timing. Seven minutes past one. It's time."

It sure as hell was. The next few moments would determine the future of the universe. This was the all-or-nothing moment for Sierra. It had to succeed.

Fifty Two

The five clasped their hands together before turning as one and gaping up at their access point.

"Are you ready? There might be no escape," Kaito said.

"Always. We're with you to the end. As you said last night, we must be fast and return to this spot. It's the only way. We can do this," one of the delegates said, lips pressed in a tight line.

Not without me.

"Three, two, one," another said. The two earth wielders opened a gap above us.

The rip was a decent size, we could easily slip through it, but it wasn't too big that the guards would notice it. As the delegates discussed their assignments, I slipped through the hole. I needed to be in front to handle any issues that might arise.

The pixie had done a decent job at getting them close. We were definitely inside the grounds, only a hairsbreadth from the palace. I tried to figure out how they expected to get in, but then wrinkled my nose at a foul odor. I didn't know whether to be impressed or to laugh. Our opening had put us right next to the drainage tunnel. Its barred gate was partially visible above ground. To get inside, it seemed we'd have to walk through shit, literally.

Leaving the gate for the delegates to worry about, I searched for any guards. There were only two. Their gray, leathery skin and dark radiance had intensified since yesterday. They were dangerous, full demonic guards from Delmore, but they still had no brains.

One by one, I laid my hands on them, flashed visible, and stared into their eyes, forcing my voice inside their empty heads. My mind recoiled at the lack of anything inside. They were only a vessel, an evil puppet of Mothers. I told them to urinate against the palace walls, right in front of the opening. That'd make it easier for the delegates to kill them. If they didn't, I'd do it once the delegates had stepped away.

One delegate eased through the opening and noticed the guards. He gestured to Kaito and the others to move forward. One of the males, who had orange eyes, opened a water bottle. Kaito's hand glowed blue as he waved it, using his water element to lift the contents out and part it into two streams. With a quick hand motion and strong force, he slammed them into the guards.

They thrashed on the floor and spat water as they gasped for air, but each time they spat out the water, more rushed into their noses, not giving them enough time to breathe. This continued until their bodies stopped moving, and they passed out. The female delegate slit their throats and threw them down the hole.

Seconds later, one of the five noticed the drainage tunnel and waved a hand in front of his scrunched nose. Once the odor had wafted toward Kaito, he cursed and said, "Guess we can't complain. We've gotten this far. Juniper and Willow, will you do the honors?"

Underneath my feet, the ground roared, waking from a deep sleep and vibrating right through my feet. With every roll, more of the bars blocking the drainage tunnel appeared. The two delegates were manipulating the earth, but only in a small area near the gate. This impressive feat had my mouth hanging wide open.

Once the ground dropped low enough for us to fit through, we faced the challenge of squeezing between the metal bars, the separation between each, only a forearm's length, if that.

A different delegate pulled out a saw and cut through the bars with minimal noise. An impossible feat until I realized how the wind wielder contributed to this mission. She'd angled her body, the left side pointing toward the drain and her right arm reaching for the river. Whatever she did had her tilting her head. Her yellow eyes shone brighter, and her mouth had fallen open a smidge. She moved the sounds of the saw into the empty forest and village so it wouldn't give us away. Nice skill.

The second Kaito worked his way toward the opening, I rushed past him. I needed to be in the lead. The space was so tight I brushed against his knee. Shit. I froze as he glanced around, hand rubbing his knee, eyes narrowed in concentration.

This couldn't end. Not now. I couldn't breathe as I waited for him to do something.

A second later, he shook his head and continued to move forward.

Once we were deeper inside the tunnel, a slow, mechanical dripping noise echoed from the iron drain. I rubbed my eyes and nose, feeling the sting caused by the strong odor.

After a few minutes, the drip faded, but the awful odor lingered due to excrement lathering our ankles.

We were one floor above the forbidden dungeon, within the caves of the palace.

Frigid air bit into our flesh, and the walls changed from metal to rock. Uncanny shadows danced on the wall from the flickering orange lights, which barely provided any illumination. Darkness still filled the area.

Deeper into the underground, the smell changed from the nasty stench to death and decay.

One delegate cursed when Kaito made a loud noise as he stepped on something, breaking it. We all studied the ground, and our hands shot to our mouths. Bones and skin littered the floor, and who or what they belonged to, I had no idea. In some places, piles of the unknown dead reached to the top of the cave.

I had always wondered what happened to Mother's subjugates or playthings. Why had it taken me so long to realize she wasn't good? I was a fool. A puppet, even. A thing for her to control and lie to, to do her bidding and be manipulated.

If it wasn't for me needing to stay hidden, I'd have destroyed the cave. I wanted to release the anger boiling inside, but more than that, I wanted to expel the extreme hurt.

The wind wielder carried the sound of our footsteps away so that the cracking of bones disappeared with each footstep, but I often heard a sniffle or sigh coming from the group.

Light shone through an opening, and I ran forward before the delegates could. It led to the servant's corridors, and five lower ranked workers, plus Demeatris, were there. I'd found him yesterday and begged for his help. He was the one who'd started me down this path, and he could help me finish it.

Two maids faced the sink, scrubbing at the dishes. One slept in a lousy cot with several holes in it. Two others brought buckets of waste from the prisoners' cells to the opening.

Demeatris stood nearby, shuffling his feet. He'd promised he'd be in the servants' corridors when I arrived.

I portaled in front of him, flickered visible in the shadows, touched his arm, and stared into his eyes before slipping into his mind. *Demeatris, the delegates are here. Please provide a distraction for them. I promise, Aris's daughter will wake soon, and she'll get you out of this place. I'll personally make sure of it.*

Tartarus, you better not be lying. You promise she's okay, at least?

I provided him with images of Sierra dancing on Halloween, us bowling, and her using her senses. For a split second, I wondered again how she was holding up back at the cave. We hadn't left on the greatest of terms.

Demeatris's lips twitched up at the corners. *I'm doing this for her. For the prophecy. One to find—two to unite.*

His thoughts changed, going to how different my voice, tone, and demeanor had become. Not wanting to hear anymore, I removed myself.

An ache formed in my chest. He was the third person I'd left alive after revealing my secret. If Mother ever found out and gained control over me again, we'd all be in hell.

"Ladies, your queen had fun with several extra poor souls this evening. Let's bring them to their places until she decides what to do with them," Demeatris said, and the servants turned to follow him.

Seconds later, the delegates appeared, jaws slack, with shock written on their faces. "This entire thing seems too easy," one of them said.

"Let's not question it. That'll only lead to problems. Kylie said my mother's prison was one floor below the servants' corridors and to the left. If anything, let's hope our luck continues," Kaito said.

I continued on, far in front, and entered the mind of each guard I came upon. At just the right moment, each one either turned their backs to the wall or dropped their eyes from the delegates. Once the delegates neared, they took them out.

We arrived at the entrance to the forbidden dungeon from the outer underground path, bypassing the main dungeon.

The next guard, the daftest of them all and clearly a demon with his slithery skin and black bulbous eyes, was clueless when I opened his mind and ordered him to clean the dirt off his shoe. He did as I'd instructed, and I remained in his head while waiting for the delegates to kill him. His mind was just like the others, empty and void.

Not learning anything from him, I escaped his mind just as his head thumped to the floor.

Kaito took the keys from the dead guard and opened the forbidden dungeon. On the left, where a metal door stood, the fragrance of honey mixed with decay wafted toward us. As Kaito opened the cell, I eased down the hall and slipped into the guards' minds, ordering them to sleep.

Once the door creaked open, I rushed inside the room. It looked as if Mother had drained all life from the woman. Panha's cheeks were sunken and her waif-like body was slumped against the wall. She was way too thin, as if no one had fed her in weeks. Chains wrapped around her entire body. Only her face, hands, and knees down remained uncovered.

I couldn't even tell her hair or skin color from the caked blood covering anything left exposed. She looked dead, unless you were close enough to catch her chest faintly rise. Her eyes remained closed. Panha was either unaware of our presence or simply keeping her eyes closed against whatever terrible torture might come next.

Kaito fell to his knees as the others tried to wake Panha.

Holy Delmore, this little moment had lasted way too long! Even though I'd messed with the guard's minds, I could've missed one, or someone else might decide to come down to the cells. They were playing with fire. If I could, I'd take Panha now, but I had to make sure they were all safe and out of this kingdom.

I couldn't portal all of us out without raising red flags.

What better way to make them move than by scaring them?

Time to alert the guards of trespassers.

Fifty Three

I picked up the guard's head that they'd hacked off and chucked it at one of the sleeping guards. The guard stirred, eyes widening, and his mouth dropped open as he sounded the alarm. I rushed back into the prison cell to find the delegates sweating and Panha still asleep but unshackled. They looked at Kaito.

"Grab her and return to where we came," Kaito said.

Two of the delegates picked up Panha and made it three feet before twenty guards appeared. Shit. I hadn't expected that many or for them to have been so fast. I just wanted to get the delegates moving.

One delegate carried Panha over their shoulder while the rest unsheathed their weapons. On Kaito's command, the delegates huddled close and started their charge. The darkness around the guards grew as they blasted their demon magic forward.

Black demon cyclones spun toward the delegates. Death was imminent. I had no choice but to portal us away. Shit. I shook my sweaty hands. There went my secrecy. But if I didn't get the delegates out of there, they'd all die, and Queen Rosalida wouldn't help me.

I shoved them next to each other, grabbed handfuls of their shirts, and imagined the fissure in the dome. I rubbed my fingers, and we landed a few feet from it.

Just like this morning, there were two guards stationed near the black humming dome. Once the delegates landed with heavy thuds, the guards whipped around, throwing their black tendrils in our direction. I used all of my strength to shove the delegates and Panha through the opening without touching the shield. As they crossed, the alarm sounded a death tune.

Black tendrils pushed through the rip and grabbed hold of one delegate, preventing them from running. Of course, I could've jumped through, pulled the delegate free, and portaled away with Panha, but I'd rather make a show, make my stand, and ensure Mother saw someone rescuing her prisoner. Though it was foolish and cost me time, I wanted, *needed*, to hurt her.

While the others tried to hack at the magic and pull the delegate away from the demonic tendrils, I portaled behind the other guard. I plucked his blade from his grasp and shoved him into the dome. Electric currents engulfed his body as he screamed.

Using this guard's blade, I hacked at the neck of the other guard, who held a grip on the delegate. He turned and faced me, a cringy grin on his face. Though I was invisible, he could somehow see me. Holy Delmore. I gulped as he pulled out a different blade.

One hand continued to hold the delegate in those evil tendrils while he battled against me with the other.

Blade clashing against blade sounded across the kingdom. Both our blows had the strength of a giant thrust upon them.

The clang of metal was deafening, and our movements were swift.

Another guard came at me from the left and joined the battle. His eyes brightened when he saw me, too.

Could the delegates see me? Or just the guards because of their demon blood? But why these ones? No one saw me this morning or when we entered earlier today. Since the alarm blared, did Mother send the best to investigate and handle the intrusion? So then, maybe these demons were special or more powerful, and that was why they saw me?

Good thing for my mind control, or this would be a tougher battle. I'd still win, though. I was better, at least when in a small fight like this. If any more appeared I might have a problem.

I leaped backward and grabbed hold of the guard on my left, his neck firmly in my grasp.

Once I dug into his mind, I ordered him to use his blade to slice the head off the other guard who'd joined us. Face scrunched up, he did as I'd ordered. Still in his mind, I had him slice through his own neck.

The first guard, still holding the delegate, exuded anger. He drew his tendrils back from the delegate and rushed me. He swiped his blade at my calf while the delegates shuffled around, gaining their bearings. Any second, they'd be gone. Shit. Forget Mother seeing. I needed to finish this and grab Panha before I lost my chance.

Just as the demon swung his blade forward, Mother's chariot bells pealed in the distance. It amped up my adrenaline as sweat dripped down my forehead. I rushed him and snapped his neck with my bare hands.

His body went slack, and I portaled back to the rip.

Just as I slid through and my body landed on the other side of the dome, Mother's wagon appeared, her thick mist almost swallowing her whole. Her blood-wrenching scream rent the air. The whole kingdom trembled, as did I, but not at her outcry. Mine was from the darkness that spewed out of her mouth in massive amounts. She became a fountain, gushing out the blackness. It spread throughout the dome and darkened it further.

If anybody saw, there was no way they wouldn't know that Mother was evil. *Good.*

I placed my hands on Panha's shoulder and yanked her free of the delegate's grip before the darkness touched us. Once she was free of their touch, I portaled us both to Queen Rosalida's bed chambers.

Fifty Four

We arrived in a chamber with beautiful light pinks and gold glistening everywhere. Queen Rosalida paced beneath the chandelier, fidgeting with her braid. Beside her oak four-poster bed, three people messed with medical equipment. Sanitary scents flooded the room.

Holy Delmore! They were preparing for Panha.

I'd assume they knew about me, then.

As I waved my hand down my body and turned visible, I coughed.

Queen Rosalida turned in our direction. Her sapphire eyes fell on Panha, and her body went rigid. "Healers! Grab Panha. Work on her, please." The three healers took Panha from my arms and rushed her to the bed. "Tartarus. I trusted you."

What the hell? I stepped back at her words.

"If you were going to portal my delegates out of the dungeon, you should've portaled them to Make Waves or anywhere else. Why allow your mother to see them taking her? For weeks, she's been preparing for a war, and you just gave her ammunition to accelerate her plans."

"I ... I ..." She wouldn't believe me if I confessed that portaling outside the kingdom wouldn't have worked. Plus, I didn't have to wait for Mother to see. But I wanted to hurt her. I hadn't thought about the consequences.

"Because of that, I'm hesitant to fix Slinger or have my lady-in-waiting go with you."

No! I fell to my knees. This couldn't be happening. This was my last chance, my alternate plan. My body shook. Queen Rosalida knelt beside me and lifted my chin.

"You've accessed the Gateway."

I scrunched my eyebrows.

"You know the rules. You can't lie once you're on the vault."

I nodded, not understanding where she was going with this.

She pushed the tufted couch at the end of her bed out of the way and moved the ancient wool rug. Underneath it was a Gateway vault. I blinked several times.

"You have access to Lukita?" Why hadn't she seen Sierra then or taken her?

"It's not Lukita's Gateway." She shook her head. "We're running out of time. The semantics don't matter. If you want my help, I request you not to lie to me."

I gulped. The pain the Gateway could inflict was torturous, as per my past experience, but I needed Queen Rosalida's help. "Deal."

I stuck out my hand, and she grabbed it. Light blue and black smoke swirled between us. It turned into a straight line and zapped into both our chests. With a strong force, it slammed me backward. A light blue knot formed in my chest next to where Sierra's lavender bond would be. Magic had just bound us.

A feat only possible between two people who had the blood of a god.

"The bond, combined with the Gateway confession, will show me if I should trust you. Are you ready?" Queen Rosalida leaned against the dresser and gestured for me to stand on the vault.

"Yes." I stepped into the circle, and a flickering gold layer formed around the perimeter and rose to the ceiling. There was no getting out without me confessing whatever she wanted. My throat closed. I knew this was a risk. I knew she could capture me. But now that she had, my heart broke as I thought of Sierra turning into the darkness.

"My name is Tartarus Obsidian of whatever kingdom Sierra's throne is. I'm no longer the queen's bodyguard. My position and allegiance are, and will always be, to protect Sierra. After capturing Sierra, my heart only reappears when I touch her, and when it does, a bond forms."

When my blood didn't boil, and the gold layer vanished, releasing me, tears streamed down my face. I already knew how I felt, but to know it was true, to know I wasn't imagining it, became overwhelming.

With my truths exposed, I gazed up at Queen Rosalida.

It was her turn.

My head tilted as I watched her expression. A smile spread across her face, and her eyes shone a bright light blue with purple specs.

"Thank you, Tarus, for your truths." She used my nickname that only Sierra and Vilo knew. Huh? "What request do you seek?"

"To have your help mending Slinger and for permission to take Panha with me, but you already know this. A deal requires something from both sides. A knot formed in my chest when we struck the deal. The bond will only disappear when I fulfill your request. So, what is it? It wasn't going into this circle. Otherwise, it would've already disappeared." My mind couldn't even fathom what it could be, which made the hairs on the back of my neck stand.

"Because you've ignited the war between your mother and me, we're running out of time. All I ever dreamed of was meeting my daughter. Without her belief, your mother will destroy us. I want to see Sierra and embrace her before I die. So, I'm giving you three days to wake her magic. On day four, you must share your location and let my delegates save her."

My lungs collapsed. I couldn't breathe. "Three days?"

"Three days. You have Panha. If that doesn't help, you're not going to be able to wake her."

"What about the image you saw of us marrying?"

"That's the thing about prophecies and the future—they aren't set in stone. They can always change. We have to accept that this one did, too." A lone tear fell on her cheek, but massive droplets poured out of me. I refused to believe our future had changed. It couldn't have.

"If I give her to you, and you already know everyone with you will die once you go up against my mother, you're committing her to death."

"Then I guess you have a lot of work ahead of you. Make her believe." Her lips turned up.

"Guess I do." My muscles tightened. Panha better be able to help.

Queen Rosalida held out her hand. "Slinger?"

I pulled Slinger's pieces out of my pocket and handed them to her. She walked to the side of her bed, placed the parts in a gray glass mixing bowl, and handed it to me. I stared at it.

She leaned over Panha, kissed her cheek, and removed her necklace. It held a small glass circle like hers, but instead of a live ember of fire, it had a small windmill rotating.

She connected the two *pieces* like a puzzle. They sizzled in her hands. Smoke rose from them and brought with it scents of marshmallows roasting on a fire.

After placing them in the bowl, she pulled a star from her dress pocket, a mini version of Slinger but with a silver rim and pink rhinestones. She sliced her palm and squeezed her blood into the bowl. A hiss resonated throughout the room.

"You can cast spells if you have all the ingredients, correct?" She glanced at me.

"Yes."

"Repeat after me. *Clima escailnt bileska ekta.*"

On the third repetition, I managed to say it. The mixture rose from the bowl in a translucent red square. The contents circled one another and fused Slinger together. Heat radiated through my chest. A part of me had been restored. All wasn't lost with Slinger, and it wasn't with Sierra either.

Having finished, the square disappeared, and Slinger thumped into the bowl.

Queen Rosalida picked Slinger up, kissed him, and handed my star back to me.

"Thank you." I bowed and hugged Slinger tightly.

"Any second, Kaito and the rest of the delegates are going to barge in. You need to go. You have three days, Tarus. I hope you wake my daughter's magic." She squeezed my hands.

"What about Panha? She isn't awake yet?" Her color had returned, her bones no longer protruded, and her black hair looked healthy, at least.

"Tell her that Rosalida said, 'One to find. Two to unite.' That phrase should make her trust you. Now go."

I placed my hand on Panha and portaled back to the Gateway.

Panha was still out of it when we appeared inside the cave. Since I didn't know where Sierra was or how Panha would react when she woke, I transported us to the farthest end of the cave, where the waterfall would diminish any sounds.

Hunched over, I leaned my back against the wall and caught my breath.

"Slinger fixed?" Lukita asked.

Unsheathing Slinger, I held him out. He looked shinier than before. I smiled and kissed the perfect star. "Good as new."

"I told you she'd help."

"Yeah, but everything comes with a price, and she had one, too." I closed my eyes and searched for the light blue bond. Sure enough, it was there.

She gasped. "What do you mean?"

"I kind of ... sort of ... f'd up." I scrunched my nose and waited for the reprimand.

"Are you talking about how your mother completed her dome?" Lukita's voice rose.

"I don't know why I was hell-bent on making Mother hurt, but now Queen Rosalida believes I've ignited a war. She gave me three days to awaken Sierra's magic. If I don't, I have to give up our location and let her delegates come and save the day." Wait. Why? Damn it. I should've asked. Why couldn't I just portal us in three days?

She whistled. "So, what's your plan?"

"Have Sierra and Panha talk. Train Sierra, like planned, to see if I can spark her magic." I rubbed my temples. Hopefully, that would do it. "How's Sierra?"

"She's seen better days. You've been gone almost forty-eight hours."

My chest tightened. I needed to see her.

"Will you make Panha comfortable? Give her a bed, couch, and things to do. But ..." My throat tightened. I hated doing this. "... keep her enclosed. We can't have her running into Sierra before I speak to her. Let me know when she wakes, please."

"Okay. What are you going to do?"

"Talk to Sierra. Before I left, things weren't good between

us." She had told me she refused to ever love me and that she thought I belonged to a cult.

"Tartarus, I'm not meant to interfere, so I won't say much, but I need Sierra's magic to awaken to be freed. When you were gone, she confessed to the wind that if she were in her fantasy books, a mating bond would've formed between you two. She loves you. But she doesn't understand how you could do this to her. Work with that."

A warmth filled my soul. She still loved me!

Fifty Five

Sierra slept without stirring, a soft noise escaping her nose. I couldn't help but gaze at her. As I watched her sleep, breathing in her scent of lavender, embers, and salt water, the lavender bond formed and hummed a sweet tune deep inside me.

Panha's awake, and she's pissed, Lukita said before I had a chance to utter a word to Sierra.

A tightness grew in my chest as I waved my hand, turning invisible, and returned to Panha. Her yellow eyes shone brightly as she punched an invisible wall in front of me. She appeared to be screaming, but I couldn't hear a thing.

What did you do? I asked Lukita.

I placed her in a soundproof box so Sierra wouldn't hear. Her screams are deafening.

Did you say anything to her?

No. That's your place.

Groaning, I placed my hands on the box and turned visible. Panha's eyes grew wide as she stumbled backward and pressed herself against the rear wall underneath a burning torch. I cupped one hand around my ear, the other to my heart ... a gesture of peace in our realm. She fell to the floor.

Remove the box so I can talk to her. Please.

Panha's sobs bounced off the wall.

"My name is Tartarus." I leaned over the buffet table, covered with an assortment of foods and coffee beans, in the corner of the room.

"I know who you are." She glared up, her teeth grinding.

"I'm not here to hurt you. I just saved you from my mother."

"Liar!" she screamed.

I gripped the edge of the table and took a deep breath. "Please believe me. Queen Rosalida knows you're here. She told me to tell you, 'One to find. Two to unite.'"

"How dare you lie about the queen!" Veins bulged on her forehead.

She wasn't going to listen to me. I raked my hand through my hair.

I don't think she's gonna help, Lukita chimed.

No shit. I rubbed my temples.

"Panha. Please." Sierra thought I was crazy. I needed someone to explain everything to her.

"Go away!" She clenched her fists.

"Will—"

"I said, go!"

I punched the wall next to me. Bones cracked. Panha and I both drew a sharp breath. Great, I'd scared her even more.

"Will you hear me out, please?" I leaned over the table again. She glared at me but kept silent. "The last part of the prophecy talks about a powerful warrior without a heart finding Sierra and uniting everyone under love. Your queen and I—"

"If you want me to listen, you won't discuss my queen." She seethed.

I could work with that. At least she wasn't screaming and telling me to go away anymore.

"Okay. I believe the last part was referring to me. Before I met Sierra, I had no heart. I haven't had one for a while, and over the last two years, I've been a bodyguard to my mother, the dark queen. Without my heart and with her as my influence, I didn't care about many people, and it didn't bother me to kill others for her. I thought they deserved it."

Panha gasped, clutching her chest, but she didn't tell me to go, so I continued, "When I met Sierra, something sparked inside me. A lavender vein formed and built me a heart. But even with that, I still struggled with betraying my mother until she killed my maiden, who was like a second mother to me. It woke me up to the truth."

Even though I knew the truth, just thinking about the betrayal and the possibility of killing Mother, my chest tightened. I didn't think I'd ever be okay with the alternate plan. I was happy Rosalida had fixed Slinger, but part of me wished she hadn't. Then I wouldn't have to kill Mother. It was clear from the prophecy it had to be Slinger that killed her.

"I no longer support the dark queen. I'm trying to wake Sierra's magic so she can reunite the realms under love. But ... a pixie cursed me, preventing me from mentioning magic to Sierra. So, I brought you here in the hope you could help." I shrugged.

"You expect me to believe that?" She stood and stalked forward but kept the table between us.

"Yes." My lips thinned.

"I need to think." She waved her hand in dismissal.

I slumped but took the hint and ventured back to Sierra.

She was at the lake. One leg lay in the water, the other folded beneath her.

"Hey, Sierra."

She flinched as I took a seat in the sand beside her.

"It was awful of me to have left with things how they were between us." I placed my hand on hers. Her breath hitched, and the lavender vein formed before she pulled away.

She said nothing in return, and as the silence dragged on, accompanied by the occasional crackle from the torches, sweat dripped down my spine. Misery, in the form of a dark shadow, fell around us despite the glow on her face from the water's reflection.

"Sierra, you bring out the good in me. Give me a chance to prove it."

"Do I really have a choice?" Her voice was distant.

"You always have a choice."

"Not really. You're going to keep me prisoner, regardless." Her eyes misted over, and she splashed her foot in the lake. Salty droplets fell on my lips as the water drenched my shirt.

"Sierra, you're not a prisoner. We're in here to protect you."

Regardless of whether Panha helped, I would still have to convince her to train. "There's something I have to tell you. I wish you were in better spirits for this conversation, but I can't wait." I blinked back the tears. I had to lie to her—make up a story about Mother coming to torture her. It was the only way she'd understand the intensity of the situation and hopefully get her to take the training seriously. Otherwise, I had no idea how to spark her magic.

"You know how I told you people are after us? Those people. I went and saw them. Begged them to stop searching for you. Said you weren't the right person."

"Did they believe you?" Sierra bit the inside of her mouth.

"Worse. They gave me an ultimatum." The thorn bush reappeared and shot sharp pain anywhere it touched.

"And?" Sierra hugged her knees close.

"I have three days to wa—" Knives stabbed my chest. The damn curse. Damn it! I groaned.

"Are you okay?" Her eyes widened.

I took a deep breath. "Yes. Sorry. I have three days to make you believe. If you don't, my mother kills us both after she's done torturing us."

Tears flowed from Sierra's eyes, stabbing me worse than the curse.

"How did I get messed up in this? I ... I ..." She rested her head in her hands.

"I am sor—"

"Tarus, those three words ..."

"I know." But I was sorry. Sorry, this was all happening. Sorry, I couldn't speak the truth. And sorry her life was in danger.

"What do we do now?" She gazed at me, her white orbs glistening.

"Make you believe."

"In the impossible? Seriously, what are we going to do?"

"Train you for a fight. It's all we can do." I gave her a moment to take it all in. "For the next three days, we train. I'll teach you everything I know."

"Starting when?" Sierra blinked, her head cocked to the side.

Lukita, can you bring down two swords? Two long swords dropped onto my lap with a loud clang. Sierra bunched her eyebrows. *Thank you.*

"Now." I handed her a sword. "Let's see how you do in combat with swords."

"Like in medieval times? Are you serious?"

"Dead serious."

The color drained from her face, and my stomach dropped.

Even though we were running out of time, I didn't want to rush her. But once my shirt had dried, time was up. I needed to get things moving. "What are you thinking about?"

"How I don't want to hate you." A tear plopped onto the sword's blade and echoed around the cave. My breathing hitched. I didn't know how to respond to that. "I want to believe you, but what does that say about me if I do?"

"It says you're smart and amazing." It was working. She was believing. Maybe I wouldn't need Panha. Or perhaps Panha would be the final push Sierra needed to believe.

"I'm smart for still liking the guy who blinded and trapped me? That sounds foolish."

"You still like me?" I smiled.

"Tarus!" She shoved my shoulder. "I don't know. It's hard not to like you, but it's also hard not to hate you. I'm confused. I'm frightened. And I want to go home." She sighed.

"You know what's great to do when you're stressed and confused?"

She turned her face to me, bags prominent underneath her crystal orbs.

"Train. Expel all the emotions in a workout."

Releasing a breath, she wiggled her lips and said, "Let's make it into a game."

Gods, this woman! "Okay."

"Answer a question for me, and I'll train."

"Deal." I braced myself for another bond to form like her mother's had, but it didn't appear. Just like it hadn't any other time we struck a deal. It wouldn't happen without her magic being active.

"If you want me to escape so badly, why won't you set me free?"

"That's complicated to answer. But please trust me, if I thought it was the right thing to do, you would've never spent a single night here."

She tilted her head but didn't say anything else. We were so close to her speaking about magic. So close to me telling her everything. But she'd dropped the conversation again.

Stiff air trapped in my lungs, and I stood, trying to shake it off. "Your turn. Let's learn offensive moves." I held out a hand.

She grabbed it with her right hand, still holding the sword with her left.

"When fighting combat, it's good to have your feet planted firmly." I stood behind her, bracing her by placing her feet in the correct position. Her body tensed under my touch. I gulped before continuing to move her into the correct position. "Place your arms here." I lifted her arms to just above waist level and shifted in front of her. "Beginners should always use two hands on the hilt to give more support while thrusting."

She nodded and thrust the sword forward.

"Good. Keep doing it until you feel at one with the sword. Like you're not just holding it, but that it's a part of you."

She did as I said. Watching her mesmerized me. The way she held it looked natural. She was a born fighter.

Once she smiled, I thrust my sword in front of her next movement, and our blades clanged. She dropped hers, pouted, and then picked it up. "Again."

My body rumbled with laughter, and the lavender vein vibrated.

Each time our swords clashed, I pushed her farther back. She tried to move forward but was no match for my strength. Our blades hit several times without her dropping hers.

"Excellent. When someone fights you, they're looking for an opening. Never give one." I tapped my sword to her side and then to her left shoulder.

She groaned. "And how am I supposed to not leave an opening?"

Yes! She was asking questions. She wanted to learn.

I taught her skills, and she listened, performing them

correctly after about three attempts. I loved how fast she picked things up.

After the next battle between us, which lasted three minutes, she hunched over, panting. Her damp hair clung to her face. "Can we take a break?"

"Let's go eat." I held out my arm, and she took it. The lavender heart beat to her rhythm, and my body warmed.

At the buffet table, I grabbed a truffle and placed it on Sierra's lips. "This is my favorite."

"Tartarus!" Panha screamed.

Sierra stopped mid bite. "What was that?"

"Nothing." My body trembled.

"Tartarus!" Panha screamed again.

"Are you sure? It sounds similar to your name." She furrowed her brow.

I didn't know whether or not to be happy. Sierra couldn't find out about Panha yet, but at least Panha was actually using my name now. Did that mean she was willing to talk to Sierra? Needing to find out, I squeezed Sierra's shoulder. "You're right. Let me check the cave to ensure everything is okay and none of Mother's minions have broken in. I'll be back."

"I want to hear your story. How did you learn about the prophecy and Queen Rosalida's phrase? After you tell me everything, I'll decide whether to help you," Panha said, the second I appeared next to her yellow tufted couch.

I shared everything with her, from the moment Demeatris took me to see Aris, right up to the present moment. Several times, she interjected, asking me questions, and I filled her in as best I could.

Once finished, I hunched over the couch, out of breath from speaking so fast, and waited for Panha's decision. She took forever to respond, and my lips trembled as I waited. What if she still didn't believe me? Would training Sierra be enough? Maybe, but I didn't have the time. I needed Panha to speed things up.

Glancing at her, I couldn't help but frown. She looked torn. Her face was ashen, and she rubbed at her temples.

Shit. I was doomed.

"If Sierra finds me, I'll speak with her." Panha smiled, and my heart burst with joy.

I couldn't help myself. I jumped up and clapped.

Amid my happy dance, Panha coughed, and my body went rigid.

"If you are the powerful warrior, I can only help up to a point. Ultimately, only you can awaken her magic."

I sighed. This prophecy really had everyone so fearful of interfering, even in the slightest. But at least she was willing to help somewhat.

"Thank you for believing me. I'll make sure she finds you." I smiled and returned to the lake, but Sierra was gone.

Sighing, I dashed to her room.

She stood next to the back wall, paints in hand. In front of her, spread across the wall, was a beautiful mural of a forest with a waterfall, trees, and flowers. She couldn't see, yet she could paint that image.

"It's beautiful." I placed my hand on her back, and she tensed.

"Since I can't see, every other sense I have has increased. It's as if holding a paintbrush or a sword is second nature." She turned, my arm still wrapped around her, and tilted her face up. My heart and bond were back, and they danced inside my chest.

"Want to see how good your sense of smell and hearing are?" Seeing the painting and hearing her talk about her senses had given me a great idea. I'd have her find something hidden near Panha. That way, she wasn't just learning to use the elements, but she was also finding Panha.

"What do you have in mind?" She grinned.

"Some say I have a scent—"

"You do."

I jerked back. Hopefully, it wasn't awful. "Please share."

"You smell like a forest." She placed the paints back on the shelf, and they clattered together.

"Huh?" I leaned against her bedframe, arms folded.

"Like oak trees, pine needles, fresh sunshine, and crisp hints of lavender."

Lavender was her fragrance. So, her mom was right. Her scent clung to me.

I took off my shirt and handed it to her.

"What's this?" She lifted it to her nose.

"My shirt." I chuckled. "I'm going to hide it, and you're going to find it."

"Okay. When?"

"Give me thirty minutes."

"I can't tell time." She raised her eyebrows.

"I'll come back for you. That's when it'll start."

"If you're near me, it'll confuse the scent of the shirt." Her lips smushed to the side.

"I'll bathe in the stream. Being in there should wash away the scents. I'll be back." I ran to the corner of the tunnel, just before Panha's cave, placed my shirt down, and returned to Sierra. She had changed into a yellow sundress, shoulders bare and legs exposed. My mouth watered.

"Ready?" Sierra asked, taking me out of my thoughts.

"Yes. I'm heading to the stream now." I dashed away before she could say anything and dipped myself into the freezing water—which also helped with my erection.

After bathing, I couldn't wait any longer. I needed to know whether she had found Panha.

With my eyes closed, I took a deep breath and searched for her scent. Within seconds, I found it—she was close to Panha.

I portaled to a section of the cave near Sierra.

She bent over to pick up my shirt and then froze. She sniffed the air and scrunched her eyebrows. Shirt in hand, she rose and headed in the direction of Panha.

My pulse quickened, and I took several steps back. With a deep breath, I looked inward at my chest. The lavender vein, the outline of my heart, my bond, and her mother's bond hadn't disappeared. A lightness filled me.

Panha gasped when Sierra came into view.

Sierra jumped. "Who's there?"

"Um ..." Panha walked closer. "My name is Panha."

"Do I know you? Are you a prisoner, too?" The hairs on Sierra's arms rose.

"No, to both. I'm actually here to help you."

"Help me? Like, escape?" Sierra's eyebrows rose.

"Not exactly. Help you to believe."

Sierra shook her head and stepped back. "You're part of his cult!"

Panha rushed to Sierra and grabbed her hands. "Shanti."

Sierra froze.

Shanti?

"H ... H ... How do you know that name? I never shared it with anyone."

"It's the name your birth mother gave you."

Sierra collapsed on the floor. Tears streamed down her face in a fierce downpour. Panha wrapped her arms around Sierra. My heart ached, but at the same time, it jumped, full of adrenaline. Panha was going to get through to her.

Sierra lifted her head. "You knew my mother?"

"Yes. She's my qu ... Ahhh!" Panha clutched her chest.

What the hell? Was the curse affecting her?

"Are you okay?" Sierra asked, her voice frantic.

"Sorry. Yeah. I'm fine." Panha took a deep breath. "I wanna try something."

Sierra tilted her head. "Okay."

"Has Tarus told you who you are?"

"In a way."

"You're a se ... Ahh!" Panha hunched over, screaming.

Shit. I collapsed to the cold floor. The pixie's unfinished curse.

Sierra shook her. "Panha. Panha."

Panha rose and grabbed Sierra's hands, but she focused on me. She shook her head at me, and a lone tear trickled down her face. "Sierra, both Tarus and I can't tell you who you are. You have to believe on your own."

A weight slammed into my chest, and I returned to my room. Once there, I destroyed everything, my frustration pushing me on. Why? Why couldn't anything be easy? With nothing left to demolish, I pounded on the wall until my hands bled.

Fifty Seven

I needed to think of a new plan, but nothing came to mind. Panha was it. There was nothing else. I kicked at the cave and rested my forehead against the cold sting of the wall.

"Don't give up. You can still train her," Lukita said.

"What's the point?"

"To protect her. But, besides that, after Panha shared that she wasn't a prisoner, and called Sierra by her birth name, it might've sparked something in Sierra to believe."

"You think so?"

"They're still talking, and Sierra's smiling. It's promising."

"Thanks. I hope you're right."

I returned to Panha's room. She and Sierra lounged on the couch, hands entwined.

"You've met Panha." I moved closer.

Panha smiled, and Sierra turned in my direction. "She knows my mom."

"I know." I chuckled.

"Why did you keep her from me?" She scrunched her eyebrows.

"After speaking with those hunting us, I found her and begged her to help me make you believe. Once she'd agreed, I wanted you to find her using your senses." I eased onto the smooth ground beside the couch.

Panha squeezed Sierra's hand. "I'm an old woman and need my sleep."

My head jerked back. Panha wasn't old. I glanced at her, and she winked.

Panha stood, pulling Sierra off the couch with her. "Go train with Tarus. You need to be prepared in case his mother finds you."

"But I have so much more I want to ask you." Sierra pouted.

"You can come back later." Panha brushed a loose strand of hair behind Sierra's ear, and Sierra smiled.

"Come on, let's fight." I took Sierra's hand and mouthed *thank you* to Panha.

"Okay, but then I'm coming back." Sierra's voice was full of excitement ... life.

Although Panha couldn't fill in the missing gaps, I was happy she'd helped improve Sierra's spirits.

Sierra and I headed back to the stream. Along the way, she shared everything Panha had said about her mom. She skipped as she did so. I couldn't help but feel elated for her.

Once at the stream, I placed the hilt of the sword in her hand. "Ready?"

"Yes." She attacked, her eyes sparking blue. The water roared around us.

Distracted by the change, she almost stabbed me in the side. I attacked her back, and the more we battled, the more a light blue shimmer followed behind her every movement. Her mother's element was speaking to her. She had to feel it.

"Tarus! Are you okay?" Sierra screamed. At the same time, something sharp stabbed into my side.

Whoa. What? I jumped. One of Sierra's hands covered her mouth while the other shook atop the sword's hilt. Following the blade of the sword, I suddenly understood why her panic—she had thrust it into my side.

Clenching my teeth, I yanked the sword out. Immediately, my speed healing took over. Odd. I thought it couldn't work in front of her. Could this mean she was starting to believe and parts of the curse were lifting? "Sierra, I'm okay. It went between my arm and my side. It didn't nick me."

"Are you sure?" She gulped.

"Yes." I grasped her hand and placed it on my bare abs.

As she moved her hands around my stomach, the tension between us spiked. Warmth spread from her touch, and I couldn't breathe. She stepped closer, so close that her breath whispered against my skin. "You're okay."

With her lips inches from mine, I wrapped her in my arms and pulled her closer. "I'm okay."

She froze for a second, biting her lip, the tension building further. I leaned in, and she pushed off my chest. "I'm still confused about us. On the one hand, I believe you, but on the other, I'm so pissed you didn't say anything before." She twirled around and stormed off.

I chased after her.

"Look, I get you need time to process everything, but that's the one thing we don't have." I grabbed her hand and whirled her around to face me. "Could we put us aside for a moment and just do one more exercise?"

She clenched her jaw. "Fine."

Yes! Having seen the colors shadow her movements, I wanted to know if they'd trail her while running. Plus, she needed to learn how to run away from the enemy, especially if she was still blind.

"Race me to your room. The first one there must answer a question for the other. Deal?"

She groaned. "You know I hate running."

"Please?"

"Ugh!" She stomped a few times and then dashed off.

At first, Sierra ran sloppily. She kept her hands outstretched to balance herself, not trusting her senses to guide her. My teeth ground. *Lukita, can you create wind around Sierra and force her off balance?*

A strong breeze blew into the cave, and Sierra almost fell but caught herself before she face-planted with the ground.

After that, she picked up speed and ran like hell. She no longer lifted her hands. I dashed in front to catch a glimpse of her eyes. They were sparking green, yellow, and purple.

Yes. Three elements.

As she grew comfortable running, colors streamed behind her, not at the same magnitude as with the sword fighting, but enough. I tensed while studying those streams of color. It meant nothing when Sierra couldn't see them unless she could *feel* them. Once we finished running, I needed to find a way to ask her.

A few minutes later, Sierra's knees buckled. She began to fall, so I ran to protect her. I sandwiched her face between my hands and rested it against my sweaty lap. Once recognition dawned that she wouldn't face-plant, she lifted her chin.

My heart sped up as we stayed there, transfixed. Overwhelming, deep-rooted need and love flowed through me. I wanted her arms around me and her lips pressed against mine.

Just as I gained the courage to be foolish yet brave, and try my luck, she passed out. What the hell? My body shook. Did I do this to her? Or was it her powers? Part of me preferred it to be my fault because if her powers could do this to her, how would she ever stand up against Mother?

I carried her back to her room and tucked her under the bedcovers, but until I knew she was all right, I waited in the recliner.

A little while later, she came to.

After reorienting herself, she whispered, "Tarus, I hope you're telling the truth." She smiled as she fell back asleep.

The next morning, Sierra wasn't in her room or near the three waters.

With spirits high, I checked Panha's room. Sure enough, they had huddled close on the couch, coffee and hash browns in their hands, smiles spread on their faces.

I was about to leave when Sierra mentioned soulmates, and my ears perked up.

"Do you think that's why I still love him?" Sierra fiddled with her cardboard coffee sleeve. My hands covered my gasp. I couldn't believe she was admitting to someone that she still loved me.

"Before we were even born, it was decided who would be, what you call, a soulmate. Then it's up to us to find them. When we do, we'll know." Panha placed her coffee on the table and rested her hand on Sierra's knee. "In your case, I don't believe you can help it or change it because it sounds like Tarus is your soulmate. Don't beat yourself up about still loving him."

At those words, my heart sank, and I couldn't hear

anything else. I returned to my room to process this information.

Sierra still loved me, but she continued to beat herself up for it, like Lukita had said. I hated that I continued to cause her pain. The feeling of sharp knives stabbed into my lavender heart a million times over.

I was awful—just like Lucifer.

With a sense of dread weighing heavily on me, I lay in bed, tossing a rock into the air, over and over. "Lukita, was there ever a good seer?"

"Depends on who you ask."

"I'm asking you."

"Yes. But many didn't believe it possible, so they got rid of her."

My mouth popped open. What if Lukita's *other half* was a seer? It'd certainly explain why she was trapped. "Why?"

"Don't you need to train with Sierra?" She sounded annoyed.

"Yes. Wait, one more question?" I grinned.

She sighed. "Why not."

"Can the person who shows Sierra magic really shape her into something of good or evil? Do they really have that much power over her? Isn't *she* supposed to be the most powerful creature?"

"That's more than one question." She laughed.

"Please." I put my hands together.

"It depends on the seer. If they're meant to have continuous visions, then the minute they learn and future scenarios flood into them, it rattles their mind, and they end up becoming lost, trying to find their way out. Whether they're meant to have poems or words for prophecy depends on how soon it floods their system and who is with them when that happens. Does this make sense?"

I shrugged. "Not really, but go on. Please?"

"If one interferes in a negative way during the first prophecy, it can turn tides. There are endless possibilities. But, since most people believe every seer is dark, the only people who have given them a chance have been those who are corrupt. But enough. Go and train Sierra. She's in her room."

"Thanks." I dashed off.

The second I reached her room, Sierra turned from her painting and smiled. The flame from the fire brightened her white orbs, a translucent rainbow reflecting off them.

She looked beautiful.

"Before training, I wanted to talk." I sat on her bed and patted the soft comforter. She eased in next to me, still smiling. Good. High spirits. "You owe me an answer to a question."

Her shoulders slumped. I knew she hated talking about the magical stuff, but I wanted to use this question to gauge her belief. We only had two days left. Time was running very thin. I needed to know just how much of her power was awakening.

"Hey, I fainted. Granted, I came close many times, but you never succeeded in catching me. I think that's a deal-breaker." She tilted her head.

Her desperation made me chuckle, but we both knew, no matter what, I'd ask. "If you had been in real danger, they wouldn't have cared about you hitting your head, nor would they have returned you to your bed. You would've been dead or captured. So, you keep the consequence."

She groaned and threw her head back. My jeans grew tight, and I shifted on the bed.

"Fine. What is the personal question you're eager to ask?"

I took a deep breath. "What makes you not want to believe?"

Sierra took so long coming up with her response that pinpricks shot down my arm, and I fidgeted with Slinger. Images of Mother capturing her reappeared. I shook them away, and thoughts of Queen Rosalida replaced them. If Sierra didn't believe, how would she react to seeing her birth mom? And what would happen when Mother declared war?

"If I believe, what'll happen to me when it comes crashing down?" A lone tear escaped.

Agony filled me, the level becoming unbearable.

My silence must've lasted too long because Sierra stood up. I grabbed her arm as gently as I could and pulled her back.

Gloom radiated from her as she waited for me to explain. "I don't have those answers for you, and I'm truly sorry. Deep down, I believe you have great instincts. If you learn to trust them, to let them guide you, whatever happens, you'll be okay."

She dropped her arm. "Let's just train."

"Okay." I sighed. "Today, there isn't going to be any action or *barely* any action. Today is going to be mostly learning. A classroom-style lesson that'll be the most unforgettable one you've ever had. This way, I don't have to worry if you'll remember anything." It took me all night to come up with this idea. I held my hand out for her. "We need to train by the stream."

"Why?" She scrunched her lip to the side.

"To see if it speaks to you." I tensed, waiting for the pixie's curse to hit me, but nothing happened. Thank the gods.

She sighed and grabbed my hand.

"Whether or not you believe, the elements are important for you to learn." By the time I'd finished speaking, all the color had drained from her.

Instead of panicking, I told myself I needed to try harder. I tucked her arm over mine and guided her out of the room. "First is wind or air. People interchange the terms. I like to use *air* because it can still be there even on windless days."

"Seriously? We're going back to the elements?" Sierra's shoulders slumped.

"When we fight or you run, do you feel anything?"

"Free." She shrugged.

"Ugh. Well, think of them like your senses. Humor me."

"Only if you answer a question for me afterward."

Sierra and her games. I loved it. "Of course."

She dashed to the stream's edge and placed her legs in the water.

Grinning, I eased in next to her. "Air has tremendous ways of helping us in battle. It warns us when to flee by telling us if explosions, fire, or gas are nearby. Air could help by hiding us, sending other scents out there to mask ours. If the wind was mighty enough, it could even help knock our opponents off their feet, stunning or shocking them in the process."

"Air sounds pretty cool." She kicked her legs in the stream.

"It is, and those are just a few of the things air can do." I shrugged.

"You know, all the examples sound too powerful. Things that could only happen in a magical world." She eased back, resting on her elbows.

"Exac—" Pain shot through my arm. The Pixie's curse appeared. A boulder-like heaviness came with it, weighing down on my chest, sucking the life out of me.

Instead of letting the panic take hold, I tried again.

Since Sierra couldn't see, it might've made her feel like we played pretend. But I wanted to know if something could happen beyond her eyes sparking and the scents roaming the room. Maybe at least one would come alive in her and do something more.

Wind was the hardest—especially since neither of her parents possessed it. So, I started there. "I need you to heal me."

She scrunched her nose.

Without hesitation, I used Slinger to slice my calf. Her nose twitched. A few seconds later, she sniffed, and yellow dots formed in her white orbs. The wind pushed the scent to her, but it wasn't enough for me to see if this was an element on which she was keen.

Was she feeling it ... the magic within? I could only hope.

"Remove your shirt." She ripped pieces off and wrapped my calf to staunch the bleeding.

Quite impressive. We did two more scenarios using wind before we moved on to water.

I told her many things that water could accomplish. We did the same for earth and fire afterward.

As I suspected, her eyes sparked with each element. Throughout the process, I couldn't tell what part sang to her the most. Her crystalized orbs lit up the same every time.

After we finished practicing, I quizzed her on what she'd learned. She only messed up a few answers, which made me happy to know she'd listened. I scored her at eighty-five percent, and she laughed a joyous sound.

This time, when we headed to her room with our food, we fell back into familiar habits, talking about books, authors, and the delightful stories they created.

Sitting on the floor, leaning against her painted wall, Sierra placed her hand on my thigh. My jaw clenched, and the lavender vein vibrated out of control.

"I played your game. I listened to your lesson. Now it's my turn. Will you please answer a question for me?"

"If I can, yes." I placed my hand on hers and squeezed tight.

"Will you tell me everything you know about your mother, including any magical fantasy things that go along with her?" Sierra asked in a hushed tone.

My heart raced. My breathing stopped. Panha had done it. Whatever they'd talked about had helped her to ask me. Hopefully, since she'd opened the door, the curse wouldn't react.

"Why her?" I asked. Although I was beyond ecstatic, I

wanted to know why she'd chosen my mother. Why not ask about seers or the magical universe?

"Because if your mother arrives the day after tomorrow and captures me, I want to know what to expect. What am I up against? What is she willing to do all this for?" She gestured to her surroundings, me, and most importantly, her white crystallized orbs.

Full of emotion, I took a deep breath before I began.

Please, Deesse, pixie gods, universe, let this work. Let me open up to her.

As if trying to be funny, Lukita blew out the fire in all but one of the torches lining Sierra's room. Shadows danced in the small, lit area, and a dim light shone on Sierra. It created a creepy-as-hell atmosphere to go along with the disturbing story I was about to tell.

I rolled my eyes, and Lukita chuckled inside my head.

Shaking my head and relaxing my shoulders, I started. "My mother used to be normal. But I use the word *normal,* loosely. Until I was about four, she was marvelous. She had tremendous energy and was always happy. As I grew older, she gradually changed, and I took it as a sign of her maturing into her role.

"For the first five years of my life, I lived in a yellow cottage full of toys and anything else I asked for. The only thing it didn't have were friends, but I had a wonderful nanny named Vilo."

"She's the woman your mother killed?" Sierra clutched her chest and stared in my direction.

"Yes," I croaked out. "She and my mother were all I needed. Vilo didn't show up often, but enough. Mother, on the other hand, spent so much time with me that I never felt lonely or asked for anyone else." My heart ached as I remembered those nights playing slapjacks with Mother and listening to her giggle.

Sierra patted my shoulder. "I'm sorry. We can talk about something else if you want."

"No. I want to do this. I've been waiting for an opportunity like this." I laid my hand on top of hers and brought it to my lap. Sharing my life with her eased the burden I held on my shoulders. So, even though it hurt, I didn't want to stop.

"At the age of five, my home changed to a dark, stone-cold palace with lava for walls. It was called Hellspace. It's the hell above ground."

Sierra gasped. Her crystal orbs cast in a scarlet glow.

"Several other boys and girls around my age lived there. None of us knew why we were there, except to train from morning till night. Mother started visiting less. Over the years, she stopped coming altogether."

"What type of training?"

"Fighting. Killing. Torturing."

Sierra pulled the comforter from her bed and drew it around her body. Was she trying to create distance between us? Had I scared her? A lump formed in my throat.

"None of us ever saw our parents. Most of us didn't even know who our fathers were. One day, Mother walked in. I don't remember why, but we all called her 'Mom' that day. It made no sense. I couldn't understand how she had that many kids or if their fathers were also the same as mine. None of them looked like me." I chewed my lip. The bad parts would follow. What would she think of me then?

Sierra squeezed my hand again and interlocked our fingers.

My breathing normalized, and the lavender heart inside my chest magnified. It shined brighter than ever before.

"Until I turned eleven, every eight or nine months, like clockwork, she'd add a new child. After that, children started arriving more frequently. Each new kid was meaner and had less willpower. If you got close enough to see their eyes, you'd notice less color. The kids arrived older now, ten-year-olds, fifteen-year-olds, and even adults in their early twenties."

"So, not all of them are your siblings?"

"I don't think so." I hoped not because I'd slept with several of them.

"Go on?" She cupped my cheek, and I brushed my face against her smooth fingertips.

"The older ones who arrived were vile. They beat the little ones into submission. No one dared to cross them. Therefore, they became the Leaders of Doom and trained everyone to be ruthless. I couldn't stand watching it. So, at the age of fourteen, I was determined to do something about it, but compared to the leaders, especially the main one, I was considered weak. Out of all of them, I had the most emotions. So, I begged our god—well, goddess—to help me. She required a sacrifice. Even though everyone warned me not to make it, I wouldn't listen. So, I made the sacrifice. It numbed me in a sense and freed me to kill the main leader and take his mantle."

Sierra's eyes widened, her lip trembling. "You k-k-illed someone?" she stuttered.

Several people, even her dad. But I wasn't about to share that. Not yet. "To survive in Hellspace, you had to kill. It's how I was raised. So yes, I killed someone."

She blinked a few times before hugging me. I jerked back. Kindness was nowhere close to what I expected. But as the lavender bond grew, I embraced her back.

"I'm sorry you lived like that." Her words warmed me.

"It's okay. Once I took over his mantle, I tried making things better, but the people there didn't want a savior. Furious that they didn't appreciate my help, I destroyed the place. Destroying everything put Mother's eyes on me. A couple of days later, she took me out of the wretched place and made me her bodyguard. She told me she'd chosen me because I was her first son and because I wasn't too corrupt, so she still had room to shape me. My thought was that after she'd held a competition to select her new assassin slash bodyguard, she'd realized they were all too unreliable. She couldn't predict their loyalties. They had no love nor humanity left in them." I winced. Their phantom claws racked against my skin.

Sierra tightened her embrace, fresh tears falling from her eyes. I wiped them away, and she placed her hand on my thigh. "Why haven't you shared this with me before?"

"One: What was I supposed to say? 'Hi, my name is Tarus. I killed people to survive.' That would've gone over so well." I bit my lip and moved my forehead against hers. "Two: I was under a cu—" Electricity zapped through me, burning my insides. I cradled my knees to my chest and howled. What the hell?

Sierra screamed. But I couldn't speak over the brutal pain.

She opened the door. I'm under the correct constraints. The pain intensified, and my roars echoed off the cave walls. *I won't mention the curse or anything other than Mother. Please stop.* Tears rushed down my cheeks.

The pain slowly eased, and Sierra's yelling became clearer. She was shaking me.

"Sorry." I swallowed. "Memories flooded in. It's still hard to talk about, but I want to." I needed to.

"You're sure?" She kept her arm wrapped around my waist as I straightened and leaned against the bed.

"Yes."

She squeezed me tightly, leaned her forehead against mine, and nodded for me to continue.

"I felt honored to have been chosen. I could tell she was different, but I hadn't seen her in years, and didn't know the difference was awful. Things I remembered about her were no longer there: the bright blue in her eyes and the joyous laughter. But it didn't matter. All I cared about was that I had my mother back. She was better than the Leaders of Doom, so I was happy. I did her bidding and never thought much about it because the sacrifice I had made to the goddess was my heart. She had ripped it out of my chest and tore it apart."

"What? Like literally?" Sierra leaned back, her nose wrinkled in confusion.

"Yes. That's another reason why I hadn't realized how dark she was. Without a heart, I didn't really care about anything."

"You speak in past tense?" She bit her lip and intertwined our fingers.

"You rebuilt it. You showed me what true love and happiness are." I squeezed her hand. She was my saving grace. My hero. "You gave me my heart back." Running my thumb over the top of her hand, I peeked up at her.

"My mother, in a nutshell, is battling with the bad kind of demons. She is very dark. She heard a prophecy, and that's how she learned about you. This prophecy claims you have the answers to unite everyone under her." There was distaste and deep hostility in my words, but deep down, one could hear the fear, perhaps even taste it.

After I shared everything, we were silent for a while. To avoid reliving all the horrors, I clung tighter to her, our connection keeping my mind clear. But too much quiet began waking my dark thoughts and horrid memories, so I broke the silence.

"Before I met you, even without a heart, I wasn't entirely

okay with some of the things my mother had me do. But they were better than the things I did in Hellspace. When this woman showed me any kind of love, I welcomed it. I wanted more, so I did her bidding, hoping to win her favor. If I messed up, she had a whole litter to choose from. Meaning, I stayed on my best behavior, always ensuring I did everything I should. Sometimes she'd scare me, but it didn't bother me much because she was still there at the end of the day. Not until I met you and she killed Vilo did I know what love truly was. Perhaps she doesn't love me. She probably never did. She probably doesn't even know how to love." I didn't realize how badly reliving my story would hurt me until my body shook with the intensity.

Sierra cupped my face between her hands and caressed my cheeks with her thumbs. My body stilled. She stood, the comforter falling to the floor, and pulled me up with her. I obliged, and she hugged me. She squeezed the living daylights, and sadness, out of me. My mind could no longer hold on to anything negative. Sierra's love filled every aspect of me.

We hadn't embraced like this since Halloween, so why did she do it now? But, for the first time, I desperately needed it. My tears flowed again, and she squeezed me harder. My heart almost hammered its way right out of my chest.

As my tears dried, I broke from her. "I didn't expect this from you. You don't know what it means to me. Sierra, if you don't wake up to your ma—" My skin boiled hot. Gods, I hated this curse.

"Can't you just free me? Please. Then your mother won't catch me," she pleaded.

"I've told you before … I can't! I wish I could." If she knew her birth mom would see her soon, she wouldn't care about training and would forget about believing in her magic.

"We must have some time left. Can you teach me how to climb while blind?"

My mouth fell open. She wanted more time with me, even though I'd just denied her.

Her ability to bewilder me kept me frozen in place without an answer.

"Please, with a cherry on top? You might even get to see my butt," she teased.

My manhood rose, nothing frozen about that, and I doubled over, laughing. "You're so romantic. You really know how to make a guy blush," I teased back, and the tension in the room dropped.

Feeling frisky, I interlocked our fingers. A pulse of electricity traveled through me, waking every nerve ending. She didn't pull away.

We climbed again and again. I taught her tricks on how to feel for a suitable rock and instructed her on how to hold better if she started to fall or lose her footing.

Sierra's distraction worked wonders. Not only did I enjoy seeing her genuine love for the lesson, but I got to glance up at her ass, getting a full view of her strong, muscular legs.

Every now and then, I couldn't help but lick my lips or give a low growl. Each time I did, Sierra lost concentration and fell, which only heightened my erection because I had to catch her by placing my hand on her ass.

More than anything, I wanted to catch her in my arms and kiss her beautiful lips. So, it was most certainly a diversion for me.

When I was rock hard, out of control, and burning tight, I ended our session and led her back to her bed. I said goodnight, thanked her again for everything, and kissed her on her forehead, lingering for a beat longer than usual before walking out.

After a cold dip in the stream, I lay there, wondering. Why did she suddenly accept my story, making me feel better? Perhaps she was becoming okay with loving me. But one thing

I knew for sure—the elements were awakening in Sierra, and her magic was growing. Soon, she'd begin feeling it, and hopefully, her belief in herself would follow suit.

Tomorrow was going to be the turning point.

We were so close. It had to be.

We only had one day left.

I spent most of the night in utter anguish, biting my cheeks raw. What would happen over the next thirty-six hours? I trusted Queen Rosalida would honor her deal because the bond hadn't disappeared. It was still light blue and attached to my heart. She also seemed too moral not to.

But her kindness would come into question when our agreement ended, and three things could happen. One: Queen Rosalida could leave me with nowhere to go, my mother after me, and my hiding place discovered. Two: I'd become her slave, and then karma would come full circle. Three: She'd let me stay by Sierra's side.

The last one seemed least likely. The second one, I wouldn't mind. There was a good chance Queen Rosalida treated her slaves differently than how my mother did. It also guaranteed I'd stay close to Sierra and could protect her, even if it wasn't my proper role.

Against my will, I fell asleep, imagining myself as Queen Rosalida's property.

When I woke, I felt refreshed, my veins full of adrenaline. I dashed to Sierra's room and wasn't surprised to find she had already left. I presumed she had gone to visit Panha, so I stayed in her room and added things from Climakru to her painting to calm my nerves. Today's lesson had to work.

Staring at the painting—at my additions of birds, water-falls, and fire for her parents' elements—I dreamed of a life together. Queen Rosalida had seen a future with us married, which meant I couldn't be too far gone.

I could be good.

I could be forgiven.

I could be different from both of my parents.

And I could be loved.

After an hour, my stomach dropped, and I frowned. Had she escaped? I didn't want her to leave without Queen Rosalida, the delegates, or me. Until Sierra believed who she was, alone out there, she wouldn't last a second.

My body tensed. "Lukita, is she still here?"

"Yes. She's with Panha."

Knowing she hadn't run away didn't help relieve the tension like I'd expected. A whole new stress emerged, one reminding me of the stakes.

It took everything in my power not to storm into Panha's room and drag her out, but that wouldn't go over well. She'd be pissed. So, instead of forcing her to train, I paced.

After a while, Sierra came in silently and headed for her bed.

I took a deep breath and met her there. With my legs touching her knees, I grabbed her hands. "I thought you had escaped."

Guilt collected in the back of my throat, dripping down my spine. Guilt over striking fear deep inside her about my mother coming and for lying to her. Since we only had a day left until the delegates came to retrieve her, why did I still hold firm to this lie? Maybe because I needed her to wake up, and I couldn't tell her that her birth mother was coming for her without explaining magic.

"I have come to terms with your mother taking me tomorrow. Now, all I can do is hold on to hope and believe everything happens for a reason. I'll find a way out of this, somehow, somewhere, just *not yet.*" She smiled, and the tension lightened as I went back in time, back to the times we had said those very words before everything changed.

"Yesterday, you had wonderful questions and ideas for training. How about you choose again?" I squeezed her hands.

Several seconds later, she asked, "Will you tell me everything you know about seers and their powers?" Her words took my breath away, and to my amusement, it also took hers.

"What makes you want to know? Are you starting to believe?" I held my breath.

"If all this happened because your mother thinks I am like Elijah and Elisha, who are, in a way, seers, then it seems wise to know more about them and understand what she thinks I can do."

I sighed, but I didn't give up all hope. Something told me there was more to this story, but I didn't push it. I could tell she was fighting to believe, yet, at the same time, trying to convince herself not to. Which meant I had to make this story count and beg the curse not to stop me.

"I'm not sure where to start. History. Power. I don't know that much."

"Anything is better than nothing," she said, encouraging me.

Silence filled the room until I took a deep, audible breath. "The information we have on seers is distorted. You see, there hasn't been one for hundreds of years. All we know is what others have written. Historians studied the books and tried to form conclusions based on the limited, contradictory information available. The only part they all agreed on was that two very powerful, royal bloodlines produced a seer.”

“Does that mean I’m royal?” Sierra’s jaw dropped.

“Yes. Your mo—” My throat started closing, and my hands flew to my neck to keep the invisible hands from choking the life from me. *I’ll keep it to seers. Please let me go.* I pleaded to whoever held the curse in place. At my plea, the grip released, but the ghost of those cursed hands remained.

“My mom, what?” Sierra touched my arm. I hated that I couldn’t share more.

“All I can say is yes. But I can’t elaborate nor explain why. I am sorry.”

She pouted and messed with the tassels on her silk pillow.

“Back to seers. Another part everyone agreed on was that they were dangerous. They were unpredictable and powerful with knowledge. Without fail, that vast knowledge led to most of them turning dark, but some got trapped inside their heads trying to dissect the future.”

“I’m not dangerous.” She winced.

“Your powers haven’t awoken yet. But I don’t think you are, or will become, dangerous. Not you. You’re full of love.”

She smiled and shook her head.

“There are rules that govern seers’ powers. Those who seek answers from seers must ask direct questions because seers are notorious for skirting the truth. Seers can also look far into the future to see a particular outcome or to learn something valuable, but only if they have enough information. The future isn’t set in stone. It can always change and adapt. Hence, some of the seers were known to have become trapped in the future. Some books even suggested they could alter the future. Others said that some seers seemed blessed and would receive messages from the gods showing them things and guiding them. No books mentioned any other powers. They all focused on their knowledge." I stopped talking and gave her time to process everything.

"What about the ones who turned evil? Why?" Sierra knotted the soft comforter in her hands.

"Historians were unsure. The books mentioned two possibilities. One: the person who woke a seer to their magic was evil, and therefore, shaped the future of the seer. Two: the seer wasn't ready for their magic and got lost in how powerful they were."

"What do you believe?" She folded her hands in her lap and kept her head down. In response, I placed my finger under her chin and lifted her head.

"Until I met you, I believed a lot of things. For the most part, I thought they were a myth. Later, after listening to my mother's stories, I believed they were dangerous. When I met you, almost everything changed. I still believe they can be dangerous, but they also have the potential to be incredibly good. It just depends on what influence molded them."

She tilted her head. While she sorted things out in her mind, we walked in silence to the stream. Water had always calmed my nerves, and maybe the rushing ripples would do that for her now.

Once next to the water, we both placed our hands in the stream. But this time, it didn't soothe the war raging inside me. I couldn't escape the fact I felt like a failure for letting her lead today's lesson. I should've been training her, not giving up.

"Does my family believe I'm evil, and is that why they sent me away?"

If it weren't for the torches reflecting off the water and illuminating the area, I wouldn't have noticed the silent tears trickling down Sierra's cheeks. I wiped them away and brought her to my chest. "I believe they sent you away to give you your best chance at living." Tomorrow, she'd get the opportunity to ask her mother.

"Let's do something." She leaned away and stared up at me.

"What would you like to do?"

"Can we just dance again?" This time, her smile reached her eyes, and my body melted.

"Dance? You want to spend your last bit of time here dancing when you should be learning ways to protect yourself? Yet you choose to dance? Women!" I said in exasperation. Though I wanted to tell her *no* and that this was serious, I couldn't deny her ... not when this could be my last night with her.

Tomorrow, when the delegates *saved her*, I might be tossed to the curb, never to feel her touch against my skin again. I couldn't pass this up. With the few hours we had left, it was doubtful she'd wake her magic. She hadn't in the whole time I'd known her. What or why would that change now?

Sixty One

We spent the next few hours dancing to ballroom, country, and even some cèilidh dances on the vinyl floor. After a while, we had to stop since we were both completely exhausted, drenched in sweat, and our breathing heavy.

"Did the dance satisfy you?"

"It was exactly what I needed, thank you." She leaned against the buffet table.

My smile spread as wide as it could at the sincerity of her words. "I'm honored to have fulfilled your request. Now, it's time for you to sleep. You have a big day tomorrow and need to be well rested for what is to come."

I couldn't hide the misery in my voice. I wasn't able to wake her magic. Either the prophecy had changed, or Aris, Vilo, Rosalida, and everyone else who believed I had a part to play were wrong. They should've never had faith in me. I shouldn't have had faith in myself.

When she didn't move, I closed the distance between us. Warmth radiated from her body, her lavender scent lingering in the air. I touched her arm, and the hair on her arms rose.

The lavender vein danced, and the bond vibrated. I placed my forehead against hers to provide some stability from the pressure building in my heart, swelling with love but also breaking with the loss of her.

I wrapped my arms around her waist and pulled her against my chest, but that didn't help. My heart thundered away as if powered by an engine. Briefly, I thought of kissing her, and boy, did I want to. But I was afraid of her reaction and what it would mean if she and I parted ways tomorrow.

She bit her lower lip, and I pulled away, slamming my body against the cave wall. The fire from the torch above my head singed a few of my hairs, and smoke filled the room.

Sierra pouted. Her reaction made me want to pull her close and kiss her with every ounce of passion I had, but all too quickly, her pout disappeared, replaced with a smile.

"We should go to sleep," she said, a little breathlessly.

My libido spiked again. What had made her so breathless?

"Yes, and Sierra, in case I don't get the chance to tell you this tomorrow, please don't let your flame of life go out." I grabbed her hand and guided her back to the bedroom.

Once in her room, feet from her bed, I kissed her hand. A tear dropped from my cheek and splashed onto her skin. I glanced up to see if she'd noticed, and she, too, had tears cascading down her face. I'd failed her. I couldn't help her to find herself. I'd never hear those words of love fall from her lips, and that alone was a torment I'd carry forever. I couldn't manage my emotions, so once I returned to my room, I fell apart.

Pulling at my hair, I fell to my knees, and my heart broke. She didn't believe in her magic, and it was all my fault. I saw the magic in her. It was there when she talked to her senses, but she couldn't see it, and therefore, she refused to accept it was real. In both a literal and figurative sense, she remained blind.

Out of nowhere, random fragmented thoughts swirled inside my head: *evil one—captured—darkness—no longer everyone's hope—their destruction.*

Were these Sierra's thoughts? Lukita's? They couldn't be Lukita's. She'd talk to me. So, if these were Sierra's thoughts, why could I hear them? It couldn't be. My magic couldn't work with her.

But if they were hers, she was breaking. And I had no time left to put her back together.

Tartarus, to save them, to prevent war, to give Sierra more time to awaken her magic with love, and to fulfill the prophecy, you're going to have to go with the alternate plan, Lukita said in my mind.

I let out a deep breath. *I know.*

Now that you're following that path ... there's something I have to tell you.

Yes? By the way Lukita spoke, this couldn't be good. My chest tightened.

I wanted to wait until we knew this was the only path left. And, to be honest, I wasn't going to tell you.

I leaned forward, eyebrows raised. *Tell me what?*

Please understand that I've been cursed, trapped in this cave for centuries. I saw my way out and leaped at the chance. However, over the weeks that I've known you, I've really come to care about you, and I don't want to hide this from you anymore.

"Spit it out, Lukita!" I screamed. My temper spiked, and I clenched my fists tightly.

Using Slinger comes at a price. It requires too much. So, you should know, and have a choice, whether you want to pay it.

Requires too much? Price? Nothing is too much if it saves Sierra. My heart pounded so hard it pulsed a current throughout my body. I looked inward, and several of my blood vessels changed from black to the most vibrant scarlet I'd ever seen. The lavender vein was still present, and it was vibrating. I still had a chance to save her, to awaken her with love.

Wait until after I've told you before you make that comment. Your opinion might change. Lukita sucked in a deep breath. *Tartarus, Slinger was wielded by the last leader of Hell-space before you, and he changed it so that he could control its extreme power. Where once anyone with demonic blood would die if they tried to brand someone with it, now anyone light with a heart full of love will die.* She paused to let the words sink in.

They did, and I slumped back down, both hands clutching my chest. *Well, maybe it won't kill me. I'm not good. I'm still demonic. No matter where my heart goes, I'll always have demon blood. I'm Lucifer's son.*

Tartarus, you cannot believe you're purely demonic anymore. Queen Rosalida, Vilo, Sierra, me, and many others can see how you've changed. Look at your heart before this happened. You didn't have one. Now you have a beautiful lavender, vibrant, beating heart. You are good, Tartarus. And I'm so proud of you and will miss you.

No, I'm not. Tears gushed down my face.

Yes, you are. Not only are you good, but you're loved, Tartarus. Sierra loves you, and so do I. And, most of all, you are forgiven.

Did Queen Rosalida know this, too? Had they both betrayed me? Had they both withheld this vital information from me?

No.

How did you learn?

Sphinx, remember?

So then, it's a sure thing? Killing Mother, kills me? I bit my lip and attempted to hold back a scream.

Yes, unless there is vampire blood in you. That might keep you alive. Might. But remember, somehow, you must find a way to behead her before you possibly ... probably, die, too.

Then, the war will be stopped, and Sierra will unite the realms under love.

Vampire blood wasn't in me. Vilo thought there was, but it was impossible. People weren't born vampires. I was a goner. Even if, for some odd reason, it was, vampires craved blood, I'd crave Sierra's. I'd be a monster.

The moment I started to live, started to dream, started to love, was the moment it all went away. Karma had come back for me. I couldn't let them die, but could I sacrifice myself, sacrifice mine and Sierra's love?

Tartarus, I won't blame you either way, and neither will anyone else, so this is solely up to you. Can you lay down your life, possibly for good, to save countless others?

When I woke, all I could think about was the promise to share Sierra's location with Queen Rosalida. The delegates would find her, but while they searched, I'd go to The Kingdom of Astal and hopefully summon up the courage to kill Mother. My stomach twisted in knots. I hated this plan.

As a lone tear escaped, I portaled to Queen Rosalida's bed chamber.

The second I landed on her ruffled rug, she smiled, and her breathing calmed. She was waiting for me, sitting on the bed, no maiden in sight.

"Greetings, Tarus. I'm happy to see you. Are you here to fulfill the deal?" She strolled over to the desk in the corner of the room and waved for me to follow.

A map was spread out on the top of the desk, showing all of Climakru.

"Yes." I pointed to the location of the Gateway at the inner edge of The Kingdom of Ondin. "The Shenak Forest, a few miles from here." The light blue bond buzzed and disappeared.

"Thank you." She squeezed my shoulder. "I'm sorry Sierra's magic didn't awaken."

"Me too." I took a deep breath and added, "Why do you want the delegates to find her instead of me drugging her and then portaling her here?"

"Call it mother's intuition."

I shook my head. "That makes no sense."

"It's a good thing I don't have to make sense." She smiled.

I sighed. "The vault underneath your rug is the same way anyone enters the Gateway, which I'm sure you already know. When Lukita and I hid her Gateway from Mother, we destroyed all the entrances, and now only I have access. But Lukita is allowing the two earth wielders in your delegate team to use their abilities to create an opening."

She nodded. "They can do that."

"The minute they let go, it'll close. If it does, there'll be no second chance. Lukita will only allow one attempt to enter the wrong way. Since you want this to be a rescue mission, she'll make it hard. That way, they won't suspect that anything had been orchestrated."

"Where will Sierra be when my delegates come through, and how do I know you won't double-cross me or go back on your word once they see her?" She leaned against the wooden desk, the chandelier light creating a beautiful glow in her blue hair.

"I won't know where Sierra is. She has free range in the Gateway and goes where she pleases. And I have somewhere else to be, so I won't be there." I took a deep breath. "About me going back on my word, or anything else negative you might ask ... do you really think I'd betray you after I was the one who came to you? If I were you, this is a situation where you have to rely on faith, hope, and the belief in my love for her." The three pillars The Kingdom of Ondin followed, as did Sierra's bible.

She chuckled as she shook her head. "Well said. When should I send my delegates?"

"Give them two hours tops, then use your Gateway to portal them to where I showed you. Good day, Queen Rosalida."

Seconds before I left, she called my name in a very inquisitive and questioning manner. I stopped, frozen, uncertain about whether I should stay or go.

"If I had the power to grant you one more request, what would it be?"

"For Sierra to believe she is a seer." My shoulders slumped.

"But what about for you, something with which I could actually help? What would it be?" She stood closer, scents of honeysuckle drifting my way.

"For Sierra to know that this was never a game. My feelings for her are genuine. I love her, and I want to be a good person." Another lone tear fell.

She massaged her chin. "Tarus, Sierra k ..."

A loud clang of something like metal dropping on the sleek ground sounded from just behind the door, along with an explicit curse. My teeth ground, and I locked murderous eyes on Queen Rosalida.

"You were stalling! How could you?" I screamed, not caring if she punished me for speaking out this way. How could she betray me? "I gave you Sierra's whereabouts. Why did you need someone to listen in on our conversation? Aren't you the one who wanted this to be a rescue mission, done in secret?"

The color drained from Queen Rosalida's face. Either she was shocked that I'd raised my voice to her, or she honestly didn't know someone had been listening.

"I ... I ..." She shook her head and gulped.

My mind raced with the worst thought possible. That wasn't *her* spy. It was Mother's! In seconds, Mother would know where Sierra was. I shook, fear threatening to drag me down, and grief flooding my system.

I stood before Queen Rosalida and grasped her arms. "Tell me you trust all your maidens. Tell me you haven't doubted anyone's loyalty. Please tell me my thought is wrong."

Her cheeks turned crimson, and her eyes filled with the tears she held at bay. I lost my balance and fell. Her nonverbal response was answer enough.

"What do we do?" Queen Rosalida asked me. Me?

This was bad.

I straightened. "Soon, Mother will know everything we just said. As far as I'm aware, she doesn't have earth wielders to open the Gateway, but she'll throw everything she has at the location in order to break through. Lukita warned me she wouldn't be able to keep Mother away if she ever tried to enter."

Sharp breaths came from Queen Rosalida, and she clutched her chest.

The only way this would work in our favor was if I really did kill Mother.

I had no choice now.

"Everyone with demon blood can portal. They'll all be near the Gateway within seconds. Mother will probably let her demons get there first to open it so she doesn't have to do the hard work. She'll also prepare her army to be everywhere, from the Gateway to your palace, so they can intercept your delegates if they manage to get past her or her demons."

Desperate to get Sierra out of the Gateway before Mother arrived, and then to make sure I was there, ready to kill her, I needed to hurry. I looked at Queen Rosalida. Her jaw was clenched.

"One last thing, tell your delegates that Mother's army will most likely be fully demon. The creatures they once were are no longer alive. They're gone, so don't be afraid to kill them."

"Go! Protect Sierra while you're waiting for my delegates."

"Since we're in a rush, why don't I just portal her here? Save the risk?"

"That's information I can't share. You must have faith and hope that there's a good reason. I apologize." She grabbed my shoulders and gave them a final shake. "Go."

I nodded and portaled to the Gateway.

Sixty Three

Lukita! I screamed inside my head the minute I landed with a thud inside the cave. I didn't dare say her name aloud in case Mother's demons were already surrounding the area. Any one of them could have enhanced hearing, and they couldn't know her name.

Yes. Take a breath and calm down before you pass out. What's wrong? Concern laced her voice.

Search my mind over the last hour and see all that has happened. I need to recover. My heart thundered as I hunched over, my hands resting on the cold cave wall.

That's not good! she screamed.

Will you scan the forest above us and get a layout of Mother's minions? They must be nearby.

A minute later, Lukita returned inside my head. *Nine in total. Scattered throughout the forest within ten feet of Sierra. The closest minion is about three feet from where she is now.*

My gut clenched. *Where's Sierra?*

She's near the waterfall.

I must protect her. How can we lead them away so the delegates have access?

You're the only sure way. You'll have to be the bait, she said solemnly.

My nostrils flared. That plan could get me captured before I had a chance to kill Mother. Was that Lukita's plan all along?

Listen, I know this sounds bad, but I promise I didn't realize this would happen. This infiltration, and you being the bait, was never my intention. But you know just as well as I do that you'll have to use yourself.

We'll use me in the worst-case scenario. Until then, let's create a diversion. Can you cause a ripple effect and destruction somewhere as far from the waterfall as possible, and can you also provide some sort of signal for the delegates of where Sierra is? I'm going to catch one last glimpse of her and ensure she's rescued. I portaled close to the waterfall.

Sierra was at the top of the cascade, her face in her hands. Anger flared from her as she kicked at the rocks. She began to climb down, looking as if defeated. Without a minute to waste, Lukita shook the cave's ceiling above her, indicating Sierra's location to the delegates.

She continued climbing down, and my heart stopped as she missed her next step. At the same time, the delegates made their presence known by opening a seam in the cave roof. Sierra regained her footing and anchored herself on the rock.

The delegates' noise increased as the roof shifted, rocks fell, and the cave's ceiling ripped wider apart.

Again, I feared for Sierra since she couldn't see the falling rocks. She could be crushed. Lukita must have sensed this, too. A small cleft formed within the stone wall of the waterfall, and Sierra slipped inside to protect herself.

"Down here! Down here!" she screamed. I didn't know whether her words hurt or impressed me. She called out to them, not knowing if they were there to save her. She paused for a moment, maybe wondering if she should trust them, but the next second, she shrugged and continued. "I'm here! I hear you," she yelled, her voice pleading, aching. It broke my heart.

The entire Gateway vibrated, especially above the waterfall. Sierra pressed tighter into the fissure. Low-pitched rumbles resonated above her as the earth wielder worked on the roof. Booms and vibrations alternated while they widened the seam and created a larger escape route.

Cool air filled the cave, and dirt rained down as the earth above loosened. Then the sunshine broke through, and Sierra turned her face up to the warm light, an over joyous smile spreading from ear to ear. She lifted her hands toward the rays but quickly dropped them.

"Grab my hand!" Kaito roared.

Sierra's face turned ashen. She was about to escape and be free, yet she appeared full of misery. I wanted to scream at her to take his hand, but if I did that, the delegates would know we'd set this up, and Queen Rosalida had been adamant about this being a *rescue mission*.

"Are you here to save me, or are you another wicked scoundrel trying to use me?" Sierra asked, shocking me.

Kaito took a step back and snorted. "We have no time for this. Regardless of who I am, do you have any better options?"

"Touché, but how do I know I'll be safe if I take your hand? Why are you here? You don't sound like anyone I know," Sierra said, pushing deeper into the fissure.

"What does it look like? I'm here to save you." Kaito's voice held a tinge of exasperation.

"Well, as a matter of fact, I'm blind, so I don't know what it looks like," she retorted with so much sass.

Why was she hesitating? It hurt watching her waste time like this.

"Let me start again," Sierra said. "I apologize for my initial response. I can't see, and I'm unsure if you look friendly.

People have lied to me too often, and my trust is fragile. Please tell me how I'm supposed to know if I should go with you?"

Even if it wasn't for Queen Rosalida, I was sure the lavender vein and the curse would've prevented me from using my magic to lift her into Kaito's waiting hand, but I was dying to try.

"The thing is, you don't know. Since you are blind, I assume you must trust your instincts. You must do the same now. Trust me, because you don't have another choice. You're going to have to take a leap of faith. Sometimes things are not done by sight but by faith alone."

While Sierra debated her response, Lukita's voice appeared in my head. *We're running out of time. I cannot hold them back much longer. She has minutes. Hurry this up ... or become the diversion.*

She has almost consented.

"There is a woman down here. I can direct you to her. Save her, please. Show me you are good, and I'll follow you. The only problem is she's about a twenty-minute journey from here. We're in a rush, so you'll have to make it quick."

Holy Delmore! Sierra and her compassion. She didn't have time for this. I wish I could tell her I'd protect Panha, but Kaito must've known it was his mother because he groaned and sent two of the delegates to find her.

Even with their speed, it'd still take at least ten minutes. I kicked the ground, infuriated. Lukita had already struggled to keep the demons at bay, which meant I was now the diversion. Shit. My veins turned to ice.

As Lukita portaled me into the forest, I longed to stay with Sierra, for my world to be different, to have at least another night with her. If only I could've felt her lips against mine one last time.

Images of us dancing filled my heart and sparked my adrenaline as I landed a few yards from the demons, huddled between two rocks. No light shone in the area due to the plethora of trees and their thick branches. Smells of decay wafted in the wind, and I almost gagged.

Unaware of whether my invisibility worked with these demons, I hid between two trees and studied my surroundings.

The demons had their backs to me, oblivious and focused, opening the ground, using all kinds of magic. Whenever they figured it was no use, Lukita would move the earth a fraction farther. This distraction gave them hope that their magic was working when, in all actuality, it really just drained them of their energy.

But even with their energy depleted, it was still nine against one. They were pure demons, immortal beings usually incapable of death except through beheading or deep slits to the throat. Some might consider me one of the greatest assassins, but against multiple full-blown demons with specific death rules, what chance did I have?

Never before had I needed to fight this many at once, so the armor I'd asked Lukita to provide was unusually light. A brass chain mail shirt, a lightweight onyx-black shield, and two double-edged machete swords. These demons had no weapons or armor, only their endless magic, which could kill me.

Silent as a mouse, I tiptoed behind the one demon separated from the others and used my right hand to cover his slimy mouth, the left slit his throat with my machete. I followed him to the ground, carefully laying him on the grass without making a sound. The next demon was a few feet away. I came up behind him, decapitating him in one swift movement. Black blood spurted everywhere. Before he fell, I caught him on my knee and eased him down.

One of the demons was caught in the cross fire. Drops of blood splattered across his cheek. He swiftly turned, grazing my arm, so I crawled into his brain and ordered him not to scream before piercing him in the jugular. I sliced back and forth, decapitating him in less than two seconds. His head flopped down, and I kicked it with all my might. It flew far away.

Three down, six to go. Blood coated my blades, and my arms were no better.

Again, I slipped into another demon's mind with the same instructions I'd given his comrade. Before I'd finished hacking off his head, two other demons turned simultaneously. My throat tightened. I couldn't slip into both their heads at once. There was a chance I couldn't win against them, but it didn't matter. I still had to fight. It had only been a few minutes, and the delegates wouldn't have made it back with Panha.

Sierra wasn't safe yet.

My legs shook as they rushed at me, and the others turned around at the commotion. I quickly finished off the first demon, but then there were five others throwing their magic in my direction and running toward me. My shield stopped one but left my side open to another. The demon's magic sliced right through my torso. It dug deep, blood gushing from the wound.

My anger grew more intense, and I roared as I moved like lightning. I slashed through one demon's neck while another came at me from behind, but before the demon's magic could hit, I spun around and threw up my shield. He stopped within inches, and I grabbed a dagger from the dead demon next to me, throwing it at his jugular before running straight for him. Enraged, I yanked on the blade and sliced his head off.

The remaining three demons circled me, poised to kill, their dead eyes glaring. I wouldn't be able to shield off all their magic. Three massive tendrils of dark mist flew at me from each direction. Great. Dear old father placed himself into them, too. Otherwise, how did they have mist? My chest and abs grew tight as I anticipated the pain. I had no choice but to take a few hits.

Determined to live, I angled my shield to protect my torso whilst shredding the guy to my right. Blood caked my face as he put up a fight before falling to the ground, dead.

While the shield protected me from one demon's magic, I couldn't avoid the other's.

Tiny razor blades hacked away at my flesh in a million different places, with one deep slash cutting through half my left bicep. My knees wobbled, almost buckling, with the intensity of the demon's magic. I flexed each finger on my left hand, but it was now hard to grip the shield or move that arm. Screams and curses coursed through me as I fought through the unbearable pain and charged at both demons, holding my shield with a shaky grip.

Strength, like I'd never known, poured through my veins. It provided me with much-needed power and gave me a new feeling of ecstasy. My nostrils flared, my teeth bared, and I beelined straight for them, a feral beast hunting its prey.

One second, I was the predator, ready to pounce on my target and devour the rest of the party. The next, the roles reversed. My ears perked up, listening for the hum of their magic, while my eyes scanned back and forth, alert to their new positions. One demon was in front and one behind me.

I needed both of them to be either behind or in front of me. Sweat dripped down my forehead, burning my eyes, as I ran from side to side, zigzagging, teeth gritting through the pain. My goal was to put them behind me so I could turn and attack.

Magic mist repeatedly bounced off the ground centimeters from me. I was playing a game of hopscotch. With them now a safe distance behind me, I swirled around to run toward them. For a brief moment, panic set into their eyes as they rushed forward.

As one demon touched me, I slid into his mind, forcing him to stop. With the other, it became a battle of magic versus blade. I shielded everything he threw at me, and his magic deflected every thrust I launched at him.

We circled one another in a synchronized attempt to murder the other. My left arm tingled with numbness, and I started to lose my grip on the shield. This couldn't last much longer. I yelled as I jumped on the demon. His magic plowed into my chest, and I groaned through the pain as I sliced straight through his skull.

There was only one left, and he stood stock-still. I approached him just as hooves and wheels sounded in the distance. Two things that meant my greatest fear was nearby. Quickly, I sliced through his neck as my every muscle twitched, and I swayed, struggling to stand.

Just as I portaled back to Sierra, a hand closed around my arm. My chest grew heavy as I realized who had a hold of me. Mother!

She had portaled with me.

Shit. I couldn't breathe.

I just brought the Destroyer of Realms to Sierra.

Once we both landed in the Gateway, a wicked laugh that filled my nightmares now echoed off the cave walls, and the temperature dropped to an icy freeze. We all shivered, except for Mother, but the sudden atmospheric change had nothing to do with that.

Her nails dug into my skin as her gaze fell on Sierra. Inwardly, I gulped and envisioned all hell breaking loose. There was no way any of us were getting out alive.

A delegate, yellow eyes blazing, aimed a hand at us. Another delegate's eyes swam with fire and stared directly at us. And Kaito's free hand stretched in our direction. My eyes widened, and my chest expanded. They were subduing Mother's strength and holding her back from Sierra. Their magic shouldn't be this powerful or work within Sierra's presence.

But now that I saw the delegates up top fighting to hold Mother away, I attempted in a whisper the barrier spell I had memorized when I researched Sierra's bound magic, "Iskla midlte."

Instead of the curse attacking me like usual, temporary shields materialized around Sierra and me, giving us a layer of protection against Mother's mist and any other magic she could try to throw at us. It worked! Hell yes.

I glanced at Sierra's face, and my tiny victory vanished. Doubt still had her immobilized. One hand stretched out to Kaito, but not close enough for him to reach. Her still white orbs scanned between where she sensed me and where the sun's warming rays poured in.

"Sierra, reach a little farther. We can rescue you. Please!" Kaito was so close to freeing her. She reached up, standing on her toes, but then she pulled back again.

What was Sierra thinking? Salvation was only a stretch away, and she hesitated. Now that the delegates had caught me disobeying Mother, who cared if they knew this was a setup? All that mattered was Sierra getting away.

"Sierra, what are you doing? Leave!" My voice rang out over all the noise and shouting.

Smack! The wretched sound of Mother's backhand slap echoed off the cave walls as she struck me. "What the hell is wrong with you? She's ours!"

Mother was foolish to think she still had any control over me. I'd never let Mother have her.

"Sierra, I can't keep her away much longer." Since my focus was on Sierra, I didn't realize I let the barrier around me drop. Mother took advantage of the opportunity and scraped her tendrils of mist across my face. Tiny invisible teeth sunk into my flesh, gnawing and gnashing at everything they touched. I groaned, and the smell of iron filled the room.

Sierra hunched over and vomited.

"Did you really think you could deceive me, you insolent fool?" Her magic began to overpower whatever the delegates were doing to hold her at bay. She held me up with one hand, choking me. But I had one last thing to say.

"Go! Run, Sierra, run!" I screamed as my vocal cords tightened.

In a raspy voice, a delegate added, "Even with all our strength combined, we can't hold her much longer. Hurry."

Kaito pleaded, "Sierra, if you stay, you'll be tortured, and she'll force you into doing terrible things. It's not a question of *if*, but a question of *when*. With us, since Panha is my mom, you must know we're the good ones, here to rescue you. We'll help you get your sight back. Take my hand, take a leap of faith, of hope."

"It's not that I don't trust you or that I'm scared, but I can't leave Tarus. She'll kill him." She wiped at the tears pouring down her cheeks.

Mother's grip tightened further on me, and the barrier around Sierra blinked. A delegate gasped as Mother snarled. Next second, a wave of power from the delegates shoved into us, freezing Mother in place. My eyes widened, and the delegates' faces looked strained. Shit, how long would this protection last?

"Once we return your sight and you learn everything, if you still wish to save Tarus, I'll help you. You must have faith and hope you'll return to free him. She'll torture him whether you stay or go. The only difference is that she'll torture you if you stay, and all the realms will be doomed. If you leave, you could help save more than one person and help us save the realms," Kaito said in a haggard voice.

Sierra chewed her bottom lip as if tormented by what path to take. My heart broke with every beat. She willingly risked her chance to escape because she loved me.

"Please, I can take you to your mom, Shanti," Sierra's element-wielding nanny from Earth begged.

Mother's face reddened, and her body started to unfreeze as the mist rose.

Sierra gasped, her breathing heavy. She glanced back in my direction and whispered, "Lord, protect him until I return."

A massive wave of tears erupted from my eyes. They covered Mother's hand, still holding firm around my throat.

The delegates at the top of the cave screamed through

gritted teeth down at Sierra to grab Kaito's hand, and her nanny kept repeating, "Please, Shanti," while others shouted, "Hurry!"

Sierra reached up to Kaito, and the minute he gripped her hand, an outer layer of lavender outlined her entire body.

It matched my lavender vein and flowed around her as if alive.

The lavender light spreading over her could only mean one thing—the seer's power was awakening, and my mother knew it. She let out a death scream of anger at the sight, and that rage pushed through the delegates' hold, and her mist darted in every direction. Water splashed, rocks flew, and smoke filled the whole cave.

Apart from the one delegate holding open the rip in the cave roof, everybody up top tugged at Sierra's arms, pulling her through. Mother's nails dug into my throat, drawing blood, and my spell faltered. Mother's tendrils seized the opportunity and clung to Sierra's legs, slicing into her.

Chaos erupted.

Mother laughed. "You fools. I have her now." Sierra struggled against the tendrils pulling her down as both sides played tug-of-war.

The delegates' magic hit Mother again, and in order to seize Sierra, she had to release me.

"Sierra, I love you," I said, out of breath and pained, as I landed heavily on the ground.

"What did I say about love, you stupid disappointment?" Mother said, as Sierra slipped farther away from the delegates and her freedom.

I had seen enough. Although the curse had broken and parts of Sierra's magic were awakening, her eyes remained white and she still didn't fully believe. To win against Mother, Sierra needed all of her power. So, unless I killed Mother, she'd capture Sierra, turn her evil, and tyranny would begin. This was my only chance to save Sierra, and Mother's comment just made it easier for me. I had to do this.

Lukita, if I don't make it, have someone behead her, please.

Of course. They know the rules. And Tartarus, you're a hero.

"Delmore welcomes you!" I slammed Slinger into Mother's chest.

My lavender heart turned red, beating as if it were new, and the lavender bond inside blossomed into a vibrant purple flame before completely crystallizing with an outline of black. The mating bond had been completed. Sierra had formed a bond! The moment I died or turned into a monster, unable to be with Sierra, it had formed. The gods were cruel.

Mother's mist freed Sierra, and the delegates pulled her to safety.

Both Mother's and my eyes gushed with blood as our hearts slowed.

The last thing I noticed before I drew my last breath were Sierra's eyes turning back to brown, with several purple specs. Tears streamed down her face, and she jumped down the waterfall to kneel beside me as she screamed my name.

If I died, at least, it'd happen with me being loved and forgiven.

The prophecy had been real.

My heart had fully and permanently returned because of her, and her powers had awakened because of the love I proved by putting her first and killing my mother. I could die peacefully now because it had been worth it. Sierra would unite the realms in peace, and eventually, she'd save Lukita, who, I was positive, was a seer.

Sierra grabbed my hand, squeezing it tightly. "I love you."

Right before Sierra leaned down and kissed my lips, Mother's arms fell lifeless at her side from Kaito decapitating her. Then, all too soon, Sierra's lips lifted away from mine, and instantly, the blood in my veins, along with my heart, stopped.

There was no doubt in my mind that I should be dead, but I could still hear Sierra sobbing, the delegates comforting her, and the pounding of the waterfall. Before I had time to consider the second impossible thing being true, that I had vampire blood flowing through me, my body lifted, swirling in a dark, smokey cloud.

Fangs erupted from my gums, a sense of hunger filled my stomach, my veins glowed scarlet, and my skin turned white as snow. The mist disappeared, and I dropped with a thud on the ground. My eyes widened, my vision turned red, and my stomach grumbled as the sweet fragrance of blood slammed into me, driving me mad.

Sierra grabbed my cheeks. Her veins, pulsing against my skin, called to me at a primal level. I could practically taste them. I clenched my jaw tight, trying to control my thirst for blood. Sierra wasn't an option ... not now, not ever. Not like that. I'd fight this. I wouldn't become a monster.

After several long, deep breaths, I calmed the need deep inside me and welcomed Sierra's smothering kisses. Her in my arms felt right. Curious of the bond and my heart, I peeked inside my chest and gasped. Crimson veins, vibrant red beating heart, and a beautiful crystallized lavender bond. It was still there. I was still alive. "I love you!" I kissed her cheeks, forehead, and mouth again. With each press of my lips to her skin, the bond brightened.

"And I you." She broke from me. "What just happened?"

"My mother ... she was a vampire. Guess I just activated it." I gasped and wrapped her in my arms. I couldn't believe I had survived, even if it was as a nasty vampire. I'd learn to control the hunger. I'd never let the bloodlust control me. I refused to turn into a monster and lose Sierra. Deesse had given me a second chance, and I wouldn't waste it.

As I would help Sierra to control her seer gifts, she'd help me manage the vampire in me. Our love could handle it—I had no doubt. My heart reforming, Sierra being my bonded mate, and me actually being the warrior from the prophecy, was proof that anything was possible together.

For several minutes, we held each other. No one interrupted. A few of them talked in the distance, but I didn't care to hear what they said. All I cared about was the beautiful woman in my arms. The woman who still loved me despite me being a monster. The woman who was my bonded mate.

Sierra's body went ridged. I released her from the hug. "Sierra!"

Her eyes changed from brown back to white. Light shone out of them, almost blinding me. I couldn't breathe. What was happening? "Sierra! Sierra!"

Panha, her nanny, and the delegates crowded around us.

"She's having a prophecy." Queen Rosalida appeared at the opening, and we all turned to face her. "I'm so proud of you, Tarus." Smiling, she jumped down and squeezed my shoulders.

"As am I," Lukita's voice echoed around the cave. Besides Sierra, Rosalida, and Panha, the others jumped. "You're a hero. And still alive. Congratulations."

The delegates nodded, Panha smiled, and Sierra's nanny grabbed my hand.

Tears streamed down my cheeks. I was a hero, and I was loved.

Before I could think more about everyone being here or the fact Queen Rosalida must've known it'd come to this, Sierra's eyes changed back to brown, and a smile spread across her face. She tugged me closer for another kiss. I kissed her back, and several people coughed behind us.

She pulled away, and her eyes widened when her gaze fell on her mom.

But before she had the much-needed moment with her family, I had to make sure she was okay and that the newest prophecy didn't foretell disaster. I gripped her shoulders. "Sierra, are you alright?"

She looked back at me. "I'm better than alright. I know how to unite the realms!"

Holy Delmore. We did it. We saved everyone, and in the process, saved each other.

First, my readers: Thank you to everyone who made it this far and read *A Bond of Blood and Lavender*, my story about love, redemption, and knowing that you're not too far gone. Each one of you who picked up this book is my hero and has helped make my dreams come true. I couldn't be more thankful. Tartarus also thanks you and is happy he got to share his life with you!

Second, overall: Thank you to my mom, my writing friends, my editors, my formatter, and my traveling buddies. Without you all, I could've never done this. You encouraged me when I needed it and convinced me never to give up even though I threatened to many times.

Third, individual shoutouts:

Mom, you're my strongest supporter and mean the world to me. Throughout my life, you have always urged me to dream. You saw my passion for writing stories when I was younger. When I gave it up, you kept fighting for me to bring it back. You went so far as to make it the only way I could get ungrounded when I was 14. At the time, I rejected the first writing idea you gave me and wrote half a book on your second topic. For 13 years, I ended up carrying around that unfinished novel titled Daughters of a Serial Killer, hoping to one day figure out what to do with the antagonist. This is where the next shout-out comes and how your first suggestion resurrected.

In December of 2021, inside a wonderful hostel in London, a guy approached me and asked me what I wanted in life. For the first time, I told someone I wanted to be an author. He looked me dead in the eyes and said it'll happen; I believe in you. When he walked away, I pulled out my laptop, and instead of finishing Daughters of a Serial Killer, I went back to my mom's first idea...a blind girl trapped in a cave, which inspired the last third of this book. I wrote 8,000 words that night. By the end of the week, I had written the entire novel. By the end of the month, I had also finished Daughters of a Serial Killer. So to that man at the hostel, I don't remember your name, but thank you! You are the one who brought my passion back to life. I'll forever remember you!

There are many more shout-outs I'd love to give, especially since this book took three years to get here, plus many conferences, writing groups, and so on; but it'd take me 20 pages just to write them all. So, I'm going to focus on the ones who helped me with this particular book.

To my darling gem of an editor, Demi Michelle Schwartz, I owe you so much thanks. I wouldn't be the writer I am today if it weren't for you! I wouldn't understand immersion if not for you. You helped explain it in a way my neurodivergent brain could understand. Then, you took it a step further and ensured I grasped it. I will never forget the day we met back in early 2024. Demi, you didn't stop by just helping me understand styles and what my stories lacked. You encourage me every day and have provided me with amazing support. My title for this story came from you. I'm so thankful to have you in my writing corner and life.

Andie Smith, another wonderful editor brought to me by Demi. Andie, you've supported me and encouraged me in tremendous ways. I will never forget the email you sent me when I wanted to throw everything away. Your edits have helped my stories, including this one. I loved reading the edit letter for this book and then talking with you about how to incorporate the changes. I thank you so much for having the phone call with me and always being there.

River Ari, without your help on my opening pages, my characters would've stayed one-dimensional. You went above and beyond with your ten-page edit letter. Thank you for helping my story get what it needed to be more captivating and bringing my characters to life.

To my formatter, proofreader, writing friend, and self-publishing/book coach, Jade Feldman, thank you for helping me cross the finish line. My story thanks you for everything you have done, and yet to do for it. Without you, I wouldn't know about the cool scene breaks, chapter designs, and so much more. My pixie also thanks you for getting her a stronger role. Without you, I'd also be lost or at least taking months to accomplish the things you have helped me with. I am beyond blown away by the encouragement, friendliness, and support. You have been such a great addition to my writing community and life. You also came from Demi. And I couldn't be more thankful.

River, Demi, Andie, and Jade, I couldn't have done any of this without you. I am so thankful for everything you do and the positive light you all have shone on my life and books. I also will forever be grateful for our phone calls. They are such a great gift you all have offered me. Being able to spitball ideas and other things with you all helped in more ways than you'll ever imagine. It also gave me so much encouragement. Never stop offering them, please.

To my copy editors and proofreaders, Melissa Rodgers and Andrew Heasman, thank you! You taught me things I never knew about commas and tenses.

To the two editors I received at the very beginning of my writing journey, thank you.

To Oana Bell, Sam W, and Leah, thank you for being my beta readers. Though this book is ten times different than when you saw it, you helped me improve so much and showed me what I was lacking. The Queen thanks you, Leah, for getting her a more parental and longer role.

To my travel buddies and hostel staff friends, thanks for letting me share my stories with you. Particular shout out to everyone who worked at Smart Russell Square Hostel and Wombats London. Also, Emma, Lissa, Naomi, and others at Hillsong Church London, thank you for being such a positive encouragement to my life and my writing.

To my sister, whom I love dearly and am always trying to impress, I really hope you read this one! I hope it makes you proud.

To Karley, thanks, mate!

To every person I've missed, thank you!

To God thank you for helping me fight through the mental breaks that came along with writing this story. Without your love, faith, and guidance, I wouldn't be here. I relied on your strength through my mom, the bible, church, therapy, and so much over the years. Thanks for never giving up on me. Thanks for being the Rock on which I stand.

About the Author

Caroline Crews is a debut novelist who loves all things fantasy, dress-up events, and games. By day, she works in the medical field, and at night, she's a writer of mostly fantasy and neuro-divergent characters, like herself, who end up partaking in lots of games. She lives in Texas in a fantasy-decorated home.

https://www.caroline-crews.com
https://x.com/carolinecrews25

www.ingramcontent.com/pod-product-compliance
Lightning Source LLC
Chambersburg PA
CBHW071141100726

47908CB00002B/211